Evorath: The Birth of Death

Second Edition, 2016.

ISBN 978-0-9978838-0-0

Free Dragon Press, LLC
www.freedragonpress.com
www.evorath.com

Book 1 of the Evorath Trilogy. Immerse yourself in a world of fantasy adventure with the Legacy of Evorath family of books.

Read free stories online and keep up with future releases.

www.evorath.com

Please see the end of this novel for an appendices section, which provides a reference for Evorath, a map, and presents additional information within the world.

Prologue

Erathal News Article 100:36
Secret Races
By Archor Sylvan

In the beginning, the world was overcome with evil. Four great demons ruled the four regions of Evorath. Each demon lord warred against the others, and chaos was the only way to live. Flames engulfed the surface. Volcanoes, treacherous mountains, and scorched terrain covered most of Evorath.

The gods looked down upon Evorath, overrun with evil and void of all good. Despite this, they saw a future on Evorath, one that was free of evil. With their vision in mind, the gods banded together, performing a sacred ritual. This ritual resulted in the immediate growth of the forests of Evorath, and in the birth of the world's dryads.

For each different type of tree that was created, a dryad was also born, each with their own talents to fight the demon lords. With their power combined, these pure mistresses had enough strength to vanquish the evil that these demons wrought, but not on their own. Despite their strength, it was clear that they could not be a match for the demons, who had the support of large armies.

Fortunately, the dryads had another gift beyond their strength and control of the newly grown forests. This unique gift gave them the power to create. With only her will to fuel her, the beautiful dryad of the hickory tree was the first to use her gift and, planting a special seed within the forest, she spawned the first of the elves.

Elves were entrusted as the first defense for the forest, protectors to keep the demons from retaking the land that had been transformed from desolation to beauty. They were to be one with the forest, learning to use her resources to defend her from evil.

Other dryads quickly followed her example, creating other protectors for the forest. The dryad of the oaks created the centaur, who were to provide great strength in the forest's defense. Satyr, Lamia, trolls, felite, lizock, and all sorts of other creatures emerged as well, each providing their own unique talents to vanquish the blight upon the land.

As evil was eliminated, elves began to explore the lands, reaching out from the forest and discovering that there were other races appearing as well. These other races were often peaceful, exchanging ideas and concepts with the elves. People lived in peace and harmony, without strife and without disease, crime, or hunger.

Everything was perfect.

Time passed, and this utopia began to fade. Races began dying of mysterious causes, illness breaking out among certain tribes. As the populations grew, food became harder to come by. Disagreements began to break out between species, and minor conflicts were the result.

Relatively speaking, everything was still peaceful, but one day, an elvish researcher crossed the line. The result: catastrophe.

This misguided sage decided to conduct an experiment, operating under the principle that the environment could actually greatly alter the genetic makeup of elves. Knowing how adaptable elves were and considering the plethora of races whose origins were unaccounted for, this researcher took it upon himself to figure out how they came into being.

He looked for volunteers to test his hypothesis but had no success. In an act of depravity, he raped a young elf and took her down a mining tunnel in the Jyrimoore Mountains. Here, he intended to stay until the child was born, his hope being that the cave environment would alter the development of the child in its mother's womb.

His plan may have worked, but the section that he planned to live in for the six months of pregnancy was unstable. After about a month, the mines collapsed as he was leaving to get food.

This collapse killed the so-called 'scientist' and was believed to have killed his subject as well. All readers must note that this story was covered by our parchment twenty years ago when the incident occurred. The fact everyone ignores is that, excluding the unnamed scientist's sin, the word 'evil' did not enter our vocabulary until five months after the report.

The dwarves withdrew from all trading agreements with our people, the gnomes began to create mechanical weapons, thieves took to the streets and our king was assassinated. All of this happened precisely six months and four days after the 'test' began, or when the baby was born.

This is no coincidence.

The Sin child was born, and as the world degrades around us, and with a kidnapper on the loose, we must look for the source. The mother lived, as did her devil-child.

3

A Hájje is among us.

-=-=-=-=-=-=-=-=-

Erathal News Article 100:38
The Power of Rumors
By High Wizard Guildpac

It is amazing how a single piece of parchment can cause the biggest panic in over a decade. This article is written today, to remind readers that this so-called news source brings views from normal individuals such as you. In other words, nothing we -as volunteer writers- say, needs to be based on fact.

I sometimes play with the idea of writing about an approaching band of rabid kobolds to hit home with this point. Everyone in the city would likely panic, causing mass hysteria and disorder: all based on some fanciful ideas of one over-energetic citizen.

Don't believe everything that is written in this parchment!

By now, some of you may realize why I am writing this. The article written two days ago, titled 'Secret Races', has no basis in fact. There is no evidence to support *anything* in that article. In fact, there is quite a bit of evidence to disprove nearly everything that Mr. Sylvan wrote.

First off, though some traditionalists believe that because we were told fairy tales as children about the great demons that we must accept them as fact, these stories are just that: stories. Secondly, the idea that dryads came into being by some ritual is just a part of Evorath's mythology, as is the idea that dryads created elves, or any other race for that matter. Thirdly, the mining collapse mentioned in Sylvan's article was investigated thoroughly, and it was determined by the city's Royal Rangers that no one could have survived.

And now we move on to perhaps the most important error.

I interviewed Lieutenant Artimus Atyrmirid, the head ranger in charge of the investigation on the recent kidnappings. When I asked him if there was a connection between these kidnappings, he replied with a simple 'yes'.

I proceeded to ask if the identity of the criminal had been discovered.

The lieutenant said, "We still haven't gotten any visual of the suspect, but mages have identified him as elvish."

Simply put, there is no strange new species, no sin child out kidnapping people. All talk about the end being near, or about nonsense such as the existence of a Hájje is pure hogwash. Anyone who says otherwise is merely disturbing the peace.

They shall be punished accordingly.

Chapter 1

Lieutenant Artimus Atyrmirid of the Royal Ranger Division stood in the home of the latest reported missing person. Brushing aside a stray strand of his luscious dirty-blond hair, he focused his attention on what he hoped would change the course of his investigation. Including this most recent kidnapping, there had been seven young elvish girls, ages fourteen to twenty-two, who had mysteriously disappeared. In the twenty years since crime had begun, nineteen of which Artimus had been an investigator, there had never been a case like this one.

What made these kidnappings so strange was the fact that there was no logical pattern. Seven days ago, a fourteen-year-old elf had been kidnapped in the slums of Erathal. A day after that, a twenty-year-old woman was taken from her rich father's villa. The following day, a sixteen-year-old, lower-class girl, then an eighteen-year-old poor girl, then a seventeen-year-old merchant's daughter, and yesterday had been another rich child. Other than their gender, no one could figure out the commonality with these kidnappings.

Last night, the criminal slipped up. The kidnapper had made things personal for Artimus and his fellow rangers; he had kidnapped a twenty-two-year-old, ranger-to-be. In doing so, this infamous kidnapper had left his first clue: black hair. This, Artimus suspected, would ultimately be the kidnapper's undoing.

The experienced inspector smiled at the strands of hair that lay atop a broken table. Unlike the other victims, this trainee, Valkyrie had been her name, had put up a desperate struggle. She must have noticed his peculiar, black hair and purposely torn some out for Artimus to find. Clever.

"Cadet, do you know anyone with black hair?"

The young elf eyed his lieutenant suspiciously but took only a moment to respond.

"No, sir." The cadet burst out his answer sheepishly.

"Neither do I," the two-century-old ranger continued his thoughts. "And I can say with certainty that there are very few elves who have black hair." He finished with a sigh, perhaps of relief, but he definitely didn't feel that way.

Even knowing that the suspect had black hair did not mean that this case was over. Every black-haired elf would have to be interrogated, and then, if none of them were guilty, every other creature in the vicinity would have to be questioned.

But the lab mages had determined that the suspect was elvish. Or had the conclusion been made prematurely?

"Cadet, I need you to fetch a lab mage immediately," Artimus ordered without turning his head.

"Sir?"

"I need to know whether or not this is elvish hair. Get me a mage!"

The young ranger hesitated for a moment but was out the door before Artimus could continue. It was hard to find anyone as experienced in this field as him, a fact that he was not happy to admit. If it meant better investigations, Artimus would have gladly given his rank to someone more qualified. Unfortunately, even King Ulagret III agreed that Artimus was the best at what he did.

Despite this, Artimus missed the old days, when his only job had been hunting to provide for the city. On the day Ulagret Jr. had been killed, everything changed, and Artimus was the first elf to change his title. With the use of his tracking techniques, he had been able to find the killer and bring him to justice. Since then, he had gained the honorary title of Chief Inspector of the Rangers; his rank remained Lieutenant.

"Excuse me, sir," a new voice interrupted, this one a young female. "Mr. Ricker would like to speak with you."

Artimus turned to see the younger ranger, whose body language showed that she had given up on stalling the disgruntled father. With a sigh, he nodded.

"Let him back in. After all, who am I to keep him out of his house?" Clearly, Artimus was not happy to be disturbed mid-investigation.

In the same instant the ranger departed, Mr. Ricker burst into the room, his face red with anger. If Artimus were to speak his mind, he would ask why the old politician had not hired some sort of security after the kidnappings began. Furthermore, he wondered how this over-inflated pig had remained asleep while his daughter had clearly put up a fight. Perhaps he was the kidnapper.

"Where is my daughter?" the enraged father asked as soon as he was within arm's length of the Chief Investigator.

"Borius, you know that it does not work like that. I am not a psychic." Artimus intentionally used the senator's first name, knowing that it would throw off his feeling of control. No civilian -no matter what position he held, he was still a civilian in this investigation- would question Artimus while he was at work.

"I-" Borius began, his rhythm clearly off. He stumbled for a moment, his face going through a range of emotions from confusion to anger.

Artimus took a step back as rage won the battle.

"You *will* FIND my daughter *immediately*, or *you* will be cast into the woods!"

That wasn't the response Artimus had expected.

Fortunately, the experienced investigator was quick on his feet, and always prepared for a verbal battle, even with a politician. He stepped back towards the senator and puffed out his chest.

"*You*, Senator, will leave this house *immediately* or *I* will personally testify that *you* are interfering in an active investigation. Do *I* need to remind you how serious an offense *that* is?"

This time he struck a nerve.

The senator's face muscles relaxed, falling down into a frown and then transitioning to a concentrated scowl.

"My apologies," the senator spat, his voice almost acidic. "Contact me if you have any leads."

"As always." Artimus nodded.

Senator Ricker stood fixed in place while Artimus crouched where he had found the strands of hair. After a moment, he could hear the senator stomp out of the room in a display of anger. Continuing the search, Artimus scanned the floor once more, looking over every inch to ensure nothing had been overlooked. Any small clue, perhaps a scuff-mark from a shoe, or, if he was lucky enough, a droplet of blood, could add to his case and make this criminal that much easier to find.

Artimus surveyed the room once more at a macro-level, looking over to the wooden desk and the cracked vanity mirror. His eyes ran across to the bed, which appeared surprisingly undisturbed. He looked up at the window, which had been left wide open after the kidnapping and then shifted his gaze back under the table where he had found the hair. If there was just some other clue that might help him locate this kidnapper, perhaps he could really crack this case open.

Almost ready to give up the search, something finally caught his eye. It was in the corner of the room. Out of place among the expensive tile floors of the senator's mansion. Just beside a small, wooden chair that had been upturned, he spotted it: specific black ash, which could only be found in one place.

The kidnapper was living in Dwarven mines.

This discovery could prove more help in his investigation than the hair, and perhaps even more useful than a blood sample.

Finding out exactly where this dust came from would allow Artimus to go straight to the kidnapper.

Up until this investigation, the criminal had left behind no traces, but like all other criminals, he got sloppy. With six successful kidnappings, it made sense that the culprit would become arrogant by the seventh. It was either this expected arrogance or the fact that he had kidnapped a ranger-in-training, that the culprit had left this evidence. Whichever it was, Artimus did not care. Evidence was evidence, and he planned on using it to find his criminal by nightfall.

Without further thought on the matter, the senior investigator took a small sample of the dust, grabbed the strands of hair, and left the girl's room.

He was now in the central room of the house, where other investigators searched and of course where Senator Ricker waited. The room was large, one of the largest that Artimus had ever seen. A mahogany table, big enough to seat twelve elves, made up the center of the room. Above the table was a gaudy chandelier, made entirely of gold. Even the purple candles within it appeared extravagant, small gems pressed into the center of all six to show just how expensive they were.

A large fireplace sat at the rear of the home, a single log burning inside to supplement the light from the chandelier. Vibrant plants of green, red, yellow, blue, and purple were positioned on either side of the fireplace, each cared for so precisely that they looked identical to one another. Finally, the floor was covered in a red carpet, and by the looks of it, one more expensive than Artimus's entire house.

11

Upon seeing the senior investigator, Senator Ricker stopped harassing a younger ranger and approached Artimus.

"What else did you find?"

It was clear that the senator was distraught by his daughter's disappearance, but something about his arrogant attitude and the way he pried, annoyed Artimus beyond anything else the young investigator could imagine.

With as much calm as he could muster, Artimus gave a reassuring smile. "As a matter of fact, I have gathered new information. When the mage arrives, I will have it verified. Until then, I must ask you to sit tight."

The senator was visibly annoyed by this evasive statement, his fists clenched as he glared daggers at Artimus. Despite this, he gave a defeated nod. Artimus was in charge of this investigation, and under the authority of the king he could give out whatever information he felt the need to. If he didn't want to share the information, that was also his prerogative.

This fact was one reason Artimus liked his job. Like any other sentient creature, power was something he found handy. Better he, a qualified hunter, have the power than some arrogant bureaucrat like the senator. This authority had been helpful in the past, but he could not help thinking how much more helpful it would be if he had his complete staff. If only his officers showed up when they were supposed to, he might actually get investigations done more quickly.

Just as this thought came to mind, the door flew open and Mage Savannah Sylvanas came stumbling in, followed closely by the cadet Artimus had sent to get her. As usual, Savannah was late.

"I'm sorry, sir," she exclaimed, gliding across the room towards Artimus, ignoring the other rangers and the senator. Like most in her profession, her manners were lacking. In many cases, she would completely ignore her peers, leaving her with a largely unfavorable reputation.

Of course, where her manners ended, her beauty began, and Artimus believed this lack of protocol was made up for by her stunning features.

Her radiant, porcelain white skin contrasted beautifully with light, brown hair. With majestic green eyes peering deeply into the soul and filling any man's heart with desire, she demanded attention. Gazing upon them, most could notice a certain glow, a magical radiance caused by her stored up power reserves.

Her body was proportioned perfectly, toned but not too muscular, curves exactly where they should be. She had the figure of an angel, with flawless dimensions. Every woman longed to look as stunning as she, and every man longed to have her -at least Artimus thought so.

To make matters worse, Savannah never wore the Ranger uniform, and being a lab mage, she was not required to do so. Artimus only wished she could wear something less distracting, but in his experience she had only one type of outfit.

Her long, flowing hair rested around her ears, showing off glowing, silver earrings. About her neck she wore a petite choker, with a green, magic stone set in the center. Her upper torso was covered by a simple, green tube top, stopping only millimeters below her breasts. She wore nothing else to cover her upper torso, leaving most of her middle uncovered, including her lithe stomach. Around her waist was something a bit more modest, but enticing, nonetheless.

The green silk was form-fitting, accentuating every curve. This enchanting skirt held firmly around her upper thighs but flowed loosely down to her smooth calves.

Naturally, Artimus struggled to resist the allure. Despite this, it was his duty to make her understand the importance of being prompt. He only wished he could gather the words.

"Well, yes. It is, uh, good that, umm." He cleared his throat. "I'm glad to see you have finally arrived."

"Of course, sir. I am sorry that I-" Savannah began before getting interrupted by the lieutenant.

"No. I mean. Of course. No need to waste time. Don't be late again," Artimus stammered. He had the distinct feeling that anyone not distracted by Savannah's features was laughing at him.

"So," Savannah started, fighting back a grin and failing. She must have known the effect she had on people.

"Is there anything new to look at?"

Artimus held up both hands and offered the samples he had gathered to the mage. "I know the ash came from a Dwarven mine, but I don't know about the hair. Is it elvish?"

Savannah took the samples in both hands, ash in one, hair in the other. She closed her eyes, blue magic pulsating around her hands. Artimus wasn't sure how it worked, but like anyone else in her field, this concentration of magic somehow allowed her to pick up on the mechanics.

"Interesting," she whispered, her left eye twitching as the magic dissipated from her hand. She did not pause for an explanation but continued to feed magic into her right hand. After only a few moments, this magic faded as well, and the lab mage opened her eyes.

"The hair is elvish in origin, but it is different somehow. I don't know how, but the hair has some slight variances from yours or mine, yet it is definitely elvish. And knowing where the ash came from, this is quite unsettling. The ash did indeed come from Dwarven mines; the Jyrimoore mining shaft to be exact. If you are not familiar with famous cases, note that-"

Artimus held up his hand, a certain dread taking over his face. "I know that name as well as anyone else. We leave for the mines immediately and pray that it is just a strange coincidence. Cadets Gharis, Sylvan and Verandas, you are with me. Savannah, you are coming as well. Corporal Cylbus, you are in charge here."

Without waiting for a response, Artimus marched out the door. He could hear his officers' footsteps following behind.

Chapter 2

Runeturk Mountains, outside Erathal
13 Neglur, 1086

Artimus dismounted his horse, sending a hand motion indicating his underlings do the same. The afternoon sun shone bright above, and with a quick glance at his riders he was able to detect their exhaustion. Most had not eaten since before the investigation began that morning, and over the past week many had also been short on sleep. Normally, he would have called for a lunch break at this point, but they had already arrived at the entrance to the Jyrimoore Tunnel. At this point it would serve little purpose.

"Cadets, you have ten minutes to rest out here. Eat if you must, and make sure your mounts are content. I will be inspecting the perimeter."

"And what about me?" Savannah asked as she slid off her horse in front of Artimus, her movements inspiring thoughts in his head that he would never share with another soul. Staying professional was something he needed, but at times he wished he could drop that professionalism and act on some of his baser instincts.

"You can come with me, or you can break. It's up to you." As Artimus walked towards the collapsed entrance, he paused. "On second thoughts, I wouldn't mind asking you a few questions if you are willing."

Savannah smiled, the happiness showing in her eyes as well as her beautiful, white teeth, sending a warm feeling through Artimus.

"I would be happy to answer some questions," she said softly.

Without waiting, she went to Artimus's side and walked along next to him. "What would you like to know?"

Artimus said nothing at first, waiting until they were at the stones that blocked the entrance and safely out of earshot of his cadets.

"Well, this is the first case we have worked together on, but I wanted to tell you that so far you have proven to be the best mage I have had the privilege to work with."

He really meant that. Most of the mages he had the experience of working with were more talk than action, always claiming to have such great powers but never delivering more than the most trivial assistance. Though she was repeatedly late, Savannah had been offering suggestions since day one of this case, showing a rare initiative without the constant air of arrogance that was so common.

"Thank you." Another smile, and Artimus felt another unprofessional sensation.

"Well, it's true. I was just wondering what kind of magic you practiced before you joined the Rangers." Artimus did his best to avoid her eyes, knowing that the pull was too strong. Instead, he looked straight at her nose, allowing him to ignore her other features.

"Wellll," she said with a smile, rocking back on her heels as she clasped her hands behind her waist.

Artimus avoided her smile as best he could. He had never felt this way about another person before, but there was something special about Savannah. Unable to put his finger on what it was, he felt childish, and completely foolish, but since working with her he had felt a strange connection. It was difficult not acting on it.

"I used to be a druid." Savannah explained. "Actually, I still practice druidic magic, but only when I have free time. Since joining the rangers, I have not been involved in an actual conflict, so I've not needed to use it beyond basic everyday tasks."

She strolled on beside him as she spoke, her hands held together behind her back, a spring in her step as she looked towards the sky innocently.

"I would love to see you use some of that magic. Maybe some time when we're both off-" Artimus cleared his throat. "I mean, uhh. If you don't mind giving a demonstration. I don't want to interfere with your personal life."

Savannah laughed, an action that sounded to Artimus like a choir of angels. "You wouldn't be interfering with anything. I will show you as soon as we finish this case, so long as you do something for me."

"And what would that-" Artimus stopped mid-sentence and held up his open palm. Kneeling, he motioned to the ground. "There are tracks here."

He traced the steps, trying to find which direction they started in. He stayed low to the ground, slowly walking back towards the forest and Erathal to the south. Then, as he moved closer to where the other rangers were taking their short break, they vanished, as if the culprit had flown to this point and then walked to the abandoned mines.

Savannah remained silent as Artimus stood back up and approached the shaft again. The entire entrance was covered, but the tracks led directly to it. Artimus went around the entrance, trying to find any tracks on the hills beyond. There was nothing.

"This is quite irregular," Artimus said. His sky blue eyes were downcast in thought, and he ran his finger along the edge of the bow that hung over his shoulder. "The tracks end here, but this entrance is sealed."

Savannah shrugged. "So he sealed it after going inside."

Artimus shook his head. "Highly unlikely, and physically impossible. The rocks resemble a typical cave-in. Most likely, if we remove the first layer, there will just be another and after that, another. Anyways, to get these rocks to be stable like this could only be the result of chance. If I move some rocks around, it may cause another collapse and allow us entry, but there would be no way to seal it in this fashion again; not from the inside anyways."

"I could move these rocks and put them all back in the same exact position." Savannah said with a wink. "Magic is quite handy."

Artimus arched an eyebrow. "I'm sure you can," he began, his tone showing some disbelief, "but you are an accomplished mage. Our friend here is a criminal, and even in criminals of his

19

caliber, there have been none to possess such advanced magic. Only a handful of all criminals know *any* magic."

"So what? There's a first for everything."

Artimus sighed, a response, he noticed, that he had begun to use quite frequently. "Indeed. There is really no sense in debating this, but I pray you are wrong. Otherwise, I hope you are ready for a challenging fight. Still, I feel I should fetch the cadets before we enter."

"Alright, I'll just move these rocks while you get them."

Artimus turned and walked back to his men. "Fine, but do not enter without me," he commanded before disappearing behind the trees.

As he walked, he decided to check for any tracks that he might have missed. He found only Savannah's and his own, a troubling fact. This criminal was great at masking his trail, he almost never left evidence, and he was, potentially, a powerful magician. If not for the fact that he outnumbered this man five to one, Artimus would be worried.

"Sir," one of his cadets began as he arrived on scene, "we are all ready to begin when you are."

"Good," Artimus said, "because I believe we've found his lair. Sylvan, I believe it is your turn to keep an eye on our steeds. Gharis, Verandas, I need you both to follow me."

Though Sylvan looked unhappy, he remained where he was. Both Gharis and Verandas grabbed their essential gear and followed their lieutenant back to the mining shaft, where Savannah had already cleared the entrance. Artimus was fascinated to see the rocks hanging suspended next to the open entrance and surprised that Savannah could actually open the entrance so easily.

"Alright then. Gharis, follow me. Savannah, you follow Gharis, and Verandas, keep to the rear. It looks pretty tight down there, so stick to this formation until further notice."

"Yes, sir," both the cadets replied simultaneously.

They were only cadets, but Artimus knew how hard the entrance exam to become a ranger was. After all, he had played a major part in designing many of the preliminary tests. Passing them meant that they were smart, capable trackers, and skilled fighters. Despite his confidence in these men and himself, he still had an uneasy feeling as he led Savannah and his cadets down the incline.

He felt a little unsteady as his boots struggled to keep traction on the slope. Sand shifted beneath his feet, and he felt a few loose pebbles sliding around. As they reached the bottom, he steadied himself and drew his longbow, notching an arrow. Both of the cadets followed suit.

"Savannah, seal the entrance."

The beautiful druid winked, and the rocks slid back into place. They fit in perfectly, just as they had when the party arrived. But as the entrance was sealed, their only source of light was lost as well.

"Savannah, I need you to create some fire," he whispered, as the light disappeared.

"I can't make fire. I'm a druid, not a pyromancer."

Artimus frowned. He could have sworn a druid had once told him about using fire. At least there was always standard procedure he could follow.

"All right. Cadets! Put away your bows and light your torches. Draw out your swords as your weapon."

As usual, the cadets responded with a "Yes, sir" and did exactly as Artimus had instructed. Light filled the entrance as they ignited their torches, revealing a long stretch of shaft, which led to darkness. Artimus noted that the debris left at the entrance appeared to be a natural collapse. Next, he noticed that the footprints he found near the entrance had reappeared; but something was wrong.

"This is quite odd," Artimus whispered as he knelt down for a closer look. "There is only one set of footprints, and absolutely no drag marks."

"And?" Savannah asked matter-of-factly. "He could carry the victims if he is strong enough, or he could have used a spell to make them lighter."

"Cadets," Artimus said in his most authoritative voice. "Why is this discovery peculiar?"

Gharis was the first to answer. "Sir. Because when you say one set you literally mean one set, total. That one set, if I am not mistaken sir, leads into the tunnel. This would suggest that whoever is down here just came down for the first time and has never left. Also, the tracks seem to be fresh; no more than an hour."

"Very good, Gharis. Those are my thoughts exactly," Artimus exclaimed with pride, a slight smile appearing on his face. These cadets were coming along nicely and being their mentor; he could not help but feel some pride.

"So what does all this mean?" Savannah asked incredulously.

"It means we are being set up," Verandas piped in.

"Indeed," Artimus verified. "We must proceed with extreme caution, but I see no need for backup. Does anyone object?" The silence that followed was a sufficient answer. "Good, then we proceed quietly. From here on out do not speak unless it's an emergency or if I address you."

Artimus looked to the three of his subordinates, who all nodded in response. Taking each step with care, the lieutenant led the other rangers forward, holding his bow with an arrow at the ready. The terrain was pretty simple to navigate, but the ceilings of mines were known to be unstable. That is why Artimus kept his vision upward. If this criminal was as smart as he seemed, he could find a structurally weak point and set that as his trap. If Artimus picked up any movement, he would yell for his men to fall back.

So far, the path had been clear, but Artimus approached this search as he did all other hunts. At any moment, he knew danger could emerge. Whatever form the trap would take - Artimus was positive there was a trap- the Rangers would be ready, and Artimus was confident that they would, as always, catch the criminal.

"Sir," Gharis whispered from behind him, no urgency present in his voice. "I think you should see this."

Artimus turned, keeping his bow at the ready and his eyes trained on the ceiling. He gasped as he looked at the wall that Gharis stood before. A greenish ore protruded from the wall, covering most the cave for as far as the torchlight extended. This metallic green vein reached out in every direction, extending further down the tunnel and even reaching out along parts of the cave floor. Why would the dwarves have abandoned these mines?

The lead investigator surveyed the wall with his eyes, following along the intricate veins of the priceless ore that was before them. His own sword was crafted of the finest mythril and enchanted to a level of superior sharpness and strength, but never before had he seen the rare metal that was before his eyes. And it was no small vein either; it was a vast web, perhaps running down for the rest of the cave until it opened up into a cavern full of this precious ore.

"What is it?" Savannah asked, running her hand along the ore.

"Adamantium." Artimus responded, leaving his mouth agape as he tried to convince himself that he was not hallucinating. No one spoke for what seemed a full minute until Savannah broke the silence.

"Do I need to pry out the details?" she asked with a grin. "What is so special about this stuff?"

"My apologies," Artimus replied with sincerity. "Adamantium is the strongest metal in existence. It's slightly heavier than mythril but remains lighter than steel. It's harder

24

than diamonds and more than twice as strong as pure mythril. To mine it, you have to completely cut around it, because no tools can break it. Any elvish blacksmith would pay a fortune for a single vein.

"Makes me wonder why the dwarves abandoned these mines in the first place." Artimus finished, lowering his bow as he pondered. Dwarves rarely abandoned a mining operation, even if conditions were hazardous. The tunnel was dug though, and it led to this adamantium. Why would they create a mining network, find adamantium, and not proceed to mine it?

"Maybe they didn't search this far." Savannah offered. "Official reports say that the dwarves abandoned these mines because they did not find anything of value."

"That just complicates this case even further," Artimus said. "If this tunnel was dug after the dwarves left, then who dug it?"

A new voice answered the question, coming from beyond the torchlight. The voice was that of a young male, but it was filled with authority and carried a demonic tone. Both Artimus and his cadets held their weapons at the ready as they looked towards the source.

"I dug it," the voice bragged. "These are my tunnels. Leave immediately or all of you will die." The voice sent chills from Artimus's feet, running up his legs and rolling around in his gut before fluttering out in all directions and spiraling back around. Each word made his hair stand on end, the tone caustic and almost painful.

"Identify yourself," Artimus insisted, ignoring the man's threat and his own discomfort. "Enter the light and give yourself up. Otherwise, I will show you why I won the last three Archery Competitions. I guarantee that your voice has given me your location and I can strike your throat with ease. We don't want violence though, so please come into the light."

"Alright," the voice mocked, this time coming from behind. As all four of Artimus's party turned, the voice laughed, coming from every direction. "But as you can see, I can project my voice where I please." As he continued, his voice shifted back to its original location.

"Listen," Artimus countered. "We have no intention of intruding, nor are we looking for conflict. We are merely investigating a series of crimes. Would you be willing to answer a few questions?"

"Crime you say? Who says that crime was committed? Better yet, how can you be the judge of what is and is not crime?"

"I am no judge," Artimus answered cautiously. "I am only a protector of what is good."

"Good? Now that, my elvish brother, is a matter of perception." As these words hit Artimus's ears, the figure slowly stepped into the light, revealing his appearance. Once again, the veteran investigator found himself staring in disbelief.

The ghastly figure before him appeared elvish, but his dimensions and features contradicted this assumption. In fact, the only true similarity was the pointy ears that were upon his head, but Artimus could feel something more. Even with his deathly pale skin, his night-black hair, his extraordinary height, and his void-like eyes, this suspect had to be elvish. All those gathered knew; this man was the first hájje, a dark elf.

The Hájje spoke in a mocking tone as he paced just within the torches' lighting. "Seven matriarchs have been gathered so far. They are all mine and now bear my children, but I need more. Four more will disappear from your village and that will be all. For the record, my name is Yezurkstal, Patriarch of all hájje. Leave me and my people alone."

Artimus was shocked by the hájje's suddenly loose tongue, but he was here for a reason. "I'm afraid I cannot comply until the seven girls are released." He held his bow steady, aimed straight for this criminal's head with intent to kill if needed.

Yezurkstal grinned, a most sinister and unsettling sight. He appeared to be pondering something.

"I like you Mr. Investigator, so I will let you and the girl live. Your two light-bearers are mine though."

As these words left his mouth, the Hájje assumed an attacking stance. Two streams of black magic shot from his hands and impacted Gharis and Verandas in their chests. A swirling mass of necrotic power enveloped the rangers and caused them to fall backwards. Both men doubled over as this necrotic energy coated their bodies. They hollered in agony, their torches rolling from their hands, the light flickering and causing Artimus to lose his target.

Both cadets were enveloped in dark energy, the tangible magic coating them in a sort of cocoon as it spread out from their centers. They seemed to phase in and out of corporeal form, their bodies shifting around violently.

Fortunately, Artimus had already released his arrow before his men had even hit the ground. His bow was already slung upon his back and he held his mythril blade in hand, the point facing towards his foe as he shifted his weight back and into a defensive stance.

Artimus could hear both Gharis and Verandas convulsing on the cave floor, their swords clanging against the walls. This Hájje had proven to be more than just a criminal; he was a demon, a dark chapter in the history of Evorath.

A tumor.

The senior investigator could feel the pain of his cadets, probably the sting of his pride at being bested by a criminal. If he did not act quickly, he feared that he would meet the same fate.

"Savannah! Run back and leave the cave. Ride to town with Sylvan and bring reinforcements." Anticipating protest, he quickly added, "That's a direct order. I will follow you shortly. Just leave the exit unsealed."

"Fine," Savannah shouted definitively. Hearing the rapid footsteps that followed, he believed she had done as expected.

The Hájje was laughing, a demonic sound bouncing off the cave walls. His arrow had obviously had no effect on the creature, so staying to fight was not an option. Turning his gaze down to the two cadets, he shuddered.

Judging by the necrotic magic that was flowing through them, Artimus was not willing to risk physical contact. So with his enemy out of sight, he backed into a wall and held his defensive stance. He watched in horror as the color faded from his cadets' skin. Their hair turned a jet-black as a ghostly white overtook their tan skin pigment. The last thing he saw before turning to flee were Gharis's black eyes.

They were being mutated.

Yezurkstal had no need for mates.

He was creating more hájje.

Chapter 3

Erathal Forest
13 Neglur, 1086

Life within the wilds of Erathal was never quiet. From the tiny termites that ate away at a rotting tree stump, to squirrels gathering up acorns, or a panther stalking its prey, movement was a constant within the forest. Even after the sun set and animals settled down, owls would hunt, and lynx would travel, keeping the forest ever-flowing with life. It was an endless cycle that would continue for all eternity, life moving throughout the thickest parts of the forest no matter the time of day. Of course, the early morning activity of this great forest was the most impressive of all.

Every type of creature stirred as the sun trickled down through the thick branches of the tallest trees. An unsuspecting snake rushed through the foliage, only to be snatched up and eaten by a brown-tailed mongoose. Unicorns grazed near the edge of a small pond, unaware of the lion pride that lurked behind the bush ready to pounce. A large rat scurried for cover, only to be scooped up and devoured by a young roc.

Many people believed that this life was chaos, but for the centaur warrior who stood observing these events, it was perfect order. As his village elders had taught him, there was a heavenly order laid down through the journey of life. On any given day, a predator could find its prey only to be consumed shortly thereafter by yet a greater predator. This was the way of the forest, and interfering meant rebelling against Evorath herself.

It had always troubled Irontail, the muscle-bound young centaur, that he was forbidden from saving a deer from its feline predators, or any other prey from its respective predator, but that was not the centaur way. As a village warrior, an honor bestowed on only the most powerful males, he needed to uphold their principles lest he cause his tribe great dishonor. Among all of centaur tribes, honor was considered the most important quality. A centaur without honor would be banished, left alone to fend for himself in the wilderness in a life of isolation and loneliness.

Like all other centaur, Irontail was devoted to his tribe, which was why he had taken this job in the first place. This loyalty would keep him bound in his place until his target was within sight. With all four legs planted in fallen leaves and moss covered rocks, Irontail waited for his objective to arrive, trying in vain to ignore the constant arrival and departure of life. Natural order was the best way for the forest; or so he reminded himself as he tightened his grip on the small tree trunk he used as a club.

Unfortunately, he had been waiting here much longer than he had expected, and the spiral of death was really starting to wear on his patience. If his charge was more prompt, he could be on his way back to Dumner village.

Of course, it was not unexpected for satyr, these base creatures being known for their tardiness and general lack of manners. From Irontail's perspective, they were all just a bunch of bipedal goats who had somehow learned how to speak. He just couldn't grasp what they could possibly have to offer to his people, or to anyone for that matter.

Finally, almost two hours after they were supposed to arrive, Irontail caught sight of the courier. They meandered their way through the light undergrowth and towards the meeting spot. Irontail counted three of them and, judging by their formation, he believed that the middle satyr was the representative he was waiting for. Now would be the difficult part.

"Hail and well met," Irontail exclaimed as the convoy stopped just a couple meters before him. "I thank Evorath for your safe arrival."

The middle satyr took the lead, brushing Irontail's greeting off with a wave of his hand.

"Enuff of ore pleasant trees. Ree-laxx. Lee-ead thee way." The satyr put a special emphasis on each syllable of his words, a habit, Irontail heard, that was quite common among his kind. It was just one of many annoying habits these creatures possessed that made them so unbearable.

The young centaur took immediate notice of the small jugs that each satyr had about their waist. Judging by their posture, he guessed that they had already consumed half of the contents. This was another habit that these base creatures stuck to without fail. Drinking was their solution to everything and oftentimes the leaders of a satyr tribe were chosen solely on their ability to consume more alcohol than any other member of the tribe. Knowing this made Irontail wonder why his elder wanted to keep the peace with any satyr.

Still, just as it was not his place to save prey from its predator, it was also forbidden for him to question an elder. With a fake smile, Irontail turned and led them through the forest. Like many journeys before, Irontail would put up with this undesirable task for the good of the tribe. He only hoped that the long journey would not drive him insane.

As they walked through the dense growth of the forest, he tried his best to ignore the drunken conversation coming from behind him. The members of the courier were all intoxicated, and it seemed that there was more laughter than there was actual conversation. With all the discipline he had within himself, Irontail held his tongue and kept his anger in check.

Kilometers of trekking through the dense forest, paired with hours of this meaningless banter, brought him to the edge of his tolerance. They were clumsy and disinterested in anything but their alcoholic conquests. Irontail was beginning to lose his patience when he finally caught sight of his relief.

"Welcome," a familiar voice came from just behind an ancient Erath, the largest species of tree in the known world. These colossal trees were native only to Erathal (which is why they kept their name) and reached sizes more than twice that of any oak. This particular Erath, which reached a height over one hundred and fifty meters and a diameter of nearly thirty, was the only way that Irontail could find his village.

The magic that was at work within his tribe was known only to the elders, but somehow this tree was the focal point. Only by knowing that this tree was the key, or by being allowed entrance by an elder, could anyone see Irontail's village. This, coupled with the half-dozen warriors and handful of druids who stood guard, kept the village safe from anyone who wished to harm it.

Irontail watched the satyrs' expressions as the village was revealed to them. What appeared to be simple foliage contained over a dozen windowless dwellings made of vines, beautiful blooms growing across their walls. Half a dozen small huts, made only of fallen trees and built into the side of large Erath served as the primary dwellings for the tribe. Finally, the center of this beautiful village was comprised of a large mound of plants.

Somehow, this mound seemed to be a conscious organism, thorny vines flowing around beautiful blossoms and moving succinctly. At the same time, the mound was stationary, a solid object surrounded by many moving ones, like a beautiful flower being swarmed by hundreds of bumblebees. Regardless of its consciousness, this sacred mound remained the most beautiful thing that Irontail had ever seen. Despite their drunkenness, even the visiting satyr seemed to admire its mysterious charm for a moment before bursting out in laughter again.

Cobolthand, the centaur who had welcomed them, moved from behind the tree, effectively blocking the mystical mound from sight.

"Well met," the small druid began. "On behalf of all of our tribe, we extend full hospitality to you and your courier."

As the wizened centaur spoke, he ignored Irontail completely, speaking only to the satyr delegates. Fortunately, Irontail was not at all saddened by this. In fact, he took the opportunity to step back and allow the smaller, older, but still more powerful centaur do the talking.

"Before we enter the sacred meeting hall," Cobolthand continued, motioning towards the great mound, "I offer you a feast. If you would be so ki-"

The satyr diplomat held up his right hand, swaying a bit as he did so.

"Tha 'tis not need ed. We ould like ta' ma' eat wi-ith your el ders an' your chief tin now."

Irontail could hardly contain himself. His tribe was offering these base creatures a welcoming feast and here they were, completely throwing away their hospitality. If not for the quick glance from his elder, Irontail may have returned the disrespect in the form of physical violence.

"Very well," Cobolthand responded. "The Council is right this way. Irontail, report to Copperfoot for a new assignment."

The satyr courier paid Irontail no heed, not any acknowledgment or sign of gratitude. They merely followed Cobolthand, swaying in their drunken somber and occasionally tripping over their own feet. As far as Irontail could tell, not one of these horrible excuses for a caretaker of the forest showed any sign of actual brain activity.

It perplexed him as he stood there, watching these base creatures, wondering why the elders would ever summon them. How could these drunken fools help his tribe? More importantly, how could they help serve Evorath?

As if on cue, Irontail felt a large hand fall upon his shoulder.

"I know what you are thinking young warrior, but you must not doubt the elders. The elders are wise."

Copperfoot removed his hand from the younger centaur's shoulder, bringing his broad body around to look Irontail in the eyes. Between his colossal shoulders and sinewy biceps, he appeared large enough to crush a boulder with his bare hands. From the stories passed on to the younger centaur, Irontail had no doubt that he could do that and much more should the need arise.

"The elders are wise," Irontail parroted. He wished to question this, to know why the elders would invite such crude creatures to their village. When had they ever helped? What could they do to benefit the village? Most importantly, how would these tiny, drunken fools do anything positive?

"Come with me," Copperfoot continued without any further consideration for the younger warrior.

Unwilling to voice his concerns, Irontail followed his elder to a small hut on the other side of the village. Unlike the mystical structure that the courier had been invited to, this was a rather simple hut. Crafted from the wood of a dead willow, this shoddy structure leaned against one of the larger Erath.

No roof covered the makeshift shelter, but the branches of the Erath offered a quasi-barrier against the elements. At its base, the undergrowth seemed to merge with the warped wood, vines, along with mushrooms and the roots of the tree itself all collaborated to give the hut an unexpected stability. Though not nearly as fantastic as the Great Mound, any foreigner would find this simple hut to be quite an intriguing sight.

Irontail took the initiative to push upon a seemingly solid log. With a light touch, the log pivoted to reveal an opening large enough for a centaur. As was proper etiquette in any centaur tribe, elders were to enter a structure before their pupils.

Apparently, despite his best efforts to appear relaxed, Irontail could not shake the annoyance he felt towards the satyr. Stopping before the opening, Copperfoot put his hand upon the younger centaur's shoulder once again.

"Do not fret." he reassured. "I will explain the situation once we are inside. For a warrior, you sure think too much."

With these words, the older centaur entered the hut, leaving the young warrior to think for a moment more.

Was it possible to think too much? Something about this made Irontail's insides turn. Wasn't thinking for oneself integral to serving the tribe? If no one thought, then how could anyone know what the tribe needed? Thinking too much...?

Irontail gave up on the internal struggle, planning to return to the matter next time he was stuck on guard duty. In the meantime, he followed his elder into the hut, allowing the door to shut quietly behind him. One thing he knew for sure was that action was more important than thought, and now was the time for action.

As he entered the deceivingly large hut, his eyes had to adjust to the increased light. There was only a single round table in the room with a bright druidic candle, the source of the increased lighting. The inside of this hut was much larger than it appeared from outside, leaving more than enough room for even the largest centaur to maneuver with relative comfort.

The walls were bare, nothing decorating the plain, wooden logs. There were small gaps in the makeshift ceiling, allowing a few inconsequential rays of light to shine through. Just like every other shelter in the village, there was no floor, but centaurs had no problem standing on grass.

Only one thing had changed in the room since Irontail had last been summoned here, and that was the people gathered around the table. Much to Irontail's surprise, some of these people held very important roles in the tribe. Other than himself, everyone in the room was a member of the Village Council.

So as he approached the table, Irontail could not help but wonder why three of his highest ranking elders would have summoned him, a lowly warrior, to the strategy hut. Without the slightest clue to why his presence here was required, the young warrior kept quiet. Confused to the point of doubting his elders, the brave warrior listened intently as Copperfoot began.

Chapter 4

Erathal Forest, outside Dumner
13 Neglur, 1086

Artimus sat atop his steed, Thoron, racing through the forest faster than ever before. The great white destrier that he rode had been his companion since his days as a hunter, but he had never driven him as hard as he did now. With fear still pumping through him, he paid no heed to the strain that he might be putting on his trusted companion. Unfortunately, he also failed to notice the thick branch that barred his path.

All the air was sucked out of his lungs as the branch tore him from his steed. A pain unlike any before left him numb, completely immobilized by the sudden impact.

Everything left his body.

All sound.

All feeling.

All sight...

-=-=-=-=-=-=-=-

A dim light began to seep through. All consciousness flowed back with a force that Artimus was unable to handle. From his chest down, he could feel nothing, a frightening numbness encompassing most of his body. But the young elf could hear, he could see, he could breathe.

His body was moving, not by his own accord, but by large, rough hands. Tilting his head slightly, Artimus tried to focus his eyes, looking towards the hands of his helpers. All he could distinguish were the outlines of horses.

As his head fell back to the soggy grass, just before his vision failed again, he saw something that filled him with warmth. Familiar legs, and beautiful ones at that, covered only by a green silk, he knew immediately who those legs belonged to. Still unsure of his condition, he allowed this sight to calm him, and once again he drifted out of consciousness.

-=-=-=-=-=-=-=-=-

A smile spread across his face while sitting in his favorite chair, watching his neighbor's child play. The village children were so innocent, playing a simple game of hide and seek. It was a beautiful day, but he expected nothing less from the greatest kingdom in Evorath, Erathal. Still, despite the great joy he received from watching these children frolic as the sun rose to take its place in the sky, something felt out of place.

Then he spotted it: an intruder.

The pale beast, with its hollow eyes and death-black hair crept behind the young boy. Artimus rose to yell, to warn the helpless child. It was too late.

The boy's skin went pale, his eyes filled with the darkness of night. Like a festering wound, all life around the boy ceased. The grass on the forest floor withered, trees shed their leaves and wasted away. Death spread like locusts, and Artimus couldn't even scream as the rot closed in on him...

-=-=-=-=-=-=-=-=-

Artimus jerked up from his dream with a sharp pain radiating from his right shoulder across his chest to his left leg. His breathing was heavy and painful, but each inhale brought about less agony. As he lowered himself back into a resting position, Artimus observed his surroundings.

Using his one sense that he was sure to be fully functioning, Artimus could smell that he was still in the forest. Judging by the strong smell of oak, he ventured to guess that he was in a crudely constructed hut. Though his entire body was a bit numb, he concluded he was lying on a makeshift bed, perhaps some moss laid out on a table for cushioning. Despite the dim light, he managed to turn his head to the right and see the forest floor, proving that the hut was indeed crudely constructed. He was also able to confirm his table theory.

As he slowly turned his neck, observing a decrease in both pain and numbness each second, he realized that the only light in the room was actually seeping through the ceiling. In fact, if his eyes did not deceive him, there was no actual roof, but only tree branches serving as a makeshift roof. The more he saw of his surroundings, the more he questioned the civility of his rescuers. But then he remembered the legs.

Those beautiful, radiant legs, covered by their flowing, green silk could only belong to one person. Knowing that Savannah was somewhere nearby, coupled with the lack of any restraints, alleviated all fears about these villagers being anything less than affable. Now all he had to do was get out of this crude bed and find out where he was.

Mindful of his injuries, Artimus worked to prop himself into a sitting position. The pain flared for a moment but diminished as he forced himself through it. His body was protesting, but it seemed the more he pushed it, the less it fought back. A hopeful thought. Or, perhaps his injuries were less extensive than he had anticipated.

Footsteps stomped behind the door as he assumed a sitting position. Fighting the urge to bolt back down and feign sleep, he glued his eyes to the spot. Listening closely, it sounded like an elf and a horse.

His heart fluttered as Savannah stepped through the door, closely followed by a medium-built centaur. His vision blurred momentarily as he shifted to face the two visitors. Refocusing, he tried to ignore the light-headed sensation that followed and completely ignored the protest from his lower back. He would not let Savannah see him in pain, much less allow a centaur warrior to think of him as weak.

"I am glad to see you are sitting up," the centaur began. "Our healers found you in pretty rough shape. Said you could have been paralyzed for life if they hadn't gotten to you so soon. You're lucky that the Erath you ran into was part of our village. Thick as a large oak, that branch was, and you hit it going faster than a frightened lynx."

Artimus took a moment to look over the centaur who was speaking to him. Judging by the studded leather that covered most of his body, it was easy to conclude that he was indeed of the warrior class. Taking into account the lack of markings, face paint, tattoos, or amulets of any kind, he could reasonably assume

42

that this muscular creature held no tribal authority. They had sent a grunt to greet their guest. Not a diplomatic choice.

"I am very much obliged," Artimus started, trying to keep his eyes away from Savannah until he had shown proper gratitude. The centaur elders might not understand diplomacy, but Artimus did.

"You have done the Erathal Rangers a great service by saving me. As a representative of the Rangers, I offer whatever service your tribe may require." Artimus paused for a moment and took a slightly less diplomatic tone.

"But first, I must ask... Is my horse safe?"

The centaur laughed, a deep rumble of a sound that startled Artimus. He also noticed Savannah jump back as the sound erupted.

"Your great steed is safely grazing in the open grass just within our protective field. It was uninjured and quickly returned to you once you had fallen. Even I can tell that you and your horse share a deep bond, and I am but a lowly warrior." The centaur spoke jovially, as if he and Artimus had been old friends.

"Thoron and I have been companions for quite some time. I have a better relationship with him than I do with most elves. But I am glad to see that our relationship is so visible. I was born a hunter, but it is Thoron who has been with me since adulthood and made me an efficient ranger."

Savannah cleared her throat quite loudly, effectively breaking Artimus's thought process and drawing his attention to her exquisite body. Quickly returning his eyes to the muscular centaur, Artimus realized that the warrior was uninterested in his ramblings.

"My apologies," Artimus said quickly, doing his best to ignore the stiffness in his neck that had surfaced. "I seem to have forgotten my most basic manners. I am Lieutenant Artimus Atyrmirid of the Royal Ranger Division and I am most grateful for your hospitality."

"I am Irontail, warrior for the Dumner tribe. You are in Dumner village, and I am here to extend our hospitality."

Savannah stepped forward and smiled. "They have been most kind hosts. Sylvan and I stopped just inside their village to catch our breath, but instead we found ourselves surrounded by centaur."

"Yes" interrupted Irontail, "your cadet nearly soiled himself from the looks of it. Almost attacked us when the elder lifted the veil."

Artimus was rather confused. "What exactly is this 'veil,' or 'field,' or whatever it is called that you keep mentioning?"

Savannah cast him a dirty look, and he couldn't blame her considering how casually he was addressing this warrior. But, then again, he didn't care. If he were talking to an elder of this tribe, or even a druid, he could speak more professionally, but all he had was a warrior. Frankly, he felt that speaking in any other manner would make it appear that he was condescending.

The centaur didn't seem to mind at any rate, and answered.

"Well, I don't exactly know how the field works, but the druids of our tribe utilize arcane magic to conceal our village from any possible threats. Basically, it just casts an illusion that makes everything within the protected area look like empty forest. The only way to see the village and its inhabitants is either if an elder wills you to see it or to know the focal point, which somehow causes its appearance."

"What about large animals?" Savannah asked, beating Artimus to his next question. "I mean, couldn't an elephant just trample through by accident?"

"You'd think so," Irontail said pensively. "But somehow the elders are able to prevent that too. I have never seen anything larger than a tiger within five kilometers of here. Some kind of enchantment placed on the forest from ancient times. That's what the elders say."

Though Artimus was indeed interested with the mechanics of this tribe, he knew that there were more urgent issues that needed to be dealt with. Amidst his pain and the story of his rescuers, he had almost allowed himself to forget about the problem at hand, about the loss of his comrades and the emergence of a most dangerous enemy. For some reason, as this warrior attempted to explain how the village worked, Artimus had allowed the recent memories to surface.

Images flashed through his head of Gharis and Verandas as the evil overtook them. The hájje's face was forever burned into his conscious, the sinister face of evil incarnate. He needed to report to Erathal immediately.

As Savannah opened her mouth to ask another question, Artimus pushed himself from the table, landing roughly on his two feet with knees bent. The room spun around him, and he was sure he heard someone yelp in pain, but he kept his footing. Savannah rushed to his aid, as did the centaur warrior. It must have been he who had screamed, for sharp pain spread through his lower back as he assumed an upright posture.

A strange warmth spread throughout his body as Savannah's hand wrapped around his own. In that moment, though he was unsure if it was real, a strange, rejuvenating energy poured from her hand into his body. All pain seemed to leave, and for just a few seconds, while her soft, warm hand held his own rough, cold fingers, he felt he could do anything.

Savannah removed her hand and the pain started anew. This time however, it seemed more bearable, as if someone was helping him carry a heavy load. As Artimus lifted his head to look into her eyes, he could tell that it had not been his imagination. Her eyes had become somewhat dull, a sign that she had exerted much of her magical energies.

"You must be more careful, Artimus! I mean, sir." Savannah immediately cast her eyes toward the ground when she noticed Artimus looking into them.

"She's right," added the centaur. "You had broken ribs, a broken neck and a fractured back. The druids were able to mend your bones, but they said it will take at least a few days until the pain goes away. Also, they said your bones are extra weak right now. Best to take it easy until the pain subsides."

46

"Thanks for the advice," Artimus replied. "But I request to speak to your elders immediately. I have horrific news, which is why I was in such a hurry. Seeing as your village is even closer than our city, I must inform the elders of the danger they are in."

Irontail looked annoyed, but he was obviously doing his best to hide it. "Yeah. The elders know about the danger. They have not requested your audience, but they want to speak to your druid."

Savannah looked at Artimus and nodded. "They kept requesting an audience with me, but I told them that you are my commanding officer. If they want any news, I told them to get it from you."

Irontail jumped right onto Savannah's thought and continued. "Which is why the elders agreed that if you were ready you could accompany your druid to the meeting hall. I would say you look ready. So please follow me."

Artimus took a moment before giving a response, trying to figure out how this conversation had taken so many turns. When the discussion started, he had been inquiring about his horse, but now he found this centaur practically demanding an audience with Savannah. Why would they want to speak with his subordinate and not him?

Regardless of why, Artimus knew that his news was urgent. They claimed to know about the danger, but he would make sure they understood the scope.

"Very well," said Artimus. "Lead the way."

Chapter 5

Erathal Forest, Dumner village
13 Neglur, 1086

Irontail took his time leading the elves to the sacred chamber. Though he respected this investigator for his pain tolerance, he could not help but be annoyed by his changing attitudes. One second, he would be speaking like a trained diplomat and then, without warning, he would act as if they were old friends. Artimus was the first elf he had really spoken to, and in their short conversation he found himself quite unimpressed.

The druid, on the other hand, was quite affable. She rarely spoke, but when she did, she got her point across without mincing words. This was a respected quality in his society, but it was nice to know that it was not a quality exclusive to his kind.

The third elf, who was probably enjoying a nice meal in one of the wooden huts, was not present, but was clearly the lowest ranking. This feeble looking excuse for a warrior seemed to have less sense than most centaur children. Perhaps he had some skill with a blade, but when it came to honor and courage, it was clear that this cadet was lacking.

"Is that the meeting hall?" Artimus asked as they approached the central mound, interrupting Irontail's thoughts.

"That is much more than just the meeting hall. Within that mound there is a passage that leads underground. Along the path, there are many turns that do not concern you. It is at the end of the passage that the meeting hall lies."

"I hope there is some place to sit in this meeting hall, because my back is killing me," the investigator joked.

Irontail looked back at him with confusion.

"I'm sure they will have something to sit on sir," Savannah interjected smiling. "I just can't believe how beautiful this is."

"Indeed. Is it alive?" Artimus asked.

"I've asked myself that same thing," replied Irontail as they neared the entrance.

"Haven't gotten an answer yet?"

"Not yet."

A new voice joined the conversation as they reached the entrance to this beautiful, moving structure. The deep voice came from within, carrying a great deal of power and authority. Irontail recognized it as the tribe's greatest elder, the legendary warrior Goldenchest.

"If you had asked, my young warrior, the answer would have been given." Both elves appeared alarmed, but neither lost his or her composure. They merely stood motionless as the voice spoke. "You should ask questions when you have the opportunity my son. Knowledge can only be gained when one is interested in gaining it. If you had revealed your interest before, you would know that this hallow ground is still living."

The pulsing mound flowed in a different direction, its vines unraveling and splitting before their very eyes. Blooms slipped underneath some of the greater vines somehow staying in perfect condition despite the rapid movement. The entire thing pulsated with life, as a strange energy flowed throughout the mound.

A path revealed itself as the living mound parted to expose the great centaur. He stood tall above them, his slightly faded, golden chest glistening in the afternoon sun. Though the leaves overhead blocked most of the sunlight, enough got through for the golden hairs on this legendary elder to shine. Both elves appeared captivated by the brilliant splendor of this unique color.

In fact, Goldenchest was the only centaur -probably the only creature- to truly have golden hair. At his birth, the elders of his time knew that he would be something special. As he grew older, he quickly proved this prediction true by excelling in both magical and physical strength. According to the other elders, Goldenchest was the most powerful centaur to have ever lived.

Irontail took a quick bow as a sign of respect.

"Thank you elder. I shall be more open with my questions in the future. These are the elves that are to join your assembly."

Goldenchest returned the bow.

"Indeed they are. But, you, too, are asked to accompany me down to the ritual chamber."

"Me? To the ritual chamber?"

"Yes, you are to come as well. This ritual has never been done on such a scope. We invite you, a promising young warrior, because we believe you should witness this event. After all, you have done much to make sure that all parties have gathered safely."

Before Irontail could respond, Artimus jumped in with his own questions.

"Hold on a second. I thought you wanted to hear about what we encountered in the old, abandoned mines. What is this about a ritual?"

"You show great disrespect to your hosts," Irontail began before being cut off by his elder.

"Young warrior, have patience with these elves. After all, they arrived only by nature's fortune. True, we have rescued this ranger, but it is the druid that will give us an even greater service than we have provided."

Irontail could tell that both elves were annoyed by the fact that his elder spoke of them as if they were not present. He couldn't much blame them either, for he had never much enjoyed being ignored. As expected, his elder must have picked up on these feeling as well, because he continued by addressing them.

"My apologies Master Artimus and Mistress Savannah. I had forgotten that you were unaware of the circumstances of your visit. If you would please follow me." Goldenchest spoke very eloquently, in a tone sounding much too gentle for such a powerful creature.

"Lead on," Artimus offered, a note of suspicion present in his voice. "Are we not going to the meeting hall then?"

"Correct," replied the elder centaur as he led them forward. "We must proceed right at the first room. Through here actually."

Goldenchest stopped abruptly, causing Artimus to wince in pain as he almost ran into the large centaur. Irontail understood that this ranger was not an invited guest for this occasion but, knowing how important this ritual was, he could not help but wonder why his elder was being so rude. With a simple order from Artimus, the druid and he would both leave, causing quite the dilemma for the others attending.

Of course, as soon as these thoughts entered his mind, he did his best to push them away. Questioning the actions of an elder could never lead to anything good. Yet this recurring thought kept creeping into his head: 'what if the elders are wrong?' Fortunately, so he thought, something always pulled him away before he was able to ponder any further.

"Irontail!"

The young warrior snapped to attention at the commanding voice of his elder.

"Yes, sir?"

"Did you hear what I said?"

"No, sir. I am sorry. I jus-"

"A warrior doesn't make excuses, Irontail. Answer any questions that our guests might have while I make sure the others are prepared." Goldenchest made his order with absolute authority and turned forward.

"Yes, sir. As you wish."

As the embarrassing exchange concluded, Goldenchest left Irontail alone with the two elves. He felt uncomfortable after being scolded by his elder, but he was mature enough to ignore the shame. His habit to think about every little order before executing it was proving to be quite a nuisance lately. Still, he had a job to do, and he wouldn't let his embarrassment interfere.

Fortunately for Irontail, both elves were much too shocked to ask any questions as their eyes traveled across the giant chamber. Even Irontail could not believe that all this was possible, but somehow the elders had gathered a druid from every sentient species of the forest.

He spotted the satyr druid he had escorted across the hall and watched as he conversed with a beautiful lamia. Not far from them were a group of lizock who seemed intent on being isolated, a practice common to their race. To the other side of the room there were felite conversing with a pair of barghest and a rather small troll. This was a gathering to be proud of and knowing that it was his elders who had organized this event reassured Irontail of their infinite wisdom. Never before had all of these races united for a single cause.

"I don't believe my eyes," Artimus exclaimed as his gaze passed over the felite and fixed in on the troll.

"Is that a troll?" Savannah asked.

"Yes it is," answered Irontail full of pride.

"What are all of these people doing here?" Artimus questioned. "And what is that dog looking creature?"

"I believe you mean the barghest, sir." Savannah interjected matter-of-factly.

"Yes, it is a barghest," Irontail confirmed. "Their elders claim that at one time they were more numerous than both our species put together."

"There are many legends about barghest being around in the age of demons, before elf, dwarf, centaur, or any other common race even existed," Savannah added.

"Don't stories also say that barghest fought on the side of the demons?" Artimus asked.

To that, Irontail had no answer. History was not one of his strong points.

"I don't know," he interjected, "But enough about the barghest. You asked why they have gathered. I shall give you an answer."

Irontail paused for a moment, trying to figure out exactly what to say. In all honesty, he wasn't even sure of the exact reason these races had gathered. All that he did know was what his elders had told him in the meeting he attended just after escorting the satyr courier. He just needed to make it look like he understood more...

"Well. You see. These nine races that are gathered represent the greatest species of the woods. These nine, including both your race and my own, will perform the first perfect druidic ritual. With your help," he said turning to Savannah, "all nine races will be present and the ritual will be done."

"Wait," Savannah began, her face losing color. "Are you talking about a Xyrloom?"

"What is that?" Artimus asked.

Savannah turned to Artimus.

"A druid circle that summons forth an avatar of Evorath." Savannah turned back to Irontail shaking her head, fear mixed with anger painted over her. "Tell your elders it won't work."

"How can you know that?" Irontail asked, confused. The druid seemed quite sure of herself, and she was visibly distressed.

"Before I moved to the city, I was a druid of these woods. I lived with a small tribe of elves, and we excelled in druidic magic. One day, years ago, eight other elves and I attempted a Xyrloom. Only three of us survived."

"Hold up," Artimus interrupted. "Give me a better explanation of this Xyrloom."

Irontail looked to Savannah, hoping she would take the initiative. He assumed that it was implied, but he never liked admitting that he was clueless. All he knew was what the elders had told him, which wasn't any more than this elf had already explained.

"Alright," said Savannah, her tone severe. "The Xyrloom is a fabled ritual. Legends say that at one time there were no forests. Long ago, when the demons held dominion over Evorath, the gods performed a Xyrloom and created the forest and the dryads to watch over it. Legends are rarely accurate."

"If you do not mind," Irontail started nervously. "How did six of you die?"

"The Xyrloom didn't create an avatar. It summoned a demon," she said angrily. "The earth within our circle collapsed in, leaving a huge chasm. One of my closest friends fell in from the tremors, and another followed when attempting to catch her. It was a bottomless pit, and before any of us could even understand what had happened, a great beast burst up from within."

Savannah's voice faltered and her face was heavy with burden. Irontail had never been a sensitive creature, but even he could tell that this story was painful for her to relive. He felt an odd sensation, one he was unfamiliar with. Was it pity?

"That's enough," exclaimed Artimus, placing an arm around his druid for support.

"I'm sure that Irontail has heard enough as well. Right?" His gaze fell upon the warrior, eyes demanding a quick response. Irontail couldn't have predicted such a powerful look from a simple elf. Perhaps there was more to this ranger.

"Indeed." His response came out rather weak. He wished to hear the rest of her tale, but courtesy to these guests was his top priority.

"Thank you." Savannah wiped the tears from her eyes.

Irontail felt that strange feeling again. He didn't know what to say, but it appeared that the elvish ranger did.

"I only count eight races in attendance here. Ourselves included."

Irontail looked at the elf in disbelief and proceeded to take the tally himself. Centaur, elf, satyr, troll, felite, lizock, lamia, barghest... It appeared the ranger was right.

"I guess the other courier has yet to arrive," Irontail offered.

"Well, then you might as well tell whoever it is to turn around, because you don't have an elf either," Savannah insisted.

"I'm sorry to hear that lady elf, but perhaps we can come to an agreement."

Irontail looked around in confusion. This soothing voice did not come from he nor Artimus, or from any of the other guests that could be seen. All conversation stopped as the voice spoke, the room falling silent. It was a feminine voice; soft and sweet yet full of great fury. Both high and low, tender and dangerous, beautiful and revolting, horrible and wonderful.

"I would ask you this, my lady," the voice continued. "What if the dryads themselves approved of this ritual?"

Irontail looked to Savannah in disbelief. Judging by her expression she was taken aback by the question, as was Irontail himself. Her face showed both disbelief and confusion, accompanied by an almost mocking posture.

"When you produce a dryad, we will talk," she said, sarcasm fermenting her voice.

Her response was not quite what Irontail expected. Judging by the room's continued silence, the other guests were as eager for a response as he was.

"So be it."

As the mysterious voice spoke, the ceiling above them pulsated with life. A tremor ran across the ground, and the outline of a woman became visible in the center of the room. Irontail took a few steps back and noticed that the others had done so as well.

Slowly, the outline grew, coming forth as if it were alive. At first, he thought it was only his imagination, but the ground continued to rise, taking the full shape of a woman. Her breasts took solid form, her abdomen, her arms, her legs, her face, and finally her hair. Irontail could not believe his eyes.

Clothed in nothing but her green skin, deep green eyes, and root-like hair, she rose into a standing position. The life of the forest could be felt radiating from her, a green glow to accent her already amazing features. Her smooth, perfectly proportioned body could only belong to a maiden of the forest. She looked just as the elders had described.

She was a dryad.

Murmurs of disbelief spread through the room, but Irontail knew it in his heart. This was a real dryad, and with her help the ritual was bound to succeed. True, he had never seen a dryad before, but he knew of them as well as anyone else and trusted in their power as much as he trusted the elders. Hoping that Savannah shared this recognition, he turned and beheld her expression of complete shock.

-=-=-=-=-=-=-=-=-

Savannah was beside herself. Looking upon the woman that appeared before her, she was unable believe her own eyes. She had asked the voice to produce a dryad, and so it had been done. The voice *belonged* to a dryad.

At least most of the attention had shifted from her to this maiden.

"What say you young elvish mistress? I am a dryad, the dryad of birch, and I wish to perform this ritual with you and seven other powerful druids. Will you save the forest?"

What could she do? She thought of her friends who had died last time she had participated in this ritual. Then she thought of the potential this ritual had, if it were done properly. They had all been young in her village, led by an elf not much older than she was today. With the guidance of a dryad, a true keeper of the forest, perhaps the ritual would obtain the proper results. Perhaps the legendary avatar could be brought into physical form.

She knew there was no time to wait. Having felt the hájje's power firsthand, she understood the urgency of this decision. The desperate eyes of everyone else in the room didn't help either. But she was torn.

"I do not choose to participate in this ritual, but I must obey my commander." She turned to Artimus, dread already clear on his face. He had feelings for her, and one day she would tell him that she shared his feelings. Now she needed his help to get through this, and she knew that was something she could count on.

"What would you have me do, sir?"

-=-.=-.=-.=-.=-.=-.=-

Irontail wanted to yell at the foolish druid. How could she question this ritual? Not only had the elders suggested it, but now a dryad supported it. It couldn't possibly fail!

He could tell he was not the only one who thought this ridiculous, for another set of murmurs quickly circulated the room. The only words he was sure that he heard were "crazy," "druid," and "dumb," but that was enough to convince him that at least some people agreed with him.

"I will not order you to perform this ritual," Artimus began.

Irontail balled his fists.

"It does not fall within my authority to order you to use any such magic. But," he added without pause, "as your friend, I ask you to participate. If only for my sake, to show me what you can do, help them perform this ritual."

Irontail relaxed. He knew these two elves shared a deeper bond than just being rangers when he had seen them interact in the hut. There was no way she could say no to his request such as it was.

"Very well," Savannah responded reluctantly. She then turned to the dryad with piercing eyes. "But first you must answer one question. Why didn't you get another elf?"

The dryad came closer, and Irontail could feel her influence enveloping him. It was a soothing touch, a relaxing, refreshing sensation that spread through his body. It was Evorath's direct caress giving him a feeling of invincibility. And then her sweet voice came again, seeming even more enticing as she was just an arm's length away.

"I have powers that no druid yet understands. I knew you would be joining us today, so I told the elders not to bother contacting the elves. Perhaps someday you will understand these powers."

Irontail wanted to reach out and touch her, to feel the full power of the woods. For a moment he considered giving in, but as she turned and walked away the feeling faded. His eyes still followed the fair mistress until she stopped beside his most revered elder, Goldenchest.

Irontail could feel his own excitement welling up inside him.

"Now that we are all ready," Goldenchest started, taking an assertive posture and stepping forward, "let us begin."

-=-.=-.=-.=-.=-.=-.=-.=-

Artimus focused his eyes on Savannah's angelic face as the conversation ensued. He refused to look at the dryad, for even her aura was giving him temptations. Somehow, he knew that this beautiful elf was all that was keeping him from running with these thoughts. Only she deserved his attention.

As the dryad walked away, he felt the temptation diminish, but still kept his eyes fixed on his lab mage. From the moment he had seen her, there was a clear attraction, but now he felt something else. She was everything he could ever look for in a partner, or was that just a side-effect of the dryad?

Was this love, or dryad-induced infatuation? But didn't a dryad's effect only cause people to be attracted to them? Artimus knew he cared about Savannah, but these feelings now were different than he had felt towards anyone before. These feelings made him wish that he could hold her in his arms and never let go.

According to myth, the only thing that could keep an elf from resisting the temptation of a nymph in close proximity was a connection with a loved one. Even that connection, if it was not on the mind, could be broken with the kind of power that nymphs, especially dryads, were rumored to have over other creatures. What did it mean that Artimus was able to focus his attention on Savannah?

Artimus let his feelings take over, and as the centaur with golden hair addressed those gathered, he continued to stare at Savannah. As her gaze met his own and their eyes locked, he felt a sudden jolt of energy. They were the only important people in the room.

"Artimus?" her tone was raised in concern as she walked closer. "Were you not listening? Goldenchest just asked everyone who isn't a druid to go to the walls of the room."

"Of course," his voice sounded distant. Was that him talking? "Good luck, Savannah. I'm sure I have quite a show to look forward to."

As the voice finished, Savannah began moving away. No. Savannah was standing in place. It was Artimus who was moving, walking away from the elf he was in love with.

There was a sharp pain in his right shoulder as he spun around straight into one of the barghest that he'd seen earlier. The great canine let out a low growl, barring his teeth as Artimus took a few steps back. Reflexes caused him to grab for his hunting dagger, tightly grasping the handle and preparing to draw.

"Watch where you're going, elf!" the barghest barked, pointing his weapon at Artimus. The small iron hatchet looked sharp enough to cleave through muscle and bone with ease and, judging by his posture, he would not hesitate to use it. Barghest were a dying race, but those that remained made some of the most ferocious warriors.

"My apologies," Artimus responded with a slight bow, removing his hand from the dagger at his waist. "I shall be more careful in the future."

The barghest grunted and walked away, heading towards the walls of the ritual hall. Artimus followed him with his eyes but waited before continuing his own movement. Two satyrs stumbled past him, humming some strange song as they followed the barghest. A couple of lizock followed, their tails dragging behind like snakes as they whispered in the reptilian dialect.

Artimus turned to meet another warrior, a lithe felite wearing only two thin pieces of cloth, one over her waist and another around her chest. A small dagger hung to her left, and a water skin to her right. Like most of her kind, she was slightly shorter than Artimus and walked with grace and finesse, a certain spring in each step showing that she was ready to pounce.

"Rarely interact well with other species, those who are tasked with tending the forest do," she said, approaching Artimus.

"My friendship, I offer," she continued after a moment's pause, "and receive yours in return, I hope I can."

Felite were known for being the most agile and dexterous creatures in all of Evorath. Like their four-legged cousins, every felite had distinctive whiskers and came in a large variety of fur colors. Warrior felite typically had stripped, or a dark black fur. Druids usually had spots, or sometimes random patches of varying hair colors.

This particular felite had fur of the purest white, which made it impossible for Artimus to guess her role. Of course, judging by the dagger she carried, he was fairly certain she was not one of the druids. That meant she must have come to protect the druid.

"I am always willing to extend my hand in friendship," Artimus began, carefully choosing each word before allowing it to escape his lips. Being in a room full of other species meant he needed to act as a representative for all elves. He was never fond of diplomats, but for now he recognized his need to act as one.

"Delighted to hear that, I am," the felite said with a slight bow. "Please allow me to introduce myself. They call me Tel' Shira of the Felite Confederacy."

Though quite unsure of what a confederacy was, he gave his own introduction.

"I am Lieutenant Artimus Atyrmirid of the Royal Rangers."

"Artimus Atyrmirid. Always amazed at the length of elvish names, I am. For a felite, Tel' Shira is quite long, but still much less of a mouthful, it is." As she spoke, she led him to the wall where the others had already gathered.

He allowed his glance to stray over to Savannah and the other druids for just a moment and saw that they were discussing details. Still, his attention remained with Tel' Shira, and he allowed himself to grin at her comment about his name.

"I hope I do not offend you," Artimus offered politely, "but how many elves have you met?"

"Well, actually, the first, you are. But at least twice as long as my own is every elvish name I have heard."

"I thought as much." Artimus replied with another grin. "You see, we have a first name, which is what we go by, and a family name, which helps identify us. So nobody actually calls me by my full name."

"I see," the felite responded, rubbing her chin as she pondered. "So, what shall I call you?"

"Artimus will do fine. With any elves you meet in the future just call them by their first names."

"Indeed. Well, most happy to have your friendship, I am. To ask you, I would like, is it true that Death, you have actually seen?"

With his peripheral vision, Artimus caught the barghest and the two lizock look up at the mention of Death. Even the two satyrs stopped laughing when the words escaped her mouth.

"Death?" Artimus asked incredulously. He knew what she was asking about. She meant the hájje.

"Yes, the source of the evil. The power that grows even as we speak. The bane of life and growth. A sin child you call him, I believe."

Irontail joined the crowd as the felite spoke, her words likely drawing his interest. Artimus didn't know what to say. Yes, he had seen the sin child, and he couldn't believe the power it possessed. How could he describe it?

It dawned on him then. How would he report the death of his cadets? Were they even dead?

"It is true," Artimus said after a short pause. "I lost two cadets as a result. His powers are unlike anything I have ever seen."

"That doesn't mean much coming from an elf now, does it?" The new voice came from behind, like the grating sound of two stones being rubbed against one another. Such a voice had to belong to one of the lizock, for only a reptile could produce such bile.

A deep laugh sounded from the barghest as Artimus turned to see his adversary. He was met by two sets of red eyes glaring at him like a tiger would stare down its prey. Since both had dark, scaly skin, Artimus found he was unable to tell them apart. The only differences he could see were perhaps an inch in height and the left lizock's lack of a weapon.

"I supposed you have seen the hájje?" Artimus questioned with an arched eyebrow.

"Seen it? Certainly not. If we had encountered him, he would be dead. This whole ritual is just a waste of time. Me and my partner here could take out anyone."

Artimus fought the urge to hit the lizard merely for his arrogance. This reptile had not seen the power the hájje possessed. After all, Artimus himself had expected he could overcome the enemy before witnessing his power firsthand.

"That challenge, I will take," Tel' Shira blurted.

She stepped in front of Artimus, lowering herself into an unfamiliar stance. It appeared she had a solid base, so he assumed that it was for defense. He had heard stories about how proficient the felite fighting arts were but had never actually seen them before. Part of him wanted the demonstration, but he knew it was foolish.

"No you won't," Artimus said assertively, not giving the lizock time to respond. "We all came here for a common goal. All we are going to do is wait until the druids complete their ritual and then go our separate ways."

"Weakling," the barghest spat. "You elves are always trying to avoid a good fight."

"There will be no fighting!" Irontail asserted as he placed himself between Tel' Shira and the lizock. Though armed only with his hooves and fists, the sheer size of a centaur was enough to discourage most challengers. The two lizock stepped back and Tel' Shira relaxed. Unfortunately, the barghest didn't consider Irontail a threat.

"How about this, you overgrown horse?" the barghest growled. "You go graze somewhere else and let the warriors play."

The lizock sniggered.

"Because you are a guest to this tribe, I cannot harm you. But be warned, anyone who harms one of our guests will be called an enemy of the tribe. Centaurs don't give second chances."

The barghest grumbled, but his face showed that he had gotten the point. Being an enemy of a centaur tribe meant being killed on sight.

This made Artimus think; nature herself was full of chaos, yet amidst it all, everything seemed to function for the better. It seemed that all those who inhabited the beauty of this forest were destined to be a part of the chaos. Lizock and barghest showed hostility towards all races, lamia and troll were as wild and savage as an untamed animal, centaur and dryads kept themselves hidden, and satyr drank their lives away. This left only elves and felite. If there was any hope for the future of the forest, it was through an alliance of felite and elf.

This thought left Artimus in an awkward position. What if this ritual didn't work? His people and the felite were the only races that were level-headed enough to actively defend the forest. The others would surely try to fend for themselves, but Artimus knew this hájje's power. No one would survive unless they all worked together.

"These people sicken me," Irontail murmured, shaking his head. Artimus looked up, removing himself from thought, and realizing that both the lizock and barghest had moved away. The centaur's threat had definitely gotten through.

"Ignorant, they are," Tel' Shira responded. "Understand the situation, they do not."

"How can they?" Artimus questioned as he looked back towards her. "How can you understand?"

68

"Seen the darkness as you have, I have not, but there are those of my race who have. Powerful abilities, the sages possess. With their gift of foresight, they have told all of my people the damage this demon will cause."

"How can they know this?" Irontail asked, stealing the words from Artimus's own mind.

"Why do you trust you elders?" Tel' Shira countered.

"Because the elders are wise," Irontail responded, a note of offense present in his voice.

"Wisdom, the sages possess in excess. As clear, no, more clear, the future is, than the present to them."

"If your sages see this power," Artimus asked, "then why do you even bother trying this ritual?"

"Many possibilities, the future holds. Power beyond that of evil this ritual could bring. Why one of our most powerful druids is here to perform the ritual, that is. Also, why chosen to protect her, I was."

"So this ritual could really work?" Artimus asked hopefully.

"Of course it could," Irontail answered. "The elders would not have called for this meeting unless they knew it would work."

"Flawed, your reasoning may be, but correct you are. Work, this ritual will, but only time will tell if it works well enough."

"Time and I have never gotten along well." Artimus finished, looking beyond both Irontail and Tel' Shira.

He watched Savannah as she discussed something with the troll that not even his elvish eyes could make out. Her full and beautiful lips moved gracefully, but he could not distinguish what she was saying. As she finished speaking, they went in separate directions and the other seven participants, including Goldenchest and the dryad, formed a circle around a small bonfire.

The ritual would soon begin.

Chapter 6

Erathal Forest, Dumner ritual hall
13 Neglur, 1086

Artimus watched carefully as all nine participants took
their place in the circle. Irontail and Tel' Shira stood silently, one
to either side of him, both entrenched as the ritual began. The
entire room fell into silence as Goldenchest extinguished the
druidic fire lighting up the room, leaving the flame at the center
of the ritual circle as the primary source of light.

It seemed strange that they would use fire for a druidic
ritual, especially one to call upon Evorath's avatar. Artimus had
expected them to gather around a tree or something, not chant
around fire. But it appeared he was mistaken, for that was
precisely what they were doing.

Artimus watched, captivated as all the druids joined hands
and circled around the fire. They all spoke in a strange tongue, a
language that must have died before elves even came to walk
upon Evorath. They proceeded in this circle for at least five
minutes, perhaps longer, but to Artimus it might as well have
been an hour.

Suddenly, the flame in the center intensified, and they
paused for just a moment before reversing direction. They were
chanting something new now, but it was still incomprehensible to
Artimus. It actually sounded like half of the participants were
chanting one thing while the other half chanted something
different. The flame weakened to its original state as they flew

around the fire like a great tornado, and Goldenchest's voice came over all the others.

"Fury of fire," he yelled in the common tongue as a gust of wind strengthened the flame again. "Power of wind," he continued without pause, the circle of druids slowing down their movement.

"Combine with the strength of the earth and be as malleable as water." As he spoke these words, the wind died, and a small geyser of water broke through the flames, putting them out.

The druids halted. Their chanting stopped. The dryad stood at what appeared to be the center of the circle. Artimus caught only a glimpse of her beauty before shielding his eyes.

"Æthrän gïœra. ßeirrô üssýr ó åft drýæds." Her language sounded the same as the one they all had been chanting just a moment before.

Artimus had no time to figure out if it was, for as she finished, the circle moved again, changing position so the barghest was now at the center.

Barghest druids looked somewhat less barbaric than their warrior brethren, but still held a certain savage terror in their eyes. This druid wore a ceremonial necklace and various other amulets made from animal bones and strung together by vines. Having a thick, brown, coat of fur, he had no need for additional clothing, but Artimus could not help thinking that he looked more like a shaman than a druid.

Unlike the dryad, this barghest let out a long series of howls and growls before the circle continued, moving on to the lizock next. This lizock looked much more peaceful than the two that Artimus spoke to earlier. He wore a simple, woolen robe with an opening for his tail and a single, metallic amulet, perhaps made of copper or bronze. The lizock spoke in his own language, which seemed harsh and incoherent.

"Aauhjra mujeraaeija jgerlyru sububurru pironilisseir vejeiauno."

The circle shifted again, now to the satyr. Surprisingly enough, especially considering how drunk the other satyr had appeared, this druid seemed quite capable of controlling his actions. If Artimus didn't know better, he would think the creature sober. Unlike the three before him, the satyr spoke in the common tongue, but with his own irritating accent placed on every word.

"Ta-ake thee ain't chent ma-gicks of thee Sat-yr."

The circle shifted back to Goldenchest now, who held a ritual staff in hand. It appeared too large for Artimus to even wield, and had a ruby planted in the head of the large, oak frame.

"Take the unyielding strength of the centaur."

The circle continued, next in line the beautiful lamia, with her great serpent form ending in the upper body of a gorgeous female. A golden necklace hung about her, a garnet beset in the center. Red hair, like the apples of the trees, hung down her entire upper torso. The only clothing she wore was a golden breastplate, and in her hand a scepter with yet another, larger garnet.

Like the barghest, she did not speak any comprehensible language, but rather used a series of hisses and clicks for her part.

The troll was next in line, the most strange of all the gathered druids. In fact, Artimus was quite sure that trolls did not have any actual druid class, and assumed this troll to be, like the barghest, some sort of shaman. His attire was similar to the barghest's, with the addition of a single, bearskin cloth about his waist. Furthermore, he held a plain, twisted oak staff.

"Shabadama ogorama zulucarma notradarma ka ugalafara."

Once again came the rotation, and now it was Savannah's turn. She looked as wonderful as ever and Artimus watched intently as her body swayed. Speaking in the beautiful elvish dialect, she continued the ritual.

"Täjé rí weadû úliritá õ rí elfé."

Artimus was glad to hear that the elves had wisdom to offer. He had always doubted the intellect of some of his brothers, but this somehow reassured him that the elves were still a strong species. Thus far, everyone that he understood had offered a quality befitting of their race, so he had to figure that wisdom was an apt quality for elves.

The ritual now came to its final participant, an orange felite with black spots clothed in a modest brown robe. She wore no jewelry but wielded an intricate staff. The base appeared to be made of gold, but every four inches there was a band of silver. Blue and white sapphires were placed between every silver ring, one color on either side of the perfectly cylindrical staff. Above the point where the felite held it, the staff became gradually thicker. At the very top was a diamond, the largest Artimus had ever seen, and around it were nine topazes, each shining radiantly as she spoke.

"Zerú ze cezerd grazé á ze feziz."

"We have offered you all we have," Goldenchest shouted as the other druids all muttered some hymn under their breath. It sounded like babble to Artimus, but he knew each word carried power.

"The dryads give you their influence over the earth, the satyr their unique magic, the centaur their strength, the barghest their ferocity, the lamia their charm, the lizock their cunning, the trolls their will, the elves their wisdom and the felite their grace. Accept these abilities and amplify them with the fury of Evorath."

The hymn stopped, all eight of the druids falling to their knees, leaving only the dryad remaining. A thick, green fog flowed from the center of the ritual circle as the dryad chanted. Both the barghest and lizock spoke in the common tongue.

"Control over a druidic fire. That you may immolate your foes without bringing harm to the forest you are sworn to protect. Use this with the strength you are granted to smite your enemies."

The dryad continued her solo chant in the sacred tongue. The lizock and barghest joined in their respective languages as both the lamia and troll spoke.

"Water, that you may provide the means for the earth to grow. Be as adaptive as this water and use it to drown any enemy who would harm the forest."

Both of them joined the quiet chant while the satyr and centaur shouted.

"Earth shall give you a solid base and never fail you. Use the strength of the ground itself to bury your foes. Manipulate every aspect of the Evorath, for you are one with her; you are Evorath."

The fog grew thicker in the center, spreading well past the circle.

Savannah and the felite joined in, their voices echoing over the chant.

"Fury of the wind, with anger provoking squalls of destruction. Move with swiftness and let the weather be on your side. All those who wish to harm you shall meet their end."

The chanting ceased, and the fog spread throughout the room. In the center, it seemed to coagulate as if ready to become solid. All nine members of the ritual circle spoke in union.

"Earth, water, wind, fire. All the power of Evorath shall be yours. The strength of all her children shall be yours. The eyes of all her growth shall be yours. So long as Evorath lives, you shall have access to all her power. Trees will bow to you, the earth will tremble. Oh great Avatar, hear our summons!"

Silence.

"Æj ós Gæa's œîrdíñ œlú üý," the dryad spoke.

The mist dissipated, sucked towards the center of the ritual circle like a powerful vacuum. All of the druids resumed their strange chant as the dryad continued in her mystic language. Perhaps this ritual would be over with quicker than Artimus expected.

He noticed that everyone else in the room was watching the ritual as intently as he. Perhaps the denizens of the forest were not all that dissimilar after all. If these nine druids could perform a ritual together, perhaps one day all nine of these races could work in unity.

"It is amazing to witness such a spectacular event." Tel' Shira whispered. "I never would have imagined a barghest helping anyone but himself."

"Indeed," Artimus responded. "I feel quite privileged."

"Quiet!" Irontail insisted. "You could disturb them!"

"Right," Tel' Shira apologized.

Artimus said nothing. He doubted their whispering could hurt the ritual, but he realized it could distract him from seeing every last detail. As far as he was concerned, the success of this ritual would leave him witness to one of the greatest events since the rise of elves. He intended to remember every last detail.

The fog had now condensed to surround only those within the ritual circle. It had become so thick that not even his elvish eyes could penetrate. Then the dryad stopped.

There was complete silence.

Time froze.

"Come forth Avatar of Evorath!"

With a great rush of air, the fog imploded on itself. It released a great flash of blinding light causing Artimus to shield his eyes.

All nine of the ritual's participants bowed down before the Avatar who now stood in their midst. The male stood in the center of the ritual circle, his muscular form casting a shadow over those before him. He was quite impressive in stature, but Artimus found himself oddly disappointed.

He expected a titan, some sort of giant amalgamated creature with such power that it could command the trees themselves. This creature, though taller than any elf he'd seen, stood at no impressive height. His arms were thick, sinewy muscles bulging from his large frame, but nothing greater than the barghest that Artimus disagreed with earlier. In fact, he figured the barghest was probably both taller and broader than this supposed Avatar. Furthermore, the Avatar looked mortal, with skin, though much tanner, very similar to that of an elf. With his bald head and hairless body, this creature looked more like an unintelligent warrior than anything else. Artimus only hoped that this outer appearance was a shell to hide some greater power.

The first words the Avatar spoke supported the warrior theory. His voice was deep; full of force and strength, but it lacked any commanding inflection.

"I am Evorath's right arm. So long as I live, Evorath will live. Why have you called upon me?"

The vines that covered most of his body seemed to move as he spoke, solidifying into what appeared to be normal clothing.

They appeared to be living, but somehow were changing form, possibly another shell for the Avatar to fit into. If his clothing could do this, maybe he did have some special power to offer.

These vines formed a brown tunic and matching pants. Simple clothing for a simple man. Perhaps it was this normal appearance that would prove so deadly.

Apparently, Artimus wasn't the only one with concerns. All nine druids seemed satisfied, but the barghest and two lizock entered the picture laughing.

"This is your mighty Avatar?" the barghest mocked. "I could wrestle him myself." Both the lizock and barghest druids gave their escorts death glares.

"Indeed," the lead lizock mocked. "How is this muscle-head supposed to be of any use? There is more than enough physical strength in this world as it is."

None of the druids knew how to respond. Even the dryad, who stepped out of the circle and stared in disapproval, was unable to offer a response. Perhaps they had failed.

Fortunately for them, this strange Avatar, even if it was lacking in power, was quite capable of defending itself verbally.

"I do not see the sense in your words. My physical strength outweighs the whole of your race barghest. I also possess magical abilities far beyond any dryad. My powers are without limit. What concern is my appearance to you?"

"Is that so?" the barghest barked in disbelief. "Show your strength then!"

"Do you doubt Evorath? Or do you not believe I represent her? All of Evorath's strength is my own."

The Avatar made no movement as the barghest walked closer. Without warning the hound leapt, but to Artimus's surprise he went nowhere. Just as the barghest's hind legs left the ground, a series of vines rocketed from the earth beneath him and wrapped around his wrists and ankles before he could even howl.

He landed with a thud, the vines tightening and reinforcing themselves as he tried to pull free. The two lizock made no movement, clearly taken aback by this display of power. Artimus could not blame them.

Druids had a certain command over the forest, but this Avatar had called these vines from nowhere. It was as if they had been buried under the earth, but Artimus knew as well as anyone that vines didn't just spring up from the ground. Vines grew on trees, or on permanent structures, or even along the forest floor in some instances. As far as underground though, vines did not grow. This was not manipulation of plant life, it was creation of it.

As the barghest struggled, the vines only tightened and new ones burst from the ground to reinforce their hold. Both the lizock looked to their fallen friend and then turned their gaze back to the Avatar. They both stood like statues as the barghest growled.

"I will release you only when you cease struggling."

Cursing just a few final times in his native tongue, the barghest stopped moving. The Avatar released his hold, letting the vines return to the ground from whence they sprung. The barghest regained his footing and wiped himself off. Artimus averted his gaze as the embarrassed warrior scanned the room. Taking this opening, the barghest druid stepped out of the circle and spoke.

"You deserve to be beaten with a club you foolish dog! Leave this room at once or I will be returning to the tribe by myself."

Artimus cringed. Calling a barghest a dog was grounds for killing unless it came from a fellow barghest. Coming from another barghest, it was probably the greatest dishonor one could suffer. It was also a challenge for a fight over honor, but in this context it would go unanswered.

No one had to watch to know that the warrior barghest left the room. The lizock followed him as far as the entrance and merely waited there, neither of them saying a word. Perhaps now, without the interruptions, they would be able to get a better idea about this Avatar's power.

"Now to more important matters," the Avatar began as if nothing had happened. "I repeat my question: Why have you summoned me?"

The dryad stepped forth from the crowd, bowing her head before addressing the Avatar.

"We find ourselves in a time of peril. Evil has made itself manifest. Not even the power of the dryads is enough to combat this harbinger of death. Though he waits outside our domain, his presence is already harming the forest."

"And what would you have me do? Lead an army against him?"

"No," Goldenchest answered coming from the circle. "We would have you shield us from the outside world. The forest has always been independent, and it shall remain as such. Keep the Hájje out of our land; this is all we ask."

"What you ask is not possible. This dark force that you speak of grows ever more powerful even as we speak. Hiding away in our forest is not an option." The Avatar's words were absolute, his inflection suggesting a sort of finality.

"What are you saying? You will not help us?" Goldenchest asked incredulously.

"I exist to serve Evorath. Isolating the forest will solve nothing. I must go and spread the word of the impeding danger. The forest cannot hide. We must raise arms."

"We cannot!" Goldenchest insisted. "Protect our villages. That is why you were summoned."

"I'm afraid not," the Avatar replied, his gaze spanning past the centaur chieftain, voice distant. "My task is set before me. If you wish to survive this darkness, take up arms and prepare to fight. No one is safe from death."

Artimus wasn't sure what to do. Even the dryad appeared dumbfounded by the speech of this Avatar. Hadn't they created him? Shouldn't he obey them?

Regardless of the answers, Artimus felt that the Avatar was right. The Hájje had power to change an elf into something horrible and monstrous with the flick of a wrist. He was smart too, smart enough to trick the ranger's head investigator. No one would be able to hide from something like this.

As the Avatar walked towards the exit, Artimus wondered something for the first time in his life. Would he live to see another year?

Chapter 7

Erathal Forest, Dumner village
14 Neglur, 1086

Irontail didn't know what to do. Under normal conditions, it was his duty to show the utmost respect to all guests of the tribe. Unless his elders gave him explicit permission to do otherwise, he would not address these guests except to cater to their needs. He just wondered whether or not these were normal circumstances.

This Avatar was denouncing the will of the elders. How did this creature justify his actions? It was the elders that brought him into existence and now he was refusing them his service. Such lack of gratitude could not belong to a true disciple of Evorath.

On the other hand, this Avatar made sense. Sitting back in their village, shielding themselves from this hájje seemed wrong. How could a powerful tribe like his sit idly by while their home was being torn apart by evil? That was what the hájje would do, was it not? He would destroy without regret. Even if this Avatar was able to hide them from the outside world, the outside world would still suffer. Was that supposed to be Evorath's plan? Just hide your head in the sand while the world around them was enslaved?

For the first time in his life, Irontail was truly questioning the elders. He had no doubt in their motives, but he doubted their foresight. Didn't they understand what this meant for the rest of Evorath? If all the forest tribes hid away, the hájje would conquer the mountains, plains, desert, and sea and then come for the forest when he had no one left to destroy. His army would grow so large that no one would be able to stand up against him.

Or maybe the elders had just exaggerated the power and intentions of the hájje. In the meeting earlier, they had described him as being more powerful even than Goldenchest, and in time they said he would surpass the tribe in its entirety. They had also described him as being wholly evil, bred from dark circumstances and raised with hatred for the world around him. He was the pure essence of evil.

It mattered not to Irontail whether the elders exaggerated the evil's power or whether they were in error now. Either way, his elders had done something he had never expected. Tradition said that the elders always knew what was best for the tribe, but somehow Irontail knew the Avatar was right. If they didn't fight the evil now, there would soon be no one left to fight.

Irontail was a warrior of the tribe, a defender of nature. For as long as he could remember he had been training to defend the tribe from any type of attack. If the elders planned to hide away from this enemy, what would they need him for? Fighting was all he knew.

"Wait!"

Irontail turned to the source and saw the elvish ranger jogging towards the exit, which the Avatar had just reached. What did he think he was doing?

"I ask you this, Avatar. What are you going to do?" His words were not harsh, but rather curious, like a young child asking his mother what he should do next.

The ranger stopped just a couple meters away from the Avatar -who had not turned to look at him- his face longing for an explanation.

"I will teach the forest to fight. I will give her children the means to defend themselves. I will bring light into the darkness." He spoke without emotion, a void, hollow, bottomless voice. His face remained as expressionless as the ground he stood on.

"But how? Where will you go? What if we want to create an attacking army with you at the lead?" Artimus's tone became stronger, trying to entice the Avatar to stay.

"Speak to Evorath. If she sees your words meaningful, I will know them."

Without giving the elf time to respond, the Avatar vanished. Irontail wasn't sure if his eyes were seeing correctly. He could swear that the Avatar had not used the exit but had somehow melted into the wall. Could he travel through the very earth in some incorporeal form and then just materialize outside? Or was he some kind of spirit, not bound by the laws of the physical plane?

Irontail's mind was turning faster than ever before, churning through these strange ideas. His elders had made a mistake. It was impossible for them to make a mistake. How could they have made a mistake?

Then again, an even worse question came to the surface of his mind: what if they didn't make a mistake?

The elders were supposed to know everything. What if they knew the will of Evorath? What if the will of Evorath was to fight, not to hide? Why did the elders choose to hide if Evorath wanted them to fight? Ignorance or hypocrisy? No matter how he looked at it, Irontail kept returning to the same conclusion.

The elders had lied.

If they did not understand the will of Evorath, they had been false in their teaching of elder infallibility. Any decision reached by the elders followed the will of Evorath and would always result in a beneficial outcome. Every centaur revered their elders, for it was taught that these wizened creatures had reached a state of harmony with nature. Was this the lie?

Even if it was not a lie and the elders did understand the will of Evorath, they still betrayed him. The one teaching more important even than the wisdom of the elders was the obedience to Evorath. Every centaur knew that Evorath's will was to be followed in all cases, never broken and never questioned. If the elders knew Evorath's will and were breaking it willingly, they were liars and hypocrites.

The other druids voiced their confusion as soon as the Avatar vanished. The room was a disoriented mob of ideas, every race trying to communicate in their own language, each trying to be louder than the other. Chaos fermented the room, like the chaos that would result if the Hájje was left unopposed. The Avatar had been correct.

Irontail watched the pair of elves flee the room as the commotion grew. He would probably never see them again, for he assumed they would head straight back to their great city and call for their own preparation against the tide of death. They had been opposed to the ritual in the first place, at least the druid had.

Still, he felt these elves would have made good allies. Unfortunately, he had no time to entertain this idea any further.

All of the druids had been rejoined by their escorts. Cries of outrage and disagreement bounced off the walls, and these parties shoved one another. Unable to distinguish one voice from another, Irontail tried to figure out his next course of action. All of these races had gathered together for a common cause, for the good of all life in the forest. Now that their plan had failed, old rivalries and racial prejudices boiled to the surface.

Irontail needed to act, and for the first time in his life he did not care what the elders wanted him to do. He would act on his own judgment.

-=-=-=-=-=-=-=-=-=-

Artimus couldn't explain the feeling that overtook him as the Avatar sunk into the wall and vanished. He needed no more proof. This man was indeed the right arm of Evorath, and Artimus intended to find him and utilize his powers to destroy the tumor now blemishing the world.

Gharis and Verandas held a special place in his heart -as did all his cadets- and the image of them being overtaken by that dark energy would be forever ingrained in his mind. The anguish, despair, and helplessness that were manifest in these brave troops as they writhed in agony could never be forgotten. If it were within his power to stop this fiend, neither of these fine cadets would have perished.

But he was helpless.

His arrows were like specs of dirt to this Hájje, his sword like a feeble twig. Though unaware of Savannah's offensive abilities, he was certain that she too was like an ant to this demon. In fact, he was certain that if everyone in the chamber he was now dragging Savannah from were to unite, they would still be no more than a bee sting to this horrible bringer of death.

The Avatar was different. He was all of the strengths of the forest without any of her weaknesses. He was the enforcer of Evorath's will, the bringer of peace and life, the protector of the weak. He was the only thing that could stop Yezurkstal.

"Artimus!"

Savannah pulled away from his grip as he pushed through the vines that acted as a door for the ritual chamber. She looked at him defiantly, holding both hands at her waist.

"What do you think you are doing?" she asked with a look that reminded Artimus of a mother scolding her child.

"We need to get back to Erathal and make our report. I fear there is little time to prepare," Artimus replied with even more authority than Savannah.

Her expression remained firm, but it adopted a pensive facade.

"I suppose you are right. But I can walk without you dragging me by the wrists you know."

"Yes, my apologi-"

"What's the rush," a gruff voice interrupted from behind, followed by a strong shove in the back.

Artimus stumbled forward, the pain from his injuries flaring. Lucky for him, Savannah was alert enough to prevent his fall, but he only wished she could have prevented his loud gasp.

"Look here," Artimus turned to face the barghest warrior, "Be a good dog and go to your druid. He's in trouble."

Fortunately, Artimus's lie worked, for his claim was followed by a loud yelp from inside the chamber. The anger that had just appeared on the barghest's face was replaced by confusion. Brushing both Artimus and Savannah aside, he grasped his axe and ran back into the chamber growling.

"That wasn't a good idea," Savannah offered.

"No time to worry about it now. It all worked out for the best. Now let's get out of this place before the fun spills out here."

Artimus made a pathetic attempt at a run, limping away as fast as he could. He didn't look to see if Savannah was following, but he could hear her soft footsteps. Ignoring the beautiful scenery the village had to offer, he stumbled through until he reached the small clearing where his horse grazed.

Doing a quick scan of the area, he saw a single centaur warrior speaking to Sylvan. All three horses were also nearby, his own Thoron grazing with both Savannah's white baroque and Sylvan's chestnut destrier. Darkness descended upon the clearing, the sun setting behind the colossal trees.

Slowing his pace, Artimus did his best to appear nonchalant as he approached Sylvan and the warrior.

"Excuse the interruption," Artimus began, "but I am afraid that we must be going Cadet Sylvan. Please excuse us, good sir," finished Artimus with a slight bow.

The centaur grunted, a low rumble contrasting with Sylvan's quick response.

"Yes, sir!" He turned back to the centaur. "Perhaps I will get a chance to prove my point in the future. Until we meet again."

Like Artimus, he gave a slight bow and proceeded to follow his commander.

"Why the urgency, sir?" Sylvan whispered as they walked back to their horses.

"Savannah can fill you in on the ride back." Knowing the centaur warrior had no reason to feel alarmed by his response, Artimus didn't even bother whispering.

Jumping onto his horse, he felt another jolt of pain, a reminder of his last mistake. This time, he would make sure not to ride faster than he could see. Of course, Thoron probably wouldn't let him repeat his mistake either, but it was better that he stay focused than rely on a horse. Regardless of how deep the bond was between a rider and his steed, it was always better that he keep his fate in his own hands.

With this in mind, he left the village at a steady pace, slowly driving Thoron onward. Savannah and Sylvan stayed close behind, speaking occasionally to one another about some animal they spotted or some abnormal plant life, which often redirected their path. As for the ritual, Savannah had told Sylvan to wait for the debriefing.

Artimus assumed that their close observation of nature was a distraction until they could discuss what had happened in the village. After all, Sylvan had no idea what occurred, but he must have known by their sudden departure that something was amiss. No matter the strength of his curiosity, he would have to wait until they were back in Erathal. For now, Artimus just had to focus on getting home as quickly as possible.

-=-=-=-=-=-=-=-=-=-

Irontail had no weapon. He had no armor. He wore only a studded leather and brown tunic about his massive figure in order to cover himself.

Fortunately for him, centaurs were natural weapons.

The verbal disputes had quickly deteriorated into a large melee. The barghest and felite were wrestling, the lamia and lizock exchanging blows, and a small golem was butting heads with the troll. Goldenchest and the dryad had refrained from any violence, but both were shouting for an end to the hostilities. Their efforts were futile. Irontail had no choice.

He lunged forward, throwing his entire mass into the golem that had been created. Dirt and rock crumbled under his shoulder as his weight propelled him through the creature. Only lifeless earth was left where the animated rocks had just stood.

Letting his momentum carry him, he allowed his elbow to impact the troll in its solar plexus. Without waiting for a reaction, he planted his hooves and pushed off towards the stunned satyr courier. He heard the troll yelp as he grabbed the two satyr guards by the throat and used his front legs to pin the druid.

"Cease these hostilities or I'll crush you like I crushed your golem!" he exclaimed with primal ferocity.

Throwing both the guards like rag dolls, he turned back towards the troll, who was recovering: fast. Not wanting to allow this shaman time to use any magic, he charged forth again, this time bringing his right fist up for a strong uppercut. He heard a prominent pop as the troll stumbled back, roaring in pain.

Warrior trolls were known for their strength, many outclassing the strongest centaur. This strength, coupled with their amazing regenerative abilities, gave the trolls great power. Fortunately for Irontail, this was no warrior troll.

As the troll was about to regain his footing, Irontail made an amazing display of dexterity, bringing himself behind the smaller opponent and placing him in an arm lock. Combining this move with a half nelson, he was able to pin his opponent in place.

"No more hostility. When I let you go, you sit down and do nothing."

Once again, he didn't bother waiting for a response. The lack of resistance, coupled with the troll's silence, was enough of an answer.

As he released his hold, he continued on to the next closest brawl between the barghest and felite druids. The smaller druid was holding her own by keeping the large canine at bay with her decorative staff. Still, she was slowly losing ground.

Fortunately for Irontail, both parties were refraining from magic, which would make his job much easier.

Irontail placed himself between the two druids. With arms outstretched, he arrived between the two fighters, his left forearm slamming into the barghest's neck. His right arm shot up to catch the expected blow from the felite's staff but found that she had stopped short of his hand.

He took a moment to look at the felite, who offered a small bow and took a few steps back, both clear signs of surrender. Before looking back at the barghest, Irontail tightened his right fist and shifted his weight around towards his foe. With the force of an arrow he let his punch fly, but just before striking his foe, another contender entered the fray.

It was Goldenchest.

Like an alligator locking its jaws on a prey, Goldenchest wrapped his massive hand around Irontail's wrist, stopping his punch before it landed. Irontail tried with all his might, but he could not budge against the vice grip of his elder. The next thing he knew, he was on all four knees, brought down by some unknown force that his elder employed.

"ENOUGH!"

Tremors shot across the room as Goldenchest's thunderous voice echoed from wall to wall. Whether from his druidic powers or from the sheer force of his voice, he had caused the ground to shudder, and everyone noticed. The room fell silent.

Irontail looked around.

The felite warrior that he was speaking with earlier had her barghest counterpart pinned to the floor just a few meters away, but she was now looking to Goldenchest, frozen in fear. The two lizock warriors were on one knee behind their master, facing the lamia -who appeared completely stunned- with looks of anger. The satyrs were all bowed with their faces to the ground, and the troll had even taken a submissive position.

Everyone seemed too scared to act, or even to speak. But someone was missing. Irontail did another scan of the room. Where was the dryad?

The pressure on his wrist disappeared, and he looked up to see Goldenchest motioning him to rise. Still somewhat shaken and confused by his elder's display of power and by the disappearance of the dryad, Irontail slowly rose, his knees buckling as he took a fully upright posture. Everyone else remained still.

"Irontail. Make sure our visitors reach the edge of the village quickly. If you are not a centaur, I expect you to be out of our village immediately. We have offered you hospitality and you repaid us with savagery. Your intolerable offense will not be forgiven."

Irontail was conflicted yet again, but this time he felt angrier than before. For the first time in his life, he wanted to make his chieftain feel pain. He felt the strongest urge to pummel Goldenchest until his arms were too heavy to move. To beat his elder until blood covered his brilliant, golden chest. That would knock some sense into him.

Then fear overtook his anger as the reality of this desire registered. Such thoughts would be grounds for banishment should another tribesman hear them. Still, there was a pit in Irontail's stomach. This feeling spread to the rest of his body. He couldn't explain it, but there was something wrong with this entire situation.

Chapter 8

Erathal City

14 Neglur, 1086

"So what you are telling me is that you are incapable of retrieving my daughter?"

Senator Ricker looked at Artimus with tremendous fury, something in his glare causing the experienced ranger an uncharacteristic discomfort.

No one could have successfully rescued those women. His team was the best, with cadets trained extensively in the art of combat and prepared for emergency situations. Savannah had a strong background as a druid, probably one of the most -if not the most- powerful lab mages in the Rangers; and of course, despite his modesty about it, Artimus knew that he was the best marksman in the entire city, possibly in the entire forest. There was no more skilled team out there.

Despite this, the look that this politician was giving him made him feel as if he had done something wrong. Had he made a mistake?

No.

"I'm sorry, Senator. There was nothing we could do. Look, I need to continue on to the castle and make my report. You know that you can always take a look at it when I am done, but I do not have time to discuss this with you right now." Artimus tried his best to remain patient.

"You will make the time then," the irritable senator insisted.

"Cadet Sylvan," barked Artimus without hesitation.

"Yes, sir!"

"Kindly escort the good senator back to his house and report to the castle when you are done."

"Yes, sir!"

Sylvan dismounted his horse, placing his hand gently on the senator's shoulder blade. Ricker pulled away, his glare bearing down on Sylvan like daggers. He jerked his head back towards Artimus, his eyes burning with fury.

"I will not tolerate this! You are mistaken to think you can ignore me. I will report this to the counsel, and you will be begging for scraps when I am done."

Artimus shook his head. He would not allow this overblown fool to upset him.

"Actually, Senator, you will be placed under arrest if you do not cooperate. You are interfering with the law, and if you do not allow Mr. Sylvan to escort you back to your home, you will be brought before the counsel as a criminal. Do you wish to challenge the law, Senator?"

"I helped make these laws!" the enraged politician yelled. "I just want you to get my daughter back!" The senator flailed his arms as he yelled, but as soon as he finished speaking he lowered them to his side. Sylvan immediately took advantage of the senator's brief calm and took him in a firm hold.

"Unhand me!"

"I am sorry sir, but your daughter is not the only victim of these crimes. Despite this, I do sympathize, so I will be tolerant. If you cease now and go home, I will not drag you to the castle prison. If you say one more word, or if you attempt to resist Sylvan as he escorts you back to your home, you will be brought before the counsel in shackles. If you must contest this, do it in the proper fashion and bring it up in the counsel later. Right now, I have a report to make."

Artimus didn't even give the senator time to respond. He did not want to arrest the man, even if he was one of the most annoying and offensive bureaucrats in the counsel. Hopefully he would cooperate. If not, Artimus was certain that Sylvan could take care of it.

"Don't you think you were a bit hard on him?" Savannah whispered as they passed just out of earshot.

"I don't enjoy that part of my job, but I have to follow the law for everyone, no matter what the circumstances. Section three, subsection two, line four of the Ranger Code states: 'anyone disrupting this investigative process shall be arrested and charged with treason.' I have to follow the Code, even if it is a bit ridiculous."

"That's more than ridiculous," Savannah suggested at a normal tone, "that is tyrannical."

"I'll pretend I didn't hear that," Artimus said, looking around startled. "Technically, under subsection five of the same section, insinuating that the governing power is not fair, is also treason."

"I guess I should keep my mouth shut then," Savannah murmured looking down. "I think I realize now why my fellow druids always spoke so poorly of city life. I'll do my best to keep my thoughts to myself."

"Don't be afraid to talk to me about it," Artimus said. "You're not the only one who thinks the system is flawed, but for now it is best to keep quiet about any doubts. The people live happy lives because the crown provides for all of their needs. One day, it will have to change. People want more than what they need and the government is already having trouble controlling the citizens. Just look at that news parchment that is released every day."

"What about the news parchment?" Savannah asked.

Artimus smiled as they passed by a man who was tending to his garden, giving him a slight nod as they passed. "Good day, sir."

"And to you, Master Artimus. Any news about the kidnappings?" the elderly elf asked in a weak, but hopeful tone.

"We have a suspect," Artimus responded positively, "but we have not yet caught him. It's only a matter of time." The man rested on his rake, a smile coming over his face.

"That is wonderful news. I can only hope you catch him soon. Good luck."

"And to you."

As they passed away from the elderly gardener, Artimus looked back to Savannah.

"We will have to discuss this in more detail some other time," he said, shifting his eyes around, making sure no elves were in earshot. "I'll just tell you now that not all of the writers work for free."

"But I thought it was a citizen's paper," Savannah whispered. "Everyone just writes to get his opinion heard."

"Not everyone necessarily writes his own opinion," Artimus whispered back. "But I'll explain more later. This is really the last thing that we need to be discussing right now. No matter what the situation is in our village, we will be unable to stop Yezurkstal without help."

"Why do you call him that?"

"What, Yezurkstal? Because that is what he called himself, remember?" Artimus looked back at his lab mage in confusion. She had been there when the Hájje had identified himself. Why did she not remember his name?

"Yeah, I guess you are right," Savannah responded as she looked down at her horse. "It is just such a demonic name. Fits him well I suppose. Still, something about it just bothers me. I prefer just calling him the Hájje or something."

Artimus shrugged.

"Call him whatever you want. That's your prerogative. I've always felt that names, especially ones as unique as his, make it easier to identify a person. Maybe just an investigator thing."

"Perhaps," Savannah sighed.

"At any rate, you saw what he was capable of." Artimus struggled to keep the emotion out of his voice, not wanting to appear weak. "Gharis and Verandas were two of the most promising cadets I have seen. They would have made excellent rangers, but Yezurkstal had to make this personal." He clutched his fists, inadvertently tightening his legs around Thoron as well.

As he was trained to do, Thoron took this tightening of the heels as a message to accelerate, and since Artimus did not release his squeeze, he continued to accelerate. At first, Artimus didn't realize what was going on, but as his trusted horse galloped towards the approaching walls, he loosened his grip. Pulling back quickly on the reigns, he yelled in his elvish tongue.

"Hælüt!"

Thoron came to an abrupt halt, giving Artimus some anticipated whiplash. His back flared as he held his position on the great destrier's back. After all of his years riding horses, he had made two stupid errors in the time span of a single day. At least this time he had avoided causing himself any serious harm.

With the relationship that Artimus had developed with his steed, there was so much loyalty that Thoron would charge into a smoldering building if he was instructed to do so. Unfortunately, he was still a horse, and to him, getting squeezed meant that he needed to move faster. He was loyal, and he was even smarter than most horses, but he was still unable to distinguish between an order and a simple sign of frustration.

"Are you alright?" Savannah asked as she reached his side.

"Yeah, I'm fine," Artimus said, patting Thoron lightly on the side. "I just need to remember that my friend here is willing to do anything for me, including running into a solid, six foot thick wall of stone reinforced with solid iron. I also need to remember that squeezing a horse is like telling him to move faster."

"How long have you been riding?" Savannah asked with sincere concern in her voice.

Artimus laughed. "Oh, I don't know. About two centuries now."

"Wow. I'm glad I wasn't around you a hundred years ago," Savannah teased with a smile.

"That's pretty good," said Artimus with another laugh, "but I would say I have gotten worse, not better. Just seems to be my luck lately. Nothing is working out the way it should."

"Well," Savannah said softly, "maybe I can help fix that." She smiled, meeting his gaze with her wonderful, green eyes. As their eyes locked, he felt as if time had frozen and he could peer into her soul. Was she feeling this too?

"So what did you have in mind?" Artimus asked, breaking away from the momentary trance.

"Since this case began, you have seemed very tense. This case has been frustrating you from the start, and with the loss of Gharis and Verandas you've been even more uptight. I get it, I really do, but you can't let it slow you down. You need to focus. Tell me, when was the last time you just relaxed and enjoyed yourself?"

Artimus didn't need to think. "Last time I finished a case. Chasing that thief down and seeing the look on his face when I locked him up. That was enjoyable. As far as relaxing, I can't tell you the last time I did that. At least nineteen years ago. When you are the lead investigator for the Kingdom of Erathal, you don't have much free time. Crime gets worse every day, and it doesn't just stay with elves. I have to prevent any crime within our borders."

Savannah shook her head. "You may be the head investigator, but you are not the only one. There are plenty of elves who can solve simple cases, yet you take on twice as many as any other ranger. Take now for example. This kidnapping case started last week, and considering how tough it has been don't you think you should have focused only on it? Instead, you have worked six other cases in that time, all of which could have been solved by someone else. All you do is work and sleep. I haven't even seen you eat anything!"

"What do you want me to say?" Artimus asked in frustration. "I don't have anything else to do. Work is what I enjoy and I'm good at it. As long as I am able to solve crimes, that is what I will continue to do."

"What about family? Don't you ever spend time with your siblings, or your parents?"

"I have no family. They were all murdered twenty years ago. Why do you think I started this job? I was a hunter, providing food for my village, but then the crime wave hit us. I came to the city and found the elf who assassinated the king. That's why they made me the lead investigator. Since then, this job has been my life. There is no point in having temporary connections outside of this."

"I'm sorry," Savannah offered sympathetically. "I didn't know. So is that why you never socialize outside of work? Most elves go to the mead hall at the end of the day and look for connections with their other rangers, but you don't. Is it because you are afraid of losing someone you care about?"

Artimus shook his head. "I was, but…" He paused. He wasn't ready. "Never mind. Yeah, I guess I am afraid."

Savannah prodded her horse and got in closer to Artimus. "You won't get away that easily. What were you going to say?"

Perhaps it was best to just come clean, to let her know how he felt about her. Maybe that would help relieve some of his stress. Keeping secrets was not any easy task, especially when part of him yearned to tell the world. But what if she felt differently?

"Maybe I am afraid that the person I care about will not care about me."

"You'll never know if you don't express your feelings," Savannah said tenderly, gazing into his eyes and filling him with a sense of strength.

"I," Artimus started, but he was unsure of what to say. "I just- I don't know."

"What is there not to know? You obviously have someone in mind. Who is it?"

"I don't know."

"Who is it? Who?"

"You!" Artimus yelled finally. "It is you that I care about. I was attracted to you since I first set eyes upon you. In fact, I requested that you be put on this case with me, because I have been observing you since you started working as a lab mage. Then, when I finally met you, I knew that there was something special about you. As we worked on those first few days, even though there was no real evidence, you were always offering ideas. You were being more thorough than any lab mage I had worked with before, and you were so light-hearted. I didn't realize until just before the ritual, but Savannah Sylvanas, I feel a deep connection with you."

As soon as these words left his mouth, he felt a strong heat overcome his body. He felt embarrassed and foolish. What had possessed him to tell her this?

Savannah appeared to be in shock. She remained seated on her own horse, her face locked in an expression of disbelief. Why didn't she say anything? Was it as he had feared? Had she never even considered the idea? What had he done?

"I'm sorry," Artimus said quickly. "I shouldn't have said that. It's not professional. I understand if you-"

Savannah held up her forefinger and middle finger, placing them gently on Artimus's lips. Slowly bringing them away, she looked at Artimus with a smile. Joy seeped from every pore of her body, and she appeared as if she might float off of her horse and begin to shine like the sun above. Artimus could feel his mouth expand into the largest smile of his memory.

"No." Savannah began. "I feel the same way. When I first moved to the city and joined the Rangers, I caught sight of you on one of the first days. It was a murder case, and you came there when one of your cadets was having trouble putting the scene together. You showed up, and by the end of the day you caught the perpetrator. Watching you work that day, with your authority and charisma, it made an impression. I've thought about you a lot, and I can't tell you how thrilled I was when I found that I would be working with you. And then, when I was really around you for all that time, I found that you were all I could hope for and so much more. I feel a deep connection with you, Artimus."

Artimus was beside himself. He didn't know what to do, or what to say, but something was drawing him towards this slightly younger, amazingly beautiful elf. He leaned forward, closing the distance between their two faces and peering deep into her eyes. She leaned towards him as well, and as their lips touched, he brought his hand up to her cheek. Pouring his passion into that one action, he pressed his lips against hers, closing his eyes as he filled with joy.

This was what it meant to be free of worry.

This was what it felt like to relax.

Chapter 9

Erathal City Castle
14 Neglur, 1086

Artimus sat at his desk, vigorously writing down the events of the previous day. He needed to recount every last detail so he could deliver it to the king. From the tracks they had found that led them to Jyrimoore, to the evil magic that had claimed both Gharis and Verandas, to the ritual that had summoned the mysterious Avatar, and finally a recommendation on what they should do next; Artimus had to include every detail.

Well, he might leave out the bit at the castle walls, and as he had promised, Senator Ricker's unprofessional behavior would be left out as well. Other than these minor omissions, which were already violations of policy, he would leave nothing out, including his embarrassing injury in the forest. So Artimus wrote as fast as he could, for the first time in his career wanting to finish this pesky paperwork so he could proceed to spend some time with another person.

Savannah had told him to arrive at her cabin around dinner time and Artimus planned on being there on time. He would have to complete this report faster than he was accustomed to, and his presentation to the senators would have to be shorter than usual, but he was sure he could pull it off. Never in his life had he failed to meet a deadline, and he didn't intend to start now.

So his quill ran across the parchment with such speed that his writing was going faster than his head. He recounted every detail, the look of torment in both Gharis and Verandas, the terrible skin pigment that overtook them, and the dark color of their hair. He described the malice in this hájje's voice, the power, the terror. He explained his injury, how Irontail had greeted them, how Goldenchest had brought them to the ritual hall, the splendor of the living chamber, the amazement of seeing all the gathered races of the forest.

His explanation of the dryad and of the mystical ritual included every last detail, recalling the order that each druid spoke, the words they chanted, and the elements that were invoked. The Avatar was also described in full detail, his massive stature, his impressive display of power, and his exact words:

Goldenchest: "We would have you shield us from the outside world. The forest has always been independent, and it shall remain as such. Keep the Hájje out of our land; this is all we ask."

Avatar: "What you ask is not possible. This dark force that you speak of grows ever more powerful even as we speak. Hiding away in our forest is not an option."

Goldenchest: "What are you saying? You will not help us?"

Avatar: "I exist to serve Evorath. Isolating the forest will solve nothing. I must go and spread the word of the impeding danger. The forest cannot hide. We must raise arms."

Goldenchest: "We cannot! Protect our village. That is why you were summoned."

Avatar: "I'm afraid not. My task is set before me. If you wish to survive this darkness, take up arms and prepare to fight. No one is safe from death."

Next, he wrote his own exchange with the Avatar:

Me: "I ask you this, Avatar. What are you going to do?"

Avatar: "I will teach the forest to fight. I will give her children the means to defend themselves. I will bring light into the darkness."

Me: "But how? Where will you go? What if we want to create an attacking army with you at the lead?"

Avatar: "Speak to Evorath. If she sees your words meaningful, I will know them."

This is why I motion that we begin to mobilize, to prepare for imminent attack from the mountains. An offensive would surely fail, but by building up our forces, we could find aid from the Avatar, who, in my opinion, is our best hope. He is truly an Avatar of Evorath, and his powers must surpass those of Yezurkstal. If we can receive his aid, I believe we will be able to overtake the hájje; otherwise, there is little hope.

And so he concluded his report, adding in that their ride back home was uneventful and that they had proceeded straight back to the headquarters where they had left their horses with the stable master, Sylvan had been ordered to go home and rest, and Savannah had written her own lab report, which was attached to his. Finally, he gathered his papers together, rising from his wooden chair and looking out the window to see the sun reaching its apex in the sky.

The council would be expecting his presentation within the hour…

-=.-=.-=.-=.-=.-=.-=.-=.

Savannah knelt in front of her flowering Yggdril tree. The splendorous silver petals sparkled in the afternoon sun, casting a luminescent glow over her hand as she cradled them. This tree was, or at least she assumed it was, the only one of its kind in the entire city, and she planned to make sure that it remained strong so it could one day produce fruit.

A Yggdril tree was not common, but in her druidic tribe, there had been three fully grown ones. When Savannah had left for Erathal, there had been none remaining, and she was gifted with one of five seedlings. As soon as she was assigned to this plot of land, she planted the seedling and nursed it, feeding it just as she had been taught. Along the way, she used her druidic abilities to enhance its growth and expedite the growing process.

It still had a few decades before it would start producing its magical fruit, a food that could sustain an elf for a fortnight and was said to offer increased strength and magical potency, but the flowers that were beginning to sprout also had their uses. By grinding up the petals and mixing them with the proper amount of water, she could produce the most stimulating salad dressing, which would be perfect for the dinner she had planned. The only problem was that she needed to coax the flower to fall off on its own accord.

Structurally, the Yggdril was nearly as strong as an oak, but pulling off any one of its flowers forcibly would surely kill it.

Exact details evaded her, but the reason seemed quite simple. As the Yggdril grew, its latent magic expanded and became more prominent. These flowers that grew were mediums for this increased magical energy, and by forcibly removing them the shock would overwhelm and kill the tree. On the other hand, if the flower was coaxed into falling off on its own accord, the magic would dissipate slowly, allowing the tree to survive.

So she waited patiently, willing the flower to leave its safe dwelling and venture into the world. Calling upon the magic of Evorath, pouring only the slightest bit into her hands, she merely concentrated on the flower falling away. Patience was the key to this exercise, for even her magical means of getting the flower could kill the tree if she was not careful.

She felt a small surge of energy and released her magical hold in a flash. A single petal fell from the flower, followed soon after by another and then another. Cupping her hands, she caught each petal in turn, watching them glisten as they fell gently into their new shelter.

This was the first time she had taken a flower from a Yggdril since before she left her village, but she had done it just as quickly, if not more so. At least she could be confident that her abilities had not suffered since becoming a lab mage. With a pronounced grin, she rose from her kneeling position and went back into her cabin.

It was a plain home, perhaps too simplistic, but it provided sufficient shelter from the elements and adequate privacy. Actually, it was an exceptionally stable house, solid in its foundation and made exclusively of oak. Furthermore, it was larger than most other houses in the vicinity, a benefit of working for the Crown.

Savannah had actually made the house herself after submitting her request to be admitted as a lab mage, passing the tests and learning the simple magic. She was then assigned an empty, but modest plot of land. Using her druidic magic, it took her only about an hour to form the house. Nature itself was on her side, and she had plenty of trees in her plot to provide enough materials. After the initial structure was laid out, she had an area cut out for the entrance, and proceeded to build some of the simple interior necessities, including the table, bed, and stools.

Parting the brown canvas that she had chosen to use as a door, she entered her home and went straight for the stove. Like most other citizens of Erathal who qualified for one, Savannah had placed a stove in the center of her home, allowing it to provide optimal heat for the cold winter nights. She had already started a small fire with the tinderbox that rested on the rough countertop next to her stove and a bucket of water hung just above the reach of the flames, the water boiling.

"Perfect," thought Savannah out loud, pulling the bucket out from the stove and placing it on the counter.

She reached beneath the counter, pulling a small mortar and pestle from an otherwise empty shelf. Dropping the Yggdril petals into the pestle, she took the mortar and began grinding them up, crushing them into a fine paste. Savannah was not used to working with her hands, and even when she had prepared this special salad for her village, she always had help for any of the manual labor. Still, this was worth her time, and she wanted to make sure that everything was perfect.

After a few minutes of grinding the petals, she shook them up a bit and, unsatisfied with the results, continued her grinding. With only a few more minutes of this work, her arm was already beginning to tire, but she persisted. Within about fifteen minutes, she had finally ground the petals to a satisfactory fine paste.

She now turned her attention to the water, which still had a small amount of steam rising from it. Bending down to the bottom shelf, which was filled with bowls, plates, and an assortment of covered containers, Savannah grabbed both a medium sized bowl and a small container. Placing both items on the counter, she opened the small container to reveal salt.

Taking the bowl, she dipped it into the bucket of water and carefully pulled it out, pouring a small amount back into the bucket so that the bowl was about three quarters full. Dumping about a fifth of the salt into her palm, she sprinkled it into the water bowl. Next, she picked up the mortar and used her fingers to scoop out the paste, finishing up with a splash of water to rinse out the mortar.

Pushing the mortar and pestle aside and placing the top back on the salt, she bent down again and grabbed a large spoon as well as another small container from the bottom shelf. This other container held thyme, which she dumped straight from the container. With all four ingredients mixed together, she stirred the dressing.

Almost instantly, the water darkened, thickening to a more milky consistency. The silver color of the petals spread through the clear liquid, mixing with the salt and thyme to cause the water to change to a honey-like color. As she continued to stir, the water bubbled slightly, a sign that the salt was bonding properly with the Yggdril petals and releasing their magic into the dressing. Finally, there was a light hiss as she ceased her stirring, the cloudy dressing still swirling within the bowl.

Savannah smiled, delighted that she had finished the most cumbersome task, she gathered the materials and returned them to their proper place. She left the bucket of water on the floor next to the stove, thinking she could utilize it later. Now she just had to cool the dressing for a while, and as that was happening she could buy the rest of the food for her meal. Artimus would have to be impressed by her ability to cook once he tasted this meal.

Leaving the dressing on the counter, Savannah walked across her cabin and reached into the cupboard that was situated by the entryway. From there, she pulled out two new containers and a clear, round bottomed flask. Returning to her countertop, she opened the two containers and dumped the contents of the first into the flask until it reached a small mark that she had left for measuring. The other container held a few small, white solids. Taking one of these deformed rocks out, she dropped it into the flask and twirled the mixture.

The barium hydroxide hydrate began reacting with the solid ammonium chloride. As the two ingredients continued their endothermic reaction, a small amount of vapor rose from the container. Holding the flask away from her nose, Savannah waited for the vapor to slow and then placed the flask directly into the dressing. She watched as a thin layer of frost formed on the outside of the flask and then reached under the counter and took out another bowl. Flipping the bowl upside down, she covered the dressing and the flask that rested within. This would help lock the cold air in.

"Now that that's done."

Savannah went through the list of ingredients in her head. She could get the lettuce and tomatoes from the Food Proctor, and if she was lucky she may even be able to get the bread there. If not, she was sure that one of the merchants would have some good loafs for sale. That only other variable was whether or not she should purchase some meat.

Having been raised a vegetarian, Savannah had never purchased meat before, which left her unsure of where she could obtain it. Furthermore, it was possible that Artimus was also a vegetarian, but not likely. To be safe, she figured that they would eat some trout. But only the proctor had the rights to offer trout, and Savannah was fairly certain that she did not qualify to receive it. Perhaps she could catch some on her own, albeit illegally.

Standing and thinking about what she could do would not solve anything, so without further delay, Savannah retrieved her identification papers and a small bag of coins from beside her bed. As she cleared her cabin, she tapped her foot twice on the ground just outside and drew the druidic symbol for rock, a small curve overlapping a jagged line. With the ever-increasing spree of crime, it never hurt to be cautious, especially when she didn't have a real door. Activating this simple enchantment would effectively remedy that problem.

Savannah proceeded on foot to walk along the simple dirt road, passing a few children playing in the open forest, a couple of small hovels, and some farmland. The city was an unremarkable sight when compared to the centaur village, or to Savannah's former village for that matter. From what she had heard, the elves were the most plain of all species in their cities, being dominated by small shacks and some open areas of farmland. Excluding the castle and the Commercial District, this city was pretty much an eyesore, a gathering place for the destitute and impoverished.

The longer she lived in Erathal, the more she wondered about its appeal. Farmers worked more than twelve hours a day and were obligated by law to hand over all of their harvest to the Food Proctor for assignment. Potters and other artisans faced the same problem, having to give any of their goods over to the appropriate proctor for assignment to those elves who needed them. If there was more than needed, a merchant, who was a direct employee of the king, would be given the merchandise to sell at a heavily taxed rate, leaving little money left for the merchant himself.

Being directly employed by the king, hunters had a slightly better lifestyle, usually working less than ten hours, but they too were unable to keep any of their spoils until it was properly distributed. Everything was done for the good of the community, but Savannah was having difficulty finding where that good came into play. Of course, she was also on a higher tier of the ladder, working only when there was need for a lab mage

117

and getting benefits greater than any hunter, merchant, farmer, or artisan, but she could hardly understand why. If they worked so much more than she did, why were they given so much less?

On top of this, the senators, who spent their time sitting in a chamber discussing laws, were given luxurious homes in the Commercial District. They had their own cooks, their own servants, and all the food they could ever want and more. From what Savannah understood, they lived almost as comfortably as the king, and they did even less work. It just didn't make sense to her that a farmer, who worked all day to provide necessary sustenance for the city, would get less than a bureaucrat, who offered as much use from his front end as he did from his rear.

With these thoughts in mind, Savannah arrived in front of the Food Distribution Warehouse, where the line extended just outside the door. Taking her place at the back of the line, she looked past to the other, large warehouses, and to the villas that lay beyond. Ornately decorated houses, easily larger than six farmer's homes, and typically housing fewer people, these giant villas wasted more resources than a band of satyr.

The line slowly proceeded: a married couple exiting with only a head of lettuce and disgruntled expressions on their faces, an old man leaving with a basket full of fruit, a younger female leaving with a single shank of beef. As Savannah made it into the warehouse, she could hear raised voices coming from the front of the line. Looking over the shoulders of the man in front of her, a middle-aged man stood, clearly a farmer by his dress, and more distinctly by the dirt that covered much of his body.

While the proctor was giving a large basket full of bread, fruit, vegetables, and another basket of round cut beef to an elderly man, this younger man stood in disbelief.

"You mean this old man gets all that and I can't even get a few slices of bread? I have kids to feed, and we don't have any food left. I've been working for a day straight and I got enough vegetables to feed the entire city, but you're telling me that I don't qualify for any more food? What has this old man done to deserve all that food?"

The old man gave the younger farmer a nasty look, hastily taking his food and retreating towards the exit. For a moment, it appeared as if the farmer would follow, but he contained his anger and kept it directed at the proctor. After all, it was not the old man's choice to keep food from him.

"Sir, I told you already," the proctor offered in his diplomatic tone, "you already got your loaf of bread for the week. I can give you your monthly shank of beef if you wish, but until tomorrow that is all you qualify for."

The farmer smacked his hand against the counter, the impact echoing through the room.

"I don't need a damn shank of beef! My kids need some bread! How the hell am I supposed to cook the beef anyways? By itself?" The man shook his fist at the proctor. "My kids can't eat something that tough. And you didn't answer my damn question, you stupid bureaucrat! Why did that old man qualify for so much damn food when my family is starving?"

"Look, sir, I am going to need you to calm down," the proctor said passively. "That old man used to be a hunter and he had a family too. He needs food to keep up his strength in his old age."

The elves in the line in front of Savannah were having their own side conversations, some agreeing with the disgruntled farmer and others merely wishing he would hurry up and leave. No one took any action though, merely watching as the argument continued.

"He needs to keep his strength? I need to make sure that my children live long enough to grow old!" He smacked his hands down on the table again, his face turning red as he shouted.

"You know what? Forget it! I will just use some of the grain on my farm to make them bread. I grew it all anyways, so why not keep it?"

"Your land belongs to the king," the proctor protested as the enraged farmer turned and strode quickly for the exit. "You will be arrested for theft of the king's property!"

"Good!" the elf yelled as he reached the door next to Savannah. "My kids will get more food if I am in prison anyways!"

With those final words, he stormed out the exit and slammed the door.

Chapter 10

Erathal City

14 Neglur, 1086

Savannah stepped up to the counter, hoping that everything would go better for her than it had for the farmer, or for the other citizens who had come before her.

"I need some lettuce, tomatoes, and bread," Savannah said placing her papers on the counter.

The proctor looked over her paperwork and nodded. He then turned to his own papers and looked them over before addressing Savannah.

"Alright, Miss Sylvanas. One loaf of bread, a head of lettuce and three tomatoes are now available to you. Would you like them all today?"

"Yes please, and I had one other matter I needed to discuss," she said as the proctor reached for the loaf of bread. "I was requested to pick up some trout for Head Investigator Artimus Atyrmirid."

"I'm sorry, but you are not eligible to receive fish except on special celebrations, and since you are not related to the investigator in any way, I cannot allow you to get his food for him."

"I understand, but Mr. Atyrmirid is extremely busy right now with the kidnapping case. He was overdue to pick up some fish, so he requested that I get it for him. The next time he is in you can ask him to verify, but didn't you notice that he has not been here the last couple of days?"

The proctor cast his gaze downward and rubbed his chin. "Well, he does usually come here to get some fish every morning, and he got all of his fruit, vegetables and bread at the beginning of the week. But still…"

Savannah praised Evorath for her luck. Just a little more coaxing and the fish was as good as hers. Time to use the aggressive approach.

"Look, the investigator really doesn't have time to be coming out here when he is working on such an important investigation. The castle is on the other side of the city in case you don't remember, and last night's kidnapping is also close to the castle. He will probably be stuck eating this fish while filling out reports. You wouldn't want to slow down his work, would you?"

The proctor adjusted his stance, trying to shake away the visible discomfort.

"Perhaps you are right," he said finally. "I know you all are working hard on this case, but Lieutenant Atyrmirid better back up this story of yours next time I see him, or even your position won't help you."

"Of course," Savannah replied with a slight bow.

The proctor gathered the rest of the food, putting the bread, lettuce, tomatoes, and a single, but exceptionally large trout, into a basket and sliding it over to Savannah. Taking both her papers and the food basket, she smiled to the proctor.

"Thank you. And the investigator thanks you as well. Have a pleasant day."

-=-=-=-=-=-=-=-=-

Artimus stood uncomfortably at the center of the Council Chambers. He had never had any understanding of what his presentations accomplished, and he had never been comfortable giving them, but as Head Investigator he was regularly required to do so. In cases such as this one, even though he had not yet been to the scene of the latest crime, he needed to brief the council on the seriousness of the situation. Like usual, he didn't think the council, nor the king, would fully appreciate the depth of this kidnapping spree.

In addition to this doubt of the council's reasoning abilities, the Chamber was extraordinarily large, adding to Artimus's discomfort. From the ornately decorated pillars, featuring sculpting of some of the early elvish political figures and standing taller than most oaks, to the checkered marble floor, which always gave him a headache; Artimus just couldn't stomach the room. Something about the way these fourteen, characteristically overweight, predominately male bureaucrats all sat in their silver chairs, surrounding him and questioning everything that he said, made him wish he could quit on the spot. It didn't help much that the king sat elevated at the front of the council, sitting in his golden throne and glaring down at Artimus like he was a prisoner.

Despite his discomfort, and the inability of the council to understand the situation, he conveyed his suggestions both calmly and assertively.

"This is why I motion that we begin to mobilize, to prepare for imminent attack from the mountains. An offensive would surely fail, but by building up our forces, we could find aid from the Avatar, who, in my opinion, is our best hope. He is truly an Avatar of Evorath, and his powers must surpass those of Yezurkstal. If we can receive his aid, I believe we will be able to overtake the hájje; otherwise, there is little hope." Artimus took a deep breath as he concluded his report, looking around at the blank faces that stared back at him.

"I'm not sure I understand," a senator began at the far left of the chamber. "I mean, what do you suggest we do to prevent further kidnappings?"

Artimus shook his head.

"Including the victim of last night, there are eight elves who have been taken from the city. Three more *will* be kidnapped. There is nothing we can do to prevent it."

"That's nonsense," Senator Ricker protested from beside the king. "We should send a Ranger unit to the Jyrimoore caves, kill the Hájje, and take the victims back by force. We can organize an assault and reach the cave before nightfall. He won't be expecting an attack, so we'll have the element of surprise on our side."

Murmurs traveled through the chamber, most of them agreeing with the senator's suggestion. Artimus needed them to understand the power of this Hájje before they sent half of the city to its death.

"The cave is sealed by rocks, and any mage of his caliber will feel us coming before we even get inside. He was expecting us when we arrived yesterday. Besides that, the cave is only wide enough for two or three elves at a time, nullifying our number advantage. An attack on his home would take the lives of our entire city and we still would not be successful."

Artimus looked around at the unconvinced faces of the senate. He needed something better, and perhaps he had an idea.

"Look," he said before anyone could respond. "This Hájje can manipulate pure dark magic and use it like a weapon. He can transform anyone we send to attack into one of his own servants. Anyone we send to his cave will become one of his troops, and that I can guarantee. Still, I can understand that it is hard to understand how powerful this mage is, so I suggest a demonstration. Is High Wizard Guildpac in the castle at this time?"

"Yes he is," the king responded. "But what of it?"

"Guildpac is the most powerful wizard in the city, is he not? I will prove that I can harm Guildpac with relative ease. If I can harm him when I was unable to harm Yezurkstal, then I believe you should have an idea of how powerful the Hájje is."

The king laughed, and most of the senate laughed with him. "The High Wizard has the magical prowess to combat half a dozen warriors. You couldn't even lay a finger on him."

"With all due respect, Your Highness, allow me to prove otherwise. If I am, as you say, unable to 'lay a finger on him' then I will lead the assault on Jyrimoore. If I am correct though, then perhaps my advice should interest you. I have been correct in all cases in the past and gamble my reputation that I am not wrong now."

"Alright," the king said with a look of approval. "You have been a great asset Artimus, and so I will allow this demonstration, so long as Guildpac agrees to it." He turned his attention to the attendant at the door. "Have the High Wizard summoned here immediately!"

The attendant nodded and exited the room, leaving the door slightly ajar.

"While he is getting the wizard, we shall discuss your suggestion in more depth." the king declared.

"Of course. Unfortunately, no matter how quickly we act, I do not see any ways that we can prevent the last three kidnappings. We should definitely prepare for a full assault, but it will take time to make the proper preparations. Meanwhile, we must send a unit to escort a diplomat to the felite tribe of the west. With their help, we should ensure that our preparations are complete. All we do then is wait for the Avatar to lead our armies."

Senator Ricker rose from his seat as Artimus finished, looking around at the rest of the senate in disbelief.

"You cannot be seriously considering his suggestion! We cannot abandon those who have been kidnapped and surely we cannot rely on some strange creature who was summoned through a legendary ritual. We must attack in full force, and we must do it immediately!" The senator scanned the room for support.

"Senator," Artimus started, "please calm yourself. I understand that you are going through a tough time right now. We all know that your daughter was one of the victims, but I must remind you that you cannot allow this to interfere with your judgment. I saw this Hájje firsthand, and I told you what he did to both Gharis and Verandas. You must realize that he has surely used this same magic on all of those he has kidnapped."

"No!" the senator protested, stomping his foot against the marble floor and shaking his head. "I cannot accept this. There must be something we can do for all of the victims!"

"That's enough!" the king shouted, sending Ricker shooting back into his chair, his face changing from deep emotional strain to that same blank stare that was expected from a senator. "Now Artimus," the king continued, "I must agree with the senator on one point. We cannot put so much faith in this supposed avatar."

"If you would allow me to speak freely sir?"

"Proceed."

"With all due respect sir, you did not witness the Avatar firsthand. Surely, though, you can appreciate the extent of his control over nature by reading my report. I have never heard of a druid who could reach anywhere near this power, yet this Avatar employed it with a simple gesture. In addition to this, there was a quality about him, a certain aura. Again, I ask you to consider my record, sir. This man, no matter how plain in physical appearance, is The Avatar of Evorath herself. If we do as he said, we will be able to defeat Yezurkstal."

"It is because of your record that I even consider your re-" The king halted mid-sentence as the door to the chamber crept open, and the attendant, followed closely by High Wizard Guildpac entered.

"Ah, Master Guildpac. I hope everything is going well for you today."

"Of course your majesty. I was told that my presence here was quite important?"

"Indeed," the king nodded. "Master Artimus would like you to participate in a little demonstration for the senate. If you would explain, Artimus."

"Of course, sir. Master Guildpac, am I correct to assume that you are carrying a wand?"

"I always do, especially when I don't have my staff," Guildpac said hesitantly.

"I would request that you allow me to use it for this demonstration."

The wizard arched an eyebrow and looked to the king. Artimus shifted his eyes to the king, who nodded in response to Guildpac's suspicion.

"Very well," Guildpac said, reaching into his robes and removing a small, wooden wand.

"Thank you," Artimus replied, approaching the wizard and taking the wand in hand. "Now, if you would please back up a few steps and prepare yourself."

"Prepare myself for what?" Guildpac asked as Artimus stepped back a few steps.

"In this demonstration, you will attempt to block a silver coin that I will be throwing at your chest. I ask the senate to note that a thrown coin travels much slower than an arrow, and that I was actually closer to Yezurkstal when I attempted to strike him. For this demonstration, I will throw the coin and then rush Master Guildpac, employing his wand as if it were my dagger. If I can bring the wizard to his knees, then I have successfully proven my point." Artimus looked out at the members of the senate, and then to the king, who all seemed to approve of his suggestion.

Turning back to Guildpac, he added, "You are to use as much force as possible to try and prevent me from reaching you. Since I had my bow aimed on Yezurkstal's head, I give you warning that I will aim for your chest with my coin, giving you the same preparation that he had. Does this all sound good to you?"

"Sounds simple enough," Guildpac said, focusing on Artimus's hand.

"Good."

Artimus reached into his pocket, removing a single silver coin and pulling his right hand back into a ready position. He focused on Guildpac's chest, preparing himself to release the coin. Without warning, he flung his arm forward, throwing the coin with all of the force he could muster.

The silver projectile cut through the air like an eagle descending upon its prey. Guildpac threw his arms forward to deflect the projectile, sending a gust of wind towards it. Artimus could feel the force of his foe's defense, but his projectile continued to fly, penetrating through the intense wind without changing course. Guildpac yelped as it struck his chest, bending over and clutching the point of impact.

Artimus wasted no time, rushing in behind his projectile and circling around the wizard. Before his opponent had time to recover from his initial attack, he pushed his heel into the back of the wizard's knee, bringing him down to the other. Holding the wand in his left hand, he grabbed Guildpac's arm and locked his shoulder blade, simultaneously positioning the wand against his throat like a knife. With only a small amount of pressure, Guildpac's other knee impacted the ground, leaving him completely vulnerable to defeat.

He held the wizard in this position for a few seconds, long enough for all of the senate to be sure that they were seeing correctly.

"Would you like to try to escape from this hold?" Artimus asked, to ensure that there was no doubt among the senate.

"No I would not," Guildpac grumbled, clearly embarrassed by his swift defeat. "I could get you off, but if that were a real knife in your hand I would probably slit my own throat in the process. Furthermore, I may break my arm if you have a firm enough hold."

"And I assure you that I did," Artimus said as he released the wizard and took a few steps back.

"If I had my wand, you would not have been able to hit me with that coin." Guildpac added as he slowly got onto his two feet.

"I'm sure you are correct, but for these purposes I could not allow it. The Hájje that I met in Jyrimoore did not have a wand, and he deflected my arrow while casting spells on two of my cadets. I hope you will forgive me for this demonstration," Artimus said, extending the wand back towards the High Wizard.

Guildpac's expression went from anger to a slim smile. "I suppose it was a humbling experience." He took his wand back and placed it into his robes. "But if it would please the senate, I would like to see a full report on this Hájje and give my assessment of his power."

"I think that would be a great idea," Artimus said turning back to the king. "And I know I need not remind the senate that because my demonstration was successful, we will not rush to an attack on Jyrimoore."

"As we agreed," the king said absolutely, not leaving any room for debate from the senate. "And I believe that your input would be most beneficial, Master Guildpac. Attendant, fetch the report and deliver it to Master Guildpac's chambers at once."

The attendant left the room once again without a word.

"Artimus. Your demonstration has been most enlightening. I have always appreciated your powers of observation, and your attention to details, but I never realized that you were such a skilled warrior. Whenever the assault does take place, I would have you be at the head of the army. Will you accept?"

131

Artimus took a low bow. "Of course, Your Majesty, but I have one request."

"And what would that be?" the king asked curiously.

"In my years of service, I have not once taken a day of leave. I would request that, until a decision is made and the preparations are complete, I can rest and have a leave from work. In the meantime, I'm more than confident that Lieutenant Argus can take my place as the temporary head of investigations."

"In lieu of what you have been through in these last couple of days, and considering your service record, I will grant you this leave without even consulting the council." The king offered a smile.

Artimus could feel the glares of the entire room falling upon him, but he didn't care. He had an important dinner to get to, and he didn't plan on being late. Having a few senators angry with him meant nothing, for tonight, he would be dinning with the most beautiful woman in all of Evorath. Over the next few days, he planned on spending as much time with her as he could.

For the first time in recent memory, Artimus was looking forward to something other than catching a criminal. He was truly happy, and as he was dismissed from the senate chambers, he could not help but wear a smile.

-=.-=.-=.-=.-=.-=.-=.-

Savannah pulled her peel from the oven, examining the trout to make sure that it was sufficiently cooked before dumping it into the empty plate that she had prepared on the counter. She leaned the peel against the oven and picked up the bucket of water that sat by her feet. Before pouring the water over the flames, she looked back to the counter. Both the bread and fish had been properly cooked, and since nothing else required cooking, she wouldn't need the oven again tonight.

With a smooth motion, she dumped the entire bucket into the stove, smoke pouring out as the cool liquid squelched the flames. She coughed a few times as she placed the empty bucket next to the peel and turned her attention to the fish once more. Following the teachings of her elder druids, she had properly gutted, scaled, skinned, and removed all of the bones from the trout, cutting it into two separate halves before proceeding to cook it.

Since Artimus would be arriving any minute, she would need to finish her preparation soon. Without any further thought she grabbed the knife that she had sitting ready. Holding the first half in place, she quickly diced through it, chopping it into many small pieces and proceeding to dice the second half in the same fashion. Taking a handful of the diced trout, she dumped it into one of the two bowls that she'd filled with lettuce.

Without any delay, she took another handful, dropping the pieces into the second bowl. She did this until both bowls had about half of the trout, and then grabbed both tomatoes, dicing them in a similar fashion and distributing them just as equally. Next, she took the loaf of bread she had cooked and began pulling off small wedges and dropping them into the bowls. The bread had hardened just as she had wanted, which would make it perfect for use in her salad.

After adding what she thought was a sufficient amount of bread, she mixed both salads with a long, wooden spoon. Finally, she had just one more ingredient to add, her dressing. Removing both the bowl that she had placed on the dressing to preserve the cool air and the flask that contained her cooling solution -which was once again room temperature- she took the bowl in hand and carefully poured out nearly half of its contents on the first salad. She did the same with the second, and then poured the remaining back into the first.

All that was left, was one more mixture, and then hopefully she would have time to clear out the room and make it more presentable. Taking the bowl that she had used to cover her dressing, she placed it on top of the first salad. Holding both bowls firmly, she lifted it and shook it vigorously, and then continued to follow this same process with the second salad. It was tedious work, and not something that she particularly enjoyed, but tonight was a special occasion.

Tonight she would have dinner with Artimus Atyrmirid, the most wonderful man that she had ever met. His determination, his intelligence, and his unbelievable charm had infatuated her since the day she laid eyes upon him. And beyond his debonair features and his renowned skills in archery, he had shown her over the last few days that he was compassionate. Tonight was not about dinner, it was about discovering whether or not Artimus was truly someone she could care about for the rest of her life.

One of the greatest things about Erathal, which was almost exclusively found among elves, was that every individual got to choose their mate. It had always seemed odd to Savannah that she could not choose the location of her house or choose that she wanted fewer tomatoes and more bread, but she was always happy in knowing that she could decide who to spend her life with. If things went well tonight, she might have a better idea of who that man might be.

As she finished clearing the counter, she thought about this, and about many of the questions she would like to ask him, and about any questions he might ask her. Thoughts were racing through her mind at a pace she did not imagine possible.

Suddenly, a magnificent voice arrived from just behind her makeshift door, interrupting her thoughts for the night. "Am I early?"

Artimus had arrived.

Chapter 11

Erathal City, Savannah's Cabin
14 Neglur, 1086

Artimus shifted uncomfortably in his shoddy wooden chair, trying not to rest his elbows on the small table as he listened to Savannah.

"So that is pretty much the story. I hope you don't mind that I used your fish in the salad. I couldn't get any of my own, and I am a vegetarian, so, you know, meat wouldn't work for me."

He shook his head, looking at the less-than appetizing meal that sat before him. Truth be told, he was never a big fan of vegetables. His meals usually consisted of some sort of meat with an apple or some other fruit. Things that grew directly from the ground just didn't sit well with him, but he felt too nervous to say so.

"No, it's fine. Truth be told, I usually give the fish to an old couple anyways. They need it more than I do." Artimus paused as he realized what he just divulged. "Please don't tell anyone. You know how the system works."

"Oh," Savannah responded sounding disappointed. "I hope you like fish."

"Of course I do," Artimus said reassuringly. He did like fish; he just preferred real meat.

"Oh, good," Savannah replied with a smile. "And, unfortunately, I got a good glimpse of how the system works today. Honestly though, I don't really understand it."

As she finished her response, she took her fork and went to work eating the salad. Artimus supposed it was time he did the same. Taking his own fork and thrusting it into the salad bowl, he speared a tomato, a few pieces of lettuce, and a small chunk of trout. Without giving a glance to Savannah, he stuffed the jumble into his mouth and chewed.

The unfamiliar taste of the enchanting dressing immediately struck him, flowing across his tongue and sending an odd sensation through his entire body. He felt as if he had just received a jolt of energy, the pain in his back flaring and then disappearing completely. Every muscle in his body seemed to relax as if he had spent the day resting. In addition to this, it tasted absolutely delicious, something he was completely unprepared for.

"Wow. Where did you say you got this lettuce?"

Savannah let out a soft giggle, a magical sound, especially in this plain cabin.

"The lettuce is from the proctor, as are the tomatoes, bread, and trout. It is the dressing that you are tasting," she said happily, placing another small fork full into her own mouth.

"I've never tasted anything like this before," Artimus replied as he examined the contents of his salad bowl more closely. "What is it?"

"That depends," Savannah said mysteriously. "Are you asking me as the Head Investigator of Erathal, or as an interested dinner guest?"

"Well, since you want me to be less guarded, I was hoping that I could become more than just a dinner guest over these next few days."

"Then I guess I can tell you, but I'm pretty sure it is illegal. You sure you won't have to lock me away?" she asked with a smile.

"If you don't get it out soon I may have to." Artimus laughed.

"Alright. Have some patience. I like to take my time with things you know. Anyways, have you ever heard of a Yggdril Tree?"

Artimus thought for a moment, racking his brain to try and recall where he had heard the term before.

"I believe so... Oh, yes! Some scholars say that they were quite common back around the Age of Demons when the forest was first born. That's about all I can remember. I know they had some sort of magical qualities to them, and they are supposed to be extinct."

"Well, they do have magical qualities," Savannah began, "but they are definitely not extinct. I have one in my yard. I used a flower off of it to make this dressing."

"I never knew that you could use flowers to make dressing," he responded with interest. "But, then again, I really don't know much about cooking. I usually just eat something simple."

"That's understandable," Savannah said between bites of lettuce. "I only really know cooking because we all learned it back in my old village."

Artimus was unsure where to go from there, so instead of trying to think of a response he merely continued to eat his salad. Contrary to his prior experience with salad, he was actually finding this quite delectable. It wasn't only the dressing either.

The lettuce seemed fresher than normal, the tomatoes softer, the bread baked in the perfect amount of spices. Even the fish seemed better, more tender than he was accustomed to. Perhaps it was all just a side effect of the dressing, somehow enhancing the flavor of the other parts of his salad. Or, though he could not be sure, perhaps it was merely an illusion caused by his present company.

"So, I know that you used to live in a druidic village, but you never told me what kind of family you left behind," he said as he finished chewing some trout.

Savannah looked up from her plate, a somewhat mild look of unhappiness present on her face.

"Well, my mother died giving birth to me and I had no siblings born before me. My father remarried shortly after my birth though, and he had a son with his new wife, so technically I have a younger brother. Both my father and brother are still in the village I left, probably still waiting for me to return and tell them that I made a mistake."

"Made a mistake? What do you mean?" Artimus asked, resting his fork in the salad bowl.

"They didn't think I should move here," she said, setting her own fork on the table. "They always thought that city life was 'evil'. They claimed that if the city had not been formed in the first place, we wouldn't have so much violence and anger in Evorath. They were ignorant."

"Well," Artimus said reassuringly, "perhaps they had a point. I mean, now that you live here, you see how the system works. Lots of people, all in one area, and all expected to live their life for the king. His every whim is given top priority, and the elf that works the hardest is the elf that has the least. Maybe your father had lived in the city before."

Savannah shook her head.

"No. He had always been 'one of Evorath's disciples'. That's what he called himself anyways. Besides, my village was just as bad. I had no freedom living there, absolutely no liberty to do anything I wanted. At least here I get some choice on what I want to do."

"It couldn't have been that bad," Artimus replied in disbelief.

"It was. Every member of the village had to learn how to perform whatever task would 'benefit the community'. I loved practicing druidic magic, but apparently that wasn't all I needed to do. They never let me practice enough, which is why there are plenty of better druids out there. So I spent more time cooking than anything else, and when I wanted to spend my spare time learning more about Evorath's magic, I would often times have to learn how to cook a new meal, or use a new gardening tool. There was no such thing as choice of job, and perhaps there was never a choice in anything. Everything I did there was because someone instructed me to do it."

"I didn't realize it was that bad. I guess living in this kingdom all my life, I had always hoped that there was a place out there that was better. Perhaps this is as good as it gets." Artimus sighed.

"I know you don't believe that," she whispered. "There must be someplace out there where people can get what they deserve, a place where justice always reigns supreme."

There was a short pause after she said this as Artimus took another forkful of his salad before responding. It was a nice notion, but it just didn't sound like something that would ever be a reality.

"If only I did." He shook his head. "But don't get me wrong," he quickly added, looking directly into her eyes. "The king is not without understanding. He was born into this system, and so he is accustomed to its workings. I have seen his attitude, and he understands justice better than most do, but he is too locked into tradition. With a bit of coaxing, and with the changing attitudes of citizens lately, there will be a change. It will take time, but people like you and me are the ones who will make a difference. By the time our children are our age, the elves will be the freest of all races."

Savannah blushed, looking down at her nearly empty salad bowl.

"Err, excuse me," Artimus added quickly. "I didn't mean *our* kids, I meant *our* kids. I mean, you know what I mean."

Savannah laughed, the most beautiful sound that any elf could possibly emit.

"I know what you meant, but maybe I thought about what *our* kids would be like," she said with a wink.

"Subversive troublemakers," Artimus suggested with a faint grin. "Just like the two of us, always looking to improve the world around them. I can see little Artimus Junior running around shooting his arrows at the rocks that he made to levitate."

"Hey," Savannah retorted, "I said that I didn't get to spend as much time as I wanted on druidic magic, but that doesn't mean that levitating rocks is my only trick. I'll show you some real druidic magic after you finish your salad and then we'll see who is shooting arrows. No one proficient in my art would need a primitive little tool like that bow of yours."

"I wouldn't want my son to be proficient in that witchcraft of yours anyways," Artimus objected sarcastically.

Savannah laughed yet again, and Artimus got that feeling that he had experienced back in the Dumner ritual hall. He felt like finishing his meal was pointless. All he wanted to do was be closer to this beautiful woman that sat across from him. As they bantered back and forth, more jokingly than seriously arguing, he felt something drawing them together. She really understood him, and he felt that he could understand her as well.

And then he thought of the possibility of their future, of the chance of having her with him every day. Their children

142

would be the best little elves to ever walk on Evorath; they had to be, with a mother like Savannah. Perhaps he did not receive praise for the work he did, nor did he receive appropriate compensation, but somehow he felt as if this was the gods telling him that he had earned something great. Without his hard work, he could never be with Savannah.

"Hello?" Savannah yelled leaning across the table. "Are you deaf or have you been possessed by some strange spirit?"

Artimus looked around the cabin and then back directly into Savannah's soothing, green eyes.

"I'm sorry," he began. "It's just that you've got me thinking of the future now too. What did you say?"

"Never mind that," she exclaimed excitedly. "What were you thinking about?"

"Well, remember when you asked me when the last time I relaxed and had fun was?" he asked.

Savannah nodded, remaining in her leaning position and waiting intently.

"Well, I don't think I have ever felt as relaxed as I do right now. And I know I have never had this much fun, except perhaps this morning."

"What was so special this morning?" she asked innocently.

"Allow me to demonstrate," he said closing the gap between their two faces and once again placing his hand upon her cheek, pressing his lips against hers.

He felt a bit awkward in his seat, so he slowly rose as the passion flew from his lips to hers, the feeling of euphoria flowing through his entire body. Running his hand slowly down her soft skin, and then back along towards her ear to move the hair from her face, he turned slightly, and then slowly backed away into his seat. Savannah remained leaning in, a satisfied smile taking over her majestic face.

Just as quickly as the smile had come, it faded to an almost cold expression, her lips straightening and eyes hardening.

"Why don't we finish eating before the salad goes bad?"

Without saying another word, she continued to eat her salad, not even looking back at Artimus to allow him to know her thoughts.

Artimus was slightly confused by this sudden mood swing, but he decided it better to eat than to try and figure it out. Perhaps this was some kind of a game to her, giving him hope one second and then pulling it away just for a few laughs later on. He had never known another elf like Savannah, and he had never thought of another elf as he thought of her. Maybe this was how all females acted when they cared about someone, or maybe she just was unsure about her feelings for him.

To him, both of their kisses had been -by quite a considerable margin- the greatest thing he had ever felt. Most men his age had already found their wives, and everyone whom he had spoken to on the matter told him he would know when he had discovered the right woman. Artimus had always been too busy with work to consider a relationship with a woman. In fact, he couldn't think of a good relationship he had with anyone, but when he kissed Savannah he felt that everything was clear. Did she not feel the same way?

As he finished his salad, the extraordinary taste being lost among his nerves, he stared uneasily at Savannah. She appeared so carefree, slowly eating her dinner without even a glance at Artimus. When her gaze did finally meet his, he relaxed and she smiled at him between bites. Did she have any idea how crazy she was making him?

"Finished already?" she asked, startling Artimus.

"Uh, yeah- I mean yes. It was very good," he added quickly.

"Well I hope it was filling enough," she said with a smile before taking another mouthful of her salad.

"Oh yes, it was more than enough," Artimus cautiously replied. Maybe she really was playing a game with him, trying to test his responses. Maybe, though she appeared to be ignoring him, she was actually watching him as carefully as he was her. And then another thought came to mind.

What if she was just as nervous as he was?

"Are you nervous too?" he asked suddenly, surprising even himself with his deliberate question. Her response did not come immediately, but rather, she waited until after taking another bite.

"Of course I am," she said quickly, pushing the words out as if saying them released a huge burden out onto the world. Perhaps it helped just to admit it.

"I'm glad to know that it's not just me," Artimus said with a sigh. "I was beginning to think that perhaps you weren't enjoying my company."

"Obviously I am enjoying your company," she exclaimed wildly. "You think I would kiss you if I didn't?"

"Well," he began a bit perplexed, "you just kind of stiffened up after I kissed you, so I thought maybe I made a mistake. I mean, we were talking, I kissed you, and then you suddenly wanted to focus on finishing your salad. I thought maybe you didn't really like it…"

Savannah let out a soft giggle, her carefree attitude, a quality that attracted Artimus perhaps more than any of her physical features, showing through. She placed her fork down on the table and looked closely into Artimus's eyes. It was quite easy to match her gaze, the green pools that filled her eyes drawing him like a bee to honey.

"You sure are clueless for an investigator, aren't you? If I didn't like kissing you, would I have invited you here for dinner after our exchange this morning?"

Artimus thought for a moment, and then smiled uneasily. He really was allowing his inexperience in this matter get the best of him. Perhaps he could try approaching this endeavor more strategically and get rid of his nervousness by applying proven methods.

"I see those gears turning. I can see it in your eyes. You are trying to look at this like another puzzle that needs to be solved. Sorry to disappoint you, mister, but feelings aren't solvable like a crime is," she exclaimed, wagging her finger in front of his face.

Artimus was taken aback by her insight. Was it really that easy to tell what he was thinking?

"Alright. I suppose you're correct. And in answer to your question, no, I don't believe you would have wanted to see me if our exchange this morning was anything less than enjoyable."

Savannah shifted her eyes back down to her salad and retrieved her fork, a slight smile remaining on her face.

"Good. So I suppose there is hope for you after all! Now if you would allow me to finish my salad. Not all of us can inhale meals as quickly as you. I guess I can add that to your list of skills."

Artimus laughed, allowing himself to relax a bit more. Perhaps there was something to this light-hearted attitude that Savannah maintained. Maybe he could adopt it and relieve some of the stress that he was constantly placing on himself.

"If they ever have a competition for eating fast, let me know. I'd be happy to enter and find out just how good I am."

Savannah smiled in between bites.

"Why don't you tell me about the news parchment? You mentioned earlier that it was not truly run by independent citizens," she said, skewering another piece of lettuce.

"Right. Well, you see, I obviously wasn't around when it was founded, so I can't personally verify the beginning, but I'll start from the top anyway. You see, about 100 years ago, before the parchment had been established, situations were already becoming tense across all of the forest. Elves in this city were getting especially upset, with food shortages, elves beginning to die, and an infection that was spreading throughout a good portion of the population, the king was worried that he might lose control.

"One of his advisors, or maybe a few of them, decided that the best way to calm the people would be to get other 'normal citizens' to tell them that everything was okay. Up until then, the king would make statements, or a group of senators would hold a hearing to try and calm the populace, but that was beginning to be inadequate. Therefore, the king and his advisors took it upon themselves to establish this parchment, which would take the name of 'Erathal News: The Independent News Parchment.'

"At first, a group of senators became the writers for this parchment, using false names in order to make the people think that they were normal citizens. They would release an article every week, making enough copies to post around the city. Of course, the success of this initial effort made people desire a news source like this more often, so they were forced to produce articles bi-weekly, and then eventually decided it was best to produce a new parchment every day. At this point, senators were not willing to put in the effort, nor did they have the knowledge to write about enough.

"You see, people wanted more than just simple news. They wanted farmers to write informed articles about farming, hunters to explain how they stalked their prey, artists to describe the subtleties of their art, etc. Since no senators could deal with this, they began hiring private citizens. With the proper compensation, these writers would remain silent and before any article was released, it had to pass through the senate for approval."

"Alright," Savannah exclaimed, putting down her fork and holding up her hand. "So you're saying that no one who writes for the parchment is actually separate from the crown? Then how did that article get published about the Hájje? That caused a lot of panic. I don't see how the senate would have allowed that article to be released."

Artimus shook his head.

"They didn't allow the article to be released. In fact, the elf who wrote that article doesn't even work for the king at all."

Savannah looked at Artimus in confusion, or at least half confusion. His hunter instincts told him there was a certain lack of sincerity.

"You see, no one knows who wrote that article, and though the king won't admit it, there is no Archor Sylvan registered in this city. In other words, the elf who wrote that article either doesn't exist, or he took a false name."

Savannah dropped her fork into the nearly empty bowl of salad and pushed it away from her.

"So how did he get the parchment distributed around town? And why didn't the king refute it? And why wasn't there a second parchment released that day; the real parchment?"

Artimus shrugged.

"All I know for sure is that since that article was written, I am on high alert looking for anyone who speaks against the crown. They also have posted night guards around town, hidden from sight, looking for anyone who might try to distribute these false parchments again. From what I have heard around the castle, the king didn't want people to know that there was someone releasing a false parchment. The counterfeits obviously got out before the deliverers from the castle could distribute the real ones, so when the fakes were discovered, they decided not to send out the approved papers.

"As I said, letting the people know that someone was releasing a fake parchment could cause real trouble for the king, and since it didn't expose the parchment for what it really was, it was decided that they would have a much easier time refuting this article than explaining how a phony got out there. Then of course, they immediately tried to locate Archor, which is why the next day was just a mundane article about how great crops were coming in. They wanted the same author who released this first parchment to refute his own work, but when he could not be found, they decided the next best thing they could do was to have our resident 'high wizard' refute it."

"So basically," Savannah continued, "the so-called independent news parchment is really just the king's propaganda?"

"More or less," Artimus confirmed with a nod. "It's scary, but with the release of this parchment, there has been strong talk within the castle walls that people are starting to understand how flawed the system is. Well, the people in the castle don't describe it as flawed, but you know what I mean. People want change, and some suspect that there are secret groups meeting to organize a rebellion against the king."

"And what do you think?" Savannah leaned in, as if she was worried that someone might try to listen in on them.

"Right now, I think everyone needs to be made aware of the threat that we face from Yezurkstal. Until he is dealt with, I pray that any secret revolutionaries remain secret. After that, I imagine that I feel the same as anyone who really thinks about it. Changes need to be made. I just hope they can be done peacefully."

"And what if you had a chance to meet with some of these revolutionaries?" asked Savannah incredulously.

"I'd explain why it's important to wait, and I'd also try and talk them out of any violent plans. But, they seem to hide pretty well, so I would probably need to find someone who is already close to introduce me."

Savannah leaned in closely, and for a moment Artimus anticipated another kiss, but she stopped just short of his lips and whispered. "I think I have some friends that you should meet."

Chapter 12

Erathal City
14 Neglur, 1086

After a brief exchange at her cabin, Artimus and Savannah departed. As they walked, Artimus observed the quality of houses decline. Though he wanted to question where they were going, he kept his mouth shut and eyes open. They soon arrived at a small hovel in the most destitute part of the city. It was made from a cheap wood and parts of the wall were worn down from the elements. The door was at a slant, left permanently ajar.

Savannah knocked on the door in a particular rhythm, and to Artimus's surprise a voice answered.

"Who is seeking entry?" it asked, the voice a deep monotone.

"Savannah," she replied.

Artimus could hear a click from the other end and a soft thud. The door sprung open.

Without delay, Savannah stepped inside and Artimus followed immediately behind her. The moment his foot hit the wooden floor, two pairs of hands grabbed his arms and slammed him against the wall.

Artimus struggled as two large elves held him pinned against the brick wall while a third frisked him for weapons. When Savannah had suggested he meet her friends, he had no idea that this was what she had in mind.

Now, as the third elf grabbed his dagger from the back of his belt and the small knife he had in his chest pocket -though missing the hidden knives he had in his boot, and sleeves- he scanned the room. Savannah stood before him with a mixture of anger and surprise on her face, and beyond her stood a fourth, unknown elf, dressed much too nicely to live on this side of town, his long silk robe, lined with gold on the cuffs, making him appear to be nobility. With the addition of his gray head of hair, wrinkled face, hardened eyes, and golden necklace that hung outside his robe, he looked almost like he could have been a former senator.

In fact, as Artimus studied his face more closely, he got the creeping suspicion that he was. But that was impossible.

"How could you bring him here?" the man who had just taken his dagger and knife asked.

"I told you," Savannah pleaded, "he is not our enemy."

"Not our enemy? Have you gone mad you crazy-"

The older elf robed in silk cast a stern glare at the speaker and interrupted him.

"That is enough! And you two, unhand him! If Savannah says that he is friendly, then he is friendly."

No one objected, and the two elves released Artimus. Artimus put out his hand to collect his weapons back, but the elf pulled them in closer and turned to the older man with a look of desperation.

"Give the investigator his weapons, though I doubt those are all he has on him. You are Artimus Atyrmirid, are you not?" he finished looking directly at Artimus.

The elf reluctantly returned his weapons, and Artimus replaced them in their proper places. He took a quick scan of the room, noting that the door he had just entered through was the only visible exit from the structure. There was no one else in the room other than the three elves who hustled him, the robed man, Savannah and himself.

"Yes, I am," Artimus started. "But you couldn't possibly be who you appear to be. I never believed in ghosts before anyways."

"And who do I appear to be?" the mysterious elf asked with a straight face.

Savannah looked between both Artimus and the older elf, worry still present on her face, but the confusion almost completely faded. She obviously hadn't expected this older elf to be here. That much Artimus could gather from her expression.

"Well, you look just like the painting of Senator Cabal that I see in the castle. But he died over one hundred years ago. At least that's what I'm told."

"You have been told correctly my friend," the old man said with a chuckle. "But, before I speak more on the matter, I must ask you why you have come here."

Artimus looked at Savannah to see if she wanted to explain, but her eyes told him that it would be better if he spoke.

"I was having a chat with our friend, Savannah, and she suggested that we come here. I was speaking of the trouble that the king is having from both outside and in, and how I would like to meet with those responsible for the fake parchment that was released just a few days ago."

"And why do you want to meet such people? Hasn't the king ordered them arrested on sight?" the old elf asked, his eyebrows raised.

"That he has. But I am not a blind follower of the king. I want to warn these people, and maybe give them some valuable information about both the king and the danger that we will soon face from the outside."

The older elf looked to Savannah. "Is this the danger you mentioned earlier?"

She didn't say a word and only nodded.

"Alright, Lieutenant. I think that you might have something to offer to this old elf and his supporters. If you would follow me."

Artimus stood in confusion as the elf walked to the other side of the room and the three others followed him. The house had only a bed that was situated right next to him, and on the other side, where the elves were gathering, a small chest. He looked to Savannah to try to figure out what was going on, and she motioned for him to follow.

As he approached the chest, he quickly understood why. The elderly elf finished a short chant and held his gold medal up to the keyhole of the chest, which popped open. There was nothing stored in this chest, for it was not a chest at all.

Artimus looked down to see a ladder, which trailed off into darkness. He could see a faint light at the end, but he could not make out how big the area was below. The old man stepped in first, followed by the man who had frisked him and then the two who had held him against the wall.

"These friends of yours seem so nice," Artimus quipped as Savannah motioned for him to go next.

She cast her head downward, trying to hide her grin and shook her head.

"They're always nice to me," she replied with a shrug.

"I guess I just don't have the right face," he joked stepping onto the ladder and beginning his descent.

"Pfft. Just keep looking down," she shouted, following him, whispering an old elvish word as she cleared the top of the chest, which caused the lid to slam shut.

As he continued his descent, he noticed the air become musty and the ladder wobbled as he made his way to the bottom. The smell of burning candle wax filled his nostrils, accompanied by a dampness that was only native to river-impacted caves. His hands became visible through the darkness as he finally reached the bottom.

They had to be at least five meters beneath the hovel, but since no light was coming from above, Artimus could not be sure exactly how far it was. As he stepped down from the ladder, he waited for Savannah to finish her descent. Just as she stepped off the ladder, he placed his left hand on her back and held out his right to help her down. She responded with a slim smile as she took his hand and stepped down from the ladder.

"The three of you should return home now. Mister Atyrmirid will not be causing me any trouble," the elderly elf stated, as he leaned on the table that sat in the middle of the room.

The three younger elves didn't respond verbally, but with downcast gazes. Two went east and the third proceed on his way west. It wasn't difficult to read the expression on all of their faces. They didn't agree with their leader, but they also didn't question him.

Artimus scanned his new surroundings as Savannah continued forward towards the older elf. This underground hideout appeared to be startlingly large, perhaps networking out to cover a great part of Erathal. Though he could not determine the exact extent, Artimus was certain that it had to span out at least through the slums. After all, the room that was situated before him had passages going in all four cardinal directions.

Of course, he was currently standing at the end of the northern passage and from his vantage point he couldn't see the end of the southern passage. As he stepped forward into the small room, a single lantern hanging above him the only immediate source of light, he looked down both the east and west passages respectively. Down the east passage, he watched as the first of the two elves turned left and disappeared. Only a few meters further, the other elf turned to his right and also vanished from sight. This confirmed that this structure -if that was what it should be considered- branched out to many different areas of the city.

Next, Artimus turned to the west, where the third elf was already gone from sight. This tunnel was much like the other two, extending out for as far as the eye could see, a torch lighting the way every four meters or so. But one thing troubled Artimus as he scanned the ceilings of each of these tunnels. How were they supported?

"Do you always need to know everything about your surroundings before you can get comfortable?" the old elf asked as he took a seat at the round table in the center of the room.

Artimus shifted his gaze to the elf as Savannah sat down in a chair across. The plain, wooden table had six chairs around it and absolutely nothing on top of it. With a quick sweep of the rest of the room, Artimus was able to confirm that there was nothing else of note within the room, save the light that he had noticed almost immediately. Certain that he had indeed figured out enough about his surroundings, he walked up to the chair next to Savannah and stood behind it.

"It's a habit that comes in handy in my line of work," he replied after a few seconds delay. "Which is why I was wondering: how is the ceiling of this place supported? I see a wooden beam every third meter, but there is no way that these could support the ground by themselves."

The old elf shook his head.

"You just can't comprehend the things that magic can do when it is employed by a competent user. All of you rangers are the same."

158

Artimus arched an eyebrow, ignoring the insult for the time being.

"You're saying that magic holds this place up? I hope whoever put the spells on this place was competent enough to make sure it would last."

"Stupid bastard. The enchantments put on the wood will never wear off, and they are what holds this place up. So just sit down and stop asking questions. I didn't allow you down here to answer your questions, at least not until you showed me that you had something useful to offer in exchange."

Artimus was taken aback by the old elf's sudden aggressive tone, and after fighting his initial reaction to respond in anger, he pulled the chair away from the table and sat next to Savannah. But as he did, he noticed something peculiar that he had missed earlier.

"I'm afraid I must ask one more question before we begin discussing the matter for which I came," Artimus said, his tone making it clear that he would not allow the elder to ignore his query. "Why is there a trap door underneath your table?"

The older elf cast a glare in Savannah's direction, whose facial expression immediately went to one of confusion as she avoided the elf's look.

"She told me nothing. I assure you," Artimus added.

This effectively shifted the elf's glare, causing it to fall on Artimus. If it had been the previous morning, this glare would have probably upset him, causing him discomfort and most likely anger. But it was not yesterday, and Artimus felt more confident than he had in years. True, this elf's gaze was powerful, but it would not shake Artimus's new confidence.

"You are too observant for your own good, Lieutenant," the older elf suggested, his tone unbelievably calm, considering the enraged facial expression that remained on his face.

"I will answer this one question, and then you will tell me all about these threats from both the king and from the outside, and give me your suggestion on what you think we should do."

The old man said this without any hesitation and with an authority unlike any Artimus was familiar with. Most politicians had arrogance, as if they were born deserving of their title and position. This man spoke with confidence, as if he knew exactly what would happen because he had earned his place of leadership.

"And then you will tell me if you really are who you appear to be, and if you are, you will explain how you pulled all this off," Artimus responded matter-of-factly.

"Alright," the older elf offered, his face softening a bit. "But I guess I should answer you. We use this system of tunnels to lead to our member's homes, though you have to navigate a maze to actually get anywhere. Most of the tunnels down here lead to dead ends at some point. We put little meeting rooms like this spread out though, to make it appear that we actually use this area for our normal meetings, but in reality it is only to interview perspective members. Therefore, as you probably already gathered, the area below us is where actual planning and discussion takes place."

160

"And much more than that I suspect," added Artimus without emotion. "But, as we agreed, I would like to spread some news to you as well. I can appreciate what you are trying to do down here, but I cannot endorse your cause, especially not in these circumstances," Artimus offered.

"You don't even know what we plan on doing. Or has Savannah developed a loose tongue?"

"No," Artimus replied flatly. "I suppose I do not know exactly what you have planned, but I understand that you don't appreciate the state of affairs in this monarchy. Taking into account your secret base, and fairly confident that it was you who wrote the fake article a few days ago, I think it is safe to assume that you intend to make some changes. And I would further venture that you plan on implementing these changes sometime soon."

"Alright. Your reasoning is sound, but what of it?" the old elf questioned.

"I think it prudent for you to wait. First, unless I am terribly underestimating your numbers, you are seriously outmatched. Second, let's assume that you have more support than I think. The question I would pose in this case: are your people really trained and experienced enough to pull off a revolution? Third, can you really say that you have a better system ready to implement? So far, I have seen all of your followers treat you like a servant would treat his king, unwilling to question your word and unable to influence your decisions."

"So you have come here to belittle me?" the older elf asked, his voice rising to suggest a hint of anger. "Perhaps before doing so, you should get an actual understanding of, first, how things work down here, and second, how I plan on making changes. I will not be the leader in our new system; the people will decide through popular decision who will lead them. And we are not a violent group. Unlike you rangers, we do not try to solve our problems with bows, steel, and mythril."

Artimus considered the elf's words carefully before continuing.

"Okay. Let's assume you have a non-violent way of changing leadership and instituting a method of popular opinion to choose a leader. Let's also assume, once more, that you are capable of doing so soon. How does that sound to you?"

"Continue," the elder commanded, his voice softer.

"Well, there is someone else out there who wants to make changes. The only problem is, he wants to change much more than just the way that this city is run. You realized, perhaps before any other elf, that there is a hájje out there, and he doesn't intend to let anything remain as it is now. This hájje, Yezurkstal as he calls himself, has more power than anything I could have imagined, easily twenty times as powerful as any magician I have seen, probably more."

"So Savannah tells me," the old man interrupted, "but what does that mean to me? Wouldn't it be better if our people were ready to meet him after a change of leadership? What if people really felt that they were fighting for something for a change? Wouldn't that make them fight harder?"

"I'm afraid it won't work that way, and you know that as well as I do. Any change in leadership will cause too many

162

problems in the short term. Besides that, getting the people to doubt their leadership in a time like this could be fatal. Things may not be perfect. Hell, it is downright nauseating the way that this city is run, but when faced with an enemy like Yezurkstal, we need people who are completely united behind the crown. Only together can we defeat this enemy. And I don't just mean elves. We need to branch out to the other races of the forest and build a unifying force in order to have any hope of winning against this Hájje. Negotiating with other races would be impossible with a newly established government. None of them would want to deal with us."

The old elf sighed. He had obviously been debating this issue already, probably due to Savannah's limited information about the Hájje. Sinking into his chair, he looked intently at Artimus.

"I'm afraid you have this dead man beat. You are obviously the right choice for head investigator. In this short time you have proven your ability to reason, your foresight, and your unbelievable observational skills. I will put off releasing any more false parchments. And to put that into perspective, I was ready to distribute another tonight. This one was good too. It was going to directly speak about the injustice of the proctors."

Artimus nodded.

"That is good to hear. And I assure you, I will be happy to read that article once it is released, but as I said, you must wait until we have dealt with Yezurkstal. I would also hope that you encourage any able-bodied followers of yours to take up arms if the Hájje makes it here. But, now I request that you finish your end of the bargain. You just referred to yourself as a 'dead man,' so I take it you are who I suspected. How did you do it Cabal?"

"I'm afraid we will have to discuss the details at a later time. I have important things to attend to, especially if I want to follow your plan of action. I have to make sure that people know not to distribute the false parchment and I have to make further preparations. This hájje could prove useful if I can spin it right. After he does attack, I should have some really good stuff, but I need to start on it now if I want to get anything done. To be fair, I'll tell you this: I faked my own death because I was sick of the way things worked. Senators were, and from what I gather from my sources, still are, just figureheads. They can offer ideas and speak to the public, but it's the king that makes choices. I felt that people should have more say, and I felt that things were getting worse, not better. Now that I am dead, I can make the changes from outside that I couldn't make from within. It just took some time to get to where I am today. But I must be going."

With that, the former senator rose from his chair, pushing it away from the table carelessly. Both Artimus and Savannah followed suit, though they did so much more slowly. Without addressing Savannah, or saying another word to Artimus, the senator placed his hand on the table and muttered something in old elvish. Without delay, the table slid to the side and the hidden trapdoor opened up.

"Remember, Senator," Artimus began, as Cabal stepped onto the ladder that led further down. "I'll support you when the time is right and I'm sure I can carry some others with me. Just wait until we are free from the terror of Yezurkstal."

The former senator said nothing, and as he disappeared beneath the ground the trapdoor slammed shut and the table slid back into place. Artimus was unsure of what he should do next, so with a smile on his face he turned to Savannah.

"You definitely have some interesting friends. But, I suppose it is about time for me to be heading home."

"Are you tired already?" Savannah asked, as they walked towards the exit.

"Well, not really, but after this meeting I figured you would want to go home and sleep."

"Why would I want to do that? The night is still young. How about we head off into the woods somewhere and find some solitude?"

Artimus grabbed the first rung of the ladder with his right and turned back towards Savannah.

"Well, from my understanding, solitude would be if you just went alone. If you want company though, I wouldn't mind joining you. Did you have somewhere in particular in mind?"

"Actually," Savannah began, her voice rising slightly in pitch. "I do. I'll lead the way. Just head up the ladder and once we get back above ground follow me."

"Why does everything have to be so secretive with you?" Artimus questioned as they climbed the ladder back towards the hovel. As he got close to the top, the exit opened without warning, startling him slightly.

"It activates on this side when you get to the third rung from the top," Savannah said as he climbed out of the chest on the other side. "And isn't it much better when you are surprised?"

Artimus offered his hand and helped Savannah as she stepped out of the chest. Savannah turned and whispered the same thing that Cabal had said earlier, causing the chest to close behind her.

"I personally prefer to know what I am getting myself into," Artimus stated as he motioned for Savannah to lead the way. "But, I suppose with you leading me it's not so bad."

"Good, because I think you'll like the place I have in mind," Savannah exclaimed with a giggle.

She winked at him as she passed and walked out the door.

Artimus usually hated not knowing his destination. Actually, certainty was something that he treasured above almost anything else in life. For some reason though, as he followed Savannah out of this dilapidated hovel, he knew that she was leading him someplace that he would enjoy.

Chapter 13

Somewhere Outside Erathal City
16 Neglur, 1086

Artimus looked up at the stars spread out across the night sky. It was an amazing sight. He was stretched out across an oak branch three meters above the forest floor. From his position, it felt as if he could almost reach out and touch the stars. He leaned back against the large trunk, Savannah situated just before him and leaning into him in a similar fashion. Since she had shown him this spot two nights ago, he had come here with her each night, watching the stars, talking about their pasts, and escaping from the frightening reality that they would have to face tomorrow.

Tonight seemed especially hard, knowing that sometime soon, or perhaps already, Yezurkstal would kidnap his final victim and make her into one of his own. Artimus wanted to try and stop him, to watch over all of the homes in Erathal and prevent him from laying a hand on anyone else. Unfortunately, he understood that such desires were impossible to fulfill, for there was no way that he could stop Yezurkstal by himself, or even with the help of an entire rangers' brigade.

No. Tonight could not be about Yezurkstal. The king had informed him that afternoon that he would be leading a contingent to Dumner tomorrow to see if Goldenchest would get on board. If not, he would proceed to the felite city, though unsure of its exact location, and work on an alliance there. But these were things he needed to push out of his head. Tonight was about him and Savannah. It was about relaxing.

167

"You're thinking about him again, aren't you?" Savannah asked, tearing him from his thoughts.

Artimus looked into her eyes and smiled.

"Yeah, I was. But, I'm ready to just focus on the present now. Thinking about the future only causes anxiety. I have a much better time talking to you."

Savannah returned his smile, and pointed up to the right corner of the sky. A few tree branches blocked some of the stars, but Artimus looked anyways.

"You see those stars there in between the branches, those four in the corner? What does that look like to you?"

Artimus tilted his head slightly as he tried to figure out what she saw in those stars.

"You mean those four, right?" he asked pointing his own finger.

"No, below that. The bottom one is almost touching the lower branch."

"Oh."

Artimus squinted. Unfortunately, he still wasn't quite sure what she could be seeing, but he tried tilting his head in the other direction. The first star was located down and to the right of the second, and both the third and fourth stars were located approximately the same point between the first two vertically but were spaced apart horizontally to the left.

"Hmm… I think I see what you're talking about. It looks kind of like a fish."

168

"Yeah! That's what I thought. I mean, it's not perfect, but I can definitely see a fish," Savannah confirmed with a smile as Artimus turned back towards her.

Artimus couldn't help but return the smile as he gazed into her beautiful green eyes.

"You know, when you brought me out here, I thought seeing the stars like this was the most amazing thing I had ever seen. It made me feel like I was someplace special and that I was someone special. But, being able to just peer into your deep, green eyes, I feel that the sky is rather mundane in comparison."

Savannah squeezed Artimus and leaned in close, laying her head upon his chest and embracing him tightly.

"I don't know how you think of these things," she whispered giddily, "but I always enjoy hearing them." She loosened her grip and backed away, before raising her head to meet his and leaning in once again.

Artimus smiled, pulled her in, and kissed her.

-=-=-=-=-=-=-=-

Felite Confederacy
16 Neglur, 1086

It was a full moon, a perfect night to look up into the night sky and watch the stars. A small shooting star shot across the horizon, passing over the moon before disappearing behind a row of trees. Of course, for the members of the felite confederacy, all of this was obscured by a thick layer of smoke that rose from the center of the village.

A large bonfire raged here, the flames reaching the tops of some smaller trees. The entire village had gathered around, waiting intently for the seers to reveal what news they had to share about the threat that lived to the west. From the smallest felite child, to the strongest warriors of the tribe, all had left their straw huts this night in order to find what their futures might hold. At the very center of this gathering, immediately before the fire and situated in a small triangle, three wizened felite elders sat.

Tel' Shira stood just two rows behind her elders, trying to be patient with the rather fowl-smelling, lion-like male that stood to her right and the jittering children that jumped up and down to her left. To make matters worse, the jet-black felite that was right before her kept moving his head from side to side, and since he was almost exactly the same height as Tel' Shira, she kept having to do the same in order to see the elders. These mobs were never something that Tel' Shira wanted to be caught in, but this one just seemed much worse than usual.

Of course, she had to consider the fact that the news they were waiting for was much more severe than usual, which could very well have contributed to her own impatience, but still, this was just ridiculous. Last night, the elders had announced that they would have a large gathering tonight because they believed the intentions of the Hájje might become fully clarified. The hope was that they would see how he could be defeated through their vision, but, short of that, they would at least be able to know where he would attack first.

This was a welcome discovery, especially considering the visions they had last night. They predicted that within seven months, fifteen children of this Hájje would be born from the eleven women that he had -or will have- kidnapped from Erathal. Furthermore, they spoke of him turning other creatures into his slaves, including barghest, lizock, and even reanimated felite that he would use to fight for him. The forest would be torn asunder, and in that vision they had seen nothing that they could use to prevent any of these tragedies.

If tonight's ritual was successful, they would have something more helpful to offer. Everyone gathered had a very good reason to be here, and everyone was ready to fight in any way that the elders advised them to. All they needed was to know what would be most helpful.

Out of nowhere, the foremost elder, Su Pau, sprang up to her two feet, her eyes shooting open. Both the other two opened their eyes as well and rose before nodding to the first elder, who responded in kind. The ritual was finished.

Su Pau stepped forward, leaving the other two standing directly behind her. She used a twisted wooden staff for support, which had a circular-cut diamond placed in the center. This staff had been passed down from all the head elders of the tribe for as long as anyone could remember, and its large diamond was said to have a hidden power that had long been forgotten. The white silk robe that she wore had also been passed down for generations, and lying over her graying fur, it gave her a look of severe authority.

"Dark, the future is for all children of Evorath," she started with a cracking voice. "Destroyed, in just two nights, the village of Dumner will be. Send aide, we must. The elves, late they will arrive. With them, our soldiers will go. Lay siege to the Hájje's home, we must. After this, the path is unclear. Act now, we must."

The crowd broke out into murmurs, some isolated panic clearly audible over the general rumble that had arisen. Tel' Shira fought the urge to hit the large male next to her, for he was currently smacking his fist into his palm, mumbling about how he would pummel the Hájje before he would allow this village to be hurt. She could appreciate his enthusiasm, but the fact that he was so obnoxious about it, didn't help his case at all.

"Silence," the sole male elder yelled from behind his leader. "Finished, we are not!"

If one compliment could be paid to the felite race as a whole, it was their discipline. As soon as their elder requested their silence, every member of the crowd fell silent, waiting for their elders to finish saying whatever it was they wanted to get across.

"By noon tomorrow, a legion will leave for Dumner. Only our greatest warriors, we will send, and at the front of this army, I will be." Before giving the crowd any time to interrupt, Su Pau raised her open palm and continued. "Question my decision, no one will. The head elder, for a long time I have been. To leave is my choice. Return, I will not."

-=-=-=-=-=-=-=-=-

Erathal City, Artimus's House
16 Neglur, 1086

Artimus lay on the floor of his cabin for the third night in a row, thinking about the wonderful day that had just concluded. Like the previous day, he spent almost the entire time with Savannah. From an early breakfast, which she prepared for him, to a long morning horseback ride, to a mid-afternoon picnic, and on to their star-gazing atop the large oak, he had not left her side. There was no way he could protect all of the elves in this city, but she was one person that he could keep safe, which is why he wanted her by him at all times until he was certain that Yezurkstal wouldn't target her as his next victim.

This is why Savannah slept silently in his bed just a few meters to his left, as she had for the previous two nights. It was hard to convince her at first, since she had initially suggested Artimus just sleep on her floor, but with the proper persuasion, he was able to infect her with his point of view. After all -as he so wisely pointed out- his house was much better protected than her quaint little hut.

She had insisted that the spell she had placed outside her entrance would be enough, but he pointed out that with Yezurkstal's magic abilities, such a spell would prove useless. Artimus's house had various enchantments placed on it by request, but in addition to these minor protections, he had set up a series of traps around every possible entrance and exit, as well as adding a few trap doors and hidden caches of weapons. If anyone tried to get into his house, he would know immediately, and even if his traps failed to harm Yezurkstal, he would be able to buy Savannah time while she escaped and got assistance.

Still, this explanation was not what convinced Savannah. So, in a last desperate attempt, he pointed out that Yezurkstal probably knew which houses had women living in them somehow. Therefore, if she remained in her home, he would be more likely to attack than if she stayed with Artimus at his house, where he had lived alone since moving to the city. Fortunately, this was enough to convince her.

Unfortunately, Artimus was not convinced. Yezurkstal had bested him once already, and he had done it with such ease that it made Artimus feel like a helpless infant. If it really came down to it, and Yezurkstal did chose to kidnap Savannah, there was really nothing Artimus could do about it. Yes, he could fight, assuming of course that Yezurkstal didn't use that same spell he had deployed against Gharis and Verandas, but there was realistically no hope for victory. How could anyone ever defeat someone who had the power to change his enemies into his own personal lackeys?

This thinking brought Artimus back to that moment once again, the look in Gharis's eyes, the pale skin pigment, the radical hair; it was all a product of evil. And he was merely a spectator, helpless to save his friends, afraid to risk physical contact, and unable to injure his enemy. Using his bow against this enemy was like trying to light a fire with water, and he doubted his short sword or any of his knives would prove any more effective. Yezurkstal had an inborn magic, drastically more powerful than anything ever imagined.

When he used his spell on Artimus's cadets, the extent of his magic became almost palpable. It was like he was dipping into an endless supply of magic, a power source of dark magic that reached beyond this universe and into another. Even being completely inept at magic, Artimus could feel the power that this

Hájje wielded as if it was a solid force, a juggernaut that could never be stopped.

There was some hope in Artimus though, even if only a glimmer, that there might be some way to reverse the effects of this spell. Recalling the expressions that he had received from both Gharis's and Verandas's families when he had reported their deaths, he wished that he could have told them his hope, or at least that he could have told them the truth. No, he was forced to lie, to tell them that they were dead.

In a way, he could rationalize this, for the personalities of both Gharis and Verandas were most definitely dead, or, as he hoped, repressed to the point that they could not break free on their own. Still, they were alive in body, and though he had no remaining family of his own, Artimus knew that this knowledge would offer some comfort. But, with the order to keep the Hájje's power limited in the public eye, Artimus could not offer these poor elves any comfort, just as he could not offer the parents of all the kidnapped victims any comfort. As far as the people of Erathal were concerned, they were all dead.

Artimus knew the truth though, and like many times before, he almost felt that it would be better if he didn't. Keeping the king's secrets, lying to his fellow elves, enforcing laws that violated the inherent rights of all living beings: these things all made him feel sick. In spite of it all, there was something in his heart that told him he had to keep going, that he had to keep offering what he could, even if it meant sacrificing his own values.

In the end, what really mattered to Artimus, the thing that made him the person he was, was his desire to protect those who couldn't protect themselves. To keep life going, and not allow any one person to harm another; this was his creed. If anyone violated this, he would use his skills, the talent that he had developed, and become more proficient at than anyone in all of Evorath, and punish the violator for his wrong-doings.

Right now, he had to protect Savannah, to keep her safe from the most evil force that had ever existed. Even understanding that he would not realistically be able to handle Yezurkstal himself, he could not turn away from his nature. So Artimus remained awake, waiting, and ready to fight, until he saw first light before finally allowing himself to drift off to sleep.

Chapter 14

Erathal Forest
17 Neglur, 1086

The felite legion stuck to the shadows, moving with great speed through the forest and towards the Dumner village. Su Pau, the elder and leader of the Felite Confederacy, rode at the head of this modest force, mounted atop her trusted roc as she rode towards her vision. Close behind traveled ten other roc riders, four of whom were skilled druids and six who carried long, wooden spears. Only a few meters back, a dozen nimble felite, armed with daggers ran, followed closely by another dozen larger warriors, each armed with a broadsword, warhammer, or battleaxe, and finally half a dozen felite armed with longbows brought up the rear.

These soldiers were the best the confederacy had to offer, most having real combat experience and all having proven themselves in training exercises. Together they could fight off an army of considerably greater size, making them more than a match for any conventional force. With their help, the warriors of Dumner would find themselves a much greater match against the darkness that approached.

Felite had stamina greater than any major race known in Evorath, only barghest even coming close to matching their endurance. This enabled the felite legion to move at a constant run for days if needed, and since the Dumner tribe was only about a day's jog from the felite village, they were able to move at an even faster pace.

Tel' Shira, a young, but experienced fighter ran at the front of the lightly armed felite, her twin daggers resting at either side of her waist. She was clothed in the same armor as the other soldiers of her class, a studded leather breastplate and matching skirt. This enabled her to utilize her amazing flexibility and speed, while effectively defending against a plethora of small arms and projectiles.

With a deep breath, she closed her eyes, doing her best to prepare for interactions with the undesirable animals that they were being forced to fight alongside. She opened and closed her fists, breathing deeply as the soldiers around her came to a complete stop. They had arrived.

.=.=.=.=.=.=.=.=.=.

Guard duty was the most undesirable task for any centaur warrior, but it was always understood how necessary it was. Of course, like most things that were supposedly understood, Irontail had a tendency to question this duty. If their village was really hidden as well as the elders suggested, a fact that Irontail now assumed could actually be fiction, then why would they need guards in the first place? No one could see their village and no wild animals traveled through the area, so what exactly was a guard's job other than just standing in place and staring out into the forest?

Today, Irontail got his first answer to this question in the form of a startling sight. Just beyond the clearing that their village occupied, a small roc came into view, but there was something following it. No, not just something, an entire legion

178

marched behind this majestic bird. More rocs flew into sight, followed by an array of felite soldiers, armed with a large variety of weapons. With just a quick head count, Irontail could see that they easily had enough members to account for Dumner's entire population.

For the first time in his life, Irontail felt that his role as a guard might actually mean something. Since they had invited a felite druid and her guard to this village a few days before, this army might actually be able to see the village, or they would at least know that it was there. If their intent was hostile, which Irontail prayed it was not, they could do some serious harm. But how was he supposed to report this?

If he left his assigned site, he would be breaking duty and if he yelled for help, the felite would probably be able to hear him. On the other hand, if he just stayed in place and waited, they could attack before anyone else in the village even knew they were coming. Granted, there were a handful of other guards on duty, but only one, possibly two of them could be seeing the felite from their positions. Unless, of course, the felite were attacking from multiple sides at once, in which case all five of his fellow guards could potentially know of the approaching army.

Once again, Irontail was forced to remind himself that action was much more helpful than thought. He dropped his makeshift club and galloped back towards the central mound. He focused on the mound and willed it to open for him, and without slowing down he ran through the vines as they extended to allow him passage. His hooves adjusted to accommodate for the downward angle, and he ran down the tunnel with as much speed as he could muster until he arrived at the elder's meeting room.

Not worrying about the potential consequences, Irontail yelled out.

"There is a felite army just outside our village! Goldenchest, the felite have a legion approaching!"

There was no response for a moment. Then, without warning, the wall before Irontail burst open to reveal his great elder Goldenchest, his eyes blazing in anger.

"Irontail! I thought you were on guard duty! What are you doing here? You should be at your post," he yelled.

"I'm sorry, sir, but this seemed the best way to warn you," Irontail pleaded.

"I don't need your excuses! Get back to your post immediately. I will alert the other elders and we will arrive shortly. Get the other guards ready for a defense but wait until you are sure their intentions are hostile. Now go!"

Irontail hesitated only a second before nodding and running back towards his post. As he approached his position, he wondered why the elders had never implemented a procedure for this. If they were going to get angry at him for leaving his post, then shouldn't they have made it possible for him to warn them without doing so? Irontail was beginning to believe that he would make a better elder than these so-called 'leaders' of his tribe.

Unfortunately, he realized that now was not the time to let himself get distracted with these kinds of thoughts. Even with the belief that he could make positive change to the tribe, this was not the proper time to be thinking about how to implement change. No, this was the time to make sure that his tribe could survive another day.

As these thoughts passed out of his mind, he slowed to a trot and approached the other guard who was stationed at the northern watch.

"Silvertoe, did you spot the approaching felite?"

The large centaur turned, resting his club over his right shoulder as he looked down at Irontail. Though much larger than Irontail, Silvertoe was slow-moving and clearly lacked any upper brain function. He stared at Irontail in confusion for at least five seconds before opening his mouth.

"Uh. Yeah. I saw them. They coming."

Irontail shook his head in frustration.

"Go tell Tungstunhand and bring him back to the front watch area. Understand?"

Once again, it took Silvertoe some time to catch up with what Irontail was saying.

"Uh. Yeah. I get him to front of village."

Irontail waited a full ten seconds before his larger counterpart turned and gradually began galloping towards the druid at the northern watch. He considered calling for the east and western guard to join him, but in case the felite were coming from multiple directions, he decided it was best to just use the guards who were posted immediately before the attackers. This of course meant Silvertoe, Tungstunhand and himself, a small but formidable force in their own right. And Goldenchest would be arriving any moment with some more soldiers, possibly some of the best, like Copperfoot or possibly Cobolthand.

Hoping that he would bring a sufficient amount of help, and also hoping that this army coming from the north was the only approaching threat, Irontail returned to his own post, retrieving his club from the foliage and moving between the trees to get a better look at the approaching army.

They had slowed down considerably since he first spotted them. In fact, they were moving at such a lax pace that it seemed improbable that they were planning an attack. Either that, or they weren't able to spot the village after all, which could provide a serious strategic advantage should their intentions be hostile.

On closer observation, none of them had their weapons drawn. Then again, perhaps that was how they caught their opponents off guard. Approach a city looking as if you intend no harm only to pounce at the last minute. That kind of attack could work out quite well for a nimble race like the felite, especially against a relatively slow-moving people, like centaur.

Irontail was also able to get a more precise count on the felite as they came closer, putting their numbers at about forty. That left them with twice as many soldiers as Dumner had to offer, and between the women, children, and non-combative elders who might be able to help, they still had fewer than forty bodies to offer. Looking purely at the numbers, there was no way that this village could survive an attack from this legion of felite.

He grasped his club, his hands gripping the leather tight, waiting in position behind a couple of large oak trees. If these felite wanted a fight, he would make sure to take out a good chunk of them before they even set foot in the village. Despite this sentiment, as Irontail waited for his elders to arrive, he prayed to Evorath that this approaching legion's intentions were not hostile.

.-=-.-=-.-=-.-=-.-=-.-=-.-=-.

The felite army came to a complete stop just before the borders of the village. Every last soldier went to attention, even the roc seeming to stand up as straight as they possibly could. They all remained silent, waiting for the centaur to emerge from their village with some sort of greeting.

Heavy humidity weighed down, storm clouds billowing above the forest's canopy. Tel' Shira almost felt that the air was palpable, making the situation feel ever the tenser with the impending storm.

Su Pau stepped towards the village with care, her arms held wide open as if offering herself as a sacrifice.

"People of Dumner, come bearing grim news we do. Approaching your village is a great army. Yourselves reveal, so that preparations can commence."

Su Pau remained stationary, waiting just a few meters ahead of her subordinates for some sort of response. Tel' Shira could not see any sign of a village, but her well-developed senses told her that the centaur could both see and hear her elder.

Tel' Shira watched her elder curiously, wondering about her prodigious perception and whether she observed even more.

183

There were tales told of Su Pau's younger days, moving with all the grace and speed of the greatest warrior. Even more impressive, were the tales of her druidic powers, her ability to control nature at a level comparable to any dryad. All of these reasons, coupled with her sincere concern for all life and her unsurpassed wisdom, made her the obvious choice as tribe leader.

She watched as her elder's ears perked up, a small rustling from the foliage ahead. Her first inclination was to grab her daggers, but she fought the temptation, knowing full well that if danger was coming, Su Pau would raise the alarm before it arrived. After a few seconds of anxiety, she saw the golden fur of Dumner's leader from behind some underbrush.

Tel' Shira felt a few drops of water from above. A crash of thunder rolled through the sky, like a beating drum.

The next moment, a great centaur emerged, followed closely by two other centaur elders, distinguished by their ceremonial dress, and a single centaur warrior. Tel' Shira did a double take of this warrior before realizing that he was the one who had been at the Xyrloom just days prior. He was undecorated, so it seemed odd that he would be joining a welcoming party. Perhaps his presence here was a mere coincidence, but she got a peculiar feeling about him, nonetheless.

Brushing this feeling aside, she turned her gaze back to Goldenchest -yes, that had been his name- and waited for some sort of greeting. Su Pau was clearly waiting for a greeting as well, for she remained in place, as if a statue, looking up at Goldenchest with anticipation.

"The people of Dumner welcome you, but I fear we do not know what you could be talking about. What is this threat that you speak of?"

Goldenchest spoke with authority, yet an almost caustic undertone stuck with each of his words, making him sound less like a leader and more like a ruffian. His arrogant tone suggested doubt in Su Pau's foresight. What a fool.

Su Pau seemed unphased by his less than tactful greeting and continued on with a genuine concern in her voice.

"For your welcoming, we thank you. Approaching your village is an army of demons, a hájje at the head of this army. Prepare for an attack, you must. To assist, we have come."

Goldenchest stepped back and looked to both of the elders beside him. Both looked back with blank faces, stupefied expressions on their simian faces. Anger flashed briefly across Goldenchest's face before he redirected his gaze to Su Pau.

"I fear I don't grasp this situation fully. Are you saying that actual demons, like those that are told of only in legends, are coming towards our village? You're saying this Hájje has the power to command demons?"

"Yes," Su Pau confirmed with a nod. "Command these demons, he does. Unknown, the exact number is, but great force, he definitely will bring. Fear we cannot succeed, I do. Much better, our chances are, if preparation, we begin now. Hours, maybe two or three, is all we have."

Tel' Shira could feel that the warrior in the rear, the one from the ritual, was getting agitated. Her sixth sense was not as developed as her elders, but any experienced felite would have to notice it. Though his face remained calm, his eyes held a certain fiery impatience. He tightened his grip on his club, squeezing the crude weapon. Even so, he remained silent, which was impressive considering the energy he gave off.

Goldenchest didn't respond immediately, nor did he turn towards either of the other elders. He stood silent, as if trying to come up with some excuse as to why Su Pau had to be wrong. Though this desire showed through quite clearly, something in his eyes revealed that he understood: Su Pau could not be wrong. Felite elders had always been known across all of Evorath for their foresight. To question her predictions would be pointless.

"As you say then, we must begin preparations immediately, though I am unsure what preparations you are suggesting."

Goldenchest turned back towards the warrior who had accompanied them.

"Irontail. Gather all of the guards back at the central mound."

He shifted his gaze back to both of the elders who had accompanied him.

"Cobolthand, you warn the citizens. Copperfoot, you gather the rest of the warriors and the other druids as well. Have all the women and children remain in their homes and bring all of the combat-ready to the central mound. Go."

Irontail was the first to go, not saying a word of confirmation but only turning and running back towards the interior of the village. Both Cobolthand and Copperfoot nodded towards their leader, and replied with a simple "yes, sir." Without another word, they both followed Irontail at a slightly slower pace.

"Like a good start, that sounds," Su Pau said softly. "Though, must be done, much more. A room large enough to fit all of your warriors as well as my own, we must go to. Discuss the proper defense, we can do there."

"Of course," Goldenchest nodded.

"Our ritual hall is large enough to fit more than double that number."

As he turned to lead the way, Tel' Shira noticed the light decrease considerably. With the whole party of felite proceeding into the village, the clouds opened up.

Chapter 15

Erathal News Article 100:43
Justice Will be Served
By High Wizard Guildpac

Since I last wrote in this insightful parchment, there has continued to be kidnapping after kidnapping. Some people are suggesting that perhaps this criminal is un-catchable, that perhaps I was incorrect in my earlier article, and our fellow citizen Archor Sylvan was right when he suggested the existence of a hájje. Today, I can say with certainty that this disgusting criminal will be brought to justice, and he will receive that justice no later than tonight.

I had the privilege once again to speak with the esteemed investigator, Artimus Atyrmirid. Apparently, he has located the whereabouts of this kidnapper, and is leading a brigade of rangers to apprehend him today. As you read this parchment, they will be making their final preparations and shall depart to dispose of this threat once and for all.

Of course, many of you are probably wondering the same thing that I was when I first received this news. Why does the investigator need an entire brigade to combat a mere criminal? Well, when I questioned Mr. Atyrmirid about this, he was more than happy to enlighten me.

These kidnappings, according to his conclusions thus far, have actually been the results of a gang of rogue lizock. When this discovery was made, the king quickly sent representatives to the nearest lizock village, where we were assured that they had not authorized any of this. In fact, they informed our diplomats that there had been a marauding gang of lizock that attacked their village only a couple of weeks before.

This discovery, as the Head Investigator informed me, set back his efforts quite a bit. The problem remained that the rangers were still unsure of where these lizock were hiding during the day. Extra guards were posted at night to hopefully catch these crooks, but it is assumed by the lab mages that they were employing some sort of camouflage in addition to their natural stealth abilities.

Finally, after the kidnapping last night, I have been informed that some evidence has been identified to reveal the lizock's location. Though he would not say where they were going, Mr. Atyrmirid said to me just this morning,

"We finally caught a break. These lizock left behind some solid indication of where they are hiding. By this time tomorrow, we'll surely have this threat neutralized."

Though this is not quite a "case solved" yet, it appears that our system has come through once again. The rangers are truly something that we should all be proud of. For me, I thank Evorath that I am a citizen of this great city, and that the king will always be there to keep me safe.

So, tonight when you go to bed, you can finally sleep soundly. In the morning, this threat will be eliminated for good.

-=-=-=-=-=-=-=-=-

Erathal Forest, Erathal
17 Neglur, 1086

Artimus finished securing his saddlebag on Thoron, giving him a final pat on the head.

"I know you don't like all the extra weight, but we will be gone for a few days. We need to be prepared for anything."

Thoron rubbed his muzzle against Artimus's cheek playfully, giving a snort as if to say he understood. It was almost strange to think about it, but Thoron was really Artimus's closest friend. He would gladly give his life for this horse, and he trusted Thoron would do the same for him.

Of course, there were still preparations to be made before he would be able to set out, not the least of which was finishing his own equipment. This was a battle they were going to fight, not just a small skirmish, or a simple scuffle, but a full-blown, bloody bedlam. People would die, and decisions would need to be made quickly. In all honesty, Artimus was quite sure he was not qualified to be leading such an engagement but being the only person who knew the extent of Yezurkstal's power, he was the only one who could do so.

He took a deep breath, the smell of the stables seeming somewhat relaxing among his chaotic thoughts. The odd mixture of horse manure, hay, old wood, and a soft afternoon breeze brought about a secure base for his feelings. It was not a pleasant smell by any measure, but it was something that he was comfortable with, and that comfort spread to his feelings about the upcoming battle.

If anyone could lead this army, it would be him. Yezurkstal had taken away too much, but it stopped here.

With a confidence in his step, he walked past the others who were preparing their own horses, mounted swordsman, spearman, and archers alike, all ready to march alongside him.

The plan was that he, Savannah, and the four dozen armored soldiers that would follow behind would go to Dumner. With any help they could solicit from there, they would then proceed to the small colony of Lamia, and then to the felite village to the north. Unsure of where any troll tribes were located, and, under Artimus's advisement, leaving the satyr, lizock and barghest out of it, they would then pray for the Avatar to join their army. Savannah seemed sure that this would be enough to get his attention, and once he was on board, they would proceed to the Runeturk Mountains and teach Yezurkstal that he could not have his way without consequences.

Artimus walked across the courtyard, observing for the umpteenth time how beautiful the blossoming flowers and single, large oak were in the early noon sun. And this was a pleasant smell, the exotic blend of flora from the grass itself to the daisies, tulips, and daffodils all filled his nose and further relaxed him. This would be a good day, and nothing that could happen would change that.

Pushing open the small wooden door to the armory, Artimus stepped in and looked around. Most of the equipment was still there, which meant everyone was, as he had, preparing their mounts before gathering their weapons. He quickly spotted the crate he was looking for just a few meters in, an *AA* written on the box to signify that it held his special equipment.

Sitting down on a neighboring crate, he slid the lid off the top, looking down at the first suit of armor he would ever wear. It was a strange feeling, excitement mixed with dread, or maybe something else that Artimus was completely unfamiliar with. Regardless, he felt rather anxious to try it all on, and even more anxious to see how well he would wield it all in battle.

He pulled out the shirt of mythril first, unbuttoning his own shirt and removing it so that he was wearing only a sleeveless, tan undershirt. Slipping the mythril over himself, he let the links fall below his waist to cover his more important lower appendages. He retrieved his green, long-sleeved shirt and buttoned it up so that the chain mail was only visible below his waist. It seemed a perfect fit, reaching down his sleeve all the way to his wrist, covering his shoulders, chest, and back and contoured to cover his crotch and buttocks without interfering with his leg movement.

Next, he reached down and pulled out the steel greaves. They were lined on the inside with leather and also had leather straps to secure them to his legs. Though he had never worn them before, he had seen them on soldiers often enough that fastening them seemed pretty simple. With a few knots on either leg, he had them securely in place, and found them, surprisingly, comfortable. Standing up, he tried walking a little.

His movement was definitely restricted, and though they were loose around the knee, they still held tight enough that he couldn't quite fully straighten or fully bend either leg. This could definitely prove detrimental in the heat of combat, but so could receiving a blow to an unprotected leg. He tried jumping a few time, doing a few simple calisthenics to see just how much it would impact him. It wasn't ideal, but after a minute of deliberation, he decided that it was safer to keep them.

Looking down at the backings that had been provided, two separate pieces of steel for each leg, he decided not to put them on. A blow to the front of the legs was quite possible, but it seemed highly unlikely that he would need to worry that much about his rear. Next was perhaps his most important piece of equipment. At least, it was the only piece of equipment that he used on a regular basis.

Pulling the mythril bracers out of the box, he looked them over closely. Typically, he used plain leather bracers, but they would not defend against any sword or even enemy archer. This chain-mail mythril, lined on the inside with leather for some added comfort, could easily be used to block an enemy's weapon strike.

Slipping both on and securing them, he found them to be quite acceptable. They were only slightly heavier than the normal bracers that he used, and he found that with a few quick movements, he could barely even notice a difference in his speed. This was ideal, for even the slightest slowdown in his reloading time would be unacceptable.

Moving right along, he pulled out the small, mythril helmet. As he had requested, the front was left almost completely open, leaving only a small bar to run down between his eyes to his mouth. This would cover his forehead and nose, while leaving his breathing free and his eyesight relatively unaffected. Unfortunately, as he put it on, he found that was not the case.

Trying to focus on different targets around the room, he found himself having to squint, move his eyes at odd angles and close one eye to get good enough focus. With a grunt, he removed the helmet and dropped it back in the box. There was no way he would wear that into battle.

Finally, he turned his attention to the simple cuirass. As he had requested, the front and back plates were separated to allow for more maneuverability. It was a bit of a tight fit, but after he slid it over his head and fit his shoulders through, he found it rather comfortable. The mythril wrapped around his sides but left a bit of extra room at the armpits to allow for a greater range of motion. At the shoulders, the plates were held together by leather straps.

To account for this lack of defense, he pulled out the final pieces, a matching pair of steel spaulders. The plated steel attached to the leather straps at his shoulders and covered any previously exposed part. With a quick rotation of both his arms, he found his movement impeded in only a minuscule degree. Though undesirable, he decided that, like the greaves, they could prove to be essential in keeping him safe.

Looking back in the box, he checked to see if they had added the other item he had requested. With a smile, he pulled out another piece of chain mail, though this one was much longer and quite a bit tighter than the other one.

"Perfect. Now I just have to convince her to wear it," he muttered to himself.

"Wear what?" came an unexpected response from the entrance of the armory.

Artimus jerked his head towards the door to the unexpected, but amazingly beautiful sight of Savannah. She was clothed in her usual attire, a tight-fitting, knee-length skirt and a matching green top. Upon closer inspection, Artimus noticed that she was also wearing leggings underneath, probably in anticipation of the long horse rides.

As he turned towards her, she continued walking in, moving to intercept him. The usual spring in her step seemed a bit shallow, a trace of fear showing through her calm exterior. Unlike the soldiers who were going on this campaign, Savannah lacked the training and mental preparedness to deal with the idea of combat. Furthermore, she had experienced Yezurkstal's power firsthand, felt his evil. With this in mind, it was understandable that she would be apprehensive.

"I thought you might want some extra protection. I know you don't usually think it is necessary, but you must know how dangerous this will be. We're venturing into uncharted territory, so it's always best to be on the cautious side." He finished by holding up the chain mail that he just taken from his equipment crate.

Savannah said nothing until she reached him, and then held out her hands to take the chain mail. Artimus appeared a bit surprised, but handed it over, thankful that it was much easier than he anticipated. It was a shame he couldn't always influence people so easily.

"I don't know," Savannah began, holding it above her head. "It doesn't look that great. Why would you think I need to wear this?"

There was the response he anticipated.

"Look. We don't really know what to expect out there, but Yezurkstal is smart enough to know that even his power is insufficient to overtake an entire army. He is going to have followers of his own, and unlike him, they will probably be using conventional weapons. If you get hit by a projectile or a small blade, this will most likely save your life."

"It will 'most likely' save my life?" she mocked. "What does that mean? And what good will it do against his magic, or against a large weapon like a spear or sword? It seems to me like this heavy piece of armor will only make me look bad and slow me down."

If there was one thing that Artimus had learned in dealing with someone as stubborn as Savannah, it was that he would get nowhere fighting her. Of course, there were other ways to convince a person.

"You're right. If you get hit with basically anything large enough, you'll die from the impact alone, even if it doesn't break through the mythril and impale you. And as it is now, it won't help against magic in the least, it does appear unattractive, and it will cause you to fatigue more easily. I just have a couple of questions for you. What if you enchanted the armor to make it protect against some magic? And what if you made it feel lighter? And lastly, what if, for argument's sake, you try on the mail and I think it looks good on you? It does have a nice color after all."

She stood there with her eyes downcast, holding the mail down at her side.

"Well, I never heard of anyone enchanting chain mail before. But I suppose it would be like enchanting a staff or wand. I guess there could be ways to improve it. And making it lighter is definitely possible. As for me looking good in it, you'll just say that I look good regardless."

The door to the armory opened up just as she finished; two young soldiers walking in and looking at both Artimus and Savannah nervously.

"Oh, uh, sorry to interrupt, sir. Can we get our equipment ready?" the first of the two soldiers asked.

Artimus laughed.

"Of course. Go ahead and get ready. Hopefully the rest of the men will be following you close behind. We need to be departing soon."

"Yes, sir. I think we were a bit ahead of the crowd, but the others should be coming here soon," the soldier said with a bit more confidence.

"Good to hear," Artimus responded before turning his attention back to Savannah. "Perhaps we can take this conversation outside? And can you please just humor me and try the mail on?"

Savannah rolled her eyes.

"Alright. If it makes you happy," she exclaimed, turning and walking to the exit. As she did, she slipped the mail over her head and lowered it onto her body, allowing it to fall into place.

Artimus followed closely behind, opening the door for her as she walked out before closing it behind him.

"Well. How do I look?" Savannah outspread her arms.

Looking her over from head to toe, Artimus could not help but grin. As she moved, there was definitely some definition to her breasts and waist, but it concealed most of her natural figure. It almost looked like she was drowning. In all honesty, Artimus could not say that he preferred this over her usual attire. However, as he looked up into her eyes, he didn't care.

"You look gorgeous. Not only do your eyes glisten like the moon reflecting off of water, but your hair hangs down with certain regality, flowing in the wind like a beautiful, majestic roc sailing through the sky."

Savannah's eyes seemed to shimmer for a moment before she curled her lips and pushed Artimus playfully.

"That's not fair! You must have had that one prepared to convince me."

She sighed and looked down at the protective garb. With a shrug, she tilted her head up back towards Artimus and glared daggers at him.

"I suppose I will wear it, but you have to let me put the same enchantments that I place on this on your armor as well. Deal?"

With a smile and a playful bow, Artimus replied, "But of course. I wouldn't have it any other way."

"You planned on asking for that anyways, didn't you?" she asked as they walked back towards the stables.

Artimus looked at the grass beneath his feet, trying to conceal his smile.

"I can't say the thought hadn't crossed my mind. After all," he continued more seriously, "this is a threat unlike any we have faced before. Yezurkstal is an unpredictable opponent, and we need every advantage we can get. Why do you think I requested that you come along in the first place? I believe your abilities will make you the most important member of this team."

Savannah stopped walking and looked at Artimus. There was something in her eyes, a certain fear that he had not seen before, a sense that she was unprepared for what lay ahead. It was as if she had just been handed a responsibility that she knew she could not handle.

"You put too much faith in my abilities. I am not even an accomplished druid. How can you expect me to be so useful?" she asked, her voice wavering.

"No. You put too little faith in yourself. Do you not remember that you participated in a ritual that was supposedly impossible only days ago? Do you not also recall some of the things you have shown me in the last few days? I have witnessed people who claim to be the greatest magicians in the world, and you are, by far, the most powerful of them all."

Artimus was good with words, but he was also honest. In the time they had spent together these last few days, Savannah had demonstrated a wide array of druidic abilities. If he doubted her abilities, he would have her hidden away somewhere in the castle rather than come along with the war party.

"You flatter me. But what about the other druids who were at the ritual? Don't you think some of them are more powerful than myself?"

"Undoubtedly, that is quite possible. Then again, I don't know for sure, and I definitely do not have any of them around to come along, now do I? Look," Artimus declared, "I can't have you thinking so negatively. You know as well as I do, that attitude is usually what makes the difference between success and failure."

Savannah remained silent, and proceeded towards the stables, her eyes downcast and feet shuffling on the ground. Artimus stood his ground, hoping that this was not how she would leave the conversation. Sure enough, she stopped after a few meters and turned back towards him with a faint smile on her face.

"Are you coming or not? I need to see what I can do with that armor of yours!" she exclaimed, her voice rising in pitch.

With a smile returning to his own face, Artimus followed, placing his right hand between Savannah's shoulder blades and motioning forward with his left. Returning his smile with one of her own brilliant displays, she continued her march onward.

They would be departing within the hour and they would march until nightfall. Judging by the clouds in the sky, it would probably be a tough night, and the following days would not be any easier. When everything was all said and done, they would be facing the most powerful foe ever imagined. In spite of all this, as Artimus walked with Savannah back to the stables, he could think only of how much he would enjoy Savannah's company.

Chapter 16

Erathal Forest

17 Neglur, 1086

Lightning flashed across the sky, illuminating the night with blinding brightness. Thunder pounded through the air like a crumbling mountain, reverberating off the tallest trees of the forest, the ground shaking with every horrendous crash. Despite the great canopy of trees that hung overhead, rain poured down with such ferocity that it mirrored a waterfall.

Between each flash of lightning and boom of thunder, the area around Artimus and his men went pitch black. Contrary to his plans, Artimus had been forced to set up camp sooner than he'd hoped. Actually, it was his initial intention that they could march through the day and arrive before nightfall; now they would have to pick up the pace to make it.

What started as a light drizzle transformed into this monsoon, blackening the sky within minutes. Without any way to see, and with a torrential downpour constantly assaulting them, they had no choice but to stop and set up camp.

Savannah proved her worth already with her quick thinking and druidic prowess. She created a natural drainage system, keeping the water from flooding everyone's tents. After two hours of such powerful rain, Artimus would have expected to be lying in water, but with her creativity, she had allowed them all to remain relatively dry. Of course, these tents were not exactly watertight, especially not with such powerful winds fueling the rain.

Artimus heard Thoron's distressed snorting from just beside his tent. Understandably, these deep snorts indicated that he was quite frightened. With his extensive training, Artimus was confident he would stay in place. He just hoped that everyone's horses would behave as well.

If the storm didn't let up soon, there was no way they would arrive at Dumner by nightfall. Every minute they delayed gave Yezurkstal another minute to expand his influence, or worse yet: stage an attack of his own.

As he struggled to relax amidst the chaos that raged outside, Artimus thought of how he would garner support from the centaur and felite, and with their support he would call for the Avatar's help. If all went according to plan, Evorath's right arm would be leading them to lay siege on Yezurkstal's cave. Everything would fall into place, and this tumor would be eradicated before it could spread and infect the world. If not...

He decided not to think about that.

-=-=-=-=-=-=-=-

Artimus awoke with a start, jumping from his makeshift mattress with startling speed. A layer of sweat covered his face, his breathing deep as he took in his surroundings. It had just been another nightmare, something that had become synonymous with his sleeping as of late. Each one felt so real, so tangible, yet every time he awoke, he felt like a fool.

Slowing his breathing to a normal rate, he poked his head outside the tent to try and see what time it was. He hadn't even remembered falling asleep, but somehow amidst the chaos of the storm, coupled with his general lack of sleep as of late, he had drifted off. How far behind schedule were they?

The storm had passed, and a few hints of sunlight broke through the canopy above. Judging by the angle, it would be setting soon. They would not make it before nightfall, but if he pushed his men, they could get there at a somewhat reasonable hour. Some of them were already packing up their tents and preparing their mounts.

Returning to the inside of his tent, Artimus found his belt and secured it about his waist, positioning his dagger so that it was on the right side of his back. After replacing his other knives in their proper locations, he turned to his boots and secured them on each foot in turn. Lastly, he lifted up the chain mail and draped it over his shoulders, allowing it to fall into place. He followed suit with his other pieces of armor as well.

After performing a final sweep of the tent, he stepped back outside and turned his attention to the spikes that were holding his tent in place. Crouching and wrapping his fingers around the large, iron peg, he yanked it out and took it in his left hand. He proceeded to all four corners in turn before going to the tree he'd used to tie the tent to and unwrapped the ropes from their respective branches.

Allowing the tent to drop, he placed the iron pegs in the center before turning his attention to Thoron's shelter. As he approached the tarp, he could hear that Thoron was happily eating the grass at his feet. With a smile on his face, Artimus pushed the tarp aside and entered, patting his trusted stead on the head as he looked around. All of his equipment appeared to have been adequately protected from the weather, including the quiver of arrows.

Thoron snorted at his owner, nudging him slightly with his nose.

"You're already eating grass! Is that not enough for you?" Artimus asked jokingly.

Giving Thoron a quick scratch behind the ears, he moved around and lifted the saddlebag from the floor. Opening up the front left compartment, he pulled out a couple of carrots and, returning the bag to the floor, went back to feed his steed. Thoron devoured the carrots held up to his mouth, giving Artimus one final lick on the hand as if to say he wanted more. Giving him a few strokes on his mane, Artimus shook his head.

"I'll give you a couple more before we leave."

With a wink, Artimus went back outside and took hold of the first support rope for the tarp. Stretching to untie his knot, he pulled it down and let the front fall. Holding up this first end, he dragged it over to the second knot and untied that as well. After unfastening all the support knots, he pulled the tarp up entirely, exposing both Thoron and his equipment to the evening air. With a sharp tug, he removed the pegs that were holding the tarp in the ground and rolled it up.

Getting on his hands and knees, he removed all the air from the quasi-tent as well as he could, condensing it down to a size just small enough to fit in its proper compartment in the saddlebag. With a glance at the tent, he sighed and retrieved the saddlebag once again, opening the back, right compartment and stuffing the tarp in as well as he could. He then turned his attention to the tent, carrying the saddlebag over with him to eliminate any unnecessary steps.

Looking at his muddy knees and sniffing in another burst of humid air, he shook his head. These conditions were undesirable to say the least, as they would slow down their march. On top of that, they wouldn't be able to eat anything solid before departing, for the wet wood would make it quite impossible to start a fire. Hopefully everyone had eaten a good breakfast that morning, because the only thing that they'd be eating before Dumner would be bread and berries.

Pushing aside his own desire for food, he turned his attention back to the tent. Careful to keep the pegs in the middle, he folded the tent in half, then again, and then a third time, pushing out as much air as he could before trying to condense it once more. Pushing down with all of his force, he got the tent into the desired form, and holding it tight he stuffed it into the front right pocket of the saddlebag.

Taking the saddlebag back over to Thoron, he placed it down beside his trusted companion. Artimus's stomach gave a low rumble, urging him to eat something. Fighting off the temptation, he went over and retrieved his water skin from between his bow and quiver. Putting the strap over his shoulder, he took a few good gulps and placed it at his side.

Casting his glance out over the camp, he counted the tents that were still standing. He could not help but feel a bit annoyed that so few had taken the liberty to even begin disassembling their shelters. The rain may have only ended within the hour, but that was no excuse for trained soldiers.

Retrieving a small metal pot from inside of his saddlebag, Artimus removed his rear dagger and banged the flat of the blade against his makeshift drum. The rancorous clanging carried throughout the camp, and anyone who was not already outside quickly emerged from their tents startled. Those who were outside scrambled and formed up around Artimus.

After a few moments of his improvised call, everyone was gathering around, and Artimus was able to pick up the three commanders making their way to the front of the crowd. Savannah remained at the back, staying somewhat outside of the group.

"All right everyone!" Artimus yelled, sure his voice was revealing his discomfort. "Perhaps no one made it clear, but the success of this mission could mean the survival of our great city! You're supposed to be the finest elves the kingdom has to offer! We hit a snag in our march, and it's understandable that we needed a break, but we should have been back on the move fifteen minutes ago. Elves! Get your act together! Get your equipment organized. We march in ten! Move out!"

It wasn't the most inspirational or maybe not inspirational at all, but it was all he could come up with on the spot. Regardless of its strength as a rallying speech, it got the job done. As he finished speaking, the soldiers all rushed to get their supplies together.

The three commanders stayed where they were, waiting for the crowd to disperse before walking up to Artimus in the clearing.

"I think maybe you should leave the motivating to us," started Commander Zeidrich, the head of the infantry unit.

He was a middle-aged elf, about four hundred and fifty years old if Artimus recalled correctly. His experience with melee combat was matched only by a handful of other soldiers in the army, all of them captains or generals by now. Having participated in skirmishes against a variety of forest-dwelling species, he had been distinguished many times over for his exemplary service.

His age showed through, perhaps a bit too much in fact, for his light hair was losing its once golden hue and receding back towards his ears. Wrinkles showed just below his steely gray eyes, which were also worn with the weight of age. Physically, he was strong, but it was more of a slow, steady strength, one that appeared could falter if pushed for too long. Mentally, he was perhaps the best tactician for this mission.

"Zeidrich," Captain Viviko, the head of the spearmen unit joked, "You couldn't motivate a bee to gather honey."

Zeidrich shook his head and pushed the captain, grinning as the younger soldier peddled backwards.

Viviko was young for a captain, around three hundred and thirty by Artimus's reckoning. Viviko was known as one of the most inspiring leaders to ever serve in the royal army and had invented an entirely different method of fighting with spears. Unlike most spear units, who excelled in a traditional spear wall to fend off mounted attackers, he devised a fighting method using the spear in a fashion similar to how most would use a fighting staff.

His entire spear unit was trained in both the traditional style and his revolutionary fighting art, making them the most effective in the kingdom, and by many accounts, in all of Evorath.

"I don't know if this is really the time to joke," the final unit head, General Fletching butted in. "I think perhaps we should just be getting on. What if this hájje decides to make an offensive? We have to get to the centaurs as quickly as possible and start working on a plan of attack."

Out of the four men in positions of leadership for this operation, Fletching was the oldest by a good amount of years. Over seven hundred years old, his once perfectly blonde hair was both thinning and now held more white and gray. He had participated in every major engagement in Elvish history and was the foremost instructor for young archers. Artimus remembered his lessons from days past, and though he never really liked Fletching while he was a student, had since learned to respect him.

Without Fletching's guidance, Artimus was sure he would not be the champion archer he was today. Everyone in the kingdom respected his ability, not only as one of the greatest archers to have lived, but also as a leader. His voice was naturally soothing, yet powerful.

"Of course, Fletching is right," Artimus spoke up, "and, I will certainly consult you on inspiration in the future."

He looked at all three of the leaders, seeing that none seemed very enthused to hear him speak.

"I understand that I am not a military leader," Artimus continued, his voice strong and resolute. "And I understand that I do not know the finer areas of war, nor have I experienced the things that you all have. I have a great respect for you all, and honor your individual accomplishments, but this mission is of the utmost importance.

"I was chosen to lead because I know the enemy better than anyone else here. I have seen him firsthand. Just as I would not begin to tell you how to lead your troops, I know that you all will respect that I know the enemy better than any. It is this qualification that has put me at the head of our current operation.

"Whatever you do though, do not confuse my position. You are the leaders of your individual units, not me. I will not tell you how to run your units, because I know not how to. I only ask that you respect my lead and command your troops accordingly. If you have advice, offer it. You know I will always be glad to hear it.

"For now though, just remember, this mission is important to the survival of our race. I want to see our kingdom survive, so let's make sure that happens. Do I have all of your support?"

All three of the unit leaders looked at one another in turn as if considering. Zeidrich was the first to speak up.

"We'll do our jobs; that much you can count on."

Viviko nodded and clapped Artimus on his shoulder.

"Just don't go trying to order us around like peons and we'll be good," Fletching added, a slight grin forming on his face.

"Alright," Artimus confirmed with a nod. "I just needed to make sure we were all on the same page. Let's get moving."

The unit leaders said nothing more, each casting a quick nod of acknowledgment and turning to tend to their gear.

As they walked away, Savannah approached somewhat cautiously. She had a faint hint of a smile, but her stride was erratic, indicating some uncertainty.

"You're looking like a natural born military leader all of a sudden," she teased.

Artimus shook his head. "I never was much for big war parties. I'm a good enough observer to notice when people aren't quite comfortable though. What is bothering you?"

Savannah cast her eyes downward, trying to avert Artimus's gaze. By now, she must have realized his powers of observation. The reality was that he noticed things that no one else did, and that included people's posture, voice inflection, minute changes in their facial expressions and a variety of other factors that, to his knowledge, no one else even paid attention to.

"You know that is actually annoying," she said, her voice scathing. "You notice way too much for your own good sometimes."

Turning her gaze back up towards him, she continued, her voice softening a bit.

"I don't know exactly what I am doing here. I know you thought I would be useful, but I can't stop thinking that we're going off to rally an army for war. This isn't just a little match to test my druidic abilities. This is something harsh and unforgiving, and I don't think I should really be here. I don't really know where I fit in. I can't follow any of those three commanders, but I don't know what I am doing on a battlefield. I feel like I will just be getting in the way by being here..."

Artimus considered her statements for a moment, wondering if maybe he was expecting too much from her. Maybe he should have just requested that the High Wizard Guildpac come along, or that he recommended someone more accustomed to battle. Gazing beyond the beautiful woman before him, he looked at the forest ahead.

The storm had been vicious, leaving debris from the larger trees, and knocking over some of the smaller ones. The ground was soaked, paths turned to mud. Trekking through the elements was difficult enough, and at the end of this path, they would be engaging an enemy of still uncertain power.

"Maybe it's not what you're used to," Artimus began, thinking carefully of every imaginable fate that could lie ahead, "and it's not what I am used to either."

He paused a moment, and made sure that she was looking at him, holding her gaze and locking in on her eyes.

"I often wish that there was someone out there better at solving cases than myself. I find myself stumped, without any idea where to go or who to question. I doubt my abilities, and I doubt that I can ever figure out some mysteries. Sometimes I fail.

"What I always remember though -no matter how tough things seem- is that I am the only one who can do some of the things that I do. No one in our kingdom can gather information from an interrogation like I can. No one follows my methods of reasoning. No one in this kingdom can out-shoot me with a bow and arrow.

"These are not boasts, they are facts. One day, I hope to meet people better than me in all of these aspects. I want to be bested, so that I can learn from their example and improve myself. And, I want to be able to step away from some situations, and trust that the entire kingdom won't fall apart in my absence.

"The reality is, our way of life is preserved by the select few who can make decisions and get things done. I do what I do because someone must do it. I enjoy it too. The thing you need to realize, Savannah, is that you are the best the kingdom has to offer."

He looked straight at Savannah, hoping to convey the strength of his words. She averted his glare, her eyes downcast as she contemplated his words. Her gears were turning, and though her doubt was almost palpable, he could tell his words had an impact.

Sometimes the best way to help someone else deal with their own doubt was to admit your own, or at least that's what he figured. Maybe it wouldn't help her much, or maybe his honesty would put the situation in perspective. Either way, being honest with Savannah just felt like it was the best choice.

Then something occurred to him, a way to relate to Savannah philosophically on a level that he could not relay to most people. He cared about Savannah, more than he had cared about anyone in a very long time, and the time they had spent together in recent days had opened him up to new possibilities, or perhaps it had just revitalized him to feel that things he once felt impossible were possible indeed.

His tone instantly changed as he continued.

"Why do you use druidic magic?" he asked plainly.

Savannah looked back up at him, her eyes meeting his once again. She could see the change in his eyes, and that must have given her some comfort.

"I was raised learning magic. That was my assignment in life, to learn how to follow in the traditional ways."

Her answer was uncertain, but it was exactly what Artimus had expected.

"No. That is why you were taught druidic magic as a child. I want to know why you continue to use it. You left your village -your home- because you believed that there was something out there besides that life. You could have decided differently, but you continued to learn and grow as a druid even after you left that environment. Why?"

Savannah's eyes softened, a spark of recognition coming through.

"Because I enjoy it. I am good at it. I love the challenge of reaching new heights, of doing something that others around me cannot do."

Artimus smiled.

"So who do you do it for?"

Savannah finally caved and allowed a faint smile to form.

"For myself."

Chapter 17

Erathal Forest, Dumner Village
17 Neglur, 1086

The sky was dark, rain pouring down upon the village of Dumner. Planning had taken place in the shelter of the ritual hall, but now as final preparations were being made, Tel' Shira found herself perched upon a branch being pelted by water.

Deployment of the defense force was complete. Thanks to her elder's foresight, they knew where to expect the assault, which would afford them a significant advantage.

Between Su Pau and Goldenchest, they had devised quite an effective deployment grid, and though she was no expert tactician, Tel' Shira was somewhat optimistic due to their predicted number advantage. Though the exact number of enemies was uncertain, Su Pau suggested it would be fewer than the sixty one bodies set up for defense.

In anticipation of the battle, every centaur who was not fit for combat had been sealed off in the center mound of the village. Unlike when she had last been here, it was now disguised as a dead mound of earth.

Like her, the other eleven lightly armed felite warriors were perched upon tree branches, prepared to pounce when the time was opportune. Higher up, the six roc-riding spearmen flew in a tight circle, preparing to descend and engage whatever threat arrived. Su Pau, the four other druids that had come from her tribe, and two centaur druids all stood behind the combined strength of twenty three heavily armed soldiers from both her own people and the centaur.

At the front of this row of soldiers, Goldenchest and his two greatest generals, Cobolthand and Copperfoot stood ready to lead the defense. At the rear of the army, the six felite archers were joined by four from the Dumner tribe. Finally, the five roc who had served as mounts for Su Pau and the other druids had their own perches upon treetops.

With the layout of the trees, they had some natural defensive cover, but beyond that they were relatively exposed. This was a familiar defensive strategy to Tel' Shira. The archers had sufficient line of sight to see the attackers before they engaged the warriors. The warriors would draw in the attacking army in a frontal assault. Once the two armies engaged, Tel' Shira's unit would spring down from the trees, followed closely be the roc riders.

The archers would provide cover and slow down the momentum of the attackers. The heavy infantry would provide a strong defense, while the druids provided magical support. The lighter infantry and aerial forces would provide a counterattack. The formula was proven in previous felite battles with other forest races.

It was not proven in combat against a force of demons.

-=.-=.-=.-=.-=.-=.-

Irontail kept his eyes fixed through the underbrush. He grasped his club tightly, anticipation building as the rain beat down upon his hide. The sound of thunder reverberated through the trees in the distance, and a flash of lightning lit up the dark skies.

In spite of all the doubt that had begun manifesting in the past days, his mind was completely free from distraction. If there was one thing he was certain he had received as a warrior of the Dumner tribe, it was preparation for a battle such as this. Though centaur villages were scattered throughout Erathal, Dumner was known as the tribe of warriors. Since his youth, Irontail had been trained to fight in frontal combat, to ignore pain, to close out his mind from distraction and to exploit any opportunity that might present itself in battle.

Never before had he gotten the chance to test his combat prowess against an outside force. The thought of battle was fueling him, causing an unfamiliar excitement to build. He was going to be a part of history, able to fight an enemy unlike any the forest had faced since the reign of demons.

This would be a true test of his strength, an opportunity to prove to himself what he was capable of. This was what he had been preparing for all his life.

-=-=-=-=-=-=-=-

They were fools.

They had no idea what they were about to be involved in.

He was building a perfect society, and this puny resistance that these felites and centaurs had pulled together would be nothing. Most of them would have to be sacrificed, but a few would be chosen to march in his army.

217

Yezurkstal cast his gaze down to his clenched fist, willing some dark energy into his hand and letting it coalesce. Forming a solid mass of magic, he opened his fist and let the energy explode outward as he pondered.

He was born into a world full of disease and conflict. His childhood had taught him how horrible Evorath was, but he had been gifted with the ability to change it all. Over the past couple of weeks, he had gained a new understanding of just how damaged society was. When he was through, the entire plane would be united under his rule, and no one would hold any higher position than any other.

Each time he mated with one of his dark queens, he had been able to incorporate her knowledge of the world into his own. The variety he had found in his mates gave him an understanding of the entire Elvish kingdom, and through that a greater knowledge of all of Evorath. These single-minded individuals knew nothing of the vision he had. How could they?

"Master, the enemy is deployed just as you have predicted."

Yezurkstal shifted his stare towards the sound of General Gharis's voice, opening his eyes to address his underling.

They stood in a clearing just outside the visual range of Dumner. Rain fell gently upon him, creating a soothing atmosphere when coupled with the darkened skies.

"Of course they have," he replied after a brief pause.

Both Gharis and Verandas had proven quite useful additions to his army, teaching him valuable military strategy and techniques his enemies would employ. More important than that, they taught him the value of the adamantium ore that he was now utilizing in abundance. Most important, they had provided him with a successful test of his grand design. His enemies would have him in superior numbers, but with the strategy he had planned, that would be completely irrelevant.

"I take it your new equipment is satisfactory?" Yezurkstal asked coldly.

"Of course, Master. Both General Verandas and I are quite pleased. With adamantium, our enemies will not stand a chance." His response was almost as cold as Yezurkstal's inquiry.

Almost.

This would be a small victory, but a victory, nonetheless. When this force was wiped out, he could regroup and lead an assault on the largest kingdom in the forest. Once Erathal was neutralized, there would be no force that could oppose him, and he could finally bring nature into a state of harmony.

"Tell our forces to proceed with the attack."

-=-=-=-=-=-=-=-

Tel 'Shira was growing impatient. It had seemed like an eternity since she had assumed her position here in this oak, and the anticipation was becoming unbearable. The incessant rain, though much lighter than before, didn't help the situation any.

She had participated in a number of engagements during her time as a warrior. From fighting a centaur tribe, to barghest, lizock, and even an engagement with a band of ogres from the mountains, she had more experience in combat than most. Still, this felt different than any engagement before, and she could not help but feel a certain apprehension.

Then it hit her.

A tingle ran down her spine. A loud shriek followed almost immediately, the sound of a roc in serious distress. She turned her head up towards the sound, catching a glimpse of a dark figure swooping just above the tree line.

One of her allies fell right before her, his spear tumbling to the ground as his lifeless body impacted a lower branch on its way down. His mount followed quickly behind, one of its wings torn clean off. The blood soaked its once regal feathers, pieces of bone and sinew sticking out of its side.

Another shriek followed from above, and another roc rider came tumbling down just across the clearing. Tel' Shira climbed, swinging branch to branch. Her claws tore into bark as she catapulted herself up.

There was a flash of lightning as she flipped herself over the top branch, arriving safely above to see her four remaining allies. The illumination from the lightning aided her in seeing the two dark figures that were flying just above. Three of her allies were closing in on one of the demons, attempting a three-pronged attack to take out their enemy.

Unfortunately, the second demon had no intention of letting this assault succeed. It quickly dropped down from above, plucking one of the three riders from his mount and tearing his legs off as if pulling a weed. With a quick spin, the demon's left claw impacted the roc and tore through with just as much ease. The blood and bodies of both its victims tumbled down through the trees and out of sight.

These demons were as large as a small drake, making the rocs that her allies rode upon look like mice by comparison. They appeared to be twins, both having leathery, black skin and demonic, yellow eyes. Each had a short tail with spikes protruding from all sides, giving them a natural weapon. Their pupils were like slits in pools of blood, and as Tel' Shira locked eyes with the demon who had just torn her ally apart, she felt as if she was trapped in a void of despair. She had to act. Now.

As the cornered demon went to defend against the rider to its left, the first demon swooped up toward the other rider. Tel' Shira sprang forward, her legs propelling her with speed and power. Flying gracefully through the air towards her unsuspecting prey, she pulled two daggers out from her belt, ready to pounce with precision and take down her much larger foe.

Through her peripherals, she caught a glimpse of the final living rider. He was descending towards the primary demon. Time slowed as the wind ran across Tel' Shira's body, each drop of rain flowing across her fur without resistance.

She landed blades first upon her prey, the daggers penetrating through the thick skin of this demon and into the flesh of his back. The demon let out a cry like none she had heard before. Following his cry of pain, he spewed out a great torrent of flame towards the nearest roc rider, instantly incinerating the unsuspecting felite and his mount.

Ignoring the shock of this frightening ability, she remained intent on her objective. Her focus shifted back to the demon she was on, averting her gaze from the two surviving riders. Whether or not they took out their target was out of her control. This one would die.

Unfortunately, the demon had other thoughts in mind, performing a barrel roll as it ascended. Grasping her daggers, she tried to strengthen her hold by digging her hind claws in but found herself unable to penetrate the demon's thick hide. Taking advantage of her exposed position, her foe reached around and grabbed hold of both her legs. She couldn't allow him to get a solid grip.

With a powerful pull on her blades, she yanked them both out and bent over backwards like only a felite could. She sunk her left dagger into the enemy's hand, causing him to loose his hold on her. That dagger was lost, and if not for her lightning reflexes she would have plummeted uncontrollably away from the fray. As she fell, she kicked off with all of her strength, causing her to rocket away from the injured demon. As she flew towards a nearby tree, she sheathed her remaining blade and sprung over in midair.

Landing feet first on the side of the tree, she dug both of her legs and her right hand into the bark for support. This demon seemed impervious to pain. It pulled the dagger out of its hand and cast it aside carelessly. Its eyes sharp, Tel' Shira's hair stood on end. The demon was angry.

She let out an instinctual hiss, anticipating his next attack. The demon's mouth opened and a torrent of flames roared towards her. Lunging off the tree just in time, she felt the intense heat of hellfire as her support platform was set ablaze. Her hands extended and she was able to flip around a nearby branch, moving on from one tree to another as the flames followed behind. This needed to end.

Running off pure adrenaline, she flipped around a branch and arched herself against the tree. Using all of the force she could muster, she pushed off a large branch and sprung forward. As she neared her enemy, she drew her remaining dagger and grasped it tightly, ready to make the final kill.

Time slowed even more for her as she approached, and she was uncertain whether or not she would make it. The demon's head was turning, the endless supply of flames still spewing forth. She would either be incinerated, or she would end her enemy's treachery now.

The heat from the demon's flames intensified as it attempted to redirect its fire on her. With both hands gripping the dagger, she landed blade first, plunging her blade through the demon's right eye socket. Yellow puss oozed from the wound. The demon clamped its jaw, stopping the flow of fire. The beast spasmed, a clear sign she had penetrated its brain.

Unfortunately, even with his death imminent, the demon seemed unwilling to succumb. The demon brought both his arms up and grabbed her. She felt its vice-like grip as it squeezed. Her breathing became labored, and she felt a rapid descent.

The demon was dead, but if she couldn't escape soon she would be as well. Wind rushed across her face, and she struggled to escape its clutch, but the more she squirmed the tighter it grasped. Her mind raced for a solution, but she could find none. She clamped her eyes shut, trying to relax her breathing.

Then, without warning, the pressure was gone.

Her eyes darted open. Two of her allies were on either side of the demon; their own weapons cut into the creature's arms and released its grip on her. With a silent look of gratitude to both warriors in turn, she took in a well-needed gasp of air and kicked off the falling corpse.

Flipping over in midair, she looked down to prepare herself for the imminent impact with the ground. Still ten meters from the ground, she needed to make sure she landed on all four to avoid injury. She was in the clearing, just behind the combined defense forces, leaving her a nice open area to land. As she neared the forest floor, she could see that the ground forces had still not engaged.

With a final adjustment, she rotated her body in an arc and pushed her arms forward just as she hit the ground. She felt a light pain as she made contact with all fours, springing off the ground and summersaulting backwards. The demon followed only moments behind, landing just a few meters in front of her as she stood upright. Its body was still spasming as it hit the ground with a crash and pushed into the muddy forest floor.

Without hesitation, Tel' Shira strode over to retrieve her dagger from the dying demon's eye. Deep crimson blood poured from the socket, mixing with a yellow puss that had come directly from the eye, but where her dagger had been only moments ago, nothing remained. She cursed and scanned the surrounding area for any sign of her blade. With the rainfall increasing in intensity, even her acute eyesight was limited, and she found her search to be in vain. With a final sweep, she did notice the corpse of one of her roc-riding allies just a few meters off.

Maybe his weapon was nearby.

As she ran over to look for her fallen ally's spear, she felt another tingling sensation. She fell into a defensive stance and observed her surroundings carefully. No one was nearby.

"There it is," she mumbled as her eyes locked on the spear.

She felt the ground tremble, and bolted over to the weapon, spinning it around in a figure eight before examining it to make sure it was undamaged. It looked good.

Another tremor.

Her gaze went ahead, out towards her allied army and beyond. Scattered cries ran through the ranks, but her ears could not distinguish what they shouted. Was it an earthquake?

No.

Just beyond the allied army, she spotted it. A tree shot out from the ground, completely uprooted as a giant behemoth came charging forward. Soil and trees alike were torn asunder as the enormous horned terror carried out its charge. Though details were a bit hazy through the rainfall, the creature definitely had three large horns upon its head, and it was easily twice the size of the demon she had just killed, probably larger.

Instinct tempted her to run and hide as even her advanced training never dealt with handling creatures such as this; they only existed in legend. Despite this, she knew exactly what she had to do, and with machine-like calm, she spun her new weapon around and grasped it between her teeth. She sprinted to the nearest tree, using her tail as a counterbalance to compensate for the tremors this behemoth created, and climbed.

If she could get behind the beast, perhaps she could penetrate its skull with her spear and kill it just as she had the demon. Her other eleven light warriors would surely have the same idea. There was nothing on Evorath a dozen felite couldn't take out.

At least, that's what she elected to believe as she ascended.

-=.=.=.=.=.=.=.=-

Irontail gazed upon the approaching behemoth in disbelief.

His heart skipped a beat as his mind struggled to understand what was happening. Where had this beast come from? What kind of power did this hájje possess to command such a creature? How would they possibly be able to fight it? This was not what he had been trained for.

The ground shook and soil was overturned as the beast charged forward, uprooting trees and tearing through the foliage towards his allies. Irontail was at a loss, and his comrades seemed to be in the same boat. Arrows began to fly, and Irontail watched as they soared overhead towards the approaching beast.

The monster charged forward, and the rain of arrows came down, but to no avail. It seemed that this beast's scales were too strong, for none of the arrows were sticking, and its charge continued without hesitation. Irontail looked to his elders for guidance; Goldenchest, Copperfoot, and Cobalthand all seemed just as surprised, unable to respond to the impending doom.

After what seemed like an eternity, Goldenchest made the first move, raising his oversized, stone axe high above his head with a war cry. As the beast approached, he charged, tucking his head and running full speed as if to meet the nightmare head on. Both Copperfoot and Cobalthand followed suit, tailing their leader in his charge. It was time to move.

Each centaur warrior, Irontail included, let out their own war cry, and galloped towards the beast. Irontail could not tell if the felite were following the charge or merely standing their ground; it didn't matter either way.

As Irontail neared the behemoth, his hooves whipping up tufts of mud, the beast's features become clearer. The creature's mouth was shaped like a beak, curving down in a sharp point and most likely without teeth. Its forehead was thick, an armored layer expanding up above its head like a shield. A serious of small spikes wrapped around this shielded crest, and protruding forward were two long horns, accompanied by a single small horn upon its beak. Thick, dark gray scales covered its entire body, affording it superior protection against smaller arms.

Despite his training in warfare, Irontail had no idea how they would take such a beast down, much less with the stone axes and wooden clubs that his tribe was equipped with. At this moment, he let other thoughts drift into his head. Why was he even here? What could he hope to accomplish? Was his devotion and loyalty really worth all of this? Pushing these questions aside, he refocused on the battle.

Goldenchest veered off to the left of the creature at the last possible moment. A wellspring of magical energy swelled up around him, his axe glowing with Evorath's force as he swung it overhead and then arched it back around. The stone head exploded on impact with the behemoth's tree-trunk sized leg, and the beast faltered.

Cobolthand and Copperfoot followed immediately behind their leader. Cobolthand's own axe slammed into the same leg as he galloped past, and Copperfoot's spiked, wooden club was left embedded as a final nail in the coffin. The beast let out a tremendous roar, its leg buckling before giving out.

The behemoth swerved to the right, collapsing upon its disabled leg and crashing to the floor with a rumble. Unfortunately for Copperfoot, this final strike came at a steep price. As a final show of defiance, the beast swung its tail around. With a loud thud, it crashed into Copperfoot's face. Nearing the fallen beast, Irontail beheld his elder in terror, blood covering his features.

Copperfoot seemed to stop in place, his body seizing for a moment as he fell to his knees. The sheer force of the blow had killed him.

The colossal beast struggled, turning its oversized head and attempting to pull the club out of its limp leg. As Irontail came to a stop only meters in front of the creature, Goldenchest circled back around and grabbed hold of his fallen comrade's weapon. Just as the behemoth tried to push itself back up, Goldenchest yanked the club out of the beast's leg and swung it in a complete circle overhead.

Cobalthand ran over to the motionless Copperfoot.

Irontail watched in awe as Goldenchest filled the new weapon with magical energy and slammed it down upon the behemoth's nearest horn. The beast let out another bellow as the club broke straight through its natural weapon. Both the horn and club split, leaving Goldenchest without a weapon once again.

"Hold it down!" Goldenchest shouted as he dropped the useless weapon and looked back towards Irontail.

Instinct kicked in, and Irontail dropped his own weapon, leaping forward and wrapping his arms around the behemoth's left, front leg. With all of the force he could muster, he yanked the leg towards himself, dropping down to contain the beast. Goldenchest grabbed the right leg, doing the same, and three of his other centaur allies each grabbed a horn and pulled down in front.

Irontail's mind raced to try and catch up with everything that was happening. The rain continued to fall as he struggled to grip this massive behemoth and hold it down. One of his elders had just been killed. Everything was happening too fast.

-=-=-=-=-=-=-

This was it.

Tel' Shira had been waiting for the moment to strike and watching as about a half dozen centaur grabbed hold of the injured beast, she knew that moment was now.

Releasing her hold on the branch, she let herself drop. She used her tail to aid in her descent, spiraling her body around as she held the spear point outstretched. Although they may have been reckless, Tel' Shira couldn't help but feel somewhat impressed with these centaurs. They were bold.

She landed spear first in the back of the behemoth's neck, the point sliding all the way through and almost halfway down the shaft. Continuing her own momentum, she spun around her weapon and dug her claws into the beast's back to avoid flying off of its side. In that instant, the beast seemed to cease its struggle to rise, and fell once more to the ground, this time defeated for good.

But the battle was far from over.

Tel' Shira felt the familiar tingle, a warning of more danger approaching. She turned just in time to see a bolo spinning straight towards her, the two metal spheres spinning through the air with amazing speed. She loosened her muscles just in time and ducked under the projectile, sliding off the side of the behemoth and taking a low defensive stance on the forest floor.

Through her peripherals, she watched as the bolo wrapped around one of the centaur warrior's necks, snapping it like a twig. Her focus shifted forward, looking through the weather to identify the new threat. One major advantage that her people had over the centaurs was that they had natural night vision. Though her field of vision was limited by the poor weather, she could still see her enemies with relative ease.

They were fifteen meters away, another half dozen demons. Unlike the ones she had engaged in the sky, these ones did not have wings but they were just as large in stature. The nearest one was the culprit behind the bolo. Its skin was burgundy in color and it wore an assorted collection of projectile weapons around its waist. Without a weapon of her own, this would be her target. She could use the demon's own blades against him and then obtain more weapons to engage her enemies with.

He obviously saw her just as easily as she saw him, for as she planned her movements, he released another bolo, this one again flying straight at her. She held her ground for a moment, and then pushed off, back-flipping over the missile and kicking down on one of the spheres. As she landed, she transitioned into a back handspring and chased after the diverted weapon.

Grasping a hold of the reclaimed weapon, she locked on to her target once again. Another bolo came rushing towards her, and she narrowly ducked underneath before continuing her charge forward.

Spinning her own bolo above her head, Tel' Shira halted her charge and let it loose. The projectile flew forward end around end, perfectly on target with her foe. Without waiting for her initial attack to hit, she resumed her charge, sprinting forward towards it. She was closing the distance: ten meters, eight meters, five meters.

The demon held up its right arm just as the bolo neared and tilted his head to the left. The bolo wrapped around the demon's arm, and it grinned as it shifted back upright. She had a split second to decide her next move: leap, or duck.

Tel' Shira slid, avoiding the demon as he swung forward to grab her. As she came up behind him, three of her allies swooped down from the trees. One landed directly on the demon's back, sliding his dagger straight into the creature's skull. The other two landed on either side of the foe, daggers leading and slicing through the demon's arms.

Tel' Shira gave her allies a look of acknowledgment as they all formed up around the fallen foe. Something wasn't right.

Before any of them had a chance to react, a stream of black energy shot out from the demon's waist and struck the felite warrior who had killed it. Tel' Shira and her other two allies backed away, unsure of what was happening. The male felite doubled over, hissing in pain as he went to his knees. Both of her allies ran to help him, but Tel' Shira hesitated.

"No!"

She couldn't react fast enough.

Her fallen comrade jolted up with a dagger in either hand, stabbing both of the other two warriors who came to his aid. They backed away and grasped the daggers that were embedded in their chests, looks of disbelief and terror on their faces as they stumbled back to die. Their previous ally was possessed, his eyes red with rage, his fur coated in dark energy.

Tel' Shira squared up against this new enemy. Her ally was gone.

She had no weapon, but neither did her foe. Her opponent made the first move, opening with a lightning fast roundhouse kick. Tel' Shira reeled back, feeling the force of the missed first kick only to receive a second straight in her waist as he spun around and followed with a back kick.

Ignoring the pain in her side, Tel' Shira kept her hands up and parried the incoming cross, countering with a swift jab to her foe's solar plexus and sidestepping to deliver a hook to his face. Anticipating his next move, Tel' Shira brought up her foot and delivered a stop kick, following up with a kick of her own to her opponent's other leg.

She followed up with a jab to the throat, cross to the face, and an uppercut to send him lurching backwards. With a backward handspring, she was on top of the fallen demon and retrieved the nearest knife from its belt. Flinging the blade forward, she flinched as it landed square in the face of her possessed attacker.

Unwilling to risk any further complications, she did not wait to see her enemy fall and summersaulted back and away from the action. Springing to the nearest tree, she scaled the branches and looked back down at the battlefield. She needed to re-assess the situation.

-=-.=-.=-.=-.=-.=-.=-

Yezurkstal strolled behind his half dozen demons, shrouded in a magical cloak of fog and darkness. His foes would

233

never see his approach, for they would be much too occupied dealing with these demonic warriors and the little surprise gift he had given them. Though surprised by the speed at which these felite had disposed of his aerial troops, he still had no doubt of victory.

These insects must have felt some form of satisfaction taking down his winged demons and disposing of his possessed behemoth. They worked quite efficiently, but no matter. They were but pawns in the grand scheme of things, and only he could know how it all would turn out.

It was time for the coup de *grâce*.

Where the felite were concerned, he would have to wipe them all out. Of the centaur, there were two remaining players that he would need to eliminate. All in all, every last one of them was a worthless maggot and it was his destiny to exterminate them.

First things first, Yezurkstal had to eliminate the two biggest threats on the battlefield.

Up ahead, he watched as one of his red-skinned demons tore through two centaur warriors. A felite joined into the mix, swinging his heavy blade down towards the demon's neck. Yezurkstal's minion parried the blow with its own sword and followed up by tackling the smaller felite to the ground. With its enemy pinned beneath it, the demon thrust forward and grabbed the felite's windpipe. Offering a quick squeeze, blood poured out from the fallen creature's throat.

The next instant, Yezurkstal's faithful servant was back on its feet, and on target for the most dangerous threat: the centaur with the golden mane. The demon rushed forward, and the golden centaur moved to meet him. Both opponents were unarmed, so this would be a shear test of strength.

Yezurkstal continued to walk towards the action, taking his time as he observed another felite get torn apart by one of his black skinned demons. To his right, two demons were engaging a concentrated group of both felite and centaur, about five of them in total. There was no need to watch. He knew what the result would be, and he was much more interested in the golden centaur.

Refocusing his attention on the important fight, Yezurkstal turned to see his demon engaged with the golden centaur. The centaur seemed to have the upper hand, his biceps bulging as he pushed the larger demon backwards. The demon struggled, pushing against the force of its stronger foe. The golden centaur clenched both the demon's wrists, slowly pushing him further and further back. Yezurkstal's minion had little hope of winning.

The demon slid through the muddy ground, its clawed feet unable to keep hold of solid footing as it struggled against the centaur. Yezurkstal could not help but feel impressed by this creature. His strength was remarkable.

With an explosion of force, the centaur threw his arms outward and opened up the demon's defense. He thrust his forehead forward, smashing the demon in the face and disorienting it. Following up with a quick cross to the demon's face, the golden centaur continued his assault.

Grabbing the demon by the throat, he dug his fingers in and squeezed. The demon only struggled for a moment before its opponent broke through its skin. With a violent pull, the golden centaur ripped the demon's windpipe from his body, leaving the hellish creature to fall lifeless at his feet.

Three.

Two.

One.

The centaur was already charging towards the next closest demon -who had just torn apart two more felite and a lesser centaur warrior- when the dark energy burst from the demons belt. Yezurkstal stopped his approach and watched as his spell bolted towards the golden creature's back.

"He's mine."

-=-=-=-=-=-=-=-

Irontail watched as a red-skinned demon tore through another two felite warriors and quickly finished off one of his fellow centaurs. These demons were strong, fast, and fought in an unfamiliar fashion. If it were brute force alone that mattered, he was confident that he could take out this demon himself, but with all things considered, Irontail just did not feel assured.

Regardless, he had one duty, and that duty was to protect his people. As he charged forward, Irontail caught a glimpse of Goldenchest tearing out one of the other demon's windpipe.

Then, a dark energy burst from the fallen demon and flew towards his leader. Irontail was not close enough to do anything.

Just before the energy could impact Goldenchest, the felite elder, Su Pau, darted out of nowhere with her staff held before her. The dark energy struck her staff, and the diamond atop it glowed a bright white before darkening. The entire staff vibrated in her hands, and one of the topaz exploded outward, spraying shards out in front of her. The diamond returned to its natural state as she stood there: stoic.

Goldenchest did not seem to even notice that his life had just been saved, for he continued his charge without hesitation. Irontail also continued moving, noting that his elder seemed to be going for the same demon he was. Then, a great yell from just a few meters behind him redirected his attention.

Irontail turned his head and looped around to watch Cobalthand and two other warriors fighting one of the demons. This demon was slightly larger than the red one and had purple skin. It wielded an oversized two-handed sword, which it had just used to decapitate a felite warrior. They needed Irontail more than Goldenchest did.

Tightening his grip on his club, Irontail turned around and charged forward. Cobalthand swung his spiked club overhead towards the demon. The other two centaur warriors flanked the foul creature from either side in a pincer maneuver, bringing their own clubs around to strike.

The demon appeared fearless, swinging his own weapon down to meet Cobalthand's strike. Its massive blade tore right through the club and continued forward to split through the elder centaur's skull. Releasing its blade, the demon shoved both of its arms outward and caught the other clubs in its palms. As the demon wrenched the clubs from the centaur's hands, Irontail struck.

With all of his might, Irontail smashed his club over the demon's skull. As the demon stumbled forward, the other two centaur grabbed for their weapons again, able to easily free them from the demon's weakened grip. The demon raised its arms to protect himself from the incoming attacks. Both the centaurs bludgeoned the demon, smashing their thick clubs into its ribs, legs, and finally its skull once again.

Irontail, meanwhile, went to his fallen elder to examine the sword wound. The blade had penetrated Cobalthand's skull and cut into his brain, killing him. Grabbing hold of the weapon, Irontail closed his eyes and yanked it from Cobalthand's skull. Focusing his attention back on the other two centaurs and the demon whose sword he had just claimed, Irontail watched as the final blow was delivered.

Both of the centaur warriors took a moment as the demon landed lifeless on the forest floor. Irontail went to turn and move onto the next demon when he saw the flash of dark energy shoot from the demon's belt. The dark magic shot up and impacted the left centaur in his chest, causing him to drop his club.

Irontail grasped his newly acquired sword and twisted his torso defensively, waiting to see what new ill this magic had in store. His ally convulsed for a few seconds, and the other centaur rushed to his aide, grabbing him for support. Irontail stood his ground.

Without warning, the first centaur stopped convulsing and grabbed his ally's face, head-butting him square in the nose. Blood poured out from the broken nose as the confused centaur stumbled backwards. Without breaking stride, the possessed centaur kept inside his opponent's guard and kept a firm hold on his head. With a violent twist, and a sickening snap, Irontail watched his ally fall lifeless to the floor.

Now was a defining moment for Irontail as a warrior. His instinct screamed for him to run, to yell in anguish and despair. What kind of power did this Hájje possess to turn his people against one another? There was no time for further thought.

As the possessed centaur redirected his attention, Irontail swung the sword in a flat trajectory. The blade cut without resistance through the centaur's throat, decapitating Irontail's former ally and ending his life. Irontail redirected the momentum of his swing and pivoted the blade around, striking the corpse with the flat of his blade and knocking it to the ground.

Irontail had just murdered one of his own kind.

He felt nothing.

-=-=-=-=-=-=-=-

Yezurkstal couldn't believe his eyes. The felite had blocked his dark magic. In the future, he would have to develop something more potent. For now, he had to focus on a closer target.

A gray-skinned demon grasped both arms of one of the felite defenders, ripping them off and casting them aside like an abandoned doll's. Yezurkstal felt pride in these creatures. They were the perfect warriors, mindlessly demolishing any enemy.

The golden centaur charged forward towards the gray demon. He would destroy this centaur himself.

Lifting his dark shroud, Yezurkstal shifted forward like lightning, his body gliding across the muddy ground to intercept the golden foe. The centaur's face was one of shock, but he still managed to bring down a swift hammer fist towards Yezurkstal's head. Yezurkstal raised his left hand, palm open.

Catching his opponent by the wrist, Yezurkstal looked up at his much taller foe with a grin. He held on as the centaur swung down with his other arm. Too predictable.

Yezurkstal caught the second hammer fist as easily as the first, holding both of his foe's wrists in an unbreakable grasp. This golden-furred creature may have been strong, but no base creature could match Yezurkstal's power. He felt his enemy struggle, trying to pull away, trying to push forward. Nothing would work.

"You will serve me."

He could feel the centaur attempting to generate his own magic, but it was fruitless. He funneled his dark magic through the creature's arms and into its very being. The dark energy coated the golden centaur's fur.

An unfamiliar feeling overtook him as he released his hold and his focus shifted to the rear. Was this pain?

Yezurkstal whipped around and saw the eldest felite standing defiantly, her intricate staff pointed tip first at him. A mass of green energy was building in the diamond and burst forth as he locked in on the weapon. He ducked down and the green energy passed harmlessly over his right shoulder.

He wasn't the target.

The green magic impacted the golden centaur and Yezurkstal's dark magic dissipated, fading away against the felite's life force. Possessing this centaur would no longer be sufficient. He needed to kill him as a demonstration of his superiority.

Yezurkstal drew his adamantium bastard sword, spinning it around and thrusting it into the centaur's chest. For good measure, he fed in some more dark magic, this time intending to kill. As he withdrew the blade, the wound immediately began to fester. The centaur rotted, fur shedding as the wound opened up and blood poured out.

Yezurkstal focused once again on the felite.

"Your life is meaningless. I am the future of Evorath you mangy cur. For your interference, I will make sure you suffer."

.=.=.=.=.=.=.=.

Tel' Shira had waited long enough. She watched as her allies fell. She witnessed Irontail slay one of his own kind, and Goldenchest take out a demon with his bare hands. Now she looked on as Su Pau challenged the Hájje.

It was time to strike.

She sprung around the branch offering her support, flipping over and landing in a run. Su Pau shot another bolt of green energy towards the Hájje, the missile flying true and fast. The Hájje swung his sword around, black energy coating the blade as he knocked Su Pau's attack away. Switching to offense, the Hájje shot forth a slashing attack with his sword, a stream of dark energy soaring towards the elder felite.

Su Pau swung her staff around just in time, creating a small barrier of invisible energy. The dark magic dissipated, but the force was too much, pushing the elder off balance and opening her up to another attack. Tel' Shira moved as fast as she could, sprinting to aide her elder in the battle against this powerful foe. The Hájje was closing in, poising himself for the kill.

Tel' Shira lunged.

She hit the Hájje square in the stomach, leading with her shoulder in an effort to wind her opponent. The Hájje was clearly taken by surprise, but Tel' Shira immediately knew that would not be enough. Tel' Shira grabbed for her enemy's blade as she pushed him back a few steps; his grip was like a vice.

The Hájje brought up his free hand, smacking Tel' Shira's jaw. She felt an immediate pop and could taste blood as she attempted to separate herself from the enemy. He let go, and she reeled back a few steps. Dazed from her broken jaw, Tel' Shira had no opportunity to reassess her plan of attack. The Hájje swung with the flat of his blade, hitting the uninjured half of Tel' Shira's face with more force than she thought possible.

Her entire face went numb, and her vision blurred as she was cast aside, tumbling off against a tree and falling flat on the forest floor. She struggled to hold onto consciousness. Her entire body felt numb, only picking up the pelting of continuous rainfall, and she watched helplessly as the Hájje continued his attack on her elder.

Su Pau swung her staff down towards the Hájje, but he dodged and countered by cutting clean through the sacred weapon. The elder felite reeled backwards, gathering more magical energy for one last effort.

It was futile.

The Hájje thrust his open hand into Su Pau's chest, penetrating her ribs.

The last thing Tel' Shira saw before losing consciousness was Su Pau's bleeding heart in the palm of Yezurkstal's hand.

.-=.-=.-=.-=.-=.-=.-

Irontail was in shock.

He stood motionless and watched as the Hájje slew his leader, the once golden fur of this great centaur graying. The flesh around Goldenchest's heart festering and falling away, his guts spilling out onto the ground. A look of disbelief was etched upon the legendary elder's face as he fell to his knees, forever stamped in place.

Irontail could not move. His entire body shook with fear and anger.

Disbelief.

The Hájje continued his vicious attack, carelessly casting Tel' Shira aside before continuing to dispose of the felite elder.

243

Irontail watched in horror as the Hájje pulled the elder's heart straight out of her chest, holding it triumphantly. The felite elder fell lifeless at the Hájje's feet.

What could Irontail do? What could anyone do?

This enemy had just eliminated the most powerful centaur to ever live and then continued, without hesitation, to take out two felite.

The entire leadership of both forces was gone. There were still a few demons tearing through what little forces remained, and the Hájje was invincible.

It was hopeless.

-=-=-=-=-=-=-=-

As Yezurkstal held the still beating heart of this pretentious cur in his palm, he felt a rush of pleasure. Up until today, claiming his wives had been the most exhilarating experience of his short life, but this rampant killing was quickly becoming his new favorite pastime.

The blood, the screams, the looks of anguish and despair that these inferior creatures gave as they drew their last breaths were priceless. And now, holding this bloody organ in his palm, he felt validated. This world was meant to be his. He was entitled to all of the pleasures of Evorath, and these creatures deserved nothing.

Yezurkstal felt the need to bask in the beauty of this day, to just let it all soak in. So he stood there, holding the now dead heart and observing as his remaining forces tore through the rest of the defenders. He surveyed the battlefield, looking to the now blackened centaur leader, past his fallen behemoth, to the dead roc lying torn on the forest floor.

It was his job to take this chaos and bring about order.

He felt the presence of one of his underlings, one of the elf warriors approaching from behind. It was Verandas.

"What do you have to report?" Yezurkstal asked without turning.

"Sir. The elvish army is approaching. Our numbers are diminished, and without a more defensible position we stand little chance. They bring a sizeable army." Verandas spoke in a dull monotone, void of emotion.

"They are ahead of schedule," Yezurkstal's cold reply came. He paused.

"No matter. We proceed as planned. You and General Gharis head back to base and prepare the other warriors for our attack. I will be right behind."

"Yes, sir."

As his general marched away, Yezurkstal took a more critical look at the field. The enemy archers were all focusing in on a single demon, taking aim as the large, hellish creature charged forward. They loosed their arrows, each landing true on target.

The demon continued its charge, ignoring the attack as the tiny arrowheads barely penetrated his thick hide. He tore into the front rank of felite archers, snapping through their longbows and clotheslining four of the six with his long arms. The other two used their mobility and backpedaled, reloading and taking aim once more.

Ignoring these two felite, the demon continued charging towards the four centaur marksmen. It was overstepping its limits. All four archers dropped their short bows and lunged forward to intercept their attacker. The demon could have easily wrestled down two of these centaurs without difficulty, but four was just too many.

The centaurs split into a pincer, two grabbing either arm and forcing the large demon to the ground. It was a struggle to be sure, but as they put the demon on his back, the two remaining felite archers took positions above the demon and fired arrows directly into his eyes. His skin may have been strong, but his eye sockets were not. The arrows penetrated into his brain, killing him.

Yezurkstal didn't bother watching what happened as his spell took effect and possessed one of the centaur archers. It would die. More importantly, Yezurkstal still had two more demons, one of which was engaging two felite heavy warriors, and one quickly approaching the enemy druids. It was time to leave.

Raising his hand up to chest, Yezurkstal did one last glance around the battlefield, taking in great pride from his handy work. With a swift flip of his hand, and a puff of smoke, he vanished.

Chapter 18

Erathal Forest, Dumner Village
17 Neglur, 1086

Artimus wiped the rain from his forehead, flinging it forward in frustration. Dumner village lay to the north, and apparently this storm was heading in the same direction. The rangers were having difficulty trekking through the muddy paths.

Captain Viviko marched to Artimus's right, and to his left was Commander Zeidrich. General Fletching was just a few strides behind, and to his left rode Savannah. The rest of the brigade kept a loose formation behind, the dozen spearman marching side-by-side behind Fletching and Savannah. The twenty archers kept a vague u-shape around the entire unit, and the sixteen warriors made up the center of the formation. Each rode atop their own horse.

Thoron let out a grunt, and Artimus felt him falter as he sloughed through some sticky mud. The closer they got to their destination, the heavier the rain became. Not ten minutes ago, they were marching through a light mist, to a slight drizzle, and now they moved into a steady rain.

Artimus kept his eyes trained low, looking for any signs of sink holes or other potential obstacles that the rain may have created. There were branches scattered all about the path, some of them as thick as Artimus's own legs. Some nasty squalls must have accompanied this storm to take such substantial branches off the trees, because upon closer observation Artimus could tell that none of them were rotting or weakened. This type of wind would be detrimental for all of the archers should they find themselves in combat.

But then he noticed something that anyone else would have missed, and immediately raised up his right fist, his glance darting to both of the troop leaders on either side. They followed suit and Artimus was confident that Fletching did the same. The entire brigade came to a halt, and Artimus dismounted Thoron.

"What is it?" Zeidrich asked, a hint of ridicule in his voice.

Artimus ignored the question, walking forward a few steps and crouching low to the ground. He wiped the rain from his forehead again, attempting to keep it out of his eyes. The rain was draining south, away from Dumner village. They were getting close, but this did not bode well for anyone.

"There's blood in the water," Artimus whispered. "A lot of blood."

He ignored the confused looks of the troop leaders and moved forward, keeping low to the ground and following the trail towards a heavy concentration of oak trees. As he approached, the blood became more apparent, the water turning a dark red. Artimus also noticed some large, brown feathers scattered about, most of them hidden from plain sight, covered up from the rain.

Artimus turned the corner and jolted his head away, forcing his eyes shut. He turned back around, and looked at the mangled body of a roc, somehow torn apart like a rag doll. Its right wing was completely severed from the rest of its body, and its guts were spilled out from a large gash. Artimus scanned the area, looking for any indication of what might have so viciously murdered such a regal creature. The 'what' could not be answered so easily, but up ahead a few meters was the answer to the 'why'.

Artimus noted the body of a felite warrior, blood covering most of her fur and a branch protruding through her torso. This roc had served as a mount, and it had been killed by the same creature that attacked its rider. The question was, what creature on Evorath could do this to such a powerful, trained bird?

He stood like a statue, listening with his superb elvish hearing. There was only the sound of falling rain. No raised voices, no clashing of weapons, absolutely no auditory indication of any kind. In fact, he couldn't even pick up the scampering of small prey or the chirping of birds. There had been a battle already, but they had arrived too late.

"Well, what is it?" Zeidrich questioned, his voice deep with concern.

Artimus came back from behind the tree, noting that each warrior had assumed a ready stance atop their steeds. They would want to stay on guard.

"It looks like Yezurkstal beat us to the punch. Stay on guard as we move forward. The village is just through these trees up ahead. Just another couple of minutes and we will be at their border. We don't know what to expect, so be ready for anything."

Artimus walked back towards Thoron, noting that as he walked the rain died back down to a drizzle. Reaching his stead, he grabbed hold and mounted, signaling for everyone to move.

"You sure it's Yezurkstal?" Viviko whispered.

"No, but I don't know what else could kill a roc and its felite rider like that." Artimus tilted his head to the right slightly and moved his eyes towards the tree as they passed.

Viviko turned away as quickly as he looked, his skin seeming to lose some color. Zeidrich shook his head.

"Keep your eyes trained ahead!" the commander barked, turning to give Viviko a look of disapproval.

Artimus glanced back and scanned over all of the warrior's faces. Save Savannah, they all had a look of intense focus and kept their glances ahead. There was certainly something to be said about their discipline training. He almost turned to distract Savannah, but she was bound to see death like this sooner or later. Maybe it was best that she look now.

There was a tangible, internal struggle in her eyes as Savannah turned her head to the right and looked upon the gruesome scene. Artimus watched her fists clench the reins of her steed as her eyes returned forward. A single tear slipped from her left eye, but an unexpected look followed. She appeared determined, and perhaps even confident. Was that a hint of familiarity in her eyes?

Artimus dismissed the thought, knowing that his focus needed to remain ahead. With the sky dark, and the rain drizzling down, it made it difficult to see much through the thick tree coverage. If the battle was still going though, they would surely hear some indication of a struggle soon enough.

Thoron drifted to the right, avoiding a tall willow before returning to formation. As they made their way around the tree, Artimus finally picked up a noise. Once again, he threw up his right fist. Turning to either side, he put his index finger over his lips, indicating for them to remain silent.

He could hear faint voices up ahead. They sounded like whispers from this distance, but the most prominent voice was that of a male. There were no artificial sounds, and no heavy footsteps, so Artimus believed that the action was over. The question was: were these voices of friends, or enemies?

.=.=.=.=.=.=.=.

Irontail gripped the arms of a red-skinned demon tightly. He dragged the creature through a patch of mud, pulling it towards the corpse of the behemoth. Only two other centaur warriors had survived, and along with the two surviving felite, heavy soldiers, they were dragging the other demons into the same spot.

The druids, only three surviving in total, along with the three centaur archers were gathering up their fallen allies. They were gathering these bodies around the central mound, which was still lying lifeless. Irontail had motioned that it was best to keep the women and children unaware of the situation for now, and no one had argued.

How had such a small force left them with so few remaining fighters? These demons had otherworldly strength, speed and toughness. It was like fighting against the flow of the river while carrying a half-ton rock. There was just no way of winning.

"Irontail!"

The despairing centaur turned towards the excited centaur voice. It was the surviving druid, who stood over one of the lightly armored, female felite warriors. The druid knelt down and put his hand gently on her stomach.

"She still draws breath! I need the felite druids."

Irontail felt the stirrings of excitement. He didn't know why, but somehow he felt if they could keep this one felite alive it would be a victory. Maybe these demons weren't all perfect killers after all.

Releasing his hold on the demon, Irontail abandoned the corpse and galloped over towards the two felite druids who were working on the northwest part of the village, where the attack had originated. The two druids were tending to a heavily armored felite who had a chunk missing from his torso. They had just flipped him onto his back when Irontail arrived.

"I need you at once," Irontail commanded. "There is an injured felite warrior over by the behemoth corpse. She is still breathing, but unconscious."

The druids came to attention, and Irontail took off towards the injured felite. He was surprised, but the felite kept right by his side, running swiftly towards their injured comrade. As they reached the injured warrior, Irontail recognized her. This was Tel' Shira, the warrior who he had met at the summoning ritual.

She lay face down, her arms outstretched as if she had been trying to lift herself back up. Her head was turned to the left, a small amount of blood pooled around her mouth. Irontail was no healer, but by his reckoning her jaw had been broken. Hopefully that was the worst of her injuries.

The felite druids motioned for the centaur to back away and he complied. One druid went on either side of Tel' Shira and knelt down, planting their hands in mirror fashion along her lower back and shoulder blade. They both closed their eyes and Irontail watched as white energy permeated their hands and spread to Tel' Shira's body.

"Flip her over, we can," the druid on Tel' Shira's right said.

"Agreed," the other druid replied in a monotone.

The centaur druid was still standing there, looking on. Why wasn't he off checking for other survivors? What was his name again?

"Woodenbrow, why are you still here?" Irontail asked with a soft nudge on the druid's arm. "Go check and make sure there are no other survivors."

Woodenbrow paused for a moment, and then strutted off north, going towards a grouping of fallen felite warriors. Maybe he would find someone else who had survived.

As Irontail turned his attention back to Tel' Shira, the druids had finished turning her, and he got visual confirmation of the broken jaw. Laid out on her back, Irontail could see that the jaw was completely dislocated, pushed off to the right. The small amount of blood had come from this injury, but it appeared that it was not too severe, as nothing more was coming from her mouth.

The druid to Tel' Shira's left laid both of his hands upon her jaw and mumbled under his breath. A lime green energy flowed from his hands, coating Tel' Shira's damaged jaw and spreading across her face. Her eyelids fluttered as the energy coated her and spread down as far as her neck.

Meanwhile, the other druid was kneading her ribs, running along both sides to, as Irontail assumed, ensure that nothing else had been broken. Irontail was glued in place, oblivious to his surroundings.

"What is your purpose here?"

Hearing the alarmed tone, Irontail jerked around. One of the other centaur warriors was asking the question. He stood to the south of the village, where he was retrieving a black and yellow skinned demon.

Standing before this warrior was a large formation of elves, and at their lead was a familiar figure. It was the elvish ranger, Artimus. Irontail had met him before the ritual only days before. But what was he doing here now?

"I am Artimus Atyrmirid of the Royal Elvish Rangers. I bring with me a brigade of Erathal's finest to fight against Yezurkstal, the bringer of death. Who of you is in charge?"

The ranger paused as he surveyed the battlefield. Without further regard to Tel' Shira, Irontail sprinted towards the elves, placing a hand on the other centaur warrior's shoulder as he arrived.

"Artimus, I remember you from the ritual. My name is Irontail. Our tribal elders have all been slain. I represent the village at the moment."

Even as the words left his mouth, Irontail wasn't sure he was saying them. He was scared, unsure of himself, and was still in shock over Yezurkstal's power. He felt completely alone and confused. Still, these words somehow felt right.

As he addressed Artimus, he knew that this was the end of his old life as a warrior. If he didn't take charge, who else would?

-=-.=-.=-.=-.=-.=-.=-

Tel' Shira jerked into a sitting position. She took in a large gulp of air through her mouth and quickly exhaled. Her right hand flew up and grabbed her jaw, the sharp pain beginning to dull. She looked down, her eyes focusing on a felite druid who was kneeling down to her left.

Spinning her head, she noted another druid to her right. The smell of damp grass filled her nostrils, mixed with the distinct taste of blood and sweat. Her fur was patched with mud, and she felt the tiny drops of rain splashing off her body.

Her neck was stiff, and there was a dull ringing in her right ear. Actually, her entire body felt stiff, but she was alive.

"Su Pau!"

Tel' Shira pushed the two druids aside and jumped to her feet. Her balance was a bit off, but with a quick adjustment of her tail and a refocusing of her eyes, she scanned the field. She felt a

255

pain in her stomach, nausea overtaking her as she remembered what had happened. It couldn't have been real.

She grabbed the druid to her right, pulling her up close. The orange furred, brown spotted druid looked frightened, her eyes dilating as she grabbed onto Tel' Shira's wrists.

"Where is Su Pau?"

The druid's eyes dropped down, her fear being replaced with sadness. That was answer enough.

Tel' Shira pushed the druid away and turned her attention to the trees. She looked behind, noting where she had been thrown by the Hájje. Turning her head back around, she noted the tree that she waited in before attacking the pestilence. Extrapolating her trajectory, she locked in on it.

Without a thought, Tel' Shira took off in a sprint, running to the fallen body of her most revered elder. She went into a slide as she reached the body, ignoring the stiffness in her limbs as she knelt over Su Pau.

How had she let this happen?

Tel' Shira ran her hand up Su Pau's stomach. She reached the bottom edge of the hole in her elder's chest where the heart had been. She felt the despair building and could not contain herself. Su Pau was the greatest of their kind, and she was dead.

Tel' Shira felt her arms buckle and she let herself fall down. She grasped on the body of her fallen elder.

Letting out a roar of pain, she wept.

-=.=.=.=.=.=.=.

Artimus regarded Irontail for a moment, unsure of what to say. Only days before, they had met at this very village. At that time, he was an undecorated warrior, but now he claimed to represent the tribe. How badly had the battle gone?

"Irontail. It pains me that we must meet again under these circumstances. Please, these are our troop leaders: Commander Zeidrich, Captain Viviko, and General Fletching. I believe you remember Savannah."

Artimus motioned towards each individual in turn, and then looked back to Irontail.

"Yes, I'm afraid there is little time for more proper introductions though. You came here to fight Yezurkstal, right? He's gone, and not many of us survived. We could use your help with the cleanup."

Irontail spoke in a monotone, his face solemn as he looked Artimus dead in the eyes. He didn't even blink.

"Of course." Artimus looked past Irontail and watched as a familiar felite warrior sprinted across towards one of the allied corpses. "I'm afraid that I am no tactician, so please talk to Commander Zeidrich here and you can coordinate the deployment."

Thoron trotted forward a few paces as Artimus gently squeezed his side. Irontail stepped aside, presumably noticing that Artimus's attention had been drawn away. Through his peripherals, Artimus saw Irontail turn and watch as the felite - Tel' Shira was her name- slid down by the corpse and began to weep.

"Go ahead," Irontail said, as he turned his attention back to the other elvish leaders.

Artimus tuned out their conversation as he guided Thoron away from the group and towards Tel' Shira. He stopped just a few meters away and slid off Thoron's side, giving his faithful mount a friendly pat on the shoulder as he walked.

Tel' Shira lay sprawled atop an elderly felite, grasping tightly to the felite's arms and sobbing. Artimus noted a gaping hole in the felite's chest, blood still trickling out of the open wound where her heart had once been. What sort of monster had Yezurkstal commanded to do this?

Artimus stopped just a couple of strides from Tel' Shira. He stood there and watched for moment, listening to the pain in her cry. He surveyed the rest of the field, noting that most of the fallen warriors were dismembered in some fashion. With his elvish eyes in the now clear field, he was able to see almost the entire village.

Three of the six huts that were within his range of sight had been destroyed, almost unrecognizable among the scattered foliage. There were arms and legs strewn about the area, most of them felite, but some belonging to the centaurs. Even stranger than this felite with her missing heart though, was the rotting centaur corpse not more than five meters from where Artimus stood. The very sight made him cringe, the bones sticking out of rotting flesh, fur grayed and peeling away. It had to have taken some serious dark magic to kill anything in this fashion.

The behemoth that had been slain was another mystery. Though there was no question about Yezurkstal's magical ability,

Artimus had to wonder where he found such a creature. Was Yezurkstal capable of just creating these beasts somehow? What other horrors did he have at his disposal?

Artimus pondered this all in a matter of seconds before refocusing on Tel' Shira.

"Who was she?" Artimus asked softly, just barely speaking above Tel' Shira's sobs.

It almost seemed as if she had not heard him at first. She continued to cry, not moving an inch save her slight shaking as she held onto the deceased felite. After a few moments, Artimus noticed her release hold with her right hand and clench her fist.

The shaking subsided, and her sobbing died down. She sniffled a few times and turned to face Artimus. Her eyes were red, her face stained with tears.

"Su Pau," Tel' Shira began, taking another sniff. "The eldest of our people, she was. And wisest."

Tel' Shira slowly rose, wiping the tears from her eyes with her left hand. Her eyes remained downcast, but she gradually rose to full height and faced Artimus. Artimus noticed that her fist had loosened somewhat.

"I am sorry for your loss," Artimus offered solemnly.

"No!"

Tel' Shira yelled violently and clenched both of her fists. Artimus took a few steps back, his hand instinctively grabbing for the dagger on his side.

"No," she repeated, this time quietly. "The one who is gone will soon be sorry. Pay, he must. Kill him, I will."

In that moment, her body shaking and fists clenched in fury, Artimus felt that she might be able to.

Chapter 19

Erathal Forest, Dumner Village
18 Neglur, 1086

Artimus stood between Irontail and Zeidrich. He glanced over at Savannah, who was standing next to Tel' Shira and Fletching. She appeared uncomfortable, but she listened as Viviko -who stood between Fletching and Irontail- finished speaking. Artimus redirected his attention back to the captain.

"My point is, we have a huge advantage if we move now. Yezurkstal has made his play, and from what you guys are telling me, his numbers are almost exhausted. With our brigade, we eliminate any defensive advantage he might have."

Zeidrich spoke next, barely waiting for Viviko to finish.

"We all see your point, Captain, but I disagree. Assuming that the force he used to attack with is all that he has, is a mistake. For all we know, he had twice the number of demons guarding that cave of his. Not to mention, his home is a CAVE. That all but eliminates any number advantage that we have. No, we have to figure out a way to flush him out of that hole of his and make him fight on our terms."

"What if we smoke him out?" Fletching offered.

"And how do you suggest we do that?" Zeidrich asked. "We don't even know how deep his cave system goes. Not only that, but how exactly do we get anything inside to provide smoke? This isn't an enemy with some wooden huts that we can set on fire to force them into the open. Again, this is a cave."

"Okay, Zeidrich, we get it's a cave!" Fletching spat sarcastically. "As you so brightly pointed out though, that's exactly why we need to get him out. We can't hope to fight him inside some tunnel system."

"You're all missing the point," Irontail exclaimed matter-of-factly. "Yezurkstal will not be brought down by any one of us. We need the Avatar."

"Here, the Avatar is not!" Tel' Shira shouted, slamming her fists on the table in the center of the room. "When this darkness came, he was not here. Absent, he still is. Count on him, we most certainly cannot. Kill Yezurkstal, I will, if into the open you can bring him."

"Last time you tried to engage him you got thrown into a tree like a rag doll," Irontail scoffed. "How exactly will you do any different next time?"

"Let's all calm down," Artimus interjected, not giving anyone else time to speak. "We need to focus on the real enemy, Yezurkstal."

He scanned the room to make sure everyone was paying attention and then continued.

"We need to look at the facts. First, Yezurkstal is fearfully powerful, more so than any one of us. Second, the only troops we are sure he has are my two former cadets who are now hájje puppets. Third, he has eleven young female elves, and judging by his transformation of the aforementioned cadets, it's safe to assume they are also on his side. Their threat to us should still be mostly limited though, as only a couple have any background to suggest they would aide him in battle.

"Finally, and most important for our purposes, Yezurkstal is young; he is arrogant. He knows he is powerful, but like anyone in his position, that power will go to his head. Irontail, you even pointed out how he just stood there in the midst of a battle, holding onto -I'm sorry Tel' Shira- Su Pau's heart as if it was a trophy. He killed the most powerful centaur and felite with his own hands, and from what witnesses recall, they were the only two kills he made.

"The reason for this seems pretty clear to me. He wanted those kills for himself, to assert his power over everyone. He believes that he is invulnerable. Though this last point is admittedly my own conjecture, these are the facts as I see them. I may not be a master of warfare, but I think it rings true across all disciplines: when it comes to making a plan, you need to stick to the facts."

"All right genius," Fletching mocked, "what exactly is your plan though? All you've done is list out some 'facts,' which still gets us nowhere."

"No," Zeidrich interrupted. "I believe he has given us a plan, based on your own idea, General."

"Precisely." Noticing that Irontail had opened his mouth to weigh in, Artimus decided it best to continue without giving him the chance.

"You suggested we smoke him out, General. I say that we do just that. Instead of using actual smoke though, we rely on his arrogance to draw him out to us."

"Do you really think that would work?"

Everyone turned to Savannah, who had, up until this point, remained completely silent. Artimus was as shocked as everyone else to hear her speak up. No one said a word for at least five seconds, so Artimus decided it was his place to answer. After all, the question was directed to him.

"Pride is a powerful force and Yezurkstal has more than just pride; he suffers from hubris. He called himself the 'patriarch of the hájje,' and in his world there is nothing beyond the Hájje."

Artimus regarded the other members at the table, noting that most of them seemed to follow. Irontail appeared to be the most skeptical of the group.

"Let me ask you something, Irontail," Artimus began, locking in on the centaur's eyes and holding his stare. "What was the name of the slightly shorter centaur with brown fur out there, the one who was helping me retrieve the dead roc?"

"What?" Irontail asked perplexed. "Umm… Woodenbrow?"

"Ah, right," Artimus mumbled, casting his eyes towards the ground. "Never mind," he continued, before returning to meet Irontail's gaze.

"What does that have to do with Yezurkstal?" Irontail questioned.

"Oh, it's nothing. Just something he said about you, but probably best that I not repeat it." Artimus darted his eyes to either side as he said this, fighting the urge to grin.

"What did he say?" Irontail shouted.

"Well, he said that he didn't think you'd make a good leader. Actually, I believe his words were that you are a 'piss poor leader'." Artimus looked down, knowing that Irontail would play right into his hand.

"Our leadership has been destroyed!" Irontail exclaimed, smashing his hands down on the table with a resounding thump. "If he wants to question my leadership, he should do it to my face. Woodenbrow is dumber than a half-witted satyr. I have half a mind to go up there now and teach him his place!"

"Alright," Zeidrich interrupted with a raised hand. "You just proved his point you nitwit."

"What?" Irontail asked, his anger replaced with a hint of confusion.

"Woodenbrow didn't say anything negative about you," Artimus stated reassuringly. "I just wanted to show everyone here what a powerful weapon we have. If we can strike a nerve with Yezurkstal, we will draw him out."

Irontail went silent, looking somewhat embarrassed as he lowered his shoulders and loosened his fists.

"That's all fine and dandy," Fletching interjected. "The question is though: where do we go from there?"

"He's right," Viviko added. "Even if we get him into the open, what are we supposed to do? From the stories everyone is telling, conventional combat is just not going to cut it with this guy. I mean, Irontail said he saw him disappear in a puff of smoke. If this guy can somehow just disappear and reappear somewhere else, how can we predict where he will jump to when we lure him out?"

"We can," Artimus interposed, not giving anyone else time to respond. "All we have to do is taunt him in the right way. Issue him a personal challenge."

"Are you suggesting that we use someone as bait?" Zeidrich asked in alarm.

"Not someone. Me."

Savannah seemed somewhat startled and the other three elves seemed intrigued. Irontail was still a bit withdrawn, but displayed some confusion, and Tel' Shira was just difficult to read.

"He's seen me before; talked to me actually. All I have to do is say how he let me go because he was afraid that if he fought me, I would have killed him. I just play that up and he'll be dying to attack me. From there, we just prepare the trap. Figure he will appear somewhere in arms reach from me."

"That sounds like suicide to me." Irontail entered back into the discussion, looking Artimus square in the eyes.

"He'll kill you before you even have time to react. Contrary to what I was supposed to believe, I know Goldenchest had his flaws, but he was more powerful a fighter than anyone in this room. His strength and dexterity were unmatched, and his magical prowess was top tier as well. I watched Yezurkstal kill him as easily as I could kill a baby deer. If he is drawn out, he will kill you."

"No," Savannah exclaimed in defiance. "We cannot let him kill anyone else."

She looked at Artimus, and he could see sadness welling up in her eyes. Breaking his gaze, she turned over to Irontail.

"If we use anyone as bait, then it is our job to make sure that he does not die. We will take precautions, both magical and non-magical, to make sure that Yezurkstal doesn't have time to do anything. He'll think he is taking us by surprise, but we'll be the ones doing the surprising this time."

Everyone looked around the room nervously, presumably unsure where to go with this. Savannah was emotional, something that could not be afforded when planning for combat. Then again, Artimus couldn't blame her. If she had just asked to be used as bait, he'd probably be just as emotional.

"Obviously we will take whatever measures we can, but what exactly are we to do?" Zeidrich was the one to finally break the silence.

"Look, if this guy is half as good as everyone says, he'll notice our traps before we even have a chance to draw him out. I can have all of our warriors ready to charge, but that won't stop Yezurkstal from killing our bait."

"If not there is our bait, to kill, what is he?" Tel' Shira asked.

Zeidrich turned to her with a look of bewilderment. Fletching did the speaking for him.

"What do you mean, if the bait isn't there? If this preposterous plan is to work, we need someone to taunt him out of his cave."

Tel' Shira glared at Fletching as she spoke. "Voice projection, we could use. The illusion, we give him, of Artimus in one place. Another place, Artimus will be. In the actual trap zone, we set actual traps."

"She might be onto something," Artimus chimed in. "The challenge is, who can use illusion magic that is powerful enough to trick Yezurkstal?"

"No one in the forest," Savannah answered dolefully.

"True, that is not," Tel' Shira responded. "Illusion mages, the lamia have some of the best. Do this, we can, if one of their more accomplished illusionists we can get."

"Okay," Zeidrich started, raising his right fist as signaling his troops to stop. "There is a Lamia village to the east. If we're going to make a move, we better get going. Now. Yezurkstal has a way of getting one step ahead of us. We need to make sure that doesn't happen here."

"He's right, of course," Viviko added.

"What about the traps?" Irontail asked. "We need to plan out what we are going to do once we trick him out of hiding."

"We'll have time for that at the Lamia village," Fletching stated.

"Yes, that will have to wait," Artimus weighed in.

"Any objections?"

-=-=-=-=-=-=-=-

Erathal Forest, Lizock Village
18 Neglur, 1086

The sun peeked over the horizon, light trickling through
the trees and down upon the log cabins of the lizock village. A
gentle breeze ran through the clearing, whipping up some dirt
from the rudimentary road system. A primitive, wooden wall
circled the perimeter of the village, offering minimal defense
should anyone chose to attack.

The village had just been settled about a year prior, but it
was already larger than many centaur tribes'. A single tower of
respectable size was stationed at the center of the village. This
served as the military headquarters for the warriors of this village
and also as a trade depot for incoming and outgoing goods.
Nearest the wooden entry gate into town, the tower had a distinct
gatehouse for convenient wagon delivery.

An open circle of grass surrounded this structure, free
from any trees or bushes. This was where merchants would park
their carts each day so they could peddle their goods. Comparing
the vibrant green grass in the back half of this circle with the
yellowish front façade, it was apparent the merchants did not
leverage that entire circle. Likely, this was intentional to keep the
receiving area free and maintain a more secure environment for
tower personnel.

A dirt road ran around this central circle and branched out
in the four cardinal directions. A small inn sat along the center

circle road for anyone who might be passing through town. Opposite the inn was a pub, and between the two buildings were a few larger log cabins. In total, there were five buildings around the central square and moving out towards the edge of the village there were two other circle roads laid out. Each of these roads contained about a dozen cabins to house the rest of the locals.

At this early hour, the roads were nearly bare. A wizened merchant wheeled his cart through the dirt road towards the center circle. His once dark scales were graying, his green eyes weighed down with the burden of age as he struggled to make his way towards the field.

After an arduous walk, he finally reached his usual spot just outside the southwestern edge of the tower. With a strong exhale, he set the cart down and allowed himself to lean back against his wares.

Yezurkstal lifted his cloak of shadows, appearing directly in front of the elderly lizock. He thrust his hand forward, grabbing the lizock's fragile neck and peering into his soul. Nothing could compare to the joy he received as he beheld the feeble creature's look of horror.

Visions flashed through Yezurkstal's head of the lizock's life. He saw a young lizock climbing trees, a female lizock, and a love affair. Glimpses of children, anticipation as their eggs began hatching flashed through afterward. Next, there were images of these children playing with their father, and of their father teaching these children his trade. There were scenes of the merchant exchanging his fabrics for gold and silver. Finally, Yezurkstal reached the memories he was looking for; soldiers performing morning drills out of the tower and weekly deliveries from barghest traders.

The dying lizock attempted to escape, grabbing Yezurkstal's arm and squeezing with his hands. He swung his tail around, aiming for Yezurkstal's ribs. Yezurkstal raised his other arm, catching the tail and watching as the old lizock struggled to draw breath. He had the information he needed.

With a rapid tightening of his hand, Yezurkstal felt the lizock's windpipe crumble in his grip. He released the corpse, allowing it to drop freely to the ground.

"I'm afraid you won't be selling any more fabric."

Flicking his wrist, Yezurkstal cloaked himself once again and walked towards the front door of the tower. The soldiers would be starting their morning route in about half an hour, which meant that he should be able to convert them all with ease. They would be completely unprepared.

Yezurkstal reached the entrance, a simple wooden door, perhaps made of oak. There was a large keyhole meant for a skeleton key, a non-issue in his plan. Placing his hand on the lock, he fed some dark energy through it and watched as it corroded away to nothing, the metal rusted, becoming as fragile as glass.

With a jerk, the door flew right open, the deadbolt snapping off as easily as Yezurkstal had just crushed that old lizock's windpipe. Looking to either side, Yezurkstal stepped inside and shut the door behind him. He observed the hallway that lay before him, another simple structure for simple people.

Based on the information he had gotten from his elvish generals, Yezurkstal had expected this structure to have more to it, but unlike the elvish buildings, this one was disappointingly simple. There was but a single hallway running through the entire tower, and with his enhanced vision, Yezurkstal could see all the way to the end. It appeared that there were five doors in total; two on either side of the hallway and one at the very end.

His intuition told him that the end hallway was where the trading would occur. Of the four side doors, one would be the preparation room, one the armory, one a strategy room and the final room would be for whoever commanded this tower. At least that is how it would be arranged in an elvish installation. Yezurkstal would structure his kingdom similarly.

Keeping himself in the shadows, Yezurkstal trekked down the hall. The walls were bare, save for a torch every three meters, the stones even appearing somewhat unfinished. It may have been lacking aesthetics, but it was somewhat attractive in its simplicity.

Yezurkstal stopped just before the first two doors, pressed against the wall on the right. He listened and heard no activity from inside. Stepping over to the left door, he listened again; still nothing. As he continued walking, he made an internal wager with himself, betting that the door on the left would contain the strategy room and also the half dozen soldiers that would be preparing for the day's patrol.

Yezurkstal approached the door on the left and noticed that it was open a crack. He could already hear voices coming from inside. Was he even capable of being wrong?

Probably not, but now was not the time to admire his own excellence. Now he needed to focus his energy. If there were, as the old lizock had led him to believe, half a dozen warriors in the next room, he would need to expend a considerable amount of energy to snag them all at once. Should he miss any, he would be forced to kill them, and that would just not work with his plans.

He would never let anyone know, not even his top generals, but he could be injured just as easily as any other creature. Well, perhaps not just as easily, but a sword to the heart or an arrow to the head was surely not something he wanted to experience. Of course, with his lightning reflexes, god-like strength and limitless magic, he could avoid this.

Taking a deep breath, he lifted his shadowy veil and focused on his magical reserves. Unlike most mages, his energy came directly from the darkness and despair that was so prevalent. Shadow, disease, and death all fueled his supply and gave him strength. It helped, of course, that he had discovered worlds beyond Evorath, worlds of darkness and despair that he could draw additional energy from. Where most mages had to draw from their immediate surroundings, he could draw from virtually anywhere.

Focusing all of his dark energy on his conversion magic, with fingers steepled just beneath his chest, he closed his eyes. The magic welled up deep in his stomach, and he could feel tingling as it coalesced around his hands. Taking a final deep breath, he felt time slow as he turned the corner and kicked the door open.

Just as anticipated, there were six lizock inside, all of them in the middle of equipping themselves. This was the armory. Flinging his hands forward, he released the dark magic in six directions, each stream of black energy impacting its own lizock.

None of the reptiles were prepared.

Yezurkstal watched with pride as they all dropped what they were doing, falling to the floor and writhing as they struggled against his control. They were being reborn, their minds being opened up to the world of Yezurkstal's own vision, a world united under his flag and his alone. Independent thought was irrelevant, and they would be subservient to him and him alone. Individual thought was no more.

The first lizock to complete his transformation was at the back of the room. He was tall and lanky, clothed in leather armor, with one gauntlet on his right hand and another on the bench next to him. A bastard sword was sheathed by his feet, and as he rose to look at his new master, Yezurkstal noted a scar across his right cheek.

Each other lizock fell into line within seconds later, one of them both tall and bulky, another short and stout and the final three all of average stature. As their new consciousness took hold, they all stood and faced their master. Their knowledge all flowed into Yezurkstal as they completed the transformation. They would serve as a welcome addition to his army.

Zumek, the tall and lanky one, was the leader of the group, and accordingly was the first to speak.

"Master Yezurkstal, what are your orders?" he asked in a monotone, ending his question with a low hiss.

"Beyond the two off-duty lizock soldiers, can anyone in this village assist in combat?" Yezurkstal already knew the answer to his question, but he needed to ensure they were loyal.

"No, sir," Zumek replied. "Most of the village is composed of traders and their families."

"That's fine. And the barghest convoy that is due to arrive this morning. How many soldiers will they have with them?" Again, Yezurkstal knew the answer.

"They usually are accompanied by four warriors." Zumek's voice remained void of all emotion.

"Excellent. Then prepare for their arrival as you would any other day," Yezurkstal commanded. "Once they arrive, you are to kill the merchants while I subdue the warriors. I will give you further instruction from there."

"Yes, sir." Their responses all came in unison, no hint of hesitation present. They would be a perfect addition to his army.

Assuming they were on schedule, the convoy would arrive in just under one hour, which gave Yezurkstal an abundance of time to kill. For a fleeting moment, he actually considered using it to kill the other villagers himself, but that could get messy. No, he would get some well needed relaxation time instead.

First things first though, he needed to move the body of the merchant he had killed. He regarded the lizock soldiers one last time before stepping out of the armory, watching them for a

275

few seconds as they equipped themselves. For such a small village, they were well armed, but that was not out of the ordinary for lizock.

In the grand scheme of things, lizock were a warrior race. A merchant village like this was quite unusual, because the large majority of lizock were fighters of some kind. Still, this village would make a good example and it was in such close proximity to his next target that he couldn't help but stop here.

As he stepped outside, he raised his right hand and shielded his eyes from the sun. He preferred to remain inside during the day. Sunlight was not pleasant.

Still, his body was more magic than it was flesh and blood, so his eyes quickly adapted to the high levels of light. Looking around, he was disappointed to see that no other merchants had left their homes yet. He would have been happy to kill another lizock or two.

As he reached the corpse, he grabbed it by the tail and dragged it back towards the entrance of the tower. Walking back inside, he thought of what Gharis and Verandas must be doing back at his cave system. He had given them both instructions to take care of his wives and make sure they would be well hidden should the enemy army approach.

It was the only logical move, they had told him, and so Yezurkstal knew that the elves would be sending an army to his home. If his timing was correct, which it was, he would arrive with his new soldiers a few hours before the elves did, so he would have plenty of time to prepare a proper defense. Then again, he had not accounted for all of his demons being slain in the battle with the centaurs.

Why had the felite shown up? This must have been a result of their pesky foresight. But, why did they care so much about the fate of a single centaur village?

Those filthy curs had really interfered with his plans. For that, he would exterminate them entirely. Clearly, a species like that was not fit to live in his perfect world.

As he contemplated the ways that he could go about their extermination, he reached the end of the hallway and entered the door opposite the armory. This was Zumek's former office, and for the short time he would be here, it was now Yezurkstal's.

Leaving the corpse just inside the room, he closed the door and looked around to see what his options were. It was very limited in its hospitalities. A wooden table and chair sat in the middle of the room. A crudely drawn map of charted territories and a delivery schedule hung on the wall to his right.

The only form of respite was positioned at the left of the desk. It was a simple cot with a plain, dirty mattress. It looked rather uncomfortable, nothing fit for someone of his status, but it would have to suffice for now. After all, he had grown up with much less.

Yezurkstal spread himself out on the cot, stretching his shoulders as he lay down. He hadn't slept for over a week, which, even with his magic, was quite a long stretch. Normally, he could go for a few days, longer than any other species, but a week was testing even his limits. He could feel his magic was somewhat limited, and his mind was a bit cloudy. Maybe that explained how he had not properly accounted for the amount of demons he would need.

With less than an hour though, was it even worth getting sleep? He figured not, but lying down and not using any magic would do him some good regardless. As he lay back in the cot, he worked on planning his next move.

-=-=-=-=-=-=-=-

Erathal Forest, Dumner Village
18 Neglur, 1086

Artimus watched a centaur warrior stack up the last demon body. Even knowing the origins of these creatures, he could not help but feel despondent at the sight of all of this death. What kind of perverse creature could cause such damage?

Between the demons, centaur and felite, the death toll was well over fifty. This had not just been a simple skirmish, but rather the start of a war. Up until today, 'war' had just been a story in myths, the battle between the dryads and the demons. Today, all of Erathal was entering a war.

The only surviving centaur druid poured the last of the oil on the pile and stepped back. Irontail stepped up to the pile of demon corpses -the behemoth laid out at the bottom- and held up his torch. He looked around at the gathering: the remaining felite, the elvish army, and all of the surviving centaur tribe, including the women and children.

"Today was a grim day in Dumner, but as our history has shown, we survive. Our tribe will continue on, and we will avenge the deaths of our loved ones. Let the gods guide our ancestors to the great forest beyond this world and drag the souls of these demons to the darkest reaches of hell."

As he completed the mini speech, Irontail dropped the torch atop the oiled-up demons. The fire roared to life, its blaze engulfing the entire pile. Red, orange and yellow flames danced around the pile, the sound of crackling skin filling the air. It was accompanied by the nauseating smell of burning flesh, something that Artimus prayed he would never have to smell again.

Savannah stood to his right. As the pile went ablaze, she turned towards him and shielded her face. Artimus noted the terror in her eyes. For a moment, he thought that she was going to embrace him, but she kept her composure enough to avoid that.

Artimus took a single step towards Savannah, which brought them close enough to whisper.

"I'm sorry you have to be here for this," he whispered, fighting his own desire to give her a hug.

Savannah raised her head and looked into his eyes. Beneath the discomfort, he could see a mountain of strength.

"This is their way. I have to be able to respect that."

Artimus nodded and looked around at the rest of the gathering. His three commanders stood in the same row as he, and they all looked ahead with blank faces. Most of the other elves just stood in place with their heads downcast. The dozen surviving felite all stood in a grouping, Tel' Shira at the front of the pride; they all looked upon the blazing corpses unfazed.

The handful of surviving centaurs all watched as the demons burned with a look of intense hatred. Not one of them was bothered by the sight or smell of the burning flesh, and they all stared as the pile slowly shrunk. Their demeanor made Artimus feel rather nauseous.

The civilian centaurs showed more eclectic emotions though. Some of them looked infuriated, some confused, some frightened, and a good portion looked downright miserable. It was the miserable ones that Artimus felt he could most relate to.

Specifically, he observed one of the children, a small female centaur with light fur. She was crying. Her face showed more than just misery though; it showed a complete and abysmal lack of hope. It was the look of someone who had forcibly had her innocence stolen from her and was left only with a harsh reality of pain and suffering.

This was the feeling that Artimus felt most equated to his own. What kind of person would start a war? Where was the motivation?

Artimus believed that life was valuable, perhaps some more valuable than others, but that each person had their own unique perspective to contribute to the world. Each creature was put on Evorath for some purpose. But what purpose could Yezurkstal possibly serve?

No.

Yezurkstal was the antithesis of life. He was anti-life. He was all that was unholy and evil. He was here to destroy the good and productive and bring about destruction. He was death.

Artimus was a normal elf, but he had spent his life training in ways that most creatures would not be willing to endure. It was this training that allowed Artimus to become the skilled hunter that he was. He had learned to track, to observe, and to fight and he was the best at what he did.

In his time as the chief investigator, he knew that there was always the possibility he would have to kill as well. Now, for the first time in his life, he was looking forward to the opportunity.

-=-=-=-=-=-=-=-

Erathal Forest, Lizock Village
18 Neglur, 1086

The barghest merchants approached the village from the south. Just as the lizock had said, there were four warriors, one marching on each of the four corners of the convoy. For such an unintelligent race, Yezurkstal found himself somewhat impressed by the size of the party.

There were three wagons in total, each large enough that it required the use of two horses to pull. The wagons themselves were predictably plain, simple wooden carts with gray covers thrown over the goods. Only one merchant rode on each of the three wagons, and like all of their species they were quite large in stature.

Yezurkstal and five of his newly recruited lizock watched from atop the tower. Zumek stood at the back of the tower, waiting to greet the merchants as they arrived. As the convoy marched towards the tower, Yezurkstal waited, gathering the necessary magical energy for their conversion.

By now, the grass field was bustling with merchants from the town, lizock selling all sorts of goods. There were a couple of merchants selling cloth, a handful selling food items, one merchant selling swords and daggers, and even a couple selling gems and jewelry.

From what he had gathered from his new recruits, these arriving barghest were not the only outsiders who traded with this booming village. It was quite common for lamia, trolls, or even the occasional rural elf to run through this town and browse the merchant's circle. This somewhat made up for the fact that the village was more merchant than not, but it still seemed unsustainable in the long run.

The barghest convoy came around the final turn and started up towards the back of the tower. Both of the front escorts picked up their pace slightly, pulling ahead of the merchants to greet Zumek at the entrance. Yezurkstal glanced at his pawns and gave them a slight nod.

They each pulled back on their bowstrings, two aiming at the farthest merchant and one each at the front two. The final solider kept his bow aimed between these first two, ready to adjust for either one should they survive the initial shot. Yezurkstal closed his eyes and focused his magic on the task at hand.

As the arrows flew, he thrust his hands forward, the dark energy shooting down and splitting apart at it headed towards the four warriors. Opening his eyes, he watched the magic from his right split apart and impact both of the front warriors. The other bolt of dark energy veered around the wagons and hit both of the rear escorts.

The four escorts fell to their knees, their fur darkening as they struggled against Yezurkstal's hold. The arrows all struck true to their mark, and not one of the three merchants showed any sign of life as they fell from their seats on the wagons.

Zumek drew his sword, pulling his weight back into a defensive stance. He wrapped his tail around, resting just in front of his left foot as an extra source of balance.

"Keep your eyes trained on the merchants. If they move, put them down." Yezurkstal ordered.

Standing upright, he stepped forward and took the plunge from the tower. As he neared the grass, he gathered up his magic and concentrated it in his legs. With a thud, his feet sunk into the grass, the magic absorbing the force of his fall and protecting him from injury.

The barghest warriors were all howling in pain, a reaction that would surely draw the attention of the town merchants. Something unexpected was happening though. As the magic took hold, their fur not only darkened in color, but their teeth and claws grew. Their muscles bulged -fast.

Yezurkstal felt an unexpected thrill as he watched, wondering how far these creatures would change. These four barghest might prove to be more lethal than a greater amount of demons. Keeping his attention on all the details, he looked to each merchant in turn.

The one most near was still clinging to life and crawled towards him. With a final breath, he let out a low growl just before an arrow impacted him in the top of the skull. Yezurkstal smiled and returned his focus to the new recruits.

They had grown by at least thirty percent, and both their teeth and claws were the size of knives. With a glance over his shoulder, he noted that Zumek looked apprehensive and was squaring up against the nearest convert. Yezurkstal waited patiently as the four creatures rose to their feet, the transformation complete.

"Do you know who I am?"

The barghest all started forward, their steps very deliberate as they neared Yezurkstal.

As the first barghest came within arm's length, he stopped and responded.

"You are master," he said simply, his deep voice booming and garbled.

"You are master," repeated the next one.

The final two lined up next to the first, repeating those three simple words. Yezurkstal smirked, glancing once again at Zumek to see that he had relaxed and returned his sword to his side. That relaxation would not last for very long.

A group of merchants stepped around the side of the tower, stopping as they took in the scene. The three dead merchants, the four mutated warriors and Yezurkstal, a complete unknown; it all must have been too much for them. Before even

Yezurkstal had time to react, one of the four merchants let out a shrill scream.

All four turned around and ran, each yelling incoherently about an attack.

The lizock already knew what to do. Zumek ran after the fleeing merchants, sword in hand as he rounded the tower. Screams filled the air, undoubtedly the result of his archers as they picked off the townspeople. Now he just needed to get the barghest involved.

"The five lizock on the roof and the one who just went running off are your allies. You will not harm them. Everyone else in the village is fair game. Kill them all."

Yezurkstal let a grin spread across his face as the four juggernauts took off, two running east and two west. With this new addition to his army, the village would be destroyed within an hour. There was only one more stop to make before returning home.

Chapter 20

Erathal Forest, Lamia Village
19 Neglur, 1086

At the advice of Zeidrich, everyone had left their horses back at Dumner. He had suggested that, though their movement would be slower, they would be better prepared should they encounter trouble along the way. The original plan had been to leave their steeds there anyways, but under the circumstances Artimus was still hoping to make better time. As things were, they had given Yezurkstal an entire day to return back to his base and prepare a defense. Or, even worse, they had given him the chance to launch another offensive.

Artimus walked behind the three commanders this time and Savannah marched to his left. They had not spoken since leaving Dumner last night, and as the sun reached its apex in the sky, he was getting anxious. He felt that he needed to clear the air before they met with the Lamia.

There were plenty of small conversations coming from the troops behind, so he wasn't too worried about privacy. The lack of general forest noise was a bit unsettling though, only a few birds chirping in the trees and no squirrels or other small prey scurrying about. He hoped it was some sort of magic around the lamia tribe that caused this effect.

"Savannah," he started glancing over at her. Her beautiful face was still weighed down with the horror of current events.

She didn't respond immediately, but Artimus noted a slight falter in her step.

"I know this has been tough," Artimus continued. "I'm out of my element just as much as you are."

A look of anger overtook her face as she glanced over at Artimus's. He had been mistaken with his word choice.

"Are you suggesting that you somehow know what I am feeling?" Savannah asked the question while still focusing on the path ahead.

Artimus knew he had to think carefully before answering this question. He had put himself in a difficult situation by having Savannah come along. As he swam through his mind for the appropriate answer, he wondered: why had he really insisted that she come?

Had he let his personal relationship influence his thought process? If she was here, he was able to personally see that she was kept safe from danger. He was also uncomfortable in his capacity leading a war party and having Savannah along helped him feel at ease. Was this the only reason he had brought her?

On the other hand, Savannah's druidic abilities could be a considerable asset on this expedition. She had demonstrated her competence as a lab mage, helped heal him after his injury and participated in the Xyrloom. Most other lab mages were much more limited in their skills, and none of them were actually soldiers anyways. Or was he just rationalizing his choice?

"I was," Artimus started his response carefully. "But I was wrong."

Savannah turned her head at this point and Artimus locked eyes with her. For a brief moment, he felt that perhaps she understood what he intended to say.

"I know that I feel unprepared for this. I'm a hunter by trade, and I was thrust into my role as an investigator because I was good. I remained in that role, because I became the best. Still, I am not a soldier. I was trained to notice the little details that everyone else misses, to note wind directions and smells, to follow tracks and note misplaced twigs. I was taught to use a bow, and I became skilled enough that I'm now a champion bowman.

"I do not know battle strategy and I was not taught how to lead a war party. I did not learn formations, marching techniques or any sort of advanced combat. I killed animals, but never anything capable of thinking. The bottom line, I simply am not prepared for a war, which is exactly what we are involved in right now."

Artimus looked over to gauge Savannah's expression. Savannah appeared to be considering his words.

"I understand," Savannah started, her voice full of sincerity.

"I understand that this is not what you want. And I know that I have to be here. I just want to move time forward and have this all over with. This Hájje kidnapped all of those girls, he indoctrinated two rangers and has brought more death and destruction than I ever imagined possible. The truth is, I'm most unhappy about how I feel; I want him dead."

She turned toward him as these final words left her mouth, a solemn look stamped upon her innocent face. In that moment, Artimus knew that she felt just as he did.

He wanted to give her a hug, to just stop walking and hold her for a moment as they were united in their mutual struggle. But he couldn't.

His attention was pulled forward as Zeidrich threw up his right fist. Fletching and Viviko immediately followed suit, and Artimus stopped dead in his tracks. He had let the conversation distract him too much, for as they stopped he noticed why.

Looking up above the tree line, he could see smoke rising ahead. The smell of burning wood caught his nostrils, and the silence of the forest suddenly made sense. Yezurkstal had beaten them to the punch yet again.

"Everyone at attention!" Zeidrich shouted in frustration.

All of the conversation ceased, and out of his peripherals Artimus watched the entire brigade stand at attention. No one could say they weren't well trained in the art of discipline. Savannah, on the other hand, allowed her attention to shift back and forth between the commanders and the ranks before looking straight at Artimus for guidance.

"I will go ahead," Artimus instructed. "Zeidrich and Fletching; you two accompany me."

Artimus pulled out his bow from over his shoulder and drew a single arrow, lining it up against the bow string and stepping in front of the two soldiers. Zeidrich drew his sword, the sound of mythril ringing out as it cleared his scabbard and he fell in line behind Artimus. Fletching also pulled his bow, taking a position at the rear.

Ignoring the clanking of armor behind him, Artimus focused all his senses ahead as he crept forward. He ducked under a branch and navigated around the foliage with care. As they pushed through the thick brush surrounding the village, he could hear the popping of a fire.

After about a minute's march, he pushed through a final bush and into the clearing. Propped up in the path was the corpse of a lamia, a single pike jabbed through the center of her skull like a toothpick in an olive. The blood upon her lips appeared fresh, still dripping from her open mouth. Her bosom was exposed, a large gash running down from above her left breast to the bottom right of her abdomen. The lower end of the pike was still visible beneath the snake half of her body, her tail wrapped around the weapon and dismembered at the end. Blood still flowed from this wound as well.

Artimus loosened his bowstring, letting it go slack as he returned the arrow to his quiver. He sent his gaze downward, away from the greeting that Yezurkstal had left for them. The river of blood from this corpse was but a few steps away, so he stepped to the right to avoid it.

"What the hell?" Zeidrich cursed as he cleared the bush and looked upon the village.

"What kind of unholy demon does this?" he continued, shaking his head as he carefully walked forward.

Fletching said nothing, but his look of disgust told more than Zeidrich's words.

Beyond the lamia corpse, there were perhaps another dozen dead in Artimus's direct line of sight. Each one was dismembered in some way, many missing arms, a couple missing their head, and one even cut clean in half. It was hard to differentiate where blood from these corpses ended and untainted land began. By the looks of things, they were taken completely by surprise.

The dwellings in this village appeared well built, solid wooden cabins and a few smaller huts. Despite this, they were all left in ruins. The nearest hut appeared to have been run clear through by some sort of juggernaut, perhaps a smaller version of the behemoth that had been used in Dumner. Most of the other buildings were in flames, roofs collapsed, walls destroyed, only ruins of their former craftsmanship.

"Well that's that then. We cannot hope to attack this monster without an illusionist. Dammit!" Zeidrich shoved his sword back in its scabbard on these last words and stomped his right foot.

"Calm yourself," Fletching demanded. "There could be a survivor. We're looking for an illusionist. Who is more likely to survive a surprise attack like this than a master of blue magic?"

"He's right," Artimus added, refusing to give up on hope. Though the odds were surely against it, there was hope.

"Is anyone still alive?" Artimus shouted as he started forward, keeping his eyes trained for any possible movement.

"We come from the Elvish Kingdom of Erathal, and we are here to fight this evil that has attacked your village. If anyone is alive, please speak up so that we might tend to your wounds."

Artimus kept walking to the right of the village, making his way to the demolished hut that was nearest. He motioned to Zeidrich, who stepped around the first lamia corpse and continued up the middle. Fletching went up the left, avoiding a decapitated lamia and approaching a flaming cabin.

Artimus focused his attention on the hut, honing in on the gaping hole in the wall. The hut was a perfect circle, about four meters in diameter and three meters tall. The walls had been weaved from thick twigs tightly knit together to make a substantial barrier against the elements. Whatever made this hole had run clean through the structure, leaving a similar exit on the opposite end.

Upon closer examination, he noticed some fur caught between the twigs around the impromptu entryway. It was a jet black in color and much thicker than any normal forest dwelling animal, but it definitely did not come from a monster like the one he had seen in Dumner. Anything was possible with Yezurkstal, so if he could get this creature identified, perhaps they would be better prepared to combat it when the time came. Grabbing a few strands, Artimus stuffed them in his right pocket; he would have Savannah work her magic and see what she could distinguish.

Unfortunately, it didn't appear this hut would reveal any survivors, for he could already smell blood and bile. With the sunlight running through the side of the hut, Artimus was able to confirm his suspicions as soon as he looked inside. The wooden floor was soaked with blood. Against the right wall of the hut, a lamia corpse lay gutted, her innards spread across the floor.

Artimus turned away and fought the immediate nausea, wondering how a creature that tore through the wall would follow up with such a precise and vicious attack. It appeared as if some clawed beast had simply grabbed her midsection and tore the guts right out of her body. Not caring to endure the odor of stomach fluids or the unsightly corpse, Artimus walked around the right of the hut, keeping his eyes trained on the outside for any further clues. At this point, he didn't figure he would get anything helpful on the inside anyways.

As he walked around the hut, he regarded both Fletching and Zeidrich. Fletching was just walking out of the burning building he had gone to investigate with a mixed look of terror and disgust. Zeidrich, on the other hand, looked like he might have something. He was at a large cabin towards the center of the village, looking in the window. For the most part, the structure appeared to be intact, but the door was torn off its hinges and part of the roof looked to have collapsed in.

Backing away from the window, Zeidrich motioned towards Artimus.

"Someone's alive in there," he barked with a hint of excitement.

Both Artimus and Fletching ran towards the commander. Zeidrich made his way towards the door as they arrived, Artimus reaching him just seconds before Fletching.

Slowing to a trot, Artimus did his best to assess the situation. The smell of burnt wood overpowered any other odor that might have given clues, but by the looks of things the fire had been extinguished. Contrary to his initial observation, he noted that the door, which had been torn clear off its hinges, was not the only damage to the building. The back right of the cabin had been demolished, and the entire area around it had collapsed.

He approached the door with care and looked back at the two military leaders.

"I'll go in. Fletching, go around back and see if entry is possible from the rear. Zeidrich, keep your eyes peeled in case any enemies are still about."

Fletching started around the side without delay, and Zeidrich nodded in reply.

Stepping through the doorway, Artimus noticed that the wooden floor had been damaged by the fire. Patches of the floor were missing, removed entirely by flame, and other areas were stained with blood and lamia entrails. His footing felt unstable as he stepped inside and took in the rest of his surroundings.

The cabin appeared to be split up into three distinct rooms, separated by a substantial wall on either side of his current position. This first room must have served as both a kitchen and dining area. A broken circular table lay in front of the doorway, two of the four legs snapped away by whatever force had come through the home. Opposite the door, stationed directly against the wall, there was a large iron stove, which was left mostly undamaged in the attack. Sitting next to the stove, there was a series of shelves, almost entirely emptied and severely damaged.

Artimus gave only a quick glance to his left, noting that the door to the room was torn out and cast on the floor by the fallen shelves. Most of the blood and what appeared to be lamia intestines was also leading into this room, suggesting that there was nothing he cared to see in that area of the house. Burnt logs were spread out in front of the stove in either direction, possibly the source of the fire. As his eyes moved to the right, he noted that the ceiling in this room was still completely intact, but the wall looked to have been damaged.

Like the door on the left, the entry to the right room was completely exposed, the door discarded in the right corner of this first room. The area around the doorway had deep claw marks, but, like the hair outside the first hut, Artimus could not accurately match them to any known creature. Creeping into the house, Artimus avoided an exposed area of the floor and stepped around a small puddle of blood.

He tried in vain to search for any other smells that might indicate something of use. The smoke smell was so strong that it must have just been extinguished, which suggested that whoever was alive in this next room must have been responsible for putting out the fire. With this in mind, Artimus crept forward, keeping his left hand extended in front of himself defensively and his right held back just above his mythril sword.

From his vantage point to the right of the doorway, he noted that the entire roof appeared to have collapsed in this next room. A large support beam blocked the lower part of the doorway, an obstacle that would make his entry dangerous if he did not first ensure that the survivor would not attack. It was time to strike up a conversation.

"Hello in there," Artimus greeted, unsure of how to address whoever was in the next room. It occurred to him as he started that he didn't know the gender or age of this lamia, or even if it spoke in the common tongue. In fact, Zeidrich had said that 'someone' was alive in there. He didn't even know if that someone was a lamia.

"My name is Artimus Atyrmirid. I am a ranger from Erathal here to help. Do you understand me?"

Artimus listened, knowing that even if the person did not respond he could get some grasp of the situation from movement. He heard the faint shifting of weight inside, but no verbal response. The indistinct rustling seemed to originate near the rear of the room, just to the right of the door he'd need to enter.

Keeping his hand on the hilt of his sword, he stepped forward and entered the next room. As the sounds suggested, a young lamia was across the room, pinned beneath a large support beam from the roof. To the left of the room, the wall was all but destroyed, and he could see Fletching peeking around back for any sign of entry. Not wanting to alarm the injured lamia, he ignored the general for the time being.

There was debris scattered about the floor, some broken pottery, stray pieces of furniture and a bed that appeared to have been set on fire, the feather pillows half burnt away from the flames. The right wall was still held up, the roof attached securely overhead of the injured lamia. A variety of different sized pieces of wood from the ceiling were scattered about in the rubble, along with some blood stains.

Artimus carefully made his way towards the pinned down lamia. She appeared to be frightened beyond her wits, struggling to escape from the beam that had her pinned down. As Artimus approached, she looked away from him and whimpered.

"You don't need to be afraid," he whispered kneeling down in front of her.

"I'm going to get some help and we're going to get you out of here. The bad guys are gone. We are here to help."

She looked pathetic, a young and frightened child. Though she had the usual ruby red hair of her people, her eyes were a distinct shade of blue, matching the scales of her beautifully patterned tail. Her pale face was stained with tears, but even in her compromised position she showed the beauty of her race in the truest sense.

Trying to get a better feel for the situation, Artimus observed that her lower torso was pinned just where the elf half of her body ended and the snake tail began, which could partially explain her silence. She could very well be in breathing distress, her lungs being restricted by the heavy weight of this support beam. If he didn't get this off of her soon, she might not survive at all.

"Alright. We need to get this off of you. I'm going to get some help from my friends," Artimus said gently.

He looked up to where the beam rested on the ceiling, still partially attached on the remaining front wall. It would be much too heavy to lift on his own, but he was pretty confident with the help of Fletching and Zeidrich that he could move it. The key was to make sure that nothing else collapsed when he did so.

"Fletching!" Fletching was clearly startled as Artimus yelled his name, jumping up and looking around before focusing in on Artimus.

"I can barely see you in there, Lieutenant. What is it?" Fletching asked.

"Go around front and grab Zeidrich. Move with haste. This lamia is trapped under some debris and I need both of you to help me move it."

Like before, Fletching did not hesitate to listen to the younger ranger. He turned and ran around front. Artimus continued to inspect the beam and the debris around it, looking for the best way to get leverage without risking anything else's integrity. The young lamia looked to be slowing her struggles, her skin changing color as if it might turn as red as her hair.

Without waiting for the other two, Artimus carefully maneuvered over the low end of the beam, getting on the other side and kneeling down towards the bottom end.

"When we lift this, you need to pull yourself out. Look at me! Do you understand?"

Whatever fear the lamia may have had of Artimus she must have realized the threat of being crushed was greater. She finally looked straight at him, her eyes pleading for help as she offered a slight nod.

Her skin was taut, her mouth open as if trying in vain to utter words. Her eyes seemed like a deep well of fear and sorrow, the blue being clouded with a void of despair. Artimus wasn't sure if there were any words that would properly describe how she looked: terror, anguish, and misery were insufficient.

Zeidrich and Fletching both stormed into the room, assessing the scene for only a moment before running to the fallen support beam. Fletching took the position opposite Artimus and Zeidrich squatted down higher up on the beam. They all looked at each other in understanding.

"We lift on three," Artimus instructed.

"One... Two... Three."

Artimus lifted with all of his strength, his legs tightening and back muscles contracting as he pulled up. He saw the strain on his two comrade's faces. They slowly lifted the beam up; one inch, and then another and another. Finally, they had cleared it of the lamia and she let out a gasp as she pushed away with her palms.

Normal color flowed back into her face as she pushed away and gasped for air. She was still badly injured.

"Take it down slowly," Zeidrich gasped as they lowered the beam back down. They didn't want to cause any other complications.

Artimus let out a sign of relief as they lowered the beam back to the floor and let it go. He held his ground for only a moment, making sure that nothing was unsettled. Confident that he could move out from behind the debris, he ducked underneath and returned to the front where the lamia was still lying.

She was breathing heavily, still trying to get more air through her lungs. Her ribs had to have been broken.

"Get Savannah!" Artimus ordered, dropping down to one knee next to the injured lamia.

He didn't bother waiting to see who went, but he heard footsteps exiting the room. Grabbing the lamia's hand, he got closer and looked into the girl's eyes. Maybe if he could get her to steady her breathing he could help ensure that she survived.

"It's alright. You are going to be OK, but you need to slow your breathing. I need you to focus on my eyes and tune out the pain in your chest."

How was this going to help?

"What do you do for fun? Do you like flowers? Just think of flowers and rolling fields on a beautiful day. Breathe in gently through your nose and let your breath out slowly from your mouth."

What was he doing?

"Just focus on now."

Was he actually helping her? She had locked in on his eyes, and it seemed as if her breathing had become less labored. Still, she was clearly in an extraordinary amount of pain. If Savannah didn't get here quickly, she would suffocate.

As if on cue with his thinking, Artimus heard a rush of footsteps from behind. He broke the lamia's gaze and released her hand, jerking around to see Zeidrich leading Savannah into the room. Artimus jumped to his feet and backed away, allowing Savannah to take a kneeling position before the struggling lamia.

Savannah placed her hand upon the lamia's side. The girl immediately pulled away, her labored breathing increasing in intensity as she used her arms to push herself toward the wall. Her eyes darted up to Artimus as if pleading him for help, a look of intense fear hardening them.

"It's alright," Artimus said reassuringly. "She is a druid. She is going to heal you. Trust me."

The girl's eyes softened and she allowed Savannah to move in closer. Placing her hands once again on the lamia's side, a vibrant green energy coated her hands and flowed into the injured lamia. Savannah was glued in place, passing the healing energy to help restore damaged bone and tissue.

Her face showed pain replaced with comfort as the energy radiated around the lamia's sternum and chest, flowing around her body like a geyser of water. The girl relaxed her breathing, going from frantic gulps for air to a normalized pattern. She took deep breaths, her chest rising steadily as the bones were set in place.

"You need to stay still," Savannah advised, keeping her hands in place and focusing more energy.

"Your ribs were broken and they damaged your lungs. I have temporarily eased your pain and infused you with healing magic that will help you breath. The damage is still there though. Just stay relaxed and don't talk. This will take a few minutes." Savannah spoke plainly, her eyes focused on the injured area, pouring green energy into the lamia.

Artimus stood watching. He had always been amazed by the idea of magic but had never been able to use any himself. Watching Savannah utilize her healing abilities was a complete mystery to him, but it was thrilling to see it actually take effect.

Just moments ago, this lamia was in the clutches of death and now she was springing back up with new life energy; all thanks to Savannah.

With the situation calmed down, Artimus reordered his thoughts. If this lamia had survived, perhaps there were others within the village that survived as well. They needed to resume their search immediately.

"We need to keep searching the village," Artimus said addressing both Zeidrich and Fletching.

"If there are other survivors in need of healing, we need to find them quickly and make sure they get it. Split up as before and meet back here."

Fletching shook his head and turned around. He walked out of the room and muttered a faint 'urgo'.

Zeidrich turned around and walked out as well but paused just as he reached the doorway.

"Let's pray she is a great illusionist. If not, we have no choice but to retreat back to Erathal."

The captain didn't wait for Artimus's reply and continued, leaving the younger ranger to ponder.

What if Yezurkstal was already on his way?

Chapter 21

Erathal Forest, Lamia Village
19 Neglur, 1086

This was unbelievable.

It was as if that demonic bastard had somehow known
that they would be coming here. He had wiped out the entire
lamia village, leaving only a helpless child. Now everyone was
talking as if they were defeated, planning on returning back to the
Elvish Kingdom to prepare a defense.

How did they know that he would attack the elvish city
next anyways? What if he was heading for her home?

Tel' Shira pondered these questions as she stood with
Artimus, Savannah, Irontail, and the three other elvish leaders in
what seemed to be the only semi-usable structure left in this
damned village.

"I say at this point we take all of our forces and return to
Erathal to prepare for a joint defense. Yezurkstal is wiping out
one village after another, and according to our surviving lamia he
now has some lamia allies." The warrior leader, Zeidrich, spoke
absolutely, as if they had no other choice of action.

"Her name is Casandra," Savannah interjected.

"Who cares?" Fletching asked dismissively. "We've been
bested, but Zeidrich is right. If Yezurkstal had any plan of
attacking the felite confederacy, he would have done so first.
They are closer to the mountains than anyone else."

This was disgusting.

"Enough of this talk, I have had," Tel' Shira shouted in outrage.

"Talk, talk, talk, all you do it is. Guesswork is all you have. Leave, my fellow felite and I shall now. Consult the elders, we must."

Artimus opened his mouth to object, but Tel' Shira turned, storming out of the hut and heading back towards the gathering of soldiers outside. In her haste, she narrowly avoided tripping over a damaged floorboard.

She was angry. She understood that she was still upset over the loss of Su Pau, but this was not the way to resolve anything. First, she would make sure that the Hájje would not attack her people. The elders would know who would be attacked next and sitting around guessing at motives was pointless.

Wherever the Hájje would be, she was going to make sure she beat him there.

-=-=-=-=-=-=-=-

Irontail couldn't entirely blame Tel' Shira for her outrage. Unfortunately, his home had already been decimated by the wrath of this horrible tumor, which was the only reason he stood here entertaining the idea of helping these elves at all. If he felt that his home was a potential target for the next attack, he wouldn't be standing here and listening either.

Dumner had been all but destroyed by Yezurkstal. This demon's power was greater than anything he had imagined, but there was one person who might be able to fight back: the Avatar.

304

During the ritual, Irontail had been convinced that this Avatar was more powerful than any other forest creature. Even though the demonstration was brief, he felt that perhaps the Avatar was even more powerful than Yezurkstal.

It was revenge, plain and simple. The Avatar had said that if the forest formed a united front to defend against Yezurkstal, he would join the cause. If Irontail did not devote the few warriors he had to Erathal's protection, what hope was there? Without the Avatar, there would be no defense against Yezurkstal.

With these things in mind, Irontail had no choice but to stick with the elves, uniting with them in hopes of gaining the Avatar's favor. Then again, would their alliance be enough? The felite were presumably out of the picture. Maybe their next course of action was to send envoys to some of the other forest tribes.

"Irontail?"

Irontail looked up to identify who addressed him. Everyone in the room was looking at him, as if expecting an answer. It was a male voice who had snapped him back to attention, but he wasn't sure who.

"Excuse me," Irontail said clearing his throat. "Please repeat the question."

Fletching shook his head and Zeidrich cast his glance towards the ground. It must have been Artimus who had asked the question, for he answered.

"I know it's a difficult time for your tribe, but can we rely on the few warriors you have to support us in our defense?"

Irontail took a moment to answer, looking around at the others to see that they were all focused on him once again.

"Without unity, there is little hope of getting the Avatar to join our cause, so the answer is yes. Still, I suggest that we send out some scouts from your city as soon as we arrive and work on getting some of the other forest denizens involved."

Irontail finished his statement with much more authority than he had expected. Now that he had taken the reins as the leading warrior, he felt a newfound confidence. All this time, his elders always told him to watch his thinking and to follow their will. Maybe the key was to think for oneself instead?

"I agree," Zeidrich chimed in.

"From what I understand, this Avatar of yours told you we needed to prepare an attacking army, right, Artimus? If that's true, what we need to do is gather our forces back at Erathal and get as many outside allies as possible. I hate to say it, but there is a lizock city to the west of our village. Also, further south of that there are barghest tribes scattered about. We have a lamia, more or less, and I think we can safely assume passing on a satyr ally would not break our deal. Heck, finding a band of trolls will be the only difficult part."

Irontail was glad that Zeidrich agreed with him on the satyr; they were a worthless race, never adding any value to anything they did and only recklessly consuming. Still, he watched Artimus for his response.

"I actually got the impression that we didn't even need that big of an alliance," Artimus replied.

"Though, it never hurts to be thorough. I agree that we should send out envoys as soon as we can." Artimus finished and regarded the others.

"Agreed," Fletching and Viviko echoed.

"I agree as well," Irontail said without much thought. It made sense.

"What about the felite?" Savannah asked.

Everyone looked around for a moment before Fletching chimed in.

"Forget the felite. Those overgrown cats are only concerned with themselves. I've dealt with them enough in my time, and unless their elders predict that it's advantageous to help us, they won't. If they are going to come to Erathal, they will come on their own."

"Agreed," Zeidrich replied.

"Alright, so," Viviko began, looking around before continuing.

"What do we tell the king? Our orders were to lead an army against Yezurkstal's home. I know we all agree, with Dumner and the destruction of this village that an attack is not a viable option, but what will he think of us bringing the fight back home?"

Irontail thought about this question for a moment. What kind of a king would take issue with this? An attack on

Yezurkstal now would only lead to the swift loss of more life and inevitably to the conversion of more soldiers. They would be shrinking their army and growing Yezurkstal's.

It was always better to fight on the home turf, which offered well-defended positions and superior knowledge of the land. At least that is what Irontail had learned in his training. Was the king not versed in military tactics?

Once again, he must not have been paying attention, because when he returned to the conversation it seemed that he had missed a piece.

"...It's our job to explain to the king why we can't lead a successful assault. It's his job, and the senate's, to explain it to the citizens." Artimus spoke in a tone quite similar to how Goldenchest used to speak to Irontail. Maybe that's how leaders had to speak?

"I'm just saying that the citizens are not going to be happy to find out that their king has been lying to them about this entire situation," Fletching responded. "And you know who the king is going to blame for that? Us."

"We get it," Zeidrich said flatly. "But the lieutenant is right. Our priority is to make sure that we can best protect the kingdom. I thought we all agreed on this. Leading an attack would be suicide."

"I'm not suggesting we lead an attack," Fletching shouted defensively. "We need to come up with something preemptive though. What if we set up a defense outside of the city? If this Avatar is one with Evorath, then shouldn't he be able to tell us where Yezurkstal will be coming from? Instead of returning to Erathal, let us all travel to the lizock city west of Erathal an–"

"That will be enough," a booming voice from the doorway interrupted.

Everyone looked confused at the introduction of the new, powerful voice. Irontail turned towards the entrance of the hut, where the voice had originated. He almost couldn't believe it.

Standing in the doorway, his large frame eclipsing the entire opening, was the Avatar.

_=.=.=.=.=.=.=.=._

Artimus turned towards the door, instinctively grabbing for his bow and immediately releasing it. This would make planning a whole lot easier.

Standing beyond the bewildered soldiers and the disheveled mess that was once a small lamia home, was the answer to their logistical problems. They must have been doing something right, because the Avatar was here.

"Who are you?" Fletching asked, his voice raised in alarm.

"He is the Avatar," Artimus replied, stepping forward towards the holy representative of Evorath.

"I know I speak for everyone," he continued, "when I say that it is a great relief to see you here now."

The Avatar took a few steps forward first to enter the cabin. He looked to each person in turn, as if sizing them all up.

His eyes were hard, a look of stern disappointment present. Upon his person, he still wore the same simple, brown tunic. His feet were still bare, but Artimus noted that he now wore some sort of amulet about his neck, the string only just peeking out the top of his shirt's neckline.

"I am saddened that Yezurkstal has brought so much destruction. My journey these last few days has shown me that Evorath's people are terribly unprepared to deal with such a tumor. Most of Evorath's creations have strayed from their once powerful and productive nature. The barghest will soon all give in to their origins and serve the Hájje. The lizock have gone from stalwart and hardy fighters to thieves and ruffians. The satyr have strayed from their artistic and creative nature and become drunken, irresponsible fools. The centaurs have split from a strong, unified race, to a disorganized bunch of superstitious tribes. You elves have become corrupted by power and control, losing sight of the strength of an individual. And the felite have suffered a similar loss, going from a proud and productive people to a lazy bunch of fools, only willing to act when their elders command it."

Artimus could tell that no one in the room was much enjoying the Avatar's little speech. Irontail looked like he was getting angry enough to attack, and the other elvish commanders were definitely on edge, particularly Fletching. Savannah was the only other person in the room who seemed to understand what the Avatar was saying.

"It is time that you all take responsibility," the Avatar continued. "It is time to use the powers that Evorath has given you and recall the work you have put in to get to where you are.

Remember, Evorath owes you nothing, for she has already given you everything that you have. Anything that you want, you must take it. Yezurkstal is a threat to us all. I will lead your forces and together we will secure victory. Now it is time to act."

"Alright buddy. You're an inspiration to us all," Zeidrich started sarcastically. "But, can you tell us where Yezurkstal is heading next? Are you suggesting we attack him?"

"No," the Avatar replied. "An attack is not advisable. Yezurkstal will be en route to Erathal city before we have time to properly plan an attack. There is a troll encampment just outside of your kingdom. I have already met with them and planned. Our defensive forces will gather there."

"We should catch Tel' Shira," Savannah began, stepping forward and brushing Artimus on his right arm.

"The felite?" the Avatar asked in monotone. "I have already halted her. She is outside with her people."

"What are we waiting for then?" Irontail pleaded, impatience clear on his face and in his voice.

Artimus looked back at the other elves. Zeidrich was standing upright, his demeanor calm and collected. Viviko looked a little out of sorts, a hint of uncertainty stamped on his face. Fletching appeared to be annoyed, his chest protruding out and his face failing to hide anger.

"Nothing," Artimus suggested after a brief pause.

"Good," the Avatar instructed. "Let us depart."

Chapter 22

Erathal Forest, Troll Encampment
20 Neglur, 1086

The distinct thud of axes chopping trees sounded out all around the troll encampment. Every one of the elvish and felite soldiers, save the commanders, was chopping down these trees. The combined dozen centaur and trolls were helping to guide the trees and drag them back towards the center of the encampment.

Being the temporary home for only a half dozen trolls, the area was certainly not an ideal defensive position. As it stood when they had arrived late last night, there were only two shoddy huts and a few large stones forming a quasi-barrier around them. According to the Avatar, they only had until nightfall to turn this clearing into a defensible position.

Sunlight was just beginning to peak over the trees as Artimus sat atop a tree stump. He ran one of his daggers against the grain of a small stone, working to hone the edge as best he could. As he listened to the soothing sound of his blade grating against the stone, he noticed a small beetle crawling up the side of the stump towards his leg.

Without a thought, he moved to hit the bug with the flat of his blade. A large hand darted out and covered the beetle; it was the Avatar. The blade bounced harmlessly off of the Avatar's hand, and Artimus jumped up and away.

"What purpose would it serve to kill this insect?" the Avatar asked, his face void of expression.

"I hadn't thought of it," Artimus replied automatically. "I just didn't want it to crawl down into my boots or up my leg."

"Everything in nature serves a purpose. Don't kill what you do not need to kill."

The Avatar spoke as if he was speaking to a young child, and after a moment's thought, Artimus understood why. To a being with all of the wisdom of Evorath, it must have seemed like everyone else was a child.

Fletching stepped out from the nearest hut, the crooked and flimsy door creaking as he did so. He was still dressed in only a simple woolen tunic, his armor and equipment left inside. Somehow, after having a proper breakfast, it seemed that his spirits were much higher than they had been yesterday.

"If all this life is so important, why do you freely chop down these trees then?" Fletching asked as he stepped closer.

The Avatar removed his hand and turned it over, allowing the beetle to crawl atop his middle finger. Standing upright, he addressed Fletching.

"There is a difference. Killing this beetle would accomplish nothing productive. Its death would be needless. These trees are being used to preserve life. Evorath intended for you to use her resources. She does not want you to waste them."

For the first time, the Avatar seemed to have a hint of sympathy in his voice, as if he was explaining to a blind man what it was like to see. As Artimus watched the beetle crawl around the Avatar's hand and onto his palm, he thought about the potential for learning this Avatar offered.

Fletching shrugged and turned back around, walking towards the further hut where the military leaders were to meet and strategize. Irontail, Tel' Shira and Viviko had already gone inside, joining the druid who was leading this band of trolls. That just left Zeidrich and Savannah in the first hut, eating.

Artimus watched the Avatar hold the beetle up and whisper something before the insect flew away. He addressed the Avatar.

"How many trees do they need to cut down?" Artimus motioned towards the soldiers as he asked.

"Only forty-seven. I marked which ones to chop. I will explain to you and the other leaders once you have all gathered in that hut." The Avatar motioned towards the hut just as Fletching stepped inside.

"Alright," Artimus said putting his dagger in the sheath on his right and dropping the stone. "Why don't you go join the others and I will find out what is taking Zeidrich and Savannah so long?"

The Avatar nodded and turned around, walking towards the planning hut. Even his stride displayed a powerful sense of calm and control.

Without delay, Artimus turned towards the other hut and walked inside.

-=-=-=-=-=-=-=-

Savannah put her fork down on the empty plate. She was pleasantly surprised to find that these trolls had such a robust selection of foods for the morning. Upon seeing the primitive nature of this encampment, she had expected nothing of substance. Instead, with a mixture of wild berries and some poached quail eggs, she was quite satisfied.

Zeidrich sat across the table, still nibbling on some berries. He seemed to be moving at a snail's pace this morning for some reason. As Savannah opened her mouth to speak, she heard the door creek open behind her.

Pivoting around on her chair, she smiled as Artimus stepped inside. Though they had only known each other for a short time, she felt a connection with this handsome ranger. Since they had left Erathal, environmental circumstances had put a definite wedge between them, but she didn't want that to damage the courtship process.

"Artimus," she exclaimed giddily as she stood up. She wished that Zeidrich wasn't in the room.

"Have you eaten anything? All of us were wondering where you were this morning."

"I had some berries," he replied dismissively. "And I always get up early. Habit formed when I was a hunter. Are you two ready for the strategy meeting. Apparently, the Avatar already has a big plan on how we can most effectively defend this place."

"Sounds exciting," Zeidrich said pushing away from the table, his chair catching on the cheap fabric thrown down as a makeshift floor.

"Damn nomads and their temporary homes," he said standing up and kicking the chair away a few inches. "Anyways, I'll see you guys next door." He clapped Artimus on the shoulder on his way out.

Artimus made a movement towards the table, and Savannah stepped in front of him.

"Artimus," she started, fighting away the nervousness. "I really enjoyed our time together before this march and everything. I hope that once this battle is over we can continue where we left off, but..." she trailed off.

Artimus looked at her as if he knew to wait for her to continue.

"But, the reality is that we could die in this battle, either one of us, or both. If that happens, well. I guess, I just want you to know that I really don't want that to happen," she finished, and cast her glance down to her feet.

Artimus placed his hand gently on her cheek, raising her gaze up to meet his own. Placing his hand on the small of her back, he pulled her in and kissed her.

"Don't let yourself worry about that. You keep a good head on your shoulders and do what you have to do. But, do me a favor and don't let yourself get hurt. I promise that I will survive." The way Artimus spoke somehow made her believe that survival was certain, but she knew it wasn't.

"Look," Artimus continued, as if anticipating her objection. "Worrying about death will do nothing but put you in a bad mindset. When the time comes, you need to keep a clear head and focus on the battle. A few days from now, we are going to be sitting in our favorite tree and looking out at the stars."

Savannah held Artimus's gaze for a few seconds, wishing that time would freeze so that she could stay in this moment longer. She leaned in and initiated another kiss, holding this one for a few extra seconds and wrapping her arms tightly around him.

Why did they have to meet during such a horrible time?

-=-=-=-=-=-=-=-

Artimus held onto the kiss, craving to keep this moment for a while longer. He wished that they could have met at a better time. Regardless, he intended to continue his courtship of this beautiful woman. Never before had he been this interested in another being. When this was all over, he would finally have something more meaningful in his life than just solving mysteries.

"We should go join the others," he whispered as they broke their embrace, their lips still only centimeters apart. "I think some of them already suspect something between us."

"Good," Savannah beamed. "I think everyone should know that you are not available for intimate encounters."

Artimus took a couple of steps back and cradled Savannah's hands. He brought them up and pulled them against his chest.

"My heart only belongs to you," he said soothingly. "Right now though, my skills are needed elsewhere."

Savannah sighed and let go of his hands, pulling away and shaking her head.

"I know," she replied with her eyes downcast. "I suppose we should get going."

She let a faint grin remain on her face, and Artimus took that as an invitation. Taking an exaggerated step backwards he bowed down and signaled for the door.

"After you, my lady," he exclaimed in an overstated tone.

Savannah let out a faint giggle and stepped in front of him, walking towards the exit. He stood upright, running in front of her and opening the door. With a wide grin, he held the door and allowed her to walk outside in front of him. Once she cleared the doorway he followed behind with haste.

"So, did you make any headway with Casandra?" Artimus asked as they walked towards the other hut.

"Actually I did," Savannah smiled. "She was training as a geomancer, learning to control all four elements of Evorath. If she were more experienced, she would probably be a greater asset in this upcoming battle than myself."

"Do you think she can help anyways?" Artimus asked. "Having some extra magic never hurts."

"I think that should be left up to her and the Avatar. I believe she wants to fight." Savannah sounded somewhat upset by this idea, but there was no time to have her elaborate, for they had arrived at the other hut.

"Ladies first," Artimus insisted, pulling open the door and signaling for Savannah to enter.

Savannah gave him one final smile before entering the hut. Like before, Artimus followed behind.

Not far from his expectations, this hut was much more open than the other one. In fact, there was no furniture within this structure and the only decoration was a bearskin rug upon the floor.

Artimus took an inventory of the room.

Going from left to right was: Zeidrich, Viviko, Fletching, Irontail, Tel' Shira, a troll, and the Avatar. Savannah took her place by Zeidrich and Artimus proceeded to stand next to the Avatar. Within their circle, Artimus noted that someone had gathered a pile of rocks and sticks.

"About time," Fletching muttered as Artimus stepped into place.

"It is time indeed," the Avatar said, the sarcasm seemingly lost on Evorath's servant. Artimus noticed both Zeidrich and Viviko fighting off a grin.

"Though most of you know one another, let us introduce ourselves. Tell us what you offer to this battle," the Avatar instructed, motioning towards Savannah.

"I am Savannah and I'm a druid," Savannah stated.

"I am Zeidrich, Captain of the Elvish Infantry."

"I am Viviko, Commander of the Elvish Spearmen."

"I am Fletching, General of the Elvish Archers." He spoke with a hint of sarcasm.

"I am Ugron, Chieftain of Troll Nomads," the troll's voice was deep and unassuming.

Artimus looked Ugron over as Irontail and Tel' Shira introduced themselves. Like most of his kind, he was tall, at least a dozen centimeters taller than Irontail. His body was muscular, but not overly so, suggesting that he was probably of the druid class. With dark gray, blemished skin and well-worn hands, he certainly looked threatening.

For clothes, he wore a simple sash across his right shoulder, which attached to a medium sized skirt reaching down to his knees. His attire was held together by a simple hemp rope, and on the rope hung a variety of charms: some wolf teeth, bird talons, a dead squirrel, and some other unidentified items. Around his neck he wore an amulet with the same string material as the Avatar. Ugron's amulet was exposed though, showing it to be an almost perfectly circular piece of tin with a green opal fixed upon the center.

Artimus heard Tel' Shira finish her introduction and returned his attention to the meeting.

"And I am the Avatar of Evorath. All of her strength manifested in physical form," the Avatar said in his signature monotone.

"And what should we call you? What is your name?" Fletching asked.

Why did he insist on being so uncooperative? Was everyone this critical at his age?

"I have no name. I merely am," the Avatar replied without hesitation.

"Okay, no-name. What is the plan?" Fletching asked shaking his head.

"Allow me to show you."

Upon finishing his reply, the Avatar opened his palms above the center of their circle and looked down. With some unseen force, he willed the sticks and stones to move about, some of them morphing into different shapes as they rearranged in the center of the room.

Artimus watched in awe as they all connected like a puzzle, the sticks piling atop one another and forming a wall around the stones. The Avatar was somehow using his control of nature to manipulate these objects to form a sort of model for what they would need to build. It was genius, something that he hoped was teachable. This type of magic could prove invaluable in future military confrontations.

Artimus allowed his eyes to wander up and observe the others gathered in the room, who were all watching just as intently. From the looks of it, no one in the room had seen anything like this before.

As he returned his eyes to the spectacle, he watched as the Avatar manipulated the twigs. It formed into a solid wall, with two distinct towers on both the left and right. He was making a tiny fort fit for ants.

In the center, he placed the stones in a pattern, three laid out evenly in one row closest to the front of the wall, two in the middle row, and then three more in the back. Finally, he placed one stone on either side outside of the wall. Artimus was no battle strategist, but he already felt he knew what the Avatar had in mind. Finally, to finish off the battle plan, the Avatar positioned two larger sticks outside the front of the wall before returning his hands to his side.

"This is a model of the defensive structure we are to construct," the Avatar offered humbly.

"Knowing your abilities as I do, this is how you shall be laid out. If you are confused, please stop me," the Avatar continued, and began by pointing to the two sticks in front of the way.

"These represent trees. We will have the felite warriors posted in the tree. On either side of the field, there will be one archer, one spear wielder, and two of your light warriors. Tel' Shira, that means you will be on one of these trees.

"The wall will be constructed of wood from the trees that are being cut down now, so the stability is not something we should count on. Still, the wall will have the twenty elvish archers stationed on top, as well as Artimus and Fletching. Additionally, we will place the two felite druids and Savannah up there. The druids' jobs are to support the wall as best they can and to heal any injuries that the archers suffer. The wall will inevitably be breached.

"Once the enemy breaches the wall, they will be met immediately by the dozen elvish spearman, as well as Viviko. Now, going outside of the wall, we have three trolls hidden behind either rock. Once the enemy is to the wall, these trolls come out from hiding and flank the enemy from the side. At this point, the felite warriors and spearman in the tree also come down and flank from behind. The archers remain in their high ground to continue their attack from above.

"The next layer of defense will be the sixteen elvish warriors, the two centaur warriors, the two heavily armed felite warriors, Irontail, and Zeidrich. For magical support, both the centaur druid and Ugron will also be at this level, ready to fight or to heal as necessary. Behind the three boulders at the rear, the three centaur archers will be ready to pick off any enemy that is threatening the integrity of our forces.

"Finally, I will be waiting for Yezurkstal to show himself. In the meantime, I will remain hidden from the enemy; if Yezurkstal figures out who I am, he will not show himself. He may be arrogant, but he is not stupid. This is how it must be."

There was silence for a good thirty seconds when the Avatar finished talking. Everyone was just staring blankly at the model that had been built, absorbing the battle plan. It made sense, at least from Artimus's prospective, but he was interested to hear if any of the military leaders had any input.

"What about Casandra?" Savannah asked after a long silence. "Where is she going to be during all of this?"

The Avatar looked to Savannah and squinted.

"This model does not account for this or the other hut. Casandra will be in one of these huts, hiding from the danger of battle. No harm shall come this far."

Artimus was quite sure this was the first time he heard the Avatar have an inflection on his voice tone; he sounded like a concerned father.

"I got to hand it to you no-name," Zeidrich said sincerely. "This is a sound strategy. Do we have any idea how many troops he has though? Last time he had winged demons. Are those accounted for?"

"My sight is limited to the world of Evorath," the Avatar began.

"I can predict that by the time he arrives either late tonight or early tomorrow, he will have upwards of a dozen mutated barghest and close to a dozen powerful lamia. He will also have half a dozen lizock, and the two hájje commanders that were taken from Artimus. Furthermore, he has, at this point in time, summoned another dozen demons from the ether. None of them have wings, but this does not mean that he will not decide to summon some winged attackers before he arrives. Remember, nature is on your side. I have an advanced scout network of birds that will report Yezurkstal's movements. We will be well-prepared when he arrives."

Artimus looked around at the other leaders. From a pure numbers stand-point, especially considering their defensive advantage, there was no way that they would lose. Despite this, no one else seemed to be in very high spirits.

"How do we ensure that he will come to our encampment and not just avoid us and head straight for Erathal?" Fletching asked.

"Every time he has traveled to Erathal, he has passed straight through this encampment. He will not go another way. Once he sees our walls, he will want to destroy us." The Avatar's answer came with a smug sense of certainty, as if there was no way he could be wrong.

"Makes sense, it does," Tel' Shira said, putting in her own two-cents.

"I agree," Irontail seconded, his tone suggesting otherwise. Artimus suspected that Irontail was still not comfortable being responsible as a decision maker. He probably felt he needed to say something to validate his position.

"Let us work then," Ugron said after a few a seconds of dead air.

Artimus locked eyes with Savannah and she nodded. Knowing that she would be nearby when the battle commenced gave him a sense of certainty. Yezurkstal's legacy would end before it began.

Chapter 23

Erathal Forest, Troll Encampment
20 Neglur, 1086

The moon was at its waning gibbous stage, still glowing brightly in the night sky. Tel' Shira stood perched in the lower branch of an oak, looking out through the tree line for any sign of the enemy. Next to her, another female warrior stood at the ready, and about a meter above both the archer and druid were perched. They were just high enough that no one on the ground would notice them in the moonlight.

The Avatar had already told them to stay on guard, for one of his bird scouts had reported Yezurkstal to be on his way. Last time she had been preparing for a battle against Yezurkstal, Tel' Shira was anxious due to unfamiliarity. This time, she knew exactly what to expect.

Fueled with the desire for revenge, she would make sure that every last one of Yezurkstal's minions was destroyed. The Avatar had been clear in telling no one to engage Yezurkstal directly and based on her last attempt to attack him she was willing to accept that recommendation. Yes, she wanted to kill him herself, but she knew this was futile.

Settling for the second best thing would work: kill every last one of his minions. From the initial scouting report, he had even more demons than expected, as well as almost a dozen possessed centaurs. All Tel' Shira had to do was to wait for the army to get underneath her tree and she would pounce.

With her night vision, she noticed some rustling of the trees off in the distance. Any other invading army would have been carrying torches to move at night, but the Avatar had already warned them that there would be no tell-tale signs of their approach. He claimed they would move quickly and quietly.

Focusing on the movement, she confirmed that this was the case. She still could not hear anything aside from the crickets, but she definitely saw the enemy. Focusing her vision, she could see two elvish figures -presumably the cadets that Artimus had told them about- marching at the lead.

As they marched forward, she tried to get a better count of everyone. She saw the lizock, the centaur, the lamia and the demons, but she could not see any barghest marching in the army. The rest of the troops seemed to count out about right, leaving around fifty enemies if her computation was correct.

Where had the barghest gone?

She scanned the surrounding area, hoping to catch a glimpse of them. She saw nothing.

The entire approaching army came to a halt. What were they doing?

Turning around, Tel' Shira looked to Fletching for some guidance. Aiming her index finger towards her eyes, then towards the approaching army and then holding up her right fist, she signaled that the army had stopped its approach.

Fletching may not have had as good of night vision as a felite, but he nodded his head in recognition. Tel' Shira watched him closely as he turned away and down towards the Avatar.

After a few seconds, Fletching turned back towards Tel' Shira and signaled for her to keep her eyes open. Did he have nothing else to report?

Turning back around, Tel' Shira locked her eyes in again on the enemy army. They were standing still about twenty to thirty meters out.

A familiar tingling came down Tel' Shira's spine and she looked around in confusion, searching for where this warning was coming from. Why did she feel like she was in danger?

The answer came in the form of an audible shriek from behind her. Tel' Shira spun around to respond. A demon, very similar in size and stature to the twins she had fought back in Dumner soared towards the elvish archers atop the wooden wall.

Her initial inclination was to abandon her perch and rush to attack, but she knew that this would only compromise their battle plan. She had to stick to formation.

Then, the answer to the missing barghest became clear. While the demon descended upon the elvish archers, the barghest came charging in from the north, a dozen of them making their way towards the rock where only three trolls stood guard. These weren't normal barghest either; they were much larger than average and charged with abandon.

If she didn't have her troops help, the trolls would be slaughtered.

-=.=.=.=.=.=.=.-

328

Artimus was amazed at how quickly they had been able to construct this makeshift wall. It was certainly not a wall fit for a fortress, but it would give them a distinct advantage against the enemy. With their forces on the high ground, they would easily be able to eliminate some of the opponent before their ground troops even had to be put in danger.

Fully armed and armored, he kept his eyes trained to the east, where the enemy would be coming from. The wall was sturdy, stretching around in a complete rectangle with towers on both the northeast and southeast corners. Artimus was stationed in the center, his bow drawn with an arrow notched and ready to pull back and let loose.

Ahead in the northeast tree, he saw Tel' Shira signaling something to Fletching. It looked like she saw the enemy halt up ahead. Tightening his grip on the bow, he raised his left arm in anticipation. From his peripherals, he saw Fletching signal for Tel' Shira to keep her eyes trained ahead. What was going on?

The answer to his question was not what he had hoped for.

Artimus turned his gaze upwards as an ear-splitting shriek echoed through the sky. He pulled his arrow back in the bowstring, ready to fire. A large demon was heading straight for them.

This one was different from the one in Dumner, its skin a dark crimson and its eyes a fiery red. The wings on its back resembled those of a dragon, and it lacked the tail of the other winged demons from before. Overall, its body shape was much more similar to that of a troll, but its arms ended in razor sharp claws similar to those of a barghest.

Even with his skills, there was no way Artimus could aim for anything vital. As the demon closed the gap Artimus fired his arrow into the beast's left wing. Before the arrow even struck its mark, he pulled out another and fired again towards the right wing.

By this time, the other archers were firing. A hail of arrows flew up towards the demon and impaled it in various parts of its body. It was not very effective. The demon continued its flight down, ignoring the arrows that stuck in its wings or the few that actually managed to penetrate its thick hide. If they didn't act appropriately, Artimus and his men would find that this gambit could completely remove their number advantage.

Fletching yelled from the northeast tower for everyone to move to the sides. The demon was heading straight towards the center of the wall, as if to break through it. He might be able to too.

Savannah was to Artimus's right, more towards the southeastern tower than the northern one. Without putting any thought into it, he slung his bow over his back and sprinted away, keeping his left eye trained on the demon. Savannah looked unsure of herself.

The demon opened his mouth, and Artimus cursed; that was his opportunity to hit a vulnerable spot. With that thought, he could feel the heat of the demon's breath as a large sphere of fire shot from its mouth and flew towards the wall. The other archers were all running for one side or another of the wall, but Savannah was locked in place.

Throwing his arms around her, he continued his momentum forward, and as the fireball impacted the wall he dove forward, spinning around in the air to keep Savannah from hitting the ground with a hard thud, he struck the wall just next to the southeast tower, Savannah landing on top of him and causing his back to flare up.

He felt the intense heat of the flames, his feet feeling like they might catch fire. Looking back into the makeshift tower, he saw one of the felite druids reach her hand out. She was standing on the ladder, which lead back down to the forest floor.

With a look at Savannah, he knew she understood what needed to be done. She reached over him and accepted the felite's grasp, pushing up and entering the tower. Once she cleared him, Artimus pushed himself up and came to his feet.

The demon came crashing down after its fireball, tearing through the now burning wall. Smoldering splinters flew in every direction, and Artimus watched two of his archers on the northern side of the barricade fall with the collapsing wall. Artimus's own footing was compromised as the wood splintered and cracked before him, causing him to lose balance and slip forward. He couldn't stop his fall.

Just as his right foot slipped and he stumbled, something darted from behind and grabbed him. A thick vine wrapped around his waist and tightened, holding him in place. Turning his neck to see what had saved him, he saw Savannah, her hand extended to control the vine.

In spite of the madness of the situation, she gave him a smile and pulled back on the vine, bringing him away from the edge and onto more solid ground. She then let the vine go slack, and it pulled back and ran down the tower.

"We're even now," she said with a wink.

"Never," Artimus responded as he turned back towards the demon. "Get down to the ground and be prepared for anything. I will join you after I am sure this demon is dead."

Savannah was obviously reluctant to obey, but with only a moment's hesitation she did.

Artimus kept his weight back but crept forward to look down at the demon. As he had hoped, Viviko and his men wasted no time. Not giving the demon a chance to stand back up and recover, they were stabbing him repeatedly with their spears. Through the flames and shattered wood, Artimus watched as the demon ceased struggling and fell down- dead.

Unfortunately, this was just the beginning.

-=-=-=-=-=-=-=-

Irontail waited patiently, grasping his club in anticipation. This battle would go differently than the last. He would slay whatever enemies he could and the Avatar would fight with Yezurkstal. They would put an end to this Hájje.

Just as this thought passed through his head, a loud shriek came from above and he watched as a demon descended upon their wall. The winged hell-spawn shot a great ball of fire out of its mouth, setting the wall ablaze. Following behind, the demon crashed through the wall and caused the entire center to collapse.

Irontail fought the urge to run forward and attack the demon himself. It was not time for him to move yet. The elvish spearmen did their part, thrusting their spears forward and slaying the great winged demon before it could rise back up and cause any more trouble.

Stupid beast.

The battle was just getting underway though. Irontail could hear howling and screams of pain coming from the northeastern tower. "Everyone hold your ground," Zeidrich commanded, taking a step forward and drawing his sword.

The Avatar walked forward as well, stepping past Zeidrich and all of the other warriors. He approached the flaming ruins of the wall and held his hand out, palms open. Water shot from his open palms, and Irontail could see a wind picking up around the flames, blowing them all inwards.

As the flames died, Irontail caught sight of oversized barghest and the rest of the charging army. Lamia, lizock, centaur and more demons like the ones from Dumner; they all charged forward towards the elvish spearmen.

There was nothing before this moment, and nothing after. All that mattered was the here and the now.

The battle had begun.

.=.=.=.=.=.=.=.

Tel' Shira couldn't wait any longer.

The demon had crashed into the wall, utterly destroying the first line of defense. With a quick glance back at the stand-still enemy army, she found that they were nowhere in sight. With a rushed survey of the area, she finally caught sight of them. They were charging forward, weaving through the trees and running straight towards the opening in the wall.

Meanwhile, the outmatched trio of trolls was engaging the dozen barghest who charged from the north. Even with their extraordinary regenerative abilities, they would be no match, especially considering that they were outnumbered four to one. She had to make a choice.

"Pounce on my mark, we shall," Tel' Shira instructed the other warrior in her tree. "Start firing, on my mark you will," she whispered above to the archer.

Looking over at the southern tree, she locked eyes with the lead warrior and slapped the top of her wrist twice before pointing down. The other felite nodded. Holding up her last three fingers, she looked down and waited.

The two hájje had fallen back in the ranks, letting the centaurs take the lead in the charge. Directly behind them, the lamia slithered and the lizock ran. The two hájje commanders charged just in front of the demons. Tel' Shira and her troops would go for the most vulnerable attackers, the lizock and the lamia.

As the centaur neared, she dropped her first finger. They drew closer, just a few meters away; she dropped her second finger. The centaur cleared the path, leaving the lizock directly below; she dropped her final finger.

Without hesitation, she reached down and unsheathed both of her daggers, releasing her hold and letting herself go into a free-fall. An arrow whizzed past her head and impacted one of the lizock in the shoulder, causing him to falter. That was her target.

Spinning around in midair, Tel' Shira flipped over and landed blades first on top of this lizock. This first lizock fell without a struggle. Extending her daggers behind her body she felt them dig into the scales of another lizock. A lamia honed in on her, swinging its flail overhead towards Tel' Shira's exposed torso.

Letting go of her blades, she dropped down underneath the attack and dug her hands into the ground behind her head. With all of the force she could muster, she kicked back up into the lamia's chest. The enemy reeled back, her flail falling from her grasp as she struggled to hold her ground. This gave Tel' Shira just enough time to spin around and retrieve her daggers from the second dead lizock.

"Trolls!" she shouted with all of her breath.

Without waiting to know if her comrades would follow, she took off to join the melee between the trolls and barghest. Sprinting to the right of the centaur, she honed in on the nearest barghest berserker. They had already engaged the trolls and the outcome did not look promising.

As she sprinted to join the fray, she watched one of the trolls swing his axe down upon a barghest. The large, stone head cut into the barghest's shoulder and through to its chest. As soon as the attack fell, another barghest tackled the troll, ripping into its side with his immense claws. Landing on top of the troll, the barghest bit down into his victim's neck, tearing out his throat in one swift motion. This was Tel' Shira's first target.

Keeping up her top speed, Tel' Shira waited until the last possible second, just as the barghest was rising from the slain troll, and dove. Her momentum afforded her enough force to knock the enemy back to the ground, her daggers digging deep into his chest and skull. She felt a tingling sensation as she landed, and turning her neck, noticed two other barghest converging on her position.

The one over her left shoulder was closer, so without hesitation, she turned towards it and threw both of her daggers. The blades cut through the air and impacted the enemy in the stomach, staining its black fur with crimson red blood. In a fluid movement, she allowed the momentum from her throwing motion to carry her off of the fallen barghest and towards the next foe, running to intercept him.

Out of the corner of her left eye, she watched a troll gutted by another of the barghest. Ignoring the gruesome sight, she continued forward and lunged into the already injured enemy. This time, her momentum was not enough to take her foe down. The wind was knocked out of her as he grasped onto her daggers, which were embedded into the foes stomach, and went falling towards the ground.

As she fell, she yanked the blades out of her enemy and grabbed onto his side, digging her claws into his thick fur. With no time to spare, she tightened every muscle in her body and yanked herself forward, throwing her body around and causing him to land face first on the forest floor.

Continuing the motion, she flung over top and landed on her feet. Without delay, she reached under the fallen barghest's body and yanked out the daggers, stabbing them once more into the creature's back for good measure. Removing the blades from the barghest's back, she turned to face the next enemy, who was only meters away. As she dropped into a defensive stance, her knees bent and daggers held outwards in front of her, she finally saw some sign of relief.

A barrage of arrows impacted this next barghest, slowing his approach and bringing him to an almost complete halt. Out of her peripherals, Tel' Shira looked and saw the elvish archers coming down from the tower, firing their arrows towards the oncoming barghest assault. In a robotic fashion, she continued to move, running towards the almost dead opponent and slashing his throat with her left dagger.

Blood spurted out of his jugular, staining her pristine fur as she repositioned herself against the rest of the barghest. There were still eight remaining. Locking in on the nearest one, she caught sight of the final troll, who wielded a large club. His efforts were noble, as he swung his club and smashed in the skull of the nearest barghest. Unfortunately, he didn't survive past that. Two more enemies tore into either side and ripped him apart, leaving his right arm to fall to the ground as he died.

With all of the trolls on this side defeated, her objective was now to ensure that the seven remaining barghest did not eliminate the elvish archers who had survived the collapse of the

337

wall. Her muscles tired and breath rapid, she focused in on the next target and charged.

-=-.=-.=-.=-.=-.=-.=-.

With a quick survey of the field, Artimus had to decide: He could stay on this small semblance of a wall and snipe enemies as they breached the perimeter, or he could climb down the ladder and help with the ground defense. From his vantage point, he could see the enemy army nearing, the possessed centaur galloping towards the breech in their wall. A handful of lizock and lamia ran behind them, each equipped with their own unique weapons. He decided.

"Savannah!" he yelled at the top of his lungs, "I need a fast way down."

Without waiting for her help, he drew his bow and notched an arrow, aiming for the head of the nearest centaur. Tracing him along his rapid approach, Artimus let his first arrow fly, and drew another. As expected, his shot landed square between the centaur's eyes, ending the enemy's life. The opposing centaur collapsed, stumbling over his own feet and falling down on the forest floor with a thud.

As the centaur landed, Artimus had already prepared another arrow, aiming for the next closest centaur and letting the projectile fly. Unfortunately, even with his champion accuracy, this arrow missed the head this time, landing square in the centaur's right shoulder.

Artimus notched another arrow and aimed for the same centaur, once again pulling for the kill shot. With a quick release, he watched as the arrows impacted the enemy in the right eye: a definite execution.

As he went to grab another arrow, Savannah's voice rang out from the tower.

"Artimus!"

Turning towards her, he signaled towards the edge of the tower.

"Send those vines of yours down the side. I need to get to the ground level."

Savannah threw her right hand forward and propelled a vine from the tower. The vine ran down the front of the remaining wall, leading all the way to the ground. Artimus grabbed a hold of the vine, the thick makeshift rope burning his hands as he thrust off of the wall and slid down the side.

As he neared the ground, he tightened his grip to slow his decent, the makeshift rope digging even more into his hand. About a meter from landing, he let go and pulled out his bow again, preparing another arrow to attack. A lizock was right before him, its sword held overhead to strike him down. Before the stroke could be made, Artimus let his arrow fly, impaling the lizock in the forehead.

Throwing his bow back over his shoulder, he drew his mythril blade and charged towards the next attacker. The next enemy was a lamia, armed with a flagged mace and a vicious demeanor.

This deranged lamia had scarlet red scales with a midnight black patterning, a dangerous contrast against her bumble bee yellow eyes. Her mace was of a greenish hue, suggesting that it was made from the adamantium that Yezurkstal had in his cavern home. If he was going to defeat this enemy, he would have to avoid her weapon.

Ducking underneath the initial attack from the mace, he swung his blade around in an arch and sliced into the lamia's arm, loosening her grasp on the powerful weapon. She somehow held onto the weapon, pulling it back and attempting to swing downward towards Artimus.

Darting to the side, Artimus brought his blade around again, this time swinging over his enemy's downward thrust. As the mace came down towards empty air, his mythril bit through skin and bone, severing the lamia's arms. Not wanting to delay victory, Artimus redirected his blade and continued forward, decapitating the enemy with a single stroke.

As the blood flowed out from the fallen foe, Artimus could not help but cringe a little. At one time, this lamia had been an innocent person; she acted only because she was controlled by Yezurkstal. Pulling his sword back and preparing to engage a nearby enemy centaur, Artimus could only think of how much he hated Yezurkstal.

The centaur that approached, had beige fur and wore only a ceremonial necklace made with both feathers and animal teeth. From the looks of it, he had been a pretty high ranking member of his tribe, because the feathers definitely came from a roc and, though he could not be certain, Artimus was pretty sure that some of the teeth came from a lynx. For a weapon, the centaur wielded a large, obsidian axe.

Running to meet this centaur head on, Artimus did a quick scan of his surroundings. Straight ahead, there was a handful of centaur and more than a dozen demons. Just to his right, he saw some more lizock and lamia, all engaging with the archers who had evacuated from the southeast tower. Savannah was fighting as well, giving Artimus a feeling of pride as he watched her hurl a large stone into one of the lamia's chest. The left side of the field was where his interest really laid.

To his left, he saw about half a dozen barghest tearing through the northern elvish archer squad. Tel' Shira and two other felite warriors, with the help of Fletching and his few remaining men, were trying to fend off the deadly dogs. Artimus needed to get over there.

As the older centaur swung down with his oversized axe, Artimus spun around and sliced into his enemy's front leg, causing him to falter and stumble forward thanks to his missed attack.

"Dammit!" cursed Artimus as he dove down and narrowly avoided the open claw of a nearby demon. In his desire to observe the entire field, he had not realized how close this enemy was. As he felt the cold dirt on his hands, he pushed himself back up and thrust the sword forward, tucking his chin and praying that he was not hit.

His move paid off, the demon's next attack breezing over his hair as his sword plunged deep into the creature's gut. Removing the blade, he swung it around overhead and decapitated this enemy. Not wanting to find himself unprepared again, he turned back towards the centaur.

Fortunately, his allies had taken the initiative, for as he caught sight of the creature it was already dead, three arrows planted firmly in his side. With a quick scan of his immediate surroundings, Artimus was confident that he could join the fray to the north. Sheathing his sword, he started to run only to be stopped mid-stride by an invisible force.

He felt the air leave his lungs as he doubled over in pain, falling to one knee. The ground beneath him was already stained with blood, and his ribs pounded with pain, probably broken from the impact. This could only be one person.

Raising his chin up, his fears were confirmed.

Yezurkstal stood over him with a sinister grin, his hands hanging loosely by his side as if mocking Artimus. Before Artimus could recover, the evil lord grabbed him by the throat and lifted him up in the air. Grasping onto Yezurkstal's wrists and trying to pull away, Artimus closed his eyes.

I'm sorry Savannah.

-=-.=-.=-.=-.=-.=-.=-

Irontail crashed through the nearest enemy centaur, his club striking his foe with such force that it left the enemy crumbled and dead. With adrenaline driving him, Irontail completely zoned in on his next target, tunnel vision taking over as he propelled himself forward and swung his club once again, this time collapsing the skull of one of the enemy lamia.

His heart pounded with fury and rage as he continued forward, coming up on a demon. This demon was large, at least half a meter taller and considerably broader than Irontail. His dark skin looked to be thick enough to stop even the strongest of blades. Good thing Irontail didn't rely on blades.

Charging towards the unarmed brute, Irontail swung his club again, this time hitting the foe square in the chest. Unfortunately, this demon was not as fragile as the centaur or lamia. As the club struck against his muscular chest, the hellspawn wrapped his arms around it and pulled backwards.

Even with his adrenaline pumping, Irontail had his wits about him and released, causing the enemy to reel backwards. Taking advantage of the demon's vulnerable position, Irontail continued forward and lifted himself up on his hind legs. With all of his weight, he kicked forward, his hooves smashing into the demon's leg with enough force to splinter a hickory tree.

A loud snap resounded as the demon's leg bent backwards in an unnatural fashion. Letting out a howl of pain, the demon fell to one knee. Irontail grabbed a hold of the demon's head and twisted it. Another snap sounded out as the demon fell dead at Irontail's hooves.

Allowing his vision to open up, Irontail looked for the next victim, but was taken by surprise as both of his arms were grabbed by a pair of lamia. Looking to either side, he watched as the scarlet haired demons held onto his arms and pulled them apart wide. Looking back in front, he found that they were setting him up for the kill. A smaller demon strode confidently forward, a long, thin blade held in its left hand.

Irontail grinded his teeth and let out a war cry. His entire body tensed up and his shoulders bulged. He felt like magical energy flowed through his body, and with a powerful jerking motion threw both of his arms forward.

The lamia were caught completely off guard, being tossed like rag dolls to sandwich the demon. Grabbing a firm hold of both of these lamia's wrists, he continued to yank them back towards his body and throw them on top of one another on the ground. They landed with a thud, and Irontail hopped forward to grab the dazed demon.

Without a thought, he took hold of the demon's wrist and wrenched it around, stabbing the creature with its own shiv. Letting go of the creature's wrist, Irontail brought his elbow around and slammed the demon in its face. He felt the warm blood on his arm as he withdrew his attack and continued pummeling the enemy.

As he finally brought himself up from the mutilated enemy, Irontail looked ahead and stopped straight in his tracks. Standing less than five meters ahead, Yezurkstal held Artimus up by the throat, smiling a sinister grin as he drew the ranger closer for the kill.

-=-=-=-=-=-=-=-

Tel' Shira landed hard on her back, breaking her fall and springing over backwards to avoid the large claw of a barghest. Anticipating the enemy's next attack, she continued her retreat, performing three consecutive reverse handsprings to get out of reach. Fighting these possessed dogs was much more challenging than one of their normal brethren.

As the barghest considered her, Tel' Shira dropped into a low stance, her right hand cocked behind her head and left held loosely in front of her face, her knees bent and spread about twice shoulder width apart. She waited, keeping her eyes wide to make sure no other opponent would try to take her off guard. After what seemed an eternity, she felt a faint tingle in her spine. The barghest leapt forward.

With all of the strength she could muster, Tel' Shira pushed herself off the ground and grabbed hold of the enemy in midair. While the barghest continued forward, she pulled herself in and removed one of her daggers, plunging it into the beast's spine. She held on as the momentum from his charge kept him going forward, and just as he was about to hit the ground she removed her blade and jumped off, flipping in midair and pulling out her other dagger.

Observing the field, she noticed one of the barghest rip the arms off of an elvish archer and continue towards Fletching. The older archer prepared another arrow and let it fly, hitting the charging opponent in the shoulder. That wouldn't stop it.

Running forward, Tel' Shira went to intercept the attack, but she was too late. Just as she planted her daggers into the beast's side, its own claws landed in Fletching's stomach. Yanking her blades out, Tel' Shira continued with the kill, slitting the beast's throat. Unfortunately, as the barghest stumbled backwards, Fletching's stomach came with him.

As his blood spilled out on the ground, he looked at Tel' Shira, his face turning pale with shock. Tel' Shira looked away as he landed with a thud. Turning around, she found the next sight was even more jarring.

Her body felt hot with rage as she watched Yezurkstal appear, grabbing Artimus by the throat and holding him up in the air. Every one of her bones seemed to vibrate with anger as she prepared to charge.

-=.=.=.=.=.=.=.=-

Savannah was completely out of her element. She was a druid, not a warrior. Though her training had included some aspects of fighting, she had only once ever had to use that training. Magic was a tricky tool, and using it for gardening, basic object manipulation, and healing was one thing; but to cause harm to someone was an entirely different matter.

By her nature, Savannah did not like causing anyone else harm. Even if they were there to hurt her, she much preferred to avoid a confrontation. Despite this, she was no pushover: this was a fight that had to be fought.

Still, as she used her magic to hurl a rock into one of the attacking lamia, she felt guilty. At one point, this lamia was probably a peaceful person. If not for Yezurkstal's control over her, she would be no threat at all.

Focusing more magical energy, Savannah targeted one of the nearby demons. As the demon ripped one of the archer's throat out, she honed in on a willow tree that stood behind him. Though unsure of how long she could sustain it, there was only one way that she could really help with this battle.

The life energy from the tree flowed into her, and she poured her own life into the tree. An invisible bond was formed as the demon turned its attention on her. She could feel the energy growing within her, the latent magic in the tree bonding with her mind.

With a crazed expression, the demon charged. The tree sprang to life, swinging its nearest branch down and intercepting the demon. As the demon reeled away, the tree continued to move, uprooting itself and shaking mounds of dirt off of its body.

The demon let out a great roar as the tree continued its attack, bringing an even larger branch down and smashing the demon across the face.

Savannah could feel her magic draining, the energy required to animate this tree too much for her body to handle. Was this really all she could do? Kill one lamia and one demon and her energy was drained?

No.

Magic was an unlimited force. All she had to do was tap into Evorath's abundance and she could sustain this as long as she needed to. It was an epiphany moment for her, a new and original thought hitting her like a ton of bricks.

If magic was drawn from one's environment, what stopped her from channeling it from multiple sources? The only limitation that a druid, or any other magical user had, was those they put on themselves. Could it be that simple?

Keeping her main focus on the tree, she thought about all of the trees in the forest, of the animals and even the fallen friends and foes. They all had magic within them. She allowed herself to reach out to all of them, a wellspring of energy building up inside of her.

As she stood in the middle of the fray, she gathered up a green energy, her mind focusing more than she ever thought possible. The world around her looked clearer; every one of her senses becoming amplified. She could hear footsteps as they hit the ground, the blades of grass crumpling underneath heavy armor and demon skin. The smell of sweat, fire, and blood flooded her nose. Every detail looked sharper and more defined.

With her newfound energy, Savannah commanded the tree, using it to smash through two more demons, crushing both of them beneath weighted branches. It was an unexpected thrill to be able to wield such power. She only wished that Yezurkstal would show up.

Commanding her creation forward, she got her wish. Standing a good ten meters away from her position, Yezurkstal stood triumphantly with Artimus held up by the throat. In that moment, it was as if all of her energy was drained.

There were only two options: he would kill Artimus or he would infect him with his magic and make him another pawn. She was powerless.

The intense fear of helplessness overtook her, and all of her newfound energy dissipated, the energy field around her fading. Without anyone to guide it, the willow took one final step, stretching its roots out without direction and stopping in place. Having no ground to hold itself up in, it tumbled over, crushing a handful of demons as well as one of the trolls.

Savannah fell to her knees, praying to Evorath for some salvation. She felt tears welling up in her eyes, her hair falling over her face to obscure her vision.

Then it happened: an unexpected party intervened.

Whatever Yezurkstal was saying to Artimus was cut short as a stream of fire struck the harbinger of death in his back. He released Artimus, the brave ranger falling to the ground helplessly. He was weakened, but still alive.

Savannah didn't even realize it, but she was running towards him, ignoring the melee that unfolded around her and heading straight for the one person she actually cared about.

Yezurkstal finished squelching the fire that had set his dark cloak ablaze and turned away towards the newcomer. It was Casandra.

Savannah's senses kicked in and she realized that she had to be cognizant of the battle around her. As she narrowly stumbled past a lizock corpse, she kept her eyes trained on Casandra and Yezurkstal. Now only a few meters away, she could hear Yezurkstal's scathing voice.

"What would cause you more pain I wonder? Should I kill you slowly, or leave you alive to watch everyone else die? Or maybe I should do both."

Without warning, Yezurkstal flung his hand forward, a bolt of dark energy flying forth towards Casandra.

Savannah arrived at Artimus's side, who had just pulled himself into a sitting position, coughing from the trauma to his throat. Grabbing hold of his armor, she pulled him away and watched the bolt cut through the air.

Just in the nick of time, the Avatar ran into sight, arriving as the energy struck. The dark magic coated his body, looking like it would take over for a moment before being overwhelmed by a field of green. In a flash of light, the dark energy dissipated and Yezurkstal stepped back, shielding his eyes.

While Savannah fed some healing energy into Artimus's throat and ribs, she stared and listened.

"And who, exactly, are you?" Yezurkstal spat with contempt.

"I am the one that shall eliminate your cancerous existence," the Avatar responded, his voice dull and emotionless.

"Apparently you don't understand who I am," Yezurkstal mocked.

"I know exactly who you. You are the Birth of Death. Evorath will not allow your existence to continue."

Yezurkstal must have been tired of listening, for as the Avatar muttered these words, the dark harbinger leapt forward with his sword in hand, blade aimed straight for the Avatar's chest. The Avatar clapped his hands around the blade, stopping it in mid stab just inches from his chest.

Savannah wished that she could see Yezurkstal's expression from her vantage point. Finally, the bastard would know what it was like to feel helpless. Ignoring the rest of the action, Savannah stayed there on the ground with Artimus, looking on to see what would happen next.

Yezurkstal looked to be struggling, yanking on the blade to pull it out of the Avatar's grasp. It wouldn't budge. With an angered yell, he let go of his sword and jumped into the air, landing with a powerful cross on the Avatar's chin. The Avatar let go of the sword, allowing it to land hard on the forest floor. His face looked stern as he peered down at Yezurkstal.

"How is this possible?" Yezurkstal shouted in a panic.

He was completely outmatched.

The Avatar made his move now, grabbing Yezurkstal's throat and pushing him down to his knees. Yezurkstal would not go down without a fight, offering a considerable amount of resistance as his legs struggled to fight against this superior opponent. After a few moments, he was down on the ground, both of his knees digging into the dirt as he struggled to stay alive. It was satisfying to see him suffer.

"Dammit!" Artimus cursed.

Savannah looked over at him and then back to the Avatar; she realized why.

Behind the Avatar, one of the barghest had grabbed a hold of Casandra, his left claw poised right in front of the young lamia's throat. Though she could not hear what Yezurkstal was whispering, it probably was something about threatening Casandra's life.

The Avatar listened, releasing his hold on Yezurkstal and stepping back. He had to have some sort of plan.

Yezurkstal rose to his feet, wiping the dirt off his pants and looking up at the muscular Avatar.

"Kill the girl," he commanded with a glance at the barghest.

The Avatar moved with lightning speed, something that looked quite unwieldy for someone of his size. With his right, he grabbed the barghest's left claw and squeezed, the shear force crushing it like a twig. Letting go of Casandra, the barghest stumbled backwards and howled. His howl was instantaneously cut short as the Avatar continued forward with a strong punch to the throat, instantly ending the beast's life.

"Get out of here," the Avatar commanded.

Casandra moved straightaway, slithering back towards the two huts.

"Let's make sure she gets to safety," Artimus suggested coming to his feet.

"Are you OK though?" Savannah asked, hoping that Artimus would want to sit out the rest of the fight.

"As good as ever," he replied, drawing his bow and preparing an arrow. "Duck."

Savannah looked to her left and saw an enemy centaur charging with an axe held overhead. Dropping down to her knees she felt Artimus's arrow fly just over her hair and watched as it impacted the centaur in the left eye socket.

"Let's move."

-=-=-=-=-=-=-=-

Artimus was still in some considerable pain as he and Savannah ran after Casandra. The Avatar was squaring off

352

against Yezurkstal, a confrontation that was going quite well so far. Even as Artimus ran, he saw Yezurkstal reeling away after another unsuccessful attempt at harming the Avatar.

The battle was bloody, and a great amount of troops had been lost on both sides already. In their immediate path, there were maimed felite, centaur, elves and even a few demons. Blood was soaking into the ground all around them, but the numbers were diminishing at such a rate that the noise of the battle was beginning to lessen.

"Casandra!" Artimus shouted as they closed distance with the young lamia.

She glanced back around in confusion, but once recognizing who had called her, she slowed to a halt.

Artimus kept his eyes wide, focusing on any enemies that were nearby. Yezurkstal and the Avatar were well enough behind him that he wasn't too worried about them. To his left and slightly back he caught sight of Irontail and a couple of spearmen fighting off a group of demons; they seemed to be in control. Just ahead and to his right, Tel' Shira was using her amazing acrobatics to dip around the remaining barghest. With the aid of a few elvish warriors and Zeidrich, they also looked to have the upper hand.

Behind him and to his right, Artimus recognized an enemy that he needed to fight. At first glance, he wasn't sure if it was Gharis or Verandas, but as the plate-armored hájje strode confidently towards him, he recognized that he was the taller of the two; it was Gharis.

"Savannah, go with Casandra and get her back to safety. I have to take care of this." Artimus's voice was solemn, a grim seriousness that left no room for debate.

Savannah took a moment, looking back at Gharis and then at Artimus. She nodded and kept moving ahead, leading Casandra away towards the huts.

Artimus tried searching Gharis for any indication of his former self. He peered into those now void-black eyes, searching for some sign. There was nothing. As far as equipment, Gharis wore full steel plate mail, including a cross helmet upon his head. For a weapon, he carried only a single adamantium longsword.

"Gharis," Artimus started, raising up his bow and notching an arrow. "You don't have to serve him. There must be something left of who you were. You were a promising cadet with a younger sister and two parents who cared about you. Don't you remember them?"

His words did nothing but antagonize. Gharis charged towards him, clasping the hilt of his sword close to his chest as he ran. Artimus took aim, deciding to go for the armpit instead of the head. With his enemy's cross-helmet, the surface area was only half as large, making it more difficult to strike accurately.

As his first arrow soared towards Gharis, Artimus drew another and refocused his aim, firing once more. Gharis was getting close. The first arrow flew true, embedding itself in the side of his chest. The second one was not as accurate, ricocheting harmlessly off the steel plates around his arm. Gharis continued forward.

Reaching back for one final arrow, Artimus found himself grasping at air; that must have been his last one. Discarding the bow, he drew his short sword and waited, stepping back and squaring up perfectly with his former ally. He wished there was another way.

Gharis moved in strong, swinging his blade around towards Artimus's head. Not the best leading move.

Artimus ducked underneath the attack, forcing his enemy off balance. Taking advantage of Gharis's vulnerable position, Artimus brought his own sword up and thrust it towards his enemy's stomach. Something in the transformation process must have enhanced Gharis's abilities, for despite his wide-open stance, he somehow repositioned his blade and parried Artimus's stab.

Spinning around to avoid a follow-up, Artimus slapped Gharis's shoulder with the flat of his blade, knocking the hájje back enough to square up once again. Following Gharis's eyes, Artimus was able to predict the next attack. Spinning his sword around, he held the blade towards the ground, blocking his foe's leg strike. Deflecting the blow back, Artimus opened his enemy up yet again, but this time he went for a different approach.

Feigning a sword strike for the head, Artimus held back his blade defensively and went for the leg sweep. Hooking his calf behind Gharis's knee, he knocked his enemy off balance and took him to the floor.

Gharis swung wildly to prevent Artimus from moving in, but Artimus took advantage of this. As the longsword passed his body, Artimus moved in and struck the blade away. While holding his enemy's weapon at bay, he fell on top of his foe, stabbing him in the chest with a dagger.

He felt the resistance die down and Gharis dropped his sword, the blade landing harmlessly by his side. Artimus pushed himself off his former cadet, leaving his dagger embedded in Gharis's chest. Re-sheathing his sword and retrieving his bow, he looked back across the field towards Yezurkstal and the Avatar.

At the onset of their fight, Yezurkstal appeared to be completely outmatched. Now, as he avoided the Avatar's attacks, he appeared to be adapting on the spot. It was as if the more he fought the stronger he became. Yezurkstal landed a punch square on the Avatar's jaw, causing the forest's guardian to falter and take a few steps back.

Yezurkstal was still outclassed and he realized it.

While the allied forces continued to wipe out the rest of the possessed centaur, lamia, lizock and barghest, Verandas rallied the demons and redirected them to converge on the Avatar. With no arrows remaining, Artimus would not be nearly as effective in aiding the fight, so his first task was to retrieve some arrows.

Keeping his attention open for any straggling enemies nearby, Artimus made his way towards the nearest elvish corpse. It was a morbid concept, but he needed more arrows.

This archer had five remaining in his quiver, which would not be enough. Artimus looked back up towards the approaching demons, Verandas taking his place at the rear and ordering them to move. They were nearing the Avatar.

Yezurkstal shot both of his hands forward, two spheres of dark energy wrapping around the Avatar and squeezing him in place. As the Avatar glowed green and broke the hold, Yezurkstal chuckled and flung his right hand up, disappearing in a puff of smoke. Verandas also turned and fled, running away from the field to leave the demons converging without guidance on the Avatar. Was Yezurkstal actually retreating, or was this some new ploy he was using?

Artimus didn't have time to ponder, rising and running to the next allied corpse to retrieve another six arrows. As he stood up and organized all eleven arrows, Ugron and Irontail arrived at either side.

"The enemy is all but defeated. Those demons are the last of their forces," Irontail said gasping for air.

"Good," Artimus responded, drawing an arrow and taking aim. "Let's put an end to this."

Before any of the trio could make their move, the Avatar made his. As the demons converged on his position, the Avatar slammed his right fist into the ground. His voice boomed out.

"Demons be gone!"

The ground opened up with a flash of light, a strange energy shooting up and pulling on the demons. Tremors continued as the ground closed, swallowing the demons whole.

They had won the battle, but Yezurkstal had escaped.

Chapter 24

Erathal Forest, Erathal City

21 Neglur, 1086

Artimus stood with Savannah at his side, watching as the rest of the bodies were carted into the re-appropriated barracks. It was a grim sight, dozens of elves, and a handful each of felite, trolls, and centaur all brought into this former armory turned mortuary. Despite the death toll and the fact that Yezurkstal escaped, Artimus still felt relieved.

He was alive, and more importantly, so was Savannah. No matter who else had died, that made everything seem less grim. Though, as he looked to his left, where Tel' Shira and Irontail were both standing solemnly, he was reminded that not everyone was so lucky.

No longer responsible for an entire brigade of troops, Artimus had no concern for what onlookers might think. So, as the last cart was wheeled into the barracks, he put his arm around Savannah's waist, pulling her in and giving her a light squeeze.

"I told you that we'd both survive," he whispered, looking down at her beautiful figure.

Savannah returned his gaze, wrapping her arm around him and exchanging a small embrace. As they peered into one another's eyes, they both shared a smile.

Hearing the hooves of Irontail approaching, he loosened his embrace and turned, looking up to the centaur warlord.

"You fought very valiantly, especially for an elf," Irontail offered. "With Yezurkstal still out there, I hope that the next time we face him, we will fight together again."

Artimus felt touched, realizing that this was probably the most heartfelt thing that a centaur warrior could say.

"The honor was mine," Artimus replied with a slight bow. "And I have no doubt that we will eliminate Yezurkstal together."

"Doubt, I have," Tel' Shira interrupted. Artimus hadn't even heard her walk up behind him.

"Honored, still, I am as well," she continued taking an almost unnoticeable bow.

From behind Savannah, Artimus heard the heavy footsteps that could only belong to the Avatar. Everyone turned to face him as he approached.

"Yezurkstal is still out there indeed," the Avatar started, his voice solemn as ever.

"But, we all have a reprieve from now. With his powers of darkness, I cannot track him precisely, but my foresight is more potent than even the wisest felite. I can tell you that he is leaving the forest. One day, and I'm not certain when that day will be, he will come back. Until then, let this battle be a lesson to all of your peoples. You know what you're up against, so prepare for his return."

"Will you aid us again when he returns?" Irontail asked, his voice conveying a hint of weakness.

"I am here to be a teacher for all of Evorath," the Avatar replied.

Artimus was expecting more of a response, and judging by the prolonged silence that followed, so had everyone else. After nearly a full minute of silence and awkward glances, Savannah spoke up.

"So, will you be sticking around Erathal?" she asked earnestly. "Because it would be a great opportunity to learn from you."

"No, I will not." The Avatar answered absolutely. "The troubles of this city will keep you quite busy in the months to come. I will be there for whoever asks for me in the correct manner though, and I can promise that you will be a student of mine one day. For now, I am needed elsewhere. You will make sure that Casandra receives the attention she needs?"

Savannah nodded. "Of course. I will make sure that she finds her way."

"Good. Then, I fare thee all well. Carve out the path that Evorath has made available, and you will all have great success in your time. I will see you all again soon."

The Avatar did not wait for anyone to respond and turned away, walking off towards the border of the city. Artimus was tempted to stop him, but he knew it was futile. If the Avatar said they would meet again, Artimus was willing to wait until that time.

"My people need me as well," Irontail proclaimed. "None of Dumner's living elders know a thing about warfare. It is my duty to make sure that Dumner survives."

"Of course," Artimus replied, turning back towards Irontail. "Know that Erathal and her people will always be on your side. Send a courier if you are ever in need of our assistance."

"Thank you," Irontail offered with a nod. "And Savannah, Tel' Shira, thank you for your bravery and service as well. I hope we have the opportunity to meet again soon."

"The bravest of your kind, you were," Tel' Shira responded as she shook Irontail's hand. "Meeting again, I too look forward to."

Savannah offered a smile to Irontail, giving him a handshake before the large centaur turned to face Artimus.

"Good luck," Artimus said shaking the warrior's hand. They locked eyes in understanding, holding a firm grasp for a few moments before releasing.

Without further exchange, Irontail was off, walking after the Avatar who had already disappeared through the tree line. Tel' Shira appeared ready to leave as well, her body pointed in the same direction.

"Tel' Shira," Artimus began. "I hope that we meet again sooner rather than later. The whole of my people morn for the loss of your elder, and I hope that next time we face Yezurkstal, it is with a formal alliance between our peoples."

361

"My hope, that is as well," Tel' Shira replied, giving Artimus a firm handshake.

Tel' Shira extended her hand to Savannah next, who took and shook it.

"Good future for you both, I predict," Tel' Shira exclaimed as she released the handshake.

"Farewell," Savannah replied with a smile.

Finally, with Tel' Shira walking off, Savannah and Artimus would have some time alone.

"Sir," an unfamiliar, high-pitched voice interrupted.

Artimus turned to see a shorter, very thin male ranger, his uniform disheveled and hair unkempt. He looked like he had just gone through a windstorm; probably was just getting scolded by one of his superiors.

"What is it, cadet?" Artimus questioned, wishing that he could just be left in peace for once.

"Sir, I'm sorry, sir. I have urgent news from the king. This morning, there was another fake news parchment distributed. The king wishes you to take over the investigation immediately." The cadet fidgeted around as he spoke, unable to stand still and looking extremely nervous. Artimus noticed that he was holding something behind his back.

"Is that the parchment?" Artimus asked.

The cadet nodded and handed it over.

Ignoring the over-eager cadet, Artimus looked down and began reading…

-=-=-=-=-=-=-=-

Erathal News Article 100:47
The Crown has Lied
By Cyboral Cabal

As you wake up this morning, I can only pray that our world is a better place than it was yesterday. Unfortunately, while you are stuck toiling with the mundane problems associated with a defunct monarchy, your dishonest governing body is living a life of opulence. They have lied to you.

While the hunter and farmer sow the food for this kingdom, while the mason provides us with materials to build, and while the blacksmith provides us with tools, the monarchy reaps all the benefits. They take everything that you produce and leave you almost nothing. They have lied to you.

Your king has kept many secrets from you. The senate has kept the most productive of you repressed and unable to live a comfortable life, robbing you of your basic rights as creatures of Evorath. They have lied to you.

While official reports told of a band of wandering lizock, the real truth is that our kingdom is plagued by a Hájje. The eleven girls who were kidnapped are not dead; they have been transformed into hájje themselves. They have lied to you.

Your king told you that he would care for you. The Council assured you that you would be kept safe against any threats. They have lied to you.

While you produced, your monarchy has consumed. They unjustly take ownership of all of your hard work and dedication. They have lied to you.

Yesterday, a brigade of this Kingdom's finest troops faced the gravest threat to have ever walked upon Evorath. The hájje, the bringer of death and destroyer of free will, was battled by a united force of elves, felite, centaur, and trolls. It is my prayer that he was defeated so that we can start focusing on the beast within.

If it were up to the king, you would not even know this threat existed. This Hájje, who put the safety of this entire Kingdom at risk, was something that the senate saw fit to hide. They did not want us to know, lest we lose faith in the supposed wisdom of the king.

The time has come for change.

No longer shall the citizens of Erathal settle for the leftovers. No longer shall we accept what is given to us by the king. No longer shall we surrender what is rightfully ours so that it can be redistributed to those who do not produce.

Now, we take a stand.

If you are like me and believe that each elf should have equal rights and equal opportunity, then you are against the king. If you are like me and believe that each elf should reap what he sows, then you are against the king. If you are like me and believe that it is the individual, not the small minority of bureaucrats, who should rule, then you are against the king.

In six days, we will take a stand.

In six days, if you are like me, we will be united as one to show the king that we are not his puppets.

In six days, if you wish to live in a world where production is rewarded and the individual gets to receive accolades for his work, we will gather together.

If you are tired of the lies, tired of the injustice and tired of the rule without cause, seek me out. Our numbers are vast, and the time is ripe. A change in leadership is in order.

Whatever you do, do not accept what you have been told. Evorath is not safe. The king cannot protect you.

If you want to see change, join me in six days at the Food Proctor when the moon is highest in the sky.

Until then, stop accepting your king's lies.

-=-=-=-=-=-=-=-

Yezurkstal may have retreated, but it's only a matter of time before he returns. Read book 2, *The Rise of Yezurkstal* now to see how Evorath's heroes fight back against this growing evil.

The Birth of Death is the first book in the Evorath trilogy. Visit us online for free access to additional stories, and to sign up for notifications about future releases. The second book, *The Rise of Yezurkstal*, is available for purchase as of July 2023.

If you enjoyed this book, please help other readers find that same enjoyment by returning to where you purchased it and leaving a positive review. Your voice matters. Leave a review on Amazon.

Appendices I - Map of Evorath, continent of Erathal

Appendices II - Glossary of Select Terms

◆ Adamantium - Also known as Admantite, Adamantine, or Adamant. Strongest metal in existence yet weighs no more than steel. This natural metal is light green in color and can be found in some of the deepest, darkest, caves.

◆ Barghest - A broad-shouldered and wide-chested species of bipedal canines. They make up some of the strongest warriors in Evorath but are nearing extinction due to their warrior nature.

◆ Centaur - Half-horse and half-man, this sentient species has many tribes scattered throughout the continent of Erathal.

◆ Demons - Not native to Evorath, demons are summoned from another realm. These creatures come in all shapes and sizes, but usually have dark, leathery skin.

◆ Destrier - A special breed of horse raised for war. They are bred to be hardy and stout, giving them great stamina and favoring strength over speed.

◆ Dryad - Guardians of the forest, there is one dryad for each type of tree on Evorath. They have untold powers over the forest and work to maintain balance in the forest.

◆ Dumner - This centaur village is located near the Elvish Kingdom of Erathal and is home to a great warrior tribe.

◆ Elf - Similar in stature to the humans of Earth, Elves are the most abundant sentient species in Evorath. They have pointy ears and almost exclusively have light features.

◆ Erathal - Name of the continent this adventure takes place in. Also the name of the major Elvish Kingdom.

- Ether - The space between different worlds. Reaching through the ether requires great magical abilities and allows a mage to summon creatures from one of these other worlds.

- Felite - One of the most populous species on the continent of Erathal, felite are a bipedal feline species that resemble their four-legged cousins. While many felite roam in small tribes, most are members of the Felite Confederacy, which sits to the northeast of the forest.

- Hájje - Elvish word for a dark elf. It comes from the elvish word Haijja, which means 'dark', or 'evil'.

- Jyrimoore Caves - An abandoned dwarven mine initially prospected for adamantium deposits. It is now the notorious site of heinous experiments conducted by a misguided elvish researcher.

- Lamia - A sentient race that still maintains a tribal nature. Their lower half resembles a snake and their upper half is that of an elf. Females greatly outnumber the males of the species, which is why their population is diminishing.

- Lizock - One of the most populous sentient species on the continent of Erathal, lizock are a bipedal reptilian race that resembles the common lizard. Though they can vary in size, shape, and color, the race is most well-known for its warriors and merchants.

- Lynx - A medium-sized wild cat with a short tail. Folklore indicates that these elusive felines have latent magical abilities.

- Mythril - A silverish-blue metal used primarily by elves and sometimes by dwarves. It is as light as aluminum and stronger than steel, making it a great option for the battlefield.

- Roc - A large, eagle-like bird with light brown feathers. Though wild roc can have wingspans over 15 meters, some species use these tamed birds as mounts for their aerial units. These tamed variety typically have a wingspan under 10 meters.

- Runeturk Mountains - Major mountain range bordering Erathal to the north. This range is populated by thousands of dwarves, some gnomes, and less civilized creatures like ogres, orcs, goblins, and wild animals.

- Satyr - A sentient species of Evorath once known for great works of art and music, they are now known more for their proclivity towards alcoholism. These bipedal creatures are half-elf, half-goat, with their upper half being the former and their lower half resembling the latter.

- Troll - A sentient species of Evorath. Nomadic in nature, trolls are both tall and menacing in their physical features, with many blemishes on their skin and a crude language. They have one of the lowest populations of any major forest-dwelling race.

- Urgo - An elvish word of affirmation. Essentially equivalent to saying "yes, sir" or "understood."

Printed in the USA
CPSIA information can be obtained
at www.ICGtesting.com
JSHW082256141123
52027JS00004B/21